KIT BRANDON

A PORTRAIT

<hr>

BY

SHERWOOD
ANDERSON

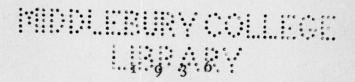
<hr>

CHARLES SCRIBNER'S SONS · NEW YORK
CHARLES SCRIBNER'S SONS · LTD · LONDON

COPYRIGHT, 1936, BY

SHERWOOD ANDERSON

✳

A

PRINTED IN THE UNITED STATES OF AMERICA

TO
MARY PRATT EMMETT

KIT BRANDON

CHAPTER ONE

K IT didn't speak much or often of her father. "Pap,"
she sometimes called him and sometimes she spoke
of him as "Father." After all, Kit when I knew her
had been made over in the big world. She had her
knowing, her way of knowing, and it seemed to me more
real than most of the ways of knowing most of us have.

And then, too, she was wanting something not culture, in
the restricted sense. "The hell with that," would have been
her word.

Her story came to me in fragments. We were together for
that purpose, that I might get her story as one more of the
multitude of curious, terrible, silly, absorbing or wonderful
stories all people could tell if they knew how.

"All right, then, I'll tell you about when I was a young
girl, if you'll let me drive the car."

This would have been when she came to me in the winter,
that time when I was doing a magazine story about conditions in South Dakota. It was the year of the long terrible dry
time in South Dakota—of the dust storms, whole farms
buried under drifting sand and dust, fences buried—during
the winter after that. Kit came up there by train, meeting me
in a little town.

"You let me drive.

"I think better when I'm driving a car. I've driven so much.

"We lived, my father, my mother and my two younger sisters and my one younger brother, in a mountain cabin in East Tennessee. My father had a little farm up there and he was quite old, for getting married I mean, when he married my mother, who was pretty young. She was only seventeen when she married him and he must have been thirty-five.

"He had been married before but he didn't have any kids by his first woman, so that didn't count.

"And it's mighty funny, when you think of it, that I haven't ever had any kids, the chances I've taken and never been careful.

"So there was a little cabin and it was down under quite a big road going over a mountain. It was on a little road that was rutty and filled with stones.

"And we had a cow and a barn right close up against the little road and there was a horse.

"There were a good many horses. My father was always trading horses."

Kit laughed—the queer cold little laugh that came only when she spoke of her father. She was a woman nearing thirty when we were together during the cold bleak days in the desolated land of South Dakota.

"He'd trade horses and trade horses. It was his fun. He loved it. It was his way of outwitting some man or being out-witted. He'd get on a bony old horse we had and ride off. It might be that some other man, a neighbor on another old horse, would go with him. He might be gone for days. He was horse trading. It was seeing people, other men, and be-

OTHER BOOKS
BY SHERWOOD ANDERSON

KIT BRANDON

ing with them. It was drinking some. It was showing how smart you are."

She described the house in which she lived as a child. It was a slovenly, dirty little house, as she described it and it was difficult to think of her as living there, she who had become what she had, really so slender and handsome, so upstanding, so curiously, in her own way, beautiful. She said she hadn't, she supposed, known or noticed much when she was a little thing.

In spite of his poverty he always wore overalls, she said, even on Sundays, and they were patched and mended . . . he patched and mended them himself she said . . . in spite of everything, he did keep neat-looking.

He, the father, Kit explained, was a small, wiry man with black hair, very stiff. It stood up straight and hard on his head and he kept it cut close. . . . "Like the grass on the front yard of a house that is mowed every week," she said, "and he was dark.

"He was like an Italian or maybe a Greek, not looking much like an American," she thought.

"He had the whitest teeth you ever saw in a man's head and they were all sound."

She had lived in the mountain house through childhood and young girlhood and, in spite of her later adventures, the figure of the father had remained sharply in her mind. "You see, I am like my mother, tall and rather skinny" . . . she smiled, using the word "skinny" to describe her slender graceful body, calling attention to it thus, as all women love to do . . . "but I'm like my father too. I'm dark like him and I've got good teeth, and my hair's black like his was."

I got little pictures of her early life, as she talked, driving my car, often over dirt roads, on bitter winter days, myself breaking the talk as we came to some town.

They were fragmentary pictures she gave me—a mountain road, going up out of an East Tennessee valley . . . this before East Tennessee became industrialized, factories coming into many of the little towns to pick up and use the cheap mountain labor. . . .

A mountain road, going up and up . . . some fifteen or twenty miles out of a valley in which there were a few rich farms and farmers—the road curling up and up. You could drive up along the road, over several mountains, through a few rich valleys, past long miles of forest, deep grown with underbrush—stopping maybe to admire the view from some mountain top—some seventy or eighty miles and you'd come to Knoxville, Tennessee. The road wasn't paved and was pretty rough when Kit was a child. It's a highway now.

"And down there, in the town in the valley, some eighteen miles from us," Kit explained, "was the first town I ever saw." She was fifteen before she ever got a chance to go to town. "There wasn't any factory down there then but there's a rayon plant now," she said.

She said also something else, that you might travel yet over the big road, going from Asheville in North Carolina to Knoxville in Tennessee . . . TVA town now . . . center of government effort to remake, recast, the lives of a whole people, the Southern Appalachian Highlanders of America . . . going some 250 miles through just the kind of country she was raised in, "and you'd say to yourself—'There don't any one live up here—they couldn't because they couldn't make a living,' you'd say, but you'd be wrong."

There were, she explained, plenty of people, thousands and many thousands of them, when she was a child, living as her family lived, "if you can call it living," she said. They hung on up there in their hills, a quite isolated, a strong enough people, in the very heart of America, sticking tight to their barren hills, "like fleas on a dog," she said.

To earth—clinging to it, to their barren enough earth, clinging.

Little pockets of flat ground, a few acres. Hillsides, planted to corn, so steep, some of them, you'd think a horse or an ox pulling a plow would fall off and be killed. Kit, although she had come to me frankly to tell her own story, grew, at times, impersonal enough . . . memories of her childhood in the hills coming back as she talked, little stories of other mountain families simply enough told, men, heads of mountain families, she said, going sometimes out of their hills, even to places as far away and strange to them as Detroit . . . employment, perhaps in the Ford plant . . . five dollars a day, a fabulous-seeming sum to them. She said that most of them couldn't stand it long. I used the expression, "The hills had them," and she nodded her head. She meant to say that the land of the skies—always the far-reaching skies—the beautiful hill lands of Southwest Virginia, West Virginia, Tennessee, Kentucky, North Carolina, called the men back as it hadn't called her. She had got, although it had apparently not touched her, a sense, in her father and other men, neighbors perhaps in her childhood, a sense of land love, hill-land love, that had made her mountaineers almost a distinct and separate people in America.

The little houses, usually very small, tucked away on some side road, very narrow, winding and stony, almost always the house standing by a mountain stream. There would be plenty of clear mountain streams. Sometimes three or four men could build a house in three or four days.

The barn would be a mere shed.

"You should have seen my father's barn," Kit said. "It was more than our house ever was. My mother, my ma, she wasn't much good.

"She was always sitting around. She had me and then, when I had grown a little and she had the others—she didn't have as many as most of the women up there in that mountain—maybe she was too lazy—she began to make me tend to the others, and do everything in the house too."

Kit thought that perhaps her mother, daughter of a near-by mountain family, named Tuttle—her own family name was Brandon—had got some disease, after she married Kit's father, hookworm perhaps, she thought.

So there was Kit, that child in that place, in that house, on the little farm, tucked away in the East Tennessee hills, with the tall indolent mother, always, Kit said, with the snuff stick in her mouth, stains of the tobacco on her broken teeth and dripping from the corners of her mouth. Not much chance for romance in the figure of that woman, as Kit spoke of her, not bitterly but with odd detachment . . . not much chance among these defeated women, slovenly and dirty, for such romances as *The Trail of the Lonesome Pine* of our Southern Highlander, John Fox, Jr. . . . these defeated women, slovenly and dirty . . . I had myself seen them. I knew them, had lived among them.

Her hair—blond it was, or had been—always uncombed, her cheap cotton dress always dirty.

"I don't see how Pa ever brought himself to sleep with her but he did," said Kit in her own curious, oddly detached way.

And then the father gone sometimes for days, on one of his horse-trading trips, usually with other mountain men, perhaps with two or three of them, a little cavalcade going along mountain trails, up and over mountain roads, stopping at some store at a crossroads—a mean enough little unpainted frame building the store would be, mountain men lounging about up there.

Every man with a bottle of moon whiskey in his hip pocket.

There would be fair, straight-shooting fellows and mean, cheap ones. All would be miserably clad. As a man goes along in life he finds out something very important to this business of living. It is that you can't go through America, or I dare say any other country, in the way so many of us do, saying, "The Highlanders are so and so, the Southerners, the workers, the rich, the poor, the proletariat, the bourgeoisie so and so," making these terrible Mason and Dixon line judgments, believing in them.

Drunken fights—stabbings, and shootings sometimes among the hill men, horse trading—thus, men always lived, horse trading. It was a part of the game being played.

Kit said, "I don't care. I think if my father—if he had been born different, in a different place, had got him a different wife—" She was implying that there was something to be said. "If he'd even had the chance I've had."

She meant to say that the father had a kind of hidden power in him, something dark perhaps (Kit was always asking, demanding, that I leap across great gaps in her account of how things were with her, what she felt about things). The man, her father, was no great talker. He, in some way, bent men to his will.

"But what about your mother, Kit? Why didn't he bend her?

"You say the house was always—unless you swept it,

cleaned it—that it was always dirty and that the dress she wore was dirty.

"Why didn't he take her in hand?"

"Oh, I guess it was because he didn't give a damn for the house or her," Kit said. She had always the times of falling into easy profanity. She went smiling off into one of her side talks, away from her own story, speaking of the great numbers of people there were in the world you had to just let go to hell, she said, not counting on them, using them when and where you could. She had got, out of her living, a philosophy common enough to a certain kind of Americans, for the most part the successful ones. More than once during my acquaintance with her I thought of Kit that she might, under other circumstances, have been one of our successful ones, another Rockefeller, a Harriman, a Gould.

"There are all kinds," she said. "You must know that! I should be telling you!

"You scare the bastards, or you bluff them out or, if you can use them in your business, you wheedle them or soft-soap them along."

"Even when you wouldn't spit on some of them?"

"Or even," she said.

(I remember a kind of shock that ran through me when Kit Brandon said this to me.)

We had stopped by a little country church that had been twisted off its foundations by a strong wind, perhaps by a tornado, out on the western plains, the windows of the little frame church all broken, the roof half twisted off.

Such a curiously pathetic little church out on wind-swept South Dakota plains.

And Kit, such a neat, slender, well-groomed thing, sitting

there at the wheel of my car. She had stopped the car and had given me one swift look.

To be sure, knowing of her what I did know, what had interested me in her as a curious American phenomenon, I did know that, having led the life she had led, having associated so long with the men with whom she had associated, she couldn't possibly have been what men mean when they say, a pure woman. Just the same she did look so neat — clad in her black jersey and in some kind of a knitted black skirt. Her slender ankles. Her good figure.

"Or even," I said, when she had stopped the car, to look at the ruined church. "What do you mean, Kit — or even?"

The reader will remember that she had been speaking of her mother, of the attitude of her mountain father toward her mother, of his indifference. She was justifying it, saying in her own way, I thought, that to live at all in life as it is, you had to get for yourself self-respect, a foundation. "You have to be strong, even pitiless some times," I thought she was trying to say.

"And a woman doing it, the thing you're talking about, Kit, a woman using the strength in herself . . . her strength might well be in her physical beauty, you know . . . her using that to get men, to make them do what she wanted done?

"Or even — you don't mean going all the way, just for that in order to gain some end of her own.

"Her own body?"

"Yes," she said, "I've gone through it with men I wouldn't spit on now. I thought I had to. I guess it just happened so, it was the break I got."

Kit, it seemed to me — being with her, having these intimate talks with her—had always the sense in her of life as a kind of game.

"For Christ's sake, Kit."

"Well, don't get up-stage on me, man," she said. "It's done every day, or at least every night, by plenty of women you've met, in the most respectable families.

"In what is called the best society."

"D'you think every woman don't know that?"

"Even with husbands, too?" I said.

"Remember, please," Kit said, "that I've had a husband. He's in prison now," she said smiling.

"Women everywhere, all the time, even the most respectable ones, taking men all the time they don't give a damn for."

"I never heard that it killed any of them yet," Kit said. "There are times," she said, "if you happen to be a working girl, as I've been, or if you've got into a gang such as I've been in, when it seems to you it's about got to be done. Why," she said, "there's some, 'scabs,' I call them, who'll do it for an automobile ride."

A mountain farm, such as has already been described, or partly described. Kit Brandon, a girl child of fifteen, on such a farm. She would have been a rather intense little worker.

She would have been out of bed at dawn. Summers came on the mountain farm and then winters. From the time she was six or seven, she went, for a few months each winter, to a mountain school.

She had to be up early in the morning. From the time when she was tall enough to stand up to the stove she got up and got the breakfast. In the winter there were corn bread and hot hog meat, and in the summer there were greens. She said her father went, in the early spring, far up somewhere into the mountains and got a kind of strange wild onion he called "ramps." That was to purify the blood from too much and too long eating of the corn bread and the fat hog meat.

Then she had to clean up the dishes and sweep out the house. She said that the house had no floor. There was just the hard earth, clay she said, made hard and even shiny by much tramping of bare and unwashed feet. There were plenty of creeping crawling things. "We had lice and bed-bugs," she said. She thought, when she was a child, they were companions every one had.

In the morning her mother stayed in bed, in the same room they ate in, and the bedding was dirty. She was lying there. By the time Kit got big enough to cook and sweep the mother started having kids again. She had Kit. Then she didn't have any, Kit said, for nearly five years. Then she started in again and in rapid succession she had three, two girls and a boy. Kit said, "I don't know why Pa suddenly warmed up to her like that. It must have been all he could get at the time."

The father was out of bed before Kit and outdoors to the little barn, he always managed to keep neat. Even in winter he stayed out there until Kit called him to come and eat his breakfast and then he ate without looking over toward the messy bed where the wife was lying in silence, just the frowsy head showing above the dirty bedclothes.

There was always plenty of work for the girl child.

To sweep out the house with a homemade broom her father had made, to wash the dishes — mend and wash her father's clothes.

To school for a few months each winter, for four or five years — to learn anyway to read and write. Spring, summer, fall, and winter.

The garden to plant and to work in. John Brandon, the father, wouldn't touch the garden. It was woman's work, he said. When she was a very little thing he said something to her about the garden that made her proud.

"It made me proud," she said when she told of it.

Her father had taken her to the garden. She might have been a girl of eight then. She said he stood with her by a low brush fence he had made. The garden was a small rich plot of ground, in a low place by the creek's edge. It was early spring and he had plowed it that day. Planting and tending it was no man's work, he said to the child. He smiled and his white teeth showed under his black mustache. He never chewed tobacco and he didn't smoke.

"It's a woman's work, planting and tending garden and, goddam it, you, kid, are as near a thing as there is to a woman around here."

That work for the child to do and plenty of other work. Doing, doing, for Kit when she was a child.

Her father taught her to milk the cow. When he was away, on one of his horse-trading trips, that were not primarily trips for gain but just trips to be away, among men, because he liked being among men, she took the cow to the bull when the cow was wanting.

"And that's one hell of a job for a child," she said, "a cow when that time comes for her.

"She just goes plumb crazy.

"She'll go slam bang, right through a fence.

"She'll drag you. She'll knock you down.

"You cry. You get so mad at her you want to kill her, but it's a thing that's got to be done." She said the nearest bull to the house was three miles away.

The garden to be taken care of—corn planting and hoe-

ing all day some days in the hillside cornfields, her own
clothes to wash and mend and those of her father and the
younger children.

"I wouldn't wash my ma's clothes. She tried to get me to
do it but I didn't. She told pap about it, tried to get him to
name it to me. I was in the barn, milking, and pap and ma
were in the yard. I heard hit. Pap only laughed. 'Is there anything else you want her to do?' he asked."

Kit, when she spoke of her childhood, occasionally fell
into the vernacular. I think she always knew when she did
it. She would look at me and laugh, saying "hit" for "it,"
and then she'd drop it again.

In the summer she went berry-picking in the woods and
she cut and carried firewood. Sometimes, when her pap went
in with some other man or men to make a run of liquor she
stood guard. There was only the one road, out of the big
road up above, that came down into the little hollow in
which the Brandon house stood, and she said there was a
clean bare place up there, no brush growing, close up to a
little wood, where it cut out of the big wood.

You had to cross the bare place to come out of the big road
into their little road. The whiskey-making would be going
on farther up the hollow, where a little stream came down,
the mountain laurel and rhododendron so thick you had
to know how or you couldn't force your way through.
Kit called the rhododendron laurel and the laurel she called
ivy.

The sheriff had a big yellow car but on the few occasions
when he came down into the hollow he left it up above. A
wagon could hardly get down into that road. When he came
to make a call on them—hardly a social call, I gathered—
the sheriff's car, the big yellow one, stayed up above.

You could see it and quite a stretch of the big road from the bare place or from a hillside cornfield and Kit stayed in one of these places. She said, even in winter, they left a few shocks of corn in the field, for her to get behind, and in cold weather to stay behind out of the wind.

And if some one came or the sheriff's car stopped up there or was on the road—she could see quite a way along the upper road, both ways—she scooted down along a path to the house. She had a bell down there her pap had got somewhere and she rang the bell. She said the sheriff only once came clear down to their house. That was in the winter and there were no leaves on the trees. You could see the still smoke a long ways off. She said her pap had arranged a pile of brush, dry and ready to burn, up at the edge of the cornfield and the woods and that when she had seen the sheriff's car coming, when it was still far down the road toward town, she got a sudden hunch and lighted the brush pile before running down to the house to ring the bell.

"I been seeing still smoke down here three or four times now," the sheriff said. The real still fire was out before he got down to the house. The sheriff was a big man and not one to crawl up a hollow through thick laurel but he had another man with him, a long lean one.

"What for was you ringing that bell?" he asked Kit, and she said she didn't answer but stayed still and looked dumb. She said her ma did the same. "It was a signal to pap to come down if any one came," she said. She said she already knew enough to let her father do the explaining but that when he didn't come she did speak.

"He's been up there clearing brush and burning it."

She got hold of the bell and rang it again.

"Never mind that now," the sheriff said and laughed.

From in front of the house, in the little road where he stood, the lean tall man standing with him, he could look up to the cornfield and see the brush burning.

"Never mind," he said. "You tell your pap I'll be back here sometime when they ain't any bells ringing." He went back up the road and to his car followed by the tall lean man, a deputy, Kit thought. "You don't need to ring no more," he said, smiling at the child. "Your pap'll have put the still fire out. You might as well look for a run-away nigger in the land of Africa," he said to the lean man as they went away.

Kit told of staying up all night once, hid in the brush near the clear place, where the little road went into the big road. That was when once her pap, with two other men, made a really big run. One of the two men Kit had never seen before. He was, she said, a man from down in the county-seat town, a man who some two or three days before had brought bags of corn meal up from town in a truck at night. He was a big, rather rough-looking man, in flashy store clothes. He took the flashy clothes off in the barn and put on overalls and when he had gone up into the brush with the other men she crept into the barn to touch the clothes. "They were pretty flashy, I guess," she said, but she spoke of the thrill she got, just touching the cloth, so beautifully and tightly woven. "So grand," she said. It was the first awakening in her of the passion, later so strong in her, for fine clothes, fine automobiles, for anything finely and well made. The man was the first of the big-town bootleggers — "blockaders" — Kit ever saw, one of a kind of man she was to know intimately enough later in life.

Afterwards, she said, he came into the house and sat by the fire smoking cigars. She was still a barefooted kid, a skinny one, she might have been thirteen. This, she said, was in the late fall, in November, and it was cold. Womanhood had just begun to show itself in her. She didn't speak of that but she did speak of something that happened.

It wasn't much, a little thing, the little thing in a girl child that first tells her she has begun as woman to attract the attention of men.

Something different in men from the other thing, the way a man touches or caresses a child.

She was in the house with the man, a big man with big shoulders and a big head.

"He had a big mouth too and a cigar stuck in the corner and he had funny red bloodshot eyes."

He was the sort of man who drinks too much and too steadily but who is so strong drink can't tear him down.

There had evidently been a deal made, Kit's pap and one or two of his horse-trading friends, in with the man from town; he in with some other more important unknown man in the liquor-running business in a big way—a big run to be made for him. Kit's pap and her ma and the younger children were out in the yard or at the barn and she brought an armload of wood from the yard for the fire in the fireplace inside.

The big man was sitting there in a chair right close to the fire and he got up. He stood looking at her and she said that there was something strange and a little startling to her in his red bloodshot eyes.

She just stood, not starting to put down the cut wood, and he came over to her. He began to take the sticks away, one by one, and put them down in a pile on the hearth.

And each time his big red fingers, as he took the sticks

from her, touched her in a peculiar way. "They'd brush
down, just lightly across my shoulders and my breasts.
They'd linger there, feeling my breasts. My breasts were
pretty small."

She stood and let him do it, frightened, she said, half-
paralyzed with a kind of fright new to her.

"It wasn't so much the thing he did. I did know and I
didn't know what he was up to, I guess."

She spoke at length of the adventure, alone there in the
mountain house with the man, wondering how many other
women had had a thing like that happen to them when they
were so young. "There are men I've been with since," she
said, "you know, all the way I mean, and, although I didn't
give a damn for them, what happened didn't seem to hurt
me like that did."

And it had been such a little thing, so half casual, the
touch of the man's fingers. She said it would have been so
easy to turn and run out at the open door and she spoke also
of sounds heard — the whole adventure lasted but a minute
— he did it three or four times and then stopped — of the
sound of her father's voice, heard coming from the yard,
near the barn, a cow, in a hillside field nearby, heard bawling
for its calf.

And she, the little mountain girl then, with the bare legs
and bare feet — thin cotton dress — slender little legs, perhaps
blue with the cold. It was only by an effort you could call up
the figure of Kit as she must have been then, knowing her
when she was a woman, so curiously self-contained.

"And I must already have known down in me somewhere
what a lot of men are like; I'd taken our cow to the bull
three times, fighting with her up along our road and to the

big road, to make her go to the man who had the bull, up
there on the big road.

"You're going to be purty. You are purty now," the big
man finally said. He was the first of the professional blockaders she was later to be in with. He'd taken the cigar out
of his mouth and she said she remembered it as such a big
mouth, with thick lips and big teeth, set wide apart, so you
could almost see into the big red cave between the teeth. "It
was like looking into a cow's mouth," she said.

"You're purty now."

His wanting, suddenly, perhaps the clean hardness, the
youth in her then.

Slenderness, hard little upright breasts, straight little legs.
Kit as a woman had slender ankles and long slender feet.

He stood looking, wanting no doubt to pounce, not daring, that other man, her father, the dark clean-looking one,
with the swarthy skin, dark, almost black eyes, white teeth,
just outside the house somewhere, within call.

Strange to look back to such a moment, for a woman like
Kit, after what she became, men she had been with, hardness, knowledge of men coming—fighting through it all
for something.

Not surely fighting afterward to keep what that man at
that moment wanted, but for something else—not womanhood either.

"I want my story told. I'll go anywhere with you. I've got
money. I'll pay my own way.

"I've been in the newspapers. I've been a notorious woman.

"You needn't be afraid I'll try to put anything over on
you.

"Nights, if you'll let me ride alone with you on this trip
you say you've got to make, I'll stay in a different hotel.

"If you try to put anything over on me it'll spoil everything.

"I want my story told."

Desire for something in Kit Brandon I thought then and still think, more akin to a thing I've oftener found in men than in women, as though to say — she never did say it to me — she wanted me to get it without saying — the sort of thing a man means when he says of another man, "Well, he's a man, he's my friend. The story you tell me of him may be true, okay. It makes no difference to me. To me he is a man and my friend."

Kit, a woman when I knew her, who perhaps felt she had quite thrown something away, something about which there has always been much of man talk . . . oh thou Purity, innocence . . . meaning too often separation from the grim reality of living . . . at last a new generation in America throwing aside much of that, what is so often false. She spoke to me of a trial, herself up for trial, after she became a notorious rum runner, in the big days of the rum runners, during the prohibition era — a trial out of which she got six months in prison. "They tried to prove I couldn't be believed, but every man they asked," she said proudly, "every man they put on the stand, crooks and honest men, they all said the same. 'When Kit Brandon tells you something it's the truth' they all said."

The woman, in her talk, trying to reach back.

"I tried to run, that time, wanted to, but I couldn't," she said. "He came over to me, close. Stood there. I could feel his breath on me. I don't know what would have happened, if we'd been somewhere, say up in the woods, just out of sight. I might have let him. I don't know.

"He touched me again and that broke it. I didn't have any more wood in my arms now.

"He put his hand, lightly, up on my shoulder again and then again ran it, his fingers down across one of my breasts. I turned and went out of the house. I didn't tell any one." It might have been, even then, that she had got that thing, so characteristic of her later.

"Goddam you, I'll take my own part. You don't need to bother to look out for me."

And afterwards, that night, and for several nights after that, while that big run of moon whiskey was being run off for the unknown big-town man who had contracted for it, Kit, barelegged, barefooted, in the cold, in the dark up there hidden in the bushes, near where the little road ran up into the big road, by the bare place, the bell with her — some rags to wind around her feet to keep them from freezing; the long dark hours of waiting and watching, her father, with the other men at work at the still—hurriedly, furiously working, that big man who had so touched her—her first— with them, smoking his cigar. "He got away with it, I let him. Maybe my father would have killed him," she said.

"I'll keep my eyes on that little gal. She'll be ripe soon."

He never got her. The long nights, half frozen up there, in that high altitude, days in the cornfield—the mother, that dirty slovenly one in the house down below.

"Getting ready to have another kid. I can't remember whether or not she'd quit having them then."

For ten years of my own life I had lived among the mountain people out of whom Kit Brandon had come. I had gone hunting with them, traded horses with them, been to wed-

dings and deaths among them. I knew the Freys of East
Tennessee and Kit's mother was a Frey. I was curious about
her leaving home, striking out for herself. Other women and
girls I knew had gone out of the hills to work in cotton-mill
towns, as Kit did, but they seldom went alone.

A family moved down out of the hills to such a town and,
when there were several children, particularly girl children,
the father often became what is known in Southern mill
towns as "a mill daddy." He put his wife and all of his
daughters to work in the mill. You will see such men in any
mill town. They are lost there. Such a man in the hills at
least kept on the move.

He went off to work in some still. He worked, occasionally,
in his corn patch. He took a bag of shelled corn on his shoulder and went to the mill to get meal. He set off on horse-
trading expeditions or walked long miles, often over high
mountain ridges to take a passel of ginseng root, dug up on
some remote mountain, to the country cross-roads store,
there to sit for an hour or two gossiping with other mountain
men.

But, in a mill village——

Such a man, too old perhaps to work in a modern high-
speed cotton or rayon mill, living in a little company house,
in a company town.

These mountain men know nothing of helping a woman
about the house, or tending a garden — "That's woman's
work" — and in a mill town they are lost souls, wandering
aimlessly about, sitting like Indians in the sun and perhaps
gazing off, all day, toward the hills out of which they have
come.

"Was it that way with you and your dad?" I asked Kit,

speaking of all this out of my own knowledge, and, "No," she said. She seemed reluctant to speak of her home leaving. "I was sixteen," she said, and stopped. She began speaking of the year she spent as a mill hand, the big light room in which she worked, of a room foreman at that place and of an adventure she had with him.

Of her going on the night shift in the mill, and the feel of the mill at night. "I got over into the loom room." Talk of the strange adventures of a young and good-looking girl, suddenly come down out of the quiet hills, to the crowded town, a strike she was in, the difficulty of learning to talk freely with people.

Of her hunger for the hills and the isolation of life in the hills. "I was glad to get over into the night shift. I couldn't sleep at night."

There were impressions remembered, fragments of adventures told about, in a cotton mill in Tennessee, later in a shoe factory in another town, sex adventures had, men who had tried, as she said, to put it over on her——

Married men and single men——

"Sometimes I let them get away with it, sometimes I didn't."

She had got her own kind of sophistication and had a theory I have heard expressed by others.

It was something about the life of women, the sort of modern women who are thrown out of homes into the world of the modern factory workers.

"It might go for any man or any woman, what I think."

"But what do you think, Kit? What are you driving at?"

She found it hard to say. "I haven't got any words for it." There was a puzzled look in her gray-green eyes. During the time she was with me Kit did practically all of the driving and she was the best driver I ever rode with, could get more out of a car without hurting the car. Like many modern people, she had got the feel of machinery down into her veins, into all of her body.

She kept trying to say something and fell into long times of silence.

She had on the little jersey. "Do you mind leaving the window open?" This love of the open, even on cold raw days, perhaps something come up out of her childhood in a mountain cabin, where doors are always left open winter and summer. Kit said, "I went barefoot, winter and summer, until I was sixteen." She went barefoot all day, out of doors, when she was a child at home, and to school—often when there was deep snow in the mountains. Sitting in there, barefooted, barelegged, on a hard bench without a back—great cracks in the floor, and between the logs of which the schoolhouse was built.

The teacher, a man, had on boots and he, she said, was always chewing tobacco and spitting into a little box beside his desk.

Snow drifting through the cracks between walls, bitter cold winds sucking up through the cracks of the floor.

Kit, in the car, as I sat looking at her profile had extraordinarily good features. The nose, mouth and chin were all cleanly drawn and she had a high white forehead. Her hair was blue-black.

She was trying to tell me. "I've often thought. It's good sometimes to tell everything."

Men can be beasts and so can women, too.

I'm not trying to reproduce her exact words. I can't.

You can go through any possible experience. A dog rolls in offal sometimes.

It doesn't change him.

She evidently wanted to say that she thought she had been something when she started life and that she was the same after the experiences she had been through.

Being a factory girl, then a clerk in a store, in a city—it was a five-and-ten-cent store, she said—then her marriage into a famous family of bootleggers in a certain Southern industrial town, her becoming, herself, first a little bootlegger, then a big one.

Her becoming a notorious woman rumrunner . . . this during prohibition, of course . . . men met, some, she frankly said, even lain with.

"Not a one of them has ever touched me yet."

"You mean you kept something?"

"Yes."

"You think you've still got it to give?"

She turned and stared at me, a peculiar long stare she had —like the stare of a gipsy woman, or of many mountain women of the American Southern Highlands. Then she smiled.

"I reckon you ain't trying to start nothing?" she asked, and "No," I said. I perhaps knew it would do me no good.

"Yes, I think I've got it," she said.

She had . . . I finally got the notion out of her broken remarks . . . the idea . . . it certainly isn't an American notion . . . I have known a few Europeans and particularly Russians and a Turk who had the same notion. . . .

"You mean, it's best sometimes to throw everything away. Is that what you're driving at, Kit?"

"Yes, something like that."

I was trying to help her say what I thought she was trying to say.

"You think all people have, well, let's say meanness, low-ness in them?"

"Yes. Sometimes, after I'd got into the newspapers, was what you call notorious—sometimes when I was in jail, other women came to see me.

"They were what is called respectable women.

"There was one I remember . . . a young one . . . she was a good looker . . . she was the daughter of a man who owned a factory in the town where they had jailed me. Her father, a rich man, was the superintendent of the Presbyterian Sunday School there.

"She managed, some way, to get into the jail and into my cell.

"It was winter and she wore very beautiful furs.

"You have to remember," Kit said, "that, at the time, I was being played up a good deal in the newspapers.

"I had driven a high-powered car, several times, at seventy miles an hour, right through the business streets of that town, the law after me.

"She had on the nicest pair of shoes I ever saw on a woman's feet," said Kit. "She was a good-looker okay." A little blush came on Kit's cheeks as she talked. "What the hell," she said. The newspapers had been playing her up. "They had told all sorts of yarns. They had said I had diamonds set in my teeth."

The woman, that young woman, daughter of the town's rich man, of the factory owner, Sunday School superintendent . . . "oh, she was so very, very respectable. . . .

"She was a virgin, she told me so," Kit said.

She wanted Kit to take her in.

"What?"

"Yes. I was in the cell there in the jail. There was another cell near by and they had thrown some drunken Negroes in there.

"They kept swearing, the kind of filthy words men say at such times — strings of them.

"It was a kind of howling profanity," Kit said, "but not any worse than the police can sling out, I'll tell you that.

"By that time I'd heard plenty of it."

She said that when the young woman, so richly clad, came in there to her at night . . . she had been brought by a young son of the jailer. . . .

"He came to the door of the cell two or three times." Kit said that he, the jailer's son, was nervous.

"I understood her all right," Kit said. "She was like me. She was a good kid."

"You mean she liked it, wanted it, what she had heard of your life at that time?"

"Yes. The third time, he — the jailer's son — came to the cell door and called to her to come out, to leave me, she swore at him. "Get the hell out of here," she said. "Goddam you, you let us alone."

"You mean, do you, she wanted, or thought she wanted, the kind of life you had, or that she thought you had, because her own life was too dull?"

"Not just that. Not just the dullness," said Kit.

She meant, obviously Kit was trying to say, that she thought it was better for all people, if they had it in them . . . she thought almost everybody did . . . to be sometime in life openly, even publicly, low. I was curious, questioning her.

"You mean," I asked, "that if you want to kill some one it's better to go and do it than to go around with killing in your heart?"

"Yes, to do that or any other low or mean thing," she said.

"Right out publicly before all the world, you mean?"

She seemed to have the notion . . . it was a kind of philosophy she had built for herself out of her experience.

"We're low and we're high. It's better to feel everything you can feel — throw it away."

I remembered, as Kit talked, a conversation I had once had with a famous artist, a painter. "A man can't really paint unless he can also be an utter skunk," the painter had said.

"You mean that the woman who came to you, the rich young woman, a virgin . . . she didn't care about that.

"You mean she would have gone through with it, taken on your kind of life?"

"She would have done it gladly," Kit said. "Some will and some won't. They haven't the guts."

"And there is something gained by it?"

"Yes," said Kit.

She said that, as regards herself, she had always kept something clear, and could keep it, she said, "in spite of hell and high water."

I gathered, however, that she hadn't encouraged the woman who had wanted to go away with her, to become a part of what she had heard of Kit's life. She had found her own life in the house of the respectable man, her father, too dull and false.

"But you didn't take her?" I said.

"I didn't. What I'm talking about, you can't do with any one else."

It was a spring day on the Brandon mountain farm and Kit was with her father in an upland field planting corn. It was on a day when the little leaves on the trees in the wood beside the field where she and her father were at work were just beginning to uncurl. The country of the Brandons—and also out of which came the Boones, the Lincolns and many other sturdy American figures—is very beautiful. Recently, within the last generation, it—the Southern Highland—has come elbowing its way into America's consciousness. There is the TVA with headquarters at Knoxville, paved roads are being built through the hills and up mountain hollows, figures of mountain men and women walk through the pages of our literature. "They are a brave people." "They are undernourished, dangerous, courteous, killers, chicken thieves," this and that.

They are people and in spite of all yet done of road building, power dam building by government, town building by government, they are an isolated people.

There are but few rich valleys and the rest of the hill country covering parts of several states is wild, and often forbidding, without roads.

Formerly the whole region—a little isolated empire in the heart of America—was covered with hardwood forests.

The great lumber companies came, the coal companies, ripping out the timber, ripping out the coal. The big companies left a wild country more wild. There are deserted mining and lumber towns, denuded hills, once covered by majestic timber, the soil now washing away with every rain, clear streams made muddy, the hills every year growing more and more bare—an old old story in America now. "We are after the money. Let the land and the people of the land go to hell."

The native people stayed on in little coves, in upland hollows—always the little cabin, often without a floor, with but one room—the Brandon cabin was of that sort.

Planting a little corn, doing a little hunting, loafing a lot—
men and women living this sort of life. Some of the families,
English, Scotch-Irish, Dutch, have been in the hills since
before the Revolutionary War.

Life, modern life, with its high-powered swift machines,
new comforts, in clothes, houses, food—all of the modern
conveniences of life—these passing on by.

The language, words coming straight down out of Eliza-
bethan England; songs—low-keyed, always sad and wistful.

Kit Brandon, when she was telling her story to me—often
broke into one of these low-keyed songs.

Her father had made himself a piece of new ground. If you
know the Blue Ridge mountain country, the Southern Ap-
palachians, you know also what that means. You work a
piece of new ground, brush-grown—angle of thirty, or even
forty-five degrees—plow it, cultivate your corn, hoe it, and
after a year or two of this, there's no ground left.

Rains come and wash your land away. It washes away,
down into the mountain streams, these after heavy rains often
running thick yellow, like molasses.

John Brandon, Kit's father, had made himself a piece of
new ground on a hilltop. He did it by ringing the trees. You
go through the standing-timber in the fall and chop a ring
completely around each tree and it dies. They stand up there,
these forests of dead trees, like ghosts. Now the sunshine can
get down, through the dead tree branches to the soil to let
the corn grow. It is hard, back-breaking plowing, roots of
killed trees catching your plow point, you, at the plow
handles, often jerked, even thrown over the plow. John Brandon kept chickens in a little shed back of his house and had
saved the chicken droppings. He saved the wood ashes from
the open fireplace in his cabin—this for fertilizer. The

younger children of the family carried the ashes up the hill, in tin pails. They dumped it in a little heap. Kit took a pailful of the mixture and went along the rows. She had a little sack, "a poke," she called it, of seed corn, slung over her shoulders.

Her father, that dark alive man, silent, working with her, making the holes for the seed corn, into which she dropped the seed. The chicken droppings scraped up and saved and the wood ashes spread over the ground. The spring day turned hot. There were cut raw places on her hands. The lye in the wood ashes burned the cut places. She was fourteen and growing tall. This was during the spring after her adventure with the man in the house. The smaller children had got their work done and had gone away. She and her father had brought their lunch up into the field and ate it sitting on the grass at the field's edge. "We didn't talk," Kit said, and I knew what she meant. Mountain people, like Indians, can work or sit together for hours without speaking. Knowing that mountain women commonly work in the fields with their men, I asked Kit about her mother.

"She was down there, in bed I guess," she said. There was contempt in her voice. "When there was work to do she was always sick." She would have been down there, in her dirty bed, lying there. Kit said her father seldom spoke to his wife. He had got her, was stuck with her, she said. Like many another man with a slovenly or ill-tempered wife he had found silence the best way out. Kit had got the breakfast for the family. She had fried fat pork and made corn bread to take up the hill to eat at the noon hour.

She was slow getting to the point, sitting in my car, telling about that day, so evidently a vitally important day in her life—she the woman of thirty, slender and good to look at.

There were rings on the fingers that had once dropped the mixture of wood ashes and chicken manure in the corn holes in the field.

She spoke of a stream that came down from a higher mountain, high beyond the one in which they were planting corn.

I had got a feeling as to what was coming as she talked.

She kept speaking of the stream, the sound the stream made, falling down over rocks, bends in the road beyond— the dead trees standing up white and gaunt, in the field. "My father was more silent than I'd ever known him to be.

"My dress was torn. I had on a thin old dress. I hadn't any underwear."

She said a cowbird kept calling in the wood near by. "It was almost time to quit for the day. I had to go on down to the house. We had two cows to milk that year," she said.

She was about to leave the field, having reminded her father of the milking to be done before darkness came, when he touched her arm. "Come on," he said, and she said also that the touch of her father's hand on her shoulder that evening did something strange to her. "Right away," she said, "I thought of that other fellow, the big man touching me that way down there in the house." Her father led the way out of the field, and over a fence into another field where thick laurel grew. Kit said she followed her father in silence, wondering a little — in a way new to her — fearful of him. They came, she said, to where the stream they could see from the field came down through a wood.

There was a little place with grass.

She said there was a place you could look through, where the stream went down. It was, as I understood her, a kind of vista.

There were thick mountain rhododendron all along the stream.

You could look through, between tall trees, just coming into leaf now, along the stream and down and far away to where there was another wood, across the little valley, the big road that went to their mountain town, the county seat, cutting across their valley farther down and disappearing in the wood beyond. "I saw a car go along the road," she said. She broke off, telling the story and I, listening, did not look at the woman telling it. We were in my car and she stopped the car beside the road, on a low hill. This in early evening. There was a silent time and I saw in fancy the hill child and her father coming through the wood and to the grassy place by the stream's edge as in a moving picture. Odd that I already knew what was coming. "I saw a car go along the road," Kit said again, and as she said it I saw a man, in a farmyard, with a woman and some children, get into a car, to drive off to some Western town, along the road we were going. Kit also saw it. "I guess maybe they're going to the movies," she said.

She broke off, breaking from the present and immediate into the past and her childhood, to speak of the bit of road she could see from between the thick bushes that grew beside the stream where she went with her father, saying that she had, at that time, been to town but once in her life. She was wanting to tell her story and not wanting. It may be that she was a little fearful that the telling would change my attitude toward her. She began sparring for time and started another story.

She had gone with her father to a trial at the courthouse where he was a witness. It was a trial of that man, the man with the cigar who had touched her breasts with his fingers, and he was being tried for liquor making.

Her father was on the stand lying.

"Didn't you make liquor with him, John Brandon?"

"No, sir, I didn't."

"He was seen at your house. He came there several times. He was seen coming and going."

"Yes, he came."

"You were in with him then? You made liquor with him? You were one of the men who made liquor with him?"

"No, sir, I wasn't."

"What was he doing at your house?"

"I dunno."

A lawyer getting facetious. "Was he courting? Was there some one to court there?"

"No, sir, there wasn't!"

"Stand aside."

They had got nothing out of John Brandon, her father. She said she did not want to tell the story of the evening with her father and, sensing a little the significance of what she was trying to get at, I tried to help her.

"At that place, by the stream, that evening, did he just . . ."

"No. He said we would wash."

"Did you know what was coming?"

"No. I did and I didn't."

There was in Kit evidence of an old terror. As she talked in a low voice, hurriedly, I had the curious feeling that the mature woman, sitting with me in the car, had gone and that the mountain girl she had once been had returned. Some-

thing happened that definitely ended her relations with her
father and that perhaps brought on a premature maturity
but it was not what I was fearing and I was intensely relieved.

There was my own imagination, leaping forward as she
talked, her words coming in low broken sentences.

They were there, father and daughter, at the creek's edge,
in the failing light, and her father took off his clothes and
bathed. He did not look at her put presently spoke. "Take
off your things," he said gruffly and she undressed. "Now
come here." There was this strange terrible moment for the
child about to become a woman. She went trembling toward him. There is a look that comes into men's eyes. It
was now almost dark in there, under the trees, and the
stream, coming down over rocks to form a little pool, made
a roaring noise.

And there had been that other experience in the mountain cabin . . . the man with the cigar and the thick fingers
on her young breasts. In these isolated families in the hills,
sometimes. . . .

He gathered cold water in his cupped hands and began to
bathe her, the cold water falling down over her slender
shoulders. His fingers touched her flesh, the figure of the
other man, with the great cow-like mouth, danced before her.

"I don't know. I guess I'll never know," she said.

She grew suddenly alarmed and ran from him. There was
a sudden snapping of the cord that had bound her to him
and she ran, snatching up her clothes. She ran through a
strip of wood and across the upland cornfield, naked in the
evening light. He didn't call to her, didn't pursue. She slipped
into her clothes, standing at the field's edge near the house.

Kit didn't say anything more, except to explain, after a

long silence, that what happened to her that evening up there
in the hills, at the stream's edge, hadn't meant much to her
and it was very evident as she gave the explanation, trying
to laugh as she did so, that she had been quite ruthless with
herself, had torn open an old sore.

She was far from clear also as she told me of how, later
that night, when it was dark in the house she came down,
silently, out of the little loft, where she slept with the younger
children, climbing silently down an outside ladder, and got
out of her father's house.

"I walked all night. I went to town and beyond."

"Did you take any food?"

"No," she said.

I was still curious.

"Did you have any money?"

"No, I hadn't a cent," she said and began, a little too
eagerly, to explain that she hadn't left her home because of
what she feared might happen.

"It wasn't that. I just thought I'd go," she said.

Kit ended her story with that declaration and then an odd
and to me quite terrifying thing occurred. She was driving
and had stopped the car under a tree beside the road but with
her story's end, she drove on. She drove desperately and rather madly I thought, the light having gone out of the day. I
remember that we went whirling, at terrific speed, through
a town. She hadn't turned on the lights. We went plunging
along thus, in darkness, for perhaps a half hour, passing cars,
people yelling at us and then, turning on two wheels into a
side road, she eased the car down and lit a cigarette.

"Perhaps I'd better turn on the lights," she said, without
smiling, and, "Yes, Kit, it would be a good idea," I answered.

CHAPTER TWO

A BUSINESS man, of a certain town of the Upper South, first told me of Kit Brandon. "Boy, God," he said, "she's a tornado.

"And so innocent looking too."

One evening quite late he was driving his car to his home through a quiet residence street in his town.

There was a sudden uproar and he pulled his car out to the side of the road and stopped.

"I was scared stiff," he said. "Great God," he exclaimed, telling me of the adventure.

Although he was on a quiet street he could go on along that street, in that particular town, past several big estates, some of them many acres in extent, the sort of places rich people affect, big stone pillars, a border of box or pine trees along the paved road, boxwood, bought at huge prices from dealers who get them for a song from old impoverished Virginia home owners not on to the racket . . . reset on wide lawns . . . a big green house, two or three gardeners employed, winding paths, an artificial lake with water lilies, wooden and stone seats under trees, stable for saddle horses.

Wife a member of the local garden club, sending off to Europe for bulbs.

"Great God," the business man said, "What the hell's broke loose now? I was scared stiff.

"Since there's been so much kidnapping going on in the country a man, who has buckled into a little dough . . . or if he has kids."

"They might even grab the wife," I said, and, "Yes," he said and smiled. "That would be an idea," he said.

It was a liquor-running fleet, six cars, all high-powered, come off a highway that led back, a hundred miles or more, to the hills and the rough country . . . this in a North Carolina cotton mill and cigarette town . . . millionaires in the town too . . . they got rich fast during the World War, the cotton mill men.

. . . big mill villages, owned by the mill men, out somewhere, in another part of the town—or beyond the town limits, rows and rows of small frame houses, just alike, flower beds in front of each door sometimes, all just alike.

"If a man can't be safe from flying bullets even in his own street, in his own town. These federal men ought to clean those people out."

The man talking to me having all through the prohibition period his own bootlegger to look out for his needs. He'd been drinking with some of his rich friends that very night. It was past midnight.

"I may even have been a little bit drunk." He thought that Kit, who was piloting the liquor cars and was several blocks ahead of them, must have been making eighty.

I gathered that the federal men, several of them, in a big fast car were after the convoy of rumrunners. They were trying to cut out cars, shoot holes in tires. The cars roared down upon my acquaintance, the rich man.

"And then?"

And then a car shot out of a side street and hit the car carrying the federal men and wrecked it. It was Kit, who must have gone whirling aside, into a side street and had doubled back. "She acted as though her life didn't mean a damn thing to her," my acquaintance said. Kit's car was also wrecked, smashed—but in a moment she crawled out of it and ran to where the federal men lay.

Luckily none of them were killed.

"I don't know whether it was lucky or not. I don't like those guys much," the rich man said. There was a man had two ribs broken and another had his head cut rather badly.

The six rum-running cars Kit had been piloting went flying on their way. They disappeared.

My own acquaintance, telling me all this later—we sat comfortably enough in a New York speakeasy—saw a slender young girl crawl out of the car that had caused the wreck. She had a long cut on one of her arms, from flying glass, he thought.

"Oh, dear. Oh, dear," she kept saying. "I lost control," she said. "There was something went wrong with my brakes."

She seemed quite cut up about the federal men, helping each other out of the wreck.

They hauled her up, of course, had her in court and she paid a fine—"for reckless driving," my man said, and laughed. "Reckless! Why it was inspired," he said. He said he thought maybe the judge was fixed.

"She had a good explanation all right," he said. At that time Kit wasn't very well known. She hadn't yet become a newspaper story.

"But just the same," said my acquaintance, a North Carolina business man . . . he is pretty shrewd, I take it for granted he must be, he has made so much money . . . I had the feeling that he was getting wise after the fact. . . . "Just

the same," he said, "I had a hunch. She was standing under a
street lamp and was going on like that. 'Oh, you poor men,
you poor men.' A hell of a lot she cared. She was a damned
good actress, I'll say."

The federal car, when she had hit it, had skidded right
across the road and into a tree and later my man had to go
and be a witness when Kit was up for trial. She had a good
story about where she'd been and how she happened to be
out alone at that time of night. "I didn't know then, not
until afterward, and the court didn't know that she was living, at that time, with the son of the biggest bootlegger in
our part of the State," my man said.

He was a little shocked. He found out later that the crowd
with which Kit was working were the very ones that brought
him his stuff.

"I had a kind of feeling for her . . . I swear I did," he said,
"seeing her standing there, so young and brave looking under
a street light." He said she had on a white blouse and that
the arm of it was all covered with blood.

"I took her and the two hurt federal men in my car to a
hospital in town and there we got out of the car, some men
from the hospital helping the man with the broken ribs. . . ."

He spoke of a light, over the front entrance to the hospital.

"She seemed such a lady to me.

"And yet.

"I found out later, that she once worked in one of my
mills."

However, he went to see her once; he had in some way
found out where she was living. It was while her cut arm
was mending. He had got a notion, perhaps a hope. He had
seen her go roaring along the street, ahead of the rum-running car, but he did not say so in court. He had seen her then

and had seen her later, standing under a street light when she had crawled out of her car. He had heard her words of sympathy for the hurt men, himself sitting in his own car at the side of the street—her declaration that her brake had gone wrong. He said he saw a little smile play over her lips as she stood wringing her hands by the wrecked car in the street. "I made up my mind I'd better let her alone," he said.

There must have been several rather dreary years for Kit Brandon—in between. When she went down out of the hills, barelegged, barefooted, after the adventure with her father, frightened and also shocked. She became a factory worker.

We spoke of the night when she ran away from home.

"And did you get down to the town, to the county-seat town before it was light?"

"Yes. I ran most of the way. It was still dark when I got to town. I went on through."

There was that picture of Kit, as girl child, so self-possessed when I knew her. Her association afterwards with men—hard-boiled enough men, most of them rumrunners and crooks—had perhaps given her her self-possession. I went afterwards to see some of her later associates, talked with several of them. They had an attitude, I thought, like men at war. There was a war on—a special race sprung up in the midst of society, in cities, in the hill country of the Upper South, gangs formed, leaders sprung up. There were native-born Americans, in the cities shrewd Jews, men from the south of Europe, Italians, Hungarians, Czechs.

Kit said, "You go to see some of the ones whose names I'll give you. You won't have any trouble finding some of them. They'll be in jail."

"Most of them, when they went into the racket, were young fellows," she said. "It was a young man's game."

"It was for them a game, like war." She told of a young man she'd known. "They never got onto Jim, didn't know who he was."

I got it that Jim was a young fellow of eighteen, going into the racket actuated by the same motives as the rich manufacturer's daughter who once came to her in a jail cell.

This one, the one she called Jim, she knew after she had herself got broken into the game.

"He was one of these bright ones." She told me Jim's story, saying that he was a kind of genius—"in book learning," she said.

He was also the son of a rich man and Jim wasn't his name.

He had got through a preparatory school at fifteen and then had two years in college.

Suddenly he quit it all. One night he was in a college town, in a speak-easy with other students, and he began talking to the proprietor. "Where do you get your stuff?" he asked. The proprietor of the speak-easy was a fellow who had been a prize-fighter. He had cauliflower ears. He hadn't made good as a fighter and had got out and had started the speak-easy.

He and the boy Kit called Jim got to be friends and Jim was taken to other men.

"He wanted excitement," Kit said. She understood that. The boy was his father's only son and the father owned a big furniture factory in a town of the upper South. A lot of factories had come down out of the North, the Middle West and out of New England into towns of Virginia, North Carolina and Tennessee—to lap up the cheap labor of hill billies and girls like Kit herself, girls who had left their mountain homes. They were wanting what they could not get at home, and "Why not?" I thought as Kit talked. Even into the most isolated of the mountain homes the catalogues of the big mail-order houses had begun to come. They were wanting what all modern girls and women are wanting. They were wanting new hats, silk stockings. They were wanting new dresses.

There was the new source of cheap labor, naturally intelligent and quick, young women and boys, out of the hills. A lot of them couldn't read and write. Kit had anyway got that far when she ran away from her father.

She had got a place in a factory, in Greenville, South Carolina, just over the line from North Carolina. It was a big and a growing town and when she was there, in the loom room of a big cotton mill, rooming in a house with a lot of other mountain people, she had gone to a night school.

She commented shrewdly. "They were taking a government census," she said. There were too many illiterates in the town and the state, and the manufacturers, having been criticized for working little children, sometimes working them sixty hours a week when they should have been in school, had paid to have out-of-work school teachers of the town and often young society women, eager to be uplifters, go to the workers at night. The idea amused her all right.

"Do you know what it means to pass as literate?" Kit asked. "It means you can read and write your own name. That's all."

The father of the young man named Jim had the big furniture factory. He made cheap furniture, the kind sold by mail-order houses and by city installment furniture stores. It is rolled out of the factories, so many millions of chairs, so

many millions of beds—beds, chairs, and tables that will
stand up and look shiny and new for a year or two. They
will stand up until the installments are paid.

In America, every day, trainloads of such furniture, knocked quickly together. There it goes. See the trains rolling
along. See the trucks on the new highways. Happy days
have come again.

The boy named Jim—Kit said he was a big laughing
young fellow, a kind of Jack Reed with gray eyes and big
shoulders . . . he had played football on his college football team.

He had been a fast, quick scholar. (She was living at that
time with a young man named Halsey, the son of Tom Halsey, one of the big rumrunners of that section of the country.)

Tom Halsey was not an Al Capone or a Legs Diamond, Kit
said, but he was big enough.

"So this kid," she said, "this Jim—you may have read about
his mysterious disappearance. It was in all of the newspapers.
His father and mother never knew what happened to him.

"He had a high-powered car. He was at the state university."

He had gone, I gathered, escorted by the ex-prize-fighter,
to Tom Halsey. "We used to pay fifty dollars for running a
big load, maybe an all-night trip, maybe less, all a car could
hold, maybe a hundred and fifty, two hundred miles." Kit
explained how it was done. "When we had to move the stuff
a long ways we had hide-out places." I gathered there was a
cache.

The gang, led by Tom Halsey, who was really a big business man, like Jim's father, got another man, one of his gang,
to rent a farm. A farm would be picked out that was in an
isolated place and that had a big barn.

Kit said that the man, so hired, or one of the gang who had been raised on a farm, would work the farm like any other farmer. She said laughing that he would be one farmer who did not have to complain about hard times, the price of hogs, the price of corn. "He'd have a woman with him, passing her off as his wife. He'd get a farm that was far away from any other place. The game was for the man to keep himself isolated. If he could get, in the neighborhood, the reputation of being mean and unneighborly, all the better. Tom Halsey might have a half dozen such places strung across the country in which he operated. Often the stuff, Kit said, had to be moved a long way.

So the man, one of the rumrunners—or there might be a fleet of cars—came to such a place at night. They loaded quickly and lit out for the next place. There were extra beds, for the rumrunners, in some of the places. A queer light came into Kit Brandon's eyes telling her story. Some of the places, isolated farmhouses, hidden away on side roads, innocent enough looking places, got, I gathered, quite lively at times.

There would be women brought in. When the liquor cache was isolated enough, Tom Halsey did not object to his men having a good time. There would be fights sometimes. She herself did not stay in these places. "There would be the goddamnedest women," she said. There would be a phonograph, drinking and dancing. The women, in such places, would get into bed with any man of the gang.

Jim, son of the rich man, the furniture manufacturer . . . he was no doubt a leading citizen of his town . . . member of the local Kiwanis or Rotary or Lions club . . . "I'll tell you, that boy of mine . . . he's a bright one all right" . . .

the father planning the future of his son. "I was a poor boy myself. I had to work my way up. That son of mine . . . I'll make a gentleman of him."

"We got quite a lot of bright young kids into our gang," Kit said. "What the hell!" she said.

She became, as she sometimes did, philosophical. She spoke again of Jim. He was one of the fastest and most daring of Tom Halsey's drivers.

"A kid like that," she said. He had been a football player in his second year in college, his name in the newspapers.

"You're a kid and you go on like that, maybe for three or four years, and then what?" she said.

"You make it pretty swell for your dad," she said.

The father could go about, among his associates, other business men, and brag,

"See, we licked them again."

I got a picture, as Kit talked, of fat middle-aged men at football games. They were sitting in grandstands with fat well-dressed women, their wives. Life had run fast for Kit after she got down out of her hills.

The young man, who had become in secret a member of Tom Halsey's gang, had, she pointed out, ahead of him the glowing prospect of going into his dad's furniture factory. He could, so easily, become a man like his dad.

Going to New York, or Chicago, seeing the buyers, buying them dinners, the theatre in the city at night. "What I like is a good musical show." There was, I thought, something surprising in Kit. She had learned fast, after she got into her racket.

The young man, the so-fortunate young American man, getting married. He would marry a rich girl, could, she said, go off to Palm Beach in the winter. He would be like one of the rich young men in a Hearst newspaper. He would be like a young man in a cigarette advertisement.

An American dream. "Jesus Maria," said Kit. The young fellow had been in revolt. He had been very educational with Kit. She said, quite frankly, that he had taken a fancy to her. "We were pals," she said.

He'd been around a good deal with his dad and made for Kit a picture of the sort of father who is forever speaking of his closeness to his son. Kit thought it nice of Jim that he seemed to have no special grouch on his father.

"They seem to like to brag," he said to Kit. "I guess it makes them feel swell." Her association with Jim had been one of the high lights in her life. Her curiosity was awakened because his whole background was something so different from her own.

And so there was Jim, one of Kit's friends, helping to make her what she became. He wanting excitement, to take chances. She said that Jim, more than many others of the Halsey gang, had understood Tom Halsey. The man Tom Halsey, as his figure was unfolded before me by Kit, became to me more and more an American figure. He became more and more an earlier American, one of our pioneers, a pioneer of business, of industry, I thought. He was like a man building a railroad across the continent in an earlier day . . . stealing land along the railroad as he went . . . corrupting legislatures of States as he went. He was like a fur trader, of an earlier day . . . breaking down the morals of Indians. He was an organizer in steel, in oil, he was a chief. Tom Halsey had begun his career in the liquor racket as driver, had fought his way up to the head of a mob, killing three or four men on the way up. Later, like all such men, when Tom Halsey had

got to the top—I got it from Kit that he never did quite become one of the great ones—he had hired others to do the
more unpleasant jobs.

Tom Halsey—I never saw him—was, at least outwardly,
a quiet enough fellow. He was even, in his own way, gentle.
It was difficult to get, from Kit, a definite picture of him.
"Oh, I don't know. He was all right in his way." That was
her word.

There was Kit, the mountain girl, with the background already suggested, with the young college man Jim. He was one
of her adventures. I have, I think, already declared that she
was herself a marvelous driver of automobiles. She and the
college boy became friends. When he was taken in with the
gang she went out with him, on two or three runs. Her doing
so made the man she was living with then—that was Gordon
Halsey, the no-account son of the big shot Tom Halsey—a
little sore but she had already grown tired of him. "I'd got
his number," she said.

"I never gave much of anything to him or any other man
I've been with that way," she said proudly. She said that a
woman, if she was onto her job, knew how to use what she
had, could go pretty far, all the way, with a man and give
nothing. "Men are pretty easy. Any woman knows about
that."

She went with the college boy on two or three runs at
night. "And could he drive!" Her eyes shining. She had—it
was as much a part of her as the hair on her head—this admiration for the skillful handling of automobiles. The boy
wasn't caring about the pay from Tom Halsey. He was doing
it for the fun, for the reckless fun of it.

Taking his chance of being shot, or killed, or caught, or
thrown into prison.

The wild plunges through the night, sometimes pursued by federal men, also in fast cars. The game often outrunning them, outwitting them. It is said that foxes, in a fox-hunting country, hearing the cry of hounds sometimes come gladly out of their holes, to get the hounds on their trail.

For the college boy it was that kind of game, to dodge sometimes into a woodland path, shut off the engine, lie low, or get into a side road or even into a strange farmyard, perhaps some farmer with a lantern coming out of his house. You put a gun to his guts. "Goddam you, lay low. Put out that light, quick, do you hear?

"And keep your trap shut."

You drive your car into an orchard beyond the farmer's barn. "He'll have something to talk about for months, the farmer will." A farmer, on such an out-of-the-way place, has a dull enough life.

"You get this straight, 'cause if you make a mistake I'll get you for sure."

Kit and that boy, on the road at night. The idea of such a boy ever shooting any one was, she said, absurd. Knowing him had helped make Kit what she was.

He had helped make her aware. He drove only at night, sometimes alone, sometimes as one of a fleet of six or eight cars, and he was keeping up his work in the school.

He was in a car with such a fleet often—Kit riding with him—and the other men, driving for Tom, were, Kit said, tough enough birds.

It was in a country he knew well. Kit said he talked and talked. He had, I gathered, given Kit, perhaps for the first time, an idea of the big world and how it is run.

"He was killed," she said, and told the story of that.

He had been unidentified after death and Kit said, smiling,

that she thought his father ought to be grateful for that. She
said it was lucky he wasn't driving his own car. He was driving a big Packard roadster belonging to Tom.

It was a stolen car and wasn't much good. There was a
fleet of liquor cars and she was acting as pilot. The boy with
the stolen car was, on that particular night, one of some six or
eight.

It made a story, simply told, Kit's tale of the rides and
talks with the boy. They would be plunging along. Two or
three times they were pursued. When they were pursued
there was a kind of fire came into Jim. Kit's eyes shone speaking of it. He was trying to tell Kit, the mountain girl, of the
world of his father, of industry and business.

He seemed to have made a study of it. She thought maybe
he was even a little cracked on the subject. He was terribly in
earnest. As they were speeding through the night, intent on
an illegal business, he spoke to her at length of men of whom
she had never heard.

There were the Rockefellers, the Morgans, the Goulds.
The boy's father, with his furniture factory, was but a little
piker. The other men, men of an earlier day—he mentioned
several of them. Kit could not remember the names.

They were such men as Tom Halsey or even bolder ones,
like Al Capone himself. They were men having a kind of
bold unscrupulousness the boy admired, and Kit said she listened to him thinking of herself.

She was thinking, she said, of her life as a factory girl and
of how she might have gone on being that and she spoke
with a kind of understanding bitterness of the fate of thousands, perhaps even millions, of such girls and women.

Giving, she said, what they had, that is to say their lives.
She had got for herself, vaguely, a kind of idea . . . her mar-

riage, to Gordon Halsey, son of the successful big bootlegger, had been a part of a kind of program she had made for herself.

She had been, after her escape from her home, what she had been, that is to say a factory girl. She had been in a cotton mill and a shoe factory. She had been a clerk in a five-and-ten-cent store.

And all the time she had been thinking and planning. She was, she said quite frankly — she knew it well enough — what woman doesn't know — quite a pretty girl. Although she had, for herself, within herself, no special call toward men, they seemed to want her. She had been specially attracted toward the college boy Jim because he made no play for her.

She had liked that and she had liked his telling her how things are run in the world. "I wanted to know," she said and spoke at length of the years when she was a working woman — men of all sorts making their plays for her.

There had been one man, son of a man who owned one of the factories in which she had worked. "I was pretty green," she said. She had let him take her out in his car.

She had gone even farther than that. It had happened to her. She had got, she said bluntly, the notion into her head that she might get him so . . . there had been talk of love . . . but it had not worked out.

Later and when she was employed as a clerk in the five-and-ten-cent store Tom Halsey's son had fallen for her, she had profited by that other experience and had driven a harder and a shrewder bargain.

"But as to Jim, the manufacturer's son?" I said, calling him back to her.

She explained that a pilot car ran on ahead of a fleet.

As I understood it, on certain occasions, when what she called "the law" was laying for them . . . often, she said, they had been tipped off . . . there would be a certain tenseness.

The law would be somewhere waiting for them. There would be cars parked on a side road, just off the big road along which they sped.

Mystery of the night. Tenseness.

And it was the business of the pilot, running on ahead, to spot the law and drop back. He let the others catch up to him and gave a signal.

The signal was for the other drivers to give her the gun, if possible to scatter, in any event to get the hell down the road.

It was a rule among liquor runners to try to have always faster and better cars than the law.

As for the individual driver, it was his business, if he got into a place where he could not escape, to wreck his car.

He was to save himself if he could. When his car was wrecked he could, if he was lucky, if there were no legs or arms broken, jump and run for it.

"He was to let the car and the load go to hell.

"And, if caught, he was to keep his mouth shut."

There was an understanding. A man like Tom Halsey, one of the big shots, if you were working for him and got caught . . .

He would put up the money to get you clear. He would hire the best lawyers. Jurors could almost always be bought.

Kit was telling the story of what had happened to her friend, Jim. He was driving the last car, that big stolen Packard, and it wasn't so good. They had planned after the one trip to leave it somewhere in the road.

There were two of the law's cars and she had cut one of them out, stalling her own car in the road before it, the law cursing at her, but the other got clear. It took out after the Packard. "We were within about two miles of a town, and the Packard wasn't so fast."

The two cars raced along the road, the law's car constantly gaining, the law shooting at the tires of the Packard. The other cars, also containing officers, the one she had managed to stop, had, with a good deal of cursing—cries, she said, of, "You wait. We'll get you, you bitch"—got clear and was following as was she.

"I was crying," she said.

She said it was bad business, crying at such a time. It was because she liked the boy in the car ahead and was afraid they would get him. She said the tears in her eyes made her drive like a punk. It was her notion that she should get in front of both cars containing the law and either stop them or wreck their cars.

She hadn't any gun, she said, because a pilot car, driven as hers was by a seemingly innocent girl . . . it was her game if caught to pull the innocent racket. . . . "I couldn't shoot," she said.

The Packard car, driven by Jim—in the game as Kit had explained only for the fun and excitement to be got out of it —had got into the main street of a town. It was a small county-seat town and there was a courthouse with a lawn in front. There was an iron fence.

And so Jim, in the stolen Packard, went right through the fence.

There were stone steps that went up to the courthouse door and Jim's car dashed for them—something may have gone wrong with the steering rod of the car. It plunged half way up the steps and turned over and Jim's body was so crushed, his face so crushed, that he could not be identified.

"He was sure killed dead," Kit said. "He was a swell kid," she added. She said there wasn't a thing on him that could be used for identification. The car he drove had been stolen. What could you make out of that?"

"And you?" I asked, when Kit had finished the tale.

"I'd turned into a side street," she said. "I went to have a look." None of the officers had recognized her as the girl who had stalled the car in the road.

It seemed to me that Kit was trying to prove to me how hard-boiled she could be.

"We buried him all right," she said. "The men of Tom Halsey's crowd had got a woman, the mother of a man of the crowd, to identify the college boy as one of her sons.

Kit said that for weeks the newspapers of the State were full of the story of a college boy who had mysteriously disappeared. His father and in particular his mother would not believe he was dead. "I guess they are still looking for him. Maybe his mother is praying for him," Kit said, and when I turned to look at her I saw, as I often did during our talks, an odd far-away light in her eyes.

CHAPTER THREE

K IT BRANDON had certainly her own nice strangeness. She talked of her experiences as a young girl, growing into womanhood, after she had run away from her home.

She was at work in the spinning-room of a big cotton mill. Afterward, in the year after she left the mill, there was a strike, a peculiarly ugly strike with several people killed. She had no part in that, no part in the agitation that led up to it. The labor movement, labor getting all the time more and more self-conscious, gaining thereby more self-respect, apparently gaining strength, obviously didn't touch her.

Kit was in the big spinning-room of the mill, having "a side" to care for, light streaming in at the windows, the walls of the big room all painted white, with the rafters up above a light blue. "A side," she explained, was one worker's section, a place of many flying bobbins.

There was a mist, a fine mist of cotton lint in the air. The employees were called "lint-heads" by the people of the town.

"We didn't live in the town. We had our own town, or rather it was a town owned by the mill."

"It was pretty," Kit said. She was impressed, had come down out of the hills, barefooted, barelegged.

"It was a Saturday when I got down there."

There had been an old man in a battered Ford who had picked her up in the road. "He was a nice old man," she said.

She had been frightened and trembling when he had stopped his car in the road but she was very tired and very hungry. In fancy I saw her thus, a half wild thing, like a little animal, a rabbit crouched in long grass in a field, a hunter with his dogs and his gun passing near. "I might have walked and run twenty miles." She said that the old man, an old worker, took her to the cotton-mill town and to his house. It was a little frame house, at the edge of the town. He was a carpenter and a small farmer, she said.

He had nieces, two young girls who worked in the mill, and they told Kit what to say when she went to apply for work and later one of the girls helped her to get the trick of it, the trick of the tying in of the broken threads on the fast-flying bobbins.

There was a little machine you held in your hand. One of the girls had loaned her shoes and stockings to wear until she got a little money ahead and could buy her own. "The girls were nice," she said. There was in them the niceness, the often almost unbelievable kindness of the poor.

She found it difficult to talk to others. "For a long time I just couldn't say a thing," she declared. I gathered she had gone for weeks about her work, the two girls, nieces of the old farmer-carpenter, having got her a place to board in the mill village. Their own house was small. She said, "I had to sleep with the two girls, all three of us in one bed. One of the girls, the older one"— they were, I gathered, mere children—"had asthma. She sat up in bed at night and fought for breath."

The mill village seemed to Kit a very pretty place. The

thing that had offended me in my studies of such places,
what I had thought the deadly sameness of the little houses,
all painted the same color, little flower beds before the doors
of many houses all alike, all of this had in no way offended
her.

"It was nice," Kit said and I gathered from her talk that
she liked something that had happened to her there.

The particular mill in which she worked was a kind of
show place, belonged, as I knew, to a company that also
owned several other big mills. During the World War the
company had made money hand over fist.

There was a big income tax to pay.

How foolish to pay all that money to government! Why
not spend the money to build more and more mills?

"We'll build a mill village that will make people sit up
and take notice."

It could be done, during the World War, and the money
so spent, often recreation houses for the workers built, tennis courts and baseball grounds laid off . . . such a feeling
of Christian virtue got . . . ministers of God hired and paid
by the mill . . . it could be done, during the World War
and the money spent, like the money spent for pages of advertising in newspapers and magazines, cost nothing. It so
cut down income taxes that it came as a gift from God. Oh
thou free and unhampered press!

And after the war, after the boom times, there remained
the new and bigger mills and the so glorified mill villages.
They both belonged to the companies. They did not belong
to the workers.

For a time Kit had loved the mill and the mill village. She
was lost there and wanted to be lost. There were so many
girls, so many men and women. She was like a young tree

in a vast forest, a blade of grass in the spring in a meadow.

She had begun from the first saving money. She worked for a few weeks on the day shift and then was shunted to the night shift. She explained, laughing, "I had to count the steps I went from the mill gate to another gate that led into the mill village." She meant that she was afraid she would get lost in the big strange place with its swarms of people. Oh, mighty world of the workers, the hundreds of thousands of men and women, even children in factory towns, mill towns, coal mining towns . . . the big factories, many of them very beautiful with a strange new kind of beauty . . . great dynamos, power out of rivers, dipped up out of earth, harnessed . . . the refinement of all this . . . speed, efficiency . . . the goods rolling out of the factories, something new, strange, wonderful . . .

Thought that we might all now go well shod, well clothed, well housed in a strange but new and comfortable world.

. . . fingers of workers willing . . .

. . . machines willing . . .

. . . the old stupidity, refusal to give to the lives of the workers the dignity that might make the revolutionized world, going on and on.

Kit turned to the right when she got to the gate of the mill. It was surrounded by a wall and there were climbing roses on the wall. She went down past four streets and turned to the left and took 273 steps and there she was at the door of the house in which she had come to live. What difference to her that it was exactly like some two or three hundred other houses in the prize mill village, so that you had to count your steps to be sure you had got to your own door?

And what strangeness, coming to that out of the lonely hill cabin!

She lived in the mill village with two older people, childless, who had both been in the mill since they were children. The woman of the house was small, silent and wiry. She was a weaver and her man a loom fixer. There were two young men workers also boarded in the house but Kit never saw them. When she was on the day shift they were working at night and when she was shunted to the night shift they were also shunted.

For some months she led a strange, silent, half-frightened life. She had to accustom herself to the new feel of people, always about her everywhere, eyes of young male workers, in the mill and in the street, as she hurried from mill to house, from house to mill, eyes taking quick account of her slim young figure, thick soft hair, straight, clean young legs . . . her young breasts, head that sat so nicely on white fleshed neck . . . other girls' eyes, often inviting her to friendship. One of the two girls, nieces of the old carpenter, was on her "side" for a time, helping her from day to day to acquire the trick of the work, and then she was sent away, ahead she went — twice she said — to the old carpenter's house, to take back the shoes and stockings she had borrowed. "I wanted to pay. I was at that house, when I first came, four or five days. I wanted to pay my board and for using the shoes and stockings. I had got some of my own." She talked, at length, of the little adventure, going to the house with the money saved and being ashamed to offer it and then going again. "I couldn't say so. There was something in them. They were so nice. They were an old pair, hard workers and childless."

"I was scared to try to say it," Kit said.

She talked of going at night, at first alone, when she had got a little accustomed to the new life, out of the mill village and down into the town. This would be on a Saturday night, the town crowded with mill girls and boys on their night off—the girl Kit, afterwards such a striking figure in the semi-criminal world of illicit liquor makers, rumrunners, liquor dealers—some of the mill girls so pretty in their clean washed and ironed dresses.

This would have been in the boom years of twenty-three and four, the mills crowded with workers, America's export business booming, huge harbors of cities full of ships, loading and unloading Coolidge prosperity.

Hoover, the engineer, who was to make the thing perpetual, put the chicken in every pot and the two automobiles in every garage, looming on the American consciousness.

"There must have been good going in the liquor racket that year in that town," Kit said laughing, as she thought back into the time of her own innocence, her greenness.

She making such a very enticing picture of herself, she still the frightened little mountain girl, straight legs, new stockings. There would be the picture of her going on one of the two trips down to the house of the old carpenter-farmer. She carried a bundle containing the borrowed shoes and stockings, under her arm. "I'd washed the stockings. They had holes in them."

She knew nothing of such little woman's tricks, darning of stocking and mending of clothes, but had watched the mill woman in the house where she had the room darn some stockings and then went and got needles and darning cotton in a five-and-ten-cent store.

"It seemed to hurt my jaws to speak, even to a clerk when I got into a store," she said, speaking thus of her first days in the big world.

She began going about, sometimes at night, in the streets

of a North Carolina town, keeping her eyes open. All the little
happenings of such nights made a deep impression on her.
At first she did not dare loiter in the streets, having an ever-
present fear that some one would speak to her, compelling
her also to say words. "As though I were hurrying to catch
a train," she said. She had started to tell me of a young boy
she met at that time in the mill but kept speaking of other
things, other adventures.

So that I would understand the strangeness, half wonder,
half terror of it all to her—coming so suddenly out of her
quiet hills, no sounds there sometimes for hours—except
perhaps the chattering of some mountain stream or the scold-
ing of a mountain boomer—the little red squirrel of the
hills.

The crowded industrial town and what being there, suddenly a part of it, had meant to her during those first weeks
and months—the bold eyes of people—girls walking the
streets with their young men—smell of the crowds, the feel
of the crowd in herself, it seemed to her at first, she said, in
the very bones and flesh of herself.

"You're so little, so lost. It's nice to be little and lost," she
said.

The eyes of a little hunted wild thing. They got bold
enough later. She began, almost at once, as soon as the first
quick terror had passed, to take note of other women and
girls, how they made their cheeks and lips red, the way they
did their hair, the clothes they wore.

"The young mill men didn't look at me much then," Kit
said smiling. "I was too countrified then."

She kept insisting upon her tale of the attempt to pay for
the use of the borrowed shoes and stockings and for the food

and the sleep had in the house of the old carpenter-farmer. She went there and went again.

"And so I went down along that street and got to where they lived. They had been so good to me, he and his wife and the two girls, his nieces."

It was out a little beyond the town.

The last time she went she stopped outside. She could hear the man talking to his wife inside the house. She didn't think she ought to be beholden to them. Her father, who had frightened her away from home, had always been saying that to her — "Don't be beholden to people," he said. She said that she thought afterwards that it was all foolishness.

Pride, often enough absurd, of a poor mountain man. Kit laughed at herself, telling of it. "It was pretty dark that night," she said. There was a fence and a gate but the gate creaked when you pushed it open and so, not wanting to be heard, she climbed over the fence. "I had a dollar. It was all I did have." She had already been at work for several weeks but had been buying clothes. "I had to, I was so near naked."

She kept saying to herself, "I'm going to thank them, I'm going to pay them." She had thought up some words to be used. "I was saying the words over aloud to myself that night while I was going down there," she explained. "Here mister is pay for my board, for the days I was here in your house, before I got my job.

"I ain't aiming to be beholden to you. You name it. How much is it I owe?"

A kind of ungraciousness in it all as a more sophisticated Kit herself later realized.

"And here's the stockings and the shoes you let me have." She said she had rubbed the shoes as clean as she could. She had tried to mend the stockings but had made a mess of the job and the woman where she boarded had seen her trying and had taken the job away from her.

"You name it—how much do I owe?"

It was at the time a great shame to her, not being able to do it. She had crawled over the fence and had got to the house door but there she stopped. There was talking going on in the house and the asthmatic niece was there and was having one of her spells. Kit could hear the queer whistling sound she made as she fought for breath. She said she laid the things she'd brought in the dark on the porch and put the dollar she'd saved inside one of the shoes. Then she got back over the fence and ran away into the darkness.

She jumped from that first tale of her life as a young mill girl to another.

She had worked for some months in the spinning-room of the big mill, that great light singing place. She said, "There was a new kind of quiet you got." She thought that even the faces of the young girls and boys working in the place changed. There was a singing roar. She had got into the night shift.

There was the white flying thread, coming down through the machines.

There you were, on your side, a little narrow passage, like the narrow hallway of a big house, light streaming down from above.

The thread came dancing, dancing. "It made you want to dance," Kit said. She began to like her life in the factory. That impulse didn't last. She thought the loss of the feeling of being a part of something big and significant came from a certain attitude toward workers by those up above. It came from society. It was in the town to which the workers trooped on Saturday night—contempt, held tight too, treasured by those not mill workers. Kit was shrewd. "It might be," she said, "that business people for example, people who lived by buying and selling—there were a lot of them—really felt cheapness, something mean in their own lives.

"So they had to pump up contempt for us."

However, at first, it was all different. "I liked it," she said.

The thread was coming down into and through the beautiful, smooth-running machines on her "side." "Go on, thread, come dancing down, run swiftly onto the bobbins, run into the great loom room, make cloth, make cloth to clothe all the world." It was dancing. It joined another thread and the two were twisted together, making one. "I don't know why it didn't break away into nothing, the so-little slender thread running so fast. It didn't often."

The thread was being spun. It was running down, at terrific speed, to be wound on to bobbins.

Come on, workers, stand together in this.

Makers of these modern beautiful machines, stand on your own dignity.

It may be the time will come, in the march of men, when your work will stand with that of other unknown men who built cathedrals in the Middle Ages.

It was all puzzling, new and strange enough to Kit Brandon, the night life in the big singing rooms in the mill, the other men and women, many girls, half children, so many of them, in the upper South, like Kit, off mountain farms, brought there from lonely quiet places . . .

. . . that they got love for the machines they tended.

. . . that they got love of factories.

Kit . . . "I liked it at night. There were two girls on a side. Mine was a tall red-haired girl.

"She was fierce. She could swear like a man.

"We had to tie in the broken threads. Sometimes a thread broke at one end of the long side and when a thread broke the machine stopped.

"You had to run there.

"Then a thread broke at the other end and you ran.

"Sometimes a lot of running, up and down, up and down.

"It was good to be young, with strong legs. It was good."

Kit spoke of how the singing noise in the mill was louder than your voice, even if you shouted. She thought it nice. You were lost in it.

She spoke of the lights at night, the way the moving shadows of machines, strange fantastic shapes, like in a dream, even shadow of the thin delicate thread, danced on the walls.

"Yes," I said, "making sometimes, lovely moving designs."

"What?" Kit said, staring at me.

The feeling workers get in the great factories of America . . . no poets among them yet to sing of it . . . the song, coming some day to be a part of the coming revolution too . . . the end of the glory of the day of the buyers and sellers, of the money men . . .

. . . the new thing in man's life, the machine in America so perfect, so intricate, doing so many marvellous things so marvellously.

Youngsters, almost children, driving modern high-speed American automobiles, over American roads—such roads never before known in all the world. Let's begin to sing this.

In the factory where Kit worked there seemed to be a

little level of sounds, a plateau, not used by the machines and
the young voices rode along this.

The night superintendent was always walking softly, un-
expectedly, through the rooms.

When one of the threads broke a machine stopped.

And there was the room foreman, Kit said he was always
snooping around.

She said the big, raw-boned red-haired girl, on her "side,"
swore viciously. In spite of all the rawness and hardness of
her earlier life Kit had never heard much profanity.

The red-haired girl spoke of the room foreman as a lousy
bastard.

"He's a goddam rat, a lousy bastard, I tell you. You look
out for him, kid."

She told Kit of how the man, who was married and had
kids, sometimes, in the middle of the night, when he knew
the superintendent had gone out of the mill to get his midnight lunch, tried to get some young girl, the younger the
better . . . he wanted to break 'em in—that was what he
wanted. The red-haired woman was named Agnes. "The
bastard's got a yen for the young ones, the green ones, the
fresh ones."

He took them into a little shut-off room, at a corner of the
big room.

"The lousy bastard . . . if he makes a proposition to a
girl, in there, and she won't, he'll lay for her, try to find
something wrong with her work——

. . . "too many machines stop on her side too often and he
gets her fired for it."

There was Agnes, the red-haired woman, who worked
with Kit on her side and Kit herself. A pale young man, concerning whom Kit had begun her tale of mill girl life, also

worked in the room. She said he was her first beau. He had already, on several occasions, come to see Kit at her rooming house, usually on a Saturday night. He came to the house and they sat together. There was a little porch at the front of the house. He was tubercular and told Kit he knew he hadn't long to live. Even a short walk tired him. Once they went down out of the mill village and sat on a bridge over a small stream. On moonlight nights they could see mountains in the distance. "He talked and talked. He liked talking to me," she said naïvely.

He thought it all wrong that he should be destined to die. The nearness of death made him talk strangely, "nicely," Kit thought. He thought a man should have at the least two hundred years of life, a hundred years, he said, to find out things and then another hundred to live—"in knowing"— he said.

There came moments between the two. "Come," he said to Kit one Saturday night . . . the mill remained closed on Saturday nights . . . they had climbed a low hill. They were in a meadow. "Lie down here on the grass with me," he said.

It was a moonlit night. "He made love to me," Kit said. She was embarrassed, trying to find words to tell of it, of what had happened. They were there, on the grass, in the meadow, not far from the mill village, and in the distance they could see the hills out of which they had both come.

But maybe they couldn't see the hills. Kit was trying to explain something that was difficult for her to get at. If she was embarrassed it was not because of what happened but because of the difficulty of finding words.

In the sick young man there was something going on,

concerned with the hills. "Why were we brought down here? Not only me but you, all of us?"

The big raw-boned, red-haired woman, Agnes, after Kit left the place, became a strike leader, a union organizer. "She was swell. She was a fighter," Kit said.

There were young men who came along the "sides" where the girls worked, tying in the broken threads. The men trundled little carts with rubber-tired wheels. They took off full bobbins and put on empties. There were conversations with the girls, flirtations started. "Some of the girls and women," Kit said, "on some of the sides, got pretty gay."

There were men who made whispered proposals to the girls. "Eh, kid, what about it, eh? If you'll come across I'll take you to the movies on Saturday night."

Or to get even gayer, pinch a girl's leg, or slap her behind, Kit said.

Some of the girls, on some of the sides, didn't care. They liked it. They'd giggle, or maybe slap the gay one's face.

"Good God," the big red-head Agnes said to Kit, "a girl had better learn fast in this dump or some of these smart guys, to say nothing of that lousy bastard of a foreman, will take it away from her fast and then she won't have it no more.

"Or she'll get something in her belly that'll make her quit jumping fences," she said.

She was out to teach Kit, but Kit said she already knew. "I guess maybe my own pap had wised me up," she said. She said that naturally she kept her mouth shut about that.

She talked of the pale young man who came, trundling one of the little carts to take off and put on bobbins on her side. He wasn't like the others. "He was pale," she said, "too pale." They became friends and that led to her walks with him.

He spoke, softly and persistently, in a low voice. Where had he got so many words? Why were we brought down? What made us come? Words about the mill and the mill village. What had got into the hill people that they trooped down out of the silent hills to the big towns?

They got lost down there . . . they were nameless ones.

He talked, even a little irrationally, of the mill, at night. "We were in there last night, all night, the night before. Six nights every week we are in there.

"There is a singing." He said. "There is a singing and I can't sing with it." He was a little feverish.

He wanted to talk to her of something, about something in the mill, the roaring song always going on in there, the speed, speed, speed of the shining machines.

"I'm so tense. I want to shout.

"If I was strong, if I wasn't sick.

"I'm a young man, I should be strong. It ain't fair.

"Sometimes if I could yell, or dance."

Odd to think that the young man, so quiet-seeming, when he was in the mill at work, could have been thinking such things, feeling such things. He was so quiet, never getting smart, trying to grab the girls, date them up. He was one of the ones who did something to Kit, one of the first ones . . .

To make her a little grown up, she thought.

He lay on the grass in the meadow beside her and swore, curses bubbling up to his lips. His face was very pale there in that light.

He cursed and it seemed to Kit, then and later, a kind of

inhuman thing—from such a gentle-seeming one, one who had always been so quiet, "so gentlemanly," she said.

As though the sky, dimly seen overhead, cursed, the ground, the blades of grass in the field cursing.

It bubbling out of him, the sick young man, half boy, so pale, so near death. He died, she said, a short time after that night.

The whole experience was to her weird but very real. She said she wasn't afraid of him. "He was lying there and I laid down beside him, quite close."

The curses that came from him, she said, had something to do with God. He broke off cursing and talked and then the cursing began again. He had been, he tried to tell her, religious, had gone to church when he was a young boy back in the hills.

They had talked of Heaven and he didn't want Heaven. He wanted to be strong—maybe a baseball player or even a prizefighter, not to be always tired and coughing . . . he stopped talking to curse for a time . . . sometimes having hemorrhages, he had had several, blood that should have been the blood of a strong young man coming up, out of his body through his throat.

It might have been the lint in the air in the mill. He had been told that. If it were true he wanted God's curses on those that let it happen.

He had an idea. He had been lying on his back, his face to the night sky, but sat up. Perhaps it was money. People were always wanting more money—like his father and mother. But they had been fools to come out of the hills for it. He said he had thought about it. What good did money do people? The mountain people got a little money in the crowded mill village but it went like water. He had heard that some of the mill owners got rich. Well, what of it? Were they taller, stronger, did their food taste better?

He was kneeling beside Kit and leaned over, looking directly down at her. "No," he said, in a half whisper, "it isn't people. It's God. Why does he put evil things in people and in things too."

He spoke in a rapid whisper, telling a tale. As a young boy, when he and his people still lived in the hills, his mother was ill. He was coming home from a mountain schoolhouse.

He said it was in the fall and he tried to tell Kit how nice-looking the hills were, the trees in their full colors. He had wanted to take some of the niceness of it home, to the mountain cabin where his mother was lying ill, and had pushed in to a place of thick bushes. There were fall flowers. There were brightly colored berries. He had made a bouquet . . . he called it, "a flower pot."

And he had got covered with poison ivy, from head to foot, was himself in bed for two weeks, writhing in misery. Why? Why?

His voice rose and he seemed about to shout. Kit was lying quietly beside him. "I didn't intend the flowers any harm, the bushes, the ivy itself . . . "I didn't intend any of it any harm. I didn't know it was there."

Kit said that, suddenly, she didn't know why she did it, she was pretty young then . . . she reached up her hand and touched his pale cheeks.

"I kept on doing it and he got quiet." She said she kept on doing it, suddenly feeling older than he was, and that presently he began touching her body with his hand. She said she didn't mind, that she let him put his hand, softly like that, all over her body. She said he got very quiet after that but kept talking, but this time without excitement or curses, of how touching her made him feel as though he were well, as though he were again a young boy in the hills, when he was strong, when he could run a long way without tiring.

A young man, from back in the hills, came to visit the consumptive young man. His name, Kit said, was Bud and the sick young man's name was Frank. Bud was Frank's cousin. Kit laughed, speaking of Bud. He was a strong young fellow, very dark and with a small bulletlike head, covered with coarse black hair.

The young consumptive, Frank, had arranged for an evening. "We're going to do something," he said. He got Kit and Agnes, the red-haired one. "She was fierce," Kit said. Frank went and brought a large bottle of moon whiskey. It was the only time Kit had ever known him to drink.

They set out, again to the fields, the four of them, in the moonlight, on a summer night. "We went out of the mill village but not to the town. We went around it." They kept circling the town, going through fields, avoiding farmhouses. "We would stop and sit down. We'd drink. The stuff burned my throat."

Kit had got a little wild. "I had been ashamed to go near any one but I wasn't any more." They were going up a little hill and she ran to the young man Bud and threw her arms about his neck. She kissed him, and Agnes and Frank both laughed. Frank didn't get a bit tired that night," she said.

There were some brush piles on top of a low hill, where some farmer had been at work, clearing land overgrown by brush, and she got some matches from Bud and ran to light them.

"Then we all ran, laughing, not to be caught by some farmer when the flames leaped up through the brush piles. Frank also ran. Kit said he seemed to forget about being ill although it was but a few weeks before he died.

They got over on another hill, to another farm, and lying on the ground watched, the four of them, their bodies close together. Kit said it was fine, watching the fires on the hill. They kept drinking out of the bottle. A farmer, with his wife and three children, came from a farmhouse and stood by the fires. He kept staring about. He had two dogs and they barked. Frank's cousin, Bud, his shyness also swept away by the drink, got to his feet. "Howdee! Howdee!" he shouted at the top of his voice.

They got up and ran farther away. She said that Agnes, who was so fierce — "She was loud-mouthed," Kit said — got very gentle.

Bud, the cousin from the hills, had a stunt he did. He was a young fellow who had a passion for horses, and as his people were very poor he could not own a horse. "At least," Frank told Kit, walking with her that night, "he couldn't own one he wanted." Frank had been drinking steadily. He was such a talker. "He got gabby," Kit said. He wanted to explain his cousin.

The cousin had gone one time on a trip with a truck. Frank told Kit that Bud lived near a town called Brevard, in North Carolina, and that there was a big tannery in a near-by town.

They had begun to take truckloads of leather through the hills and up through the Shenandoah Valley of Virginia to the eastern cities and Bud knew a fellow who drove one of the trucks.

"I bet you don't know how big the world is," Frank said to Kit. The sick young man was very gay. He seemed strong. His cousin had told him the story of his trip out into the big world and it was as though it had been an experience of his own. "He was that kind," Kit said. "He could imagine things."

They all sat down on the grass in a field and Frank kept talking. Agnes and Bud sat some distance away. They began playing. First they wrestled and then they chased each other about the field. Frank was proud of his cousin. "He's smart. He's seen a lot," he said.

"I'll bet you don't know how big the world is." In their wanderings that night the four people had got back to where they could see, in the distance, the lights of their mill town. Frank pointed toward it.

"There must be a thousand, a million towns, bigger'n that," he said. He pointed to the sky. There's as many towns as the stars up there," he said.

"And people too." He tried to tell Kit of the people Bud had seen in city streets, of the crowds of people, well-dressed people, he said. He thought it must have been wonderful for Bud seeing all that and getting suddenly sad, said he'd give anything, even one of his arms or a leg, have them sawed off, just to be well himself and go out like that to see so much.

Frank's sadness didn't last long that night. The fellow Bud was with, an older man of the mountain town, had got the job as truck driver after working in a garage. He had been on the trips to eastern cities several times. He had planned to go to Philadelphia but he went the long way, to show Bud Baltimore and Washington.

And somewhere in Pennsylvania, or Frank said it might

have been in Virginia, there was a big horse farm where
fine saddle horses were trained and knowing how Bud felt
about horses the man had stopped the truck.

"There were people, beautifully dressed, and horses, more
beautiful than the people." Frank spoke as though he had
seen everything himself. Kit said he was like a fellow reading something out of a book. There were the people in a
field, walking around . . . there were white fences like
a house — painted . . . well-dressed men and beautiful
women. "The grass was just like on a lawn," Bud had said.
There were shining thin dresses with flowers on them."

"They didn't charge anything to get in." If it hadn't been
for the truck Bud and the man could have gone in. He
didn't want to leave his truck.

"So they stopped the truck in the road and Bud crawled
up and sat on top of it."

There were barns as big as a factory. There was an old
man, with a white beard and with a young woman on his
arm. They were walking in the field but came down near
the fence by the road where the truck was. They passed so
close to the fence that the young woman's gown touched it.
"She smelled like a flower or like a Balm of Gilead tree
when it is in bloom, or like sassafras," Bud had said.

They were bringing horses into the field and they were
being put through their gaits, shown off. They trotted,
freely, fiercely. They racked. They single-footed and gal-
loped. Some of the riders shouted as though with delight at
being on such beautiful beasts and all the people standing
and watching clapped their hands. There was one rider, all
in black, with a shiny black hat and a white stiff-looking
shirt. The shirt was very white and he had a long whip.

"Hi-hi," he called to his horse in a shrill voice. "He had the best horse of them all, the most beautiful one."

Frank thought that very likely the man with the best horse owned the place where the horses were being shown.

He explained that Bud, having had always a passionate interest in horses, had remembered about the exhibition in the field more than all the rest seen during the trip. He couldn't own such a horse, couldn't get one and so, Frank said, he became a horse and when Kit laughed, thinking perhaps he had again gone a little out of his head, like that other time when he cursed so, he called to Bud.

"Come here, Bud, and you, Agnes," Frank called and the couple came across the field. "Now, Bud, you be a horse," he said, and Kit and Agnes both laughed. "We howled," Kit said. "It was such a crazy idea."

But she said Bud did it. There was a grassy bare place before them and Bud took something from his pockets. It was, she said, a pair of hoofs. "They were made of leather and Bud could strap them on his hands." The cousin strapped the hoofs on his hands and got down on all fours.

"He was a horse," she said.

"He was a bear."

She had never seen a bear. "I know anyway that's the way a bear looks.

"The cousin was small and big too. He was black almost," Kit said.

He could shamble. He could walk like a bear.

He could walk like a dog.

He could prance like a horse. "You take a horse, a stallion, when he's excited. He could go like that." She got excited, speaking of it, saying it was so strange to see, so uncanny.

He could walk on eggs and not break the shells.

"It may be all men would rather be horses," Kit said, telling of the odd experience that night in the field. As she told of it she kept laughing, a high shrill laugh, unlike herself.

There was white moonlight on a little sloping field, with a flat place below, where she, Frank and Agnes sat, Kit said.

She said there was white moonlight and green grass. "I think there must have been sheep, or maybe cows pastured in there, in that field, but we didn't see them.

"Does a sheep ever want to be a man?" she said.

"Does a cow ever want to be a man?"

The little dark squat man from the mountains had a shambling gait, going across an open moonlit place, on green cropped grass—sight of a Southern mill town in the distance . . . electric lights showing down there. He could prance, trot, single-foot, pace. He could do the slow gallop and the fast gallop.

The town in the distance, the lights of it were against a night sky. "We've got industries, we've got progress," I kept thinking irrelevantly enough, as Kit told of her extraordinary evening.

The man Bud, young yet, a mountain boy, was short, dark, and squat.

"We've got big factories, in North Carolina, owned by the Dukes. There is a Miss Duke who has more millions of dollars than any young woman who ever lived in the world.

"We've got cigarette factories, we've got cotton and silk and rayon mills," I thought.

There was a man, in a field, in the moonlight, being a
horse. He had caught just the horse rhythm. He could rack
fast, across the green earth, in the moonlight, throwing his
horse legs out . . . his arms, strong, young and muscular,
that had become legs. They were very strong, his muscular
brown, swarthy arms that had become horses' legs, with
hoofs.

Kit said he could prance. "He could trot, rack, single-
foot," she kept saying, a kind of wonder in her voice.

"He was beautiful. He frightened you," she said. "He
was so in earnest about it." He was determined, absorbed in
being a horse — not a common horse but a highly trained,
highly bred, aristocrat among horses.

"Look, I'm doing it. I am being a horse, I am a horse."

The pale tall cousin, Frank, the consumptive one, got terribly excited and, for some reason, so also did Kit and
Agnes. The man, who was a horse, was in the green flat
place where the moonlight was. There was a fence beyond
the flat place and he went, with the bright sharp trot of a
horse toward it. He leaped on all fours. The consumptive,
Frank, got to his feet. Kit thought he might have been a little drunk. He was very proud of his cousin. Agnes held the
bottle. She stood up and waved it above her head.

There was another flat meadow beyond the one where the
horse-man had trotted, single-footed, pranced, and again he
trotted back toward them. Again he leaped on all fours and
again he cleared the fence. "A high one," Kit said.

Frank was standing. He was trembling. He might have
been drunk. He was weaving back and forth. "See!" he
shouted. "He can do it. He can be it."

Kit was terribly afraid that Frank would suddenly become
ill and so she began to protest. "Don't. Quit it now," she

cried. She ran and put her arms about Frank's shoulders. "I knew he wanted so to be strong, to be a horse like that," she explained. She stood holding the young man Frank, and the big red-haired woman Agnes ran down a little slope to where Bud, absorbed, was still prancing, on all fours, in the moonlight . . . he was preparing to leap the fence again and Agnes swore as she ran.

"Now quit it," she called, "goddam you, you quit it." She was terribly in earnest, although she laughed. There had been enough of it.

"Why you little black son-of-a-bitch," she said, when she had caught Bud and had made him quit it. She was standing near him and he was unstrapping the hoofs from his hands and stowing them away in his pockets. Kit said that Agnes kept swearing at him. She wasn't really angry. She liked him a lot. Agnes kept laughing and swearing while Bud put the hoofs away in his pockets and they both came back up the slope.

"We sat on the ground and finished the bottle," Kit said, "but Frank and I didn't talk any more about Bud."

It was Agnes who talked. "She wasn't going to miss that chance," Kit said. Agnes was a big vital woman — woman enough, Kit afterward thought, but not the kind most men would fall for. She was too big, too strong and vital. She thought too much. When Kit had left the mill, when she had been through many adventures, was a bit older, and, in her own way sophisticated, Kit spent a good deal of time thinking of Agnes.

She always spoke of her, however, with a smile. It was an affectionate smile. What were such women as Agnes to do? Most of the men, the workmen, young and old, in the cot-

ton mill . . . so many of them like the consumptive Frank
. . . if they were not tubercular they were at least stoop-
shouldered men, many with narrow chests . . . they had
spent too much of their young lives eating cotton lint, breath-
ing it into their lungs.

It might be that Agnes needed and even wanted gentling
by life, by intimacy with some man, but where among the
mill men was she to find one to do it to her? If she had
been married to a farmer, say somewhere out on the Western plains, heavy hard work to do, shoulder to shoulder
with a man, her partner and lover. . . .

Unlike the others in the field that night she had read
books, she had been to meetings. Although she was still
young she had worked in several mills, had been in strikes
and at strike meetings. There had been socialist agitators in
the mill towns and the communists had come in. Later, after
Kit left the mill, Agnes was a figure in the communist
strike at Gastonia in North Carolina.

She had been playing with Bud, the horse-man, in the
field as Frank had talked to Kit but had overheard some of
the talk. Once or twice she had left Bud. They had been
wrestling, laughing and pushing each other about, but suddenly stopped. She gave Bud a push that sent him sprawling. "Now quit. Let me alone. I don't want to," she said,
and there was something in her voice that commanded. It
was always there when she wanted to use it.

She left Bud standing, or sprawled thus . . . he was
laughing. The play between them had been like two pup-
pies at play. She walked away from him.

She came to stand near where Kit and Frank were sitting. Frank was telling of Bud's trip into the East, of the

things he had seen, of the men and women of the saddle-
horse farm, and Bud's excitement, lying on top of the truck
parked in the road. She had stood near them for a moment,
listening intently, saying nothing and then, with a shrug of
her shoulders, had walked away. She began again the play
with Bud.

The four people were seated on the grass on the little hill
and had finished the bottle. Agnes looked at Bud, who had
stowed away his leather hoofs. "Why, you little black bastard . . . that you should have learned to do that," she said,
and, having said it, laughed. She was wanting to tell Kit
and the two men something of what she thought the significance of what Bud had seen on his trip into the East
— down out of the hill country and into the low country
— and hesitated because she was trying to find words for
what was in her mind. She was an odd and a striking figure
sitting thus. Her legs, like strong pillars, were spread apart
and she had big shoulders and a strong neck.

Her neck was like the necks of men Kit saw later, when
she was married and went with her husband to professional
wrestling matches and, although her head looked small, it
was covered with a mass of thick yellow hair that had become disarranged during her wrestling bouts with Bud and
now hung in a thick mass over her shoulders.

"It is just so, everywhere," she said suddenly. She had
lighted a cigarette — she was the only one of the little party
that smoked — and when she talked her arms moved about,
as though she were addressing an audience, making ges-
tures, like one of the professional speakers, the agitators she
had heard. The lighted end of the cigarette kept making
little bright arches before the eyes of the others.

They had all become silent and she told them of her
thoughts. There was, she said, something rotten in the fact
that Bud, with his love of fine horses and wanting one,
had to come down to being a horse. "What the hell — I'll
bet you he works harder than any of the guys who own the
horses," she said and, reaching over to where Bud sat,
grasped his arms. She gave him a little push so that he fell
over and lay on his side and then began again to attempt to
put her thoughts into words.

Agnes was excited and although the others did not understand some of the words and thoughts that came pouring
out of her they also got excited. She talked a little inco-
herently and brokenly. She was young and strong. Perhaps
she felt within herself the conviction growing that in the life
of the factory there was no chance for something within herself to grow, that it was choked there, the conviction that is
in so many younger Americans now, that the day of opportunity is gone here, an old myth that in America any one
may rise to dizzy heights of splendor quite exploded. She
tried passionately to express the thing most wanted, by all
men and women, not only in America but over the entire
earth. She thought it was some basis of self-respect. The
performance of Bud in the field, his becoming for the time
a horse, not a man, had in some odd way hurt her. "It isn't
that we want, to give up manhood." She could not put her
thoughts into such straight words but Kit and perhaps
Frank, for all his pride in his cousin's performance, had
been shocked as well as amused. "The thing we want, the
thing we want." Agnes was struggling for words. In spite
of the jumble of words that came from her she did in some
way get her thoughts into the others.

The thing most essentially wanted by all men and women,

always, everywhere. "Give me some basis of self-respect. Let me stand on my own feet."

The thing felt sometimes by even the poorest little mountain farmer, working as young Bud did his tiny bit of poor mountain land.

"See! Look! I did it!" In the factories, Agnes said, growing coherent and for a moment talking coherently, a man or woman got too much lost, was made to feel too small. She was remembering her experience in union struggles in factories, the right of the workers to organize, to feel themselves as having even a small part in the running of the factories and the conditions under which they labored, this right always being denied and ridiculed. Kit thought Agnes was thinking at the moment not of Bud and his performance but of the tubercular Frank. In the factory she said great care was taken to keep the dust from accumulating on the machines. Hoods came down over the machines to suck the dust from them while the workers were left to breathe it into the lungs.

The Farmer . . . "See! Look! I did it!"

"I have made the corn stand up on this poor little piece of land. I have worked here and something has resulted."

"I went, in the winter, up into the woods. I brought down leaf mould. I gathered together brush and burned it. I had no money to buy fertilizer. I put the leaf mould from the woods and the ashes from the fires on the land and plowed them in. I made something grow. Look! It is the best stand of corn in all of this neighborhood."

Pride in work, in something done. Kit thought later that Agnes had been hurt by Bud's performance, by something not very healthy she had felt in it. It might have been too much humility. She did not understand what it was that night in the field. The night was, however, educational to her.

Man wanting so little really. See the farmer, even on poor land, who has raised a small patch of good corn. He can walk a little more proudly. Something grows in man through work. It can be killed when his work is degraded.

Workers in factories also wanting—Agnes was terribly in earnest. "She was more educated than the rest of us," Kit said. The thing most wanted is so little, so seldom, understood. "They think we want revolution, to kill some one," Agnes said. "It is all nonsense," she declared. She had begun talking over the heads of the others but, in a dim way, they did all understand. Kit when she told of Agnes' talk had been through a lot. She was older and shrewder than the hill girls in the field.

"Why even—it is seldom any one speaks of it—we want love, understanding, respect. Do not do that to man which takes from him his self-respect.

"Do not do it."

"Do not do it."

In the woman worker Agnes, in the field with the others, there was something perhaps half man.

And also, Kit knew, something that could be made tender.

Kit remembered an incident in the factory. There was a young girl with her hand hurt in one of the machines and the profane strong Agnes had been deeply touched by the suffering of another. Afterwards Agnes had gone up and down on her "side," doing her work, but there were tears in her eyes and she cursed as she worked. The girl who had been hurt was very pretty and she would lose two or three fingers.

"She'll be maimed. It will spoil her chance of getting what she wants."

Kit had understood that. She herself was attractive to men.

Something, more deeply felt, Agnes was trying to put into words. She didn't succeed very well. She had heard speakers talk. She had read books. The factory workers in America were, after all, not as yet too far away from their fathers and grandfathers. Agnes called them "our old people." She also had come to the factories out of a mountain home. For the most part the people of the mountains had been in America for many generations. They were not too far away from something else, something once very much alive . . . individuality . . . the day of America's greater richness . . .

Day of the farmers on their own land . . . plenty of free land to be had for the taking . . .

Day of the craftsman too . . .

"There is that wagon, carriage, suit of clothes . . . worn by that dude you see going along the street there . . . the pair of shoes . . . that chair, bed . . . this table at which we sit eating the food grown on our own land here . . .

"The cotton from our fields, flax and the wool from our sheep. In the log cabin that was my father's house there stood an old spinning wheel. It still stands there, in a corner, forgotten. Let it stand. I do not want it back . . .

"It is, however, a symbol . . . day of our participation . . . of our own hands doing completely. They could give us the feeling back, in the factories, if they would. They won't. They are stupid. They don't want to understand.

"The big factories, so huge, so magnificent. Who are they making cloth for?" Agnes turned fiercely upon Kit. "Say, you swell kid, you want silk stockings to wear, now don't you?" She awoke, made real a hunger that was in Kit. It was a hunger that influenced all her later life. . . .

The big factories, so huge, so magnificent, the thousands of fast beautiful machines. . . .

"They have a way of making us feel, too much, just a part of the machines. Why do they want to do it? It hurts. It eats in.

"The continual strutting of those up above . . . they think, they believe, they are above us . . . the way their women do it . . . why do they do it, the fools?

"They want us to be humble. Are they humble?

"We come out of the factory after one of the long days or a longer night. Do they think we are blind? Can't we see? We see so much blossoming in America, fine roads being built, the automobiles, always getting faster, more beautiful. We see rich women, richly gowned. We see beautiful houses built for those who never made anything with their hands."

Agnes spoke fiercely of Bud's experience, of his seeing the rich men in the field showing off the beautiful saddle horses. Who were they? Had they a right to such creatures? Bud became uncomfortable. He sat with head down muttering words the others could not hear.

"Fools, why don't they give us a chance?" Agnes spoke of labor leaders who had come to factories where she had been employed. Why didn't they get more down to the guts of things, why didn't they? They were always talking about wages and hours. "I don't care about that, not first of all," Agnes said. She jumped to her feet and stood over the others. Her cigarette had been thrown aside. "I want . . . I want . . . Oh, hell," she said. There was a moment of silence and then she looked down at the others and laughed. "Well, come on. Let's get out of here. I've blown off steam long enough. Time to go home," she said, and the others got to their feet and followed her, across the field and over a fence into the road.

They walked down along the road, the four of them, an oddly mixed lot. It was a dirt road, gravelled and smooth, and presently they came to a place of houses. It was quite near the town, some two or three miles outside the town limits, their own mill village, as were other mill villages, quite separated from the real town. . . .

Place of others, their lives, of the lawyers, doctors, individual workmen . . . what was left of these in such towns . . . shoe repair men, house painters, clerks in stores, men who delivered milk and eggs to houses, truck drivers, carpenters, plumbers. . . .

The mill workers, in their own company-owned place, always so oddly separated from all of these.

They were in a place of estates, off a main road, all the land for a mile up and down the road having been bought up by a few families . . . big houses with plenty of land, little clumps of forest. Their own mill village would have been off to the right. As they were on high ground they could see its lights in the distance.

They had come to this place of big estates and Kit thought that Agnes, although by lecturing the others she had got something off her chest, was still a little high. She went striding ahead of the others and there was something fierce and determined in her figure. She did not speak to the others. They had come to one of the big houses, built in that separated place, and there was a dance going on inside. There were others, beside themselves, out for a night of it.

Agnes stopped in the road and they all stopped. She was the dominant one. They passed the entrance to a particular estate, the house a huge one, brightly lighted . . . sounds of music coming from the house . . . shining automobiles parked along a driveway . . . wide green lawn with occasional trees. . . .

There was a hedge built around the estate and Agnes stopped in the road.

There was excitement in her voice, in her manner. "Come on, all of you," she said and bolted through the hedge. The others followed. They were puzzled.

They had got into a place near some stables where, no doubt, fine saddle horses were also kept. Kit thought she heard the sound of horses moving restlessly in stalls in the stables. There was a new building, being constructed of brick. Piles of brick were lying about. For a moment they stood in silence near the stables and then Agnes, making a motion to the others, went on toward the house, the others following.

They went along a green lawn. Kit said there were flowering bushes. They were now all excited and followed Agnes with thumping hearts. What an adventure, to be in such a place! What was Agnes up to?

She led them along, their figures stooping, running forward, keeping behind the bushes, until they had got near the house. There was a little open place, with more flowering bushes, and they could look directly in.

Inside there was a dance going on. They were all young people in there, Kit explained. No doubt they were the sons and daughters of the rich and the well-to-do, of the "nice" people of the Southern town, sons and daughters of mill owners, of holders of stock in the mills. There were a half dozen mill villages near that particular Southern town. . . .

The young people were revelling in the big country house,

the sons and daughters of the owners of mill villages and mills, sons of corporation lawyers, young college men and women, home for the summer, sons and daughters of bankers. There were beautiful young women and tall young men in evening clothes. Whoever was giving the party and, for all Kit knew, it might have been the wife of the president of the mill for which the three mill workers in the party outside labored, had got in an orchestra.

Kit herself did not know how long she stood there, in the open place by the bushes, so near the house. She said that Agnes had disappeared and that presently all became conscious of her absence. They were puzzled. They were frightened. They stood looking at each other, wanting to escape, to run for it, realizing, all of them, the enormity of the fact of being there. In another moment they would all have bolted but Agnes suddenly and silently reappeared. She had crept back to where the building was being erected and had a brick in her hand. If she had been excited, a little high, earlier, she was more so now. "Wait," she said, commanding the others.

She was high. She was on edge and suddenly, inside the house, the dance came to an end. She had taken a stand a little in front of the others.

There was a moment of waiting, an intense moment to all of the little party outside. The dance had ended and the orchestra, brought in for the occasion . . . they had been half concealed behind palms and great bouquets of flowers in a corner of the big room . . . the men of the orchestra, also in evening clothes, stood up and stretched. The people of the party outside could hear the sound of the voices inside. Young women laughed, they chattered. There was the sound of the voices of young men.

"It is a swell party."

"How about coming with me for a little walk outside?"

"It is a swell night."

Oh, fortunate ones!

And now the people were moving out of the big room. In a moment more couples would be coming out to walk on the lawn. There would be flirtations, young men and women walking across a well-kept lawn in the soft darkness. It was evident that Agnes was very high. What was she up to? She was dancing about in a kind of ecstasy. There was a large plate-glass window that separated those outside from the revellers. Agnes swung wide one of her great arms and the brick went smashing through the window. There was an intense moment. Kit and her friends could see the startled faces of a group of people near an outer door and then they all ran. They were led by Agnes who kept exclaiming, "Hot dog! Hot dog!" as she ran. "Did you see their faces? Did you see their faces?"

They got to the hedge and through it to the road. It was dark out there. They could see over the hedge. On the opposite side of the road—a low fence to be got over—there was an open field and just beyond a small clump of trees. There were other fields beyond the trees. They stood in the road waiting, all but Agnes wanting to continue the flight at once. She, however, still dominated them. "No. Wait," she said, and they all stood looking toward the house.

There was a furore at the house. Men were running about. They ran to the parked cars and got flashlights. They called back and forth. The excitement in the house and on the green lawn and under the trees before the house went on and on. All in the party, except Agnes, were nervous and jumpy and then, to increase their alarm, two young men with flashlights in their hands came through the hedge and stood in the road. They were some two hundred yards away and Frank was sick with nervousness. He began pleading in a whisper. "Come. Come. We'll be caught. We'll be arrested. They'll send us to prison," he pleaded.

The men in the road were coming toward them. They were throwing the light from the flashlights along the road and into the hedge. They were young men in evening clothes. They might have been young college men, home for the summer, young football players. Agnes leaned over and began whispering rapidly to Bud. "We'll be over there. We'll wait over there." She was pointing to the trees, just seen, across the fields. They all knew there were fields beyond. They had come that way.

The young mountain man, Bud, did not have time to strap on his leather hoofs. He went down on all fours. The young men in the road were advancing. They came in silence.

And now Bud was rushing down upon them. He was on all fours. He shambled along. He also had an idea. There was a low growling guttural sound coming from his lips. It was very uncanny to hear, there in the darkness.

It was something terrible, Kit said. There was a spot of light from one of the flashlights in the road and he shambled across it. There was a cry from the lips of the young men. They bolted and he followed. When they crashed through the hedge he leaped over, still on all fours.

He was down thus on all fours.

He went with amazing rapidity.

He was a huge dog.

He was a bear.

He was a horse.

He went shamble, shamble, growling as he went.

And now the others of the party ran. They got over a low fence and ran quickly across the field to the trees. They waited there and, Kit said, Agnes was nervous. She walked up and down before the others. "He's all right. He'll take care of himself," she muttered.

They stayed in the little grove until, at last, Bud came back to them and went directly to Agnes. Agnes threw her arms about his neck and embraced him. She held him in her arms and danced in the darkness. "Oh, Bud, Bud," she cried, "oh, my darling."

"Oh, you darling little son of a bitch," she cried.

They went on but the adventures of the night were not over. They had crossed several fields, working their way around toward their own village, but sat down by a creek. Frank had become ill. For a time he couldn't go on and they stayed there, Frank lying on the grass at the creek's edge. He had whispeerd to Kit, asking her to hold his head. There were several outbreaks of coughing. They came, he became quieter, and then they came again. None of the others knew afterwards how long they stayed in the field but at last there was a hemorrhage. Kit was holding Frank's head and the moon had come up. He was at the creek's edge and asked Kit to hold his head over the creek. The moon was shining on the waters of the little creek and Kit, so close to him, could see his blood gushing from between his lips and coloring the water of the stream.

![decorative border]

CHAPTER FOUR

KIT BRANDON was sometimes a good deal moved, something restless within her was stirred, by the speeches of her friend Agnes. The two young women had become close friends although Agnes was several years older than Kit. Agnes felt in Kit something more feminine than in herself while Kit wanted more of Agnes's boldness. They walked about together, worked together. The consumptive Frank died and winter came and they went to the mill—both being still on the night shift—in the darkness of winter evenings. Like hibernating animals they had both slept through the short winter days.

Staleness of little crowded houses. Kit and Agnes did not room in the same house with the same mill family but their rooms, like the houses, were alike. Another worker slept in Kit's bed at night. Then the sheets were changed and she crept in. She got out of bed in the afternoon, slipping into her clothes. Already she was beginning to want better clothes and a better room. She ate in the kitchen. There would be the older workers about, older men and women. Sometimes in such a house the man didn't work. He was too old to get a job when he brought his family down out of the hills. He was known as a "mill Daddy." His children made his living for him.

It was something new, degenerating, to older mountain men who, in the hills, although poor, had always been kings in their own houses. There is a staleness, a weariness that gets into the blood and bone. It isn't only factory workers who have it. You see it, feel it, in white-collar workers in cities, sometimes in successful men, the money makers in business. It accounts for golf, for the passion for sports in which you do not participate . . . vicarious excitement got . . . crowds of business men, young and old, at baseball games, at football games. "Aha, we won!"

"What do you mean, we?"

Agnes said: "All right. Swell! Some day we'll get it"— meaning a three, a four, a five-hour day in the mills. She had such moments of optimism. New dream of labor when Kit was a mill girl. Agnes got angry and swore. "Goddam, why shouldn't they all work!" This came from having been to socialist and communist meetings. She had in mind places like their mill, become public institutions, to serve, classes broken down, "liquidated," as the Russians might say . . . every man and woman, at least while he was young, serving a certain number of years in some such institutions, places where cloth was woven, shoes made, clothes made. . . .

Others working on farms, in mills, on railroads . . . if there were any railroads left. Sometimes Agnes went around in a kind of dream . . . "Goddam, to mine coal, make steel, make automobiles, make tires for automobiles." She rubbed her hands together thinking of it. "Some of these goddam swell, big-bellied dames we see" . . . she meant some of the well-to-do wives of the mill officials who drove to the mill offices to pick up husbands. "Such a dame down in a coal mine for once, eh, kid?" Agnes grinned with joy thinking of it.

"At that, it might not be so bad for them. Look, they'd wear off the big hips, big bellies.

"You got some figure yourself, Kid. I wish I had it."

The thought of people at last finding each other through a universal participation. She wanted something wiped out. "It might wipe out, once and for all, this idea that there are certain people born different from others, as though God had made them special things" . . . idea of aristocracy, of birth, etc. Agnes like all of the mill girls felt deeply a kind of contempt in which all the workers were held by the town people. For some reason it didn't cut quite so deeply for Kit.

"Why should all of our people, when they get a little older than we are, always become so tired?" She felt the weariness in others deeply, having herself a vast energy. By "our people," she meant her fellow workers. Kit knew that. Agnes declared that the work of the world, given modern fast machines, could be done and no one need get tired.

The two women — Kit was fast becoming a woman; men who saw her felt her as woman — used to meet at a certain corner in the mill village. They went together to their work, walking out of the mill village and along a paved road to the mill gate. There was a high wire fence around the mill yard and a man, an old crippled one — injured sometime in the mill — was there to check them in. In their mill they had identification buttons, to be worn on the coat, buttons the size of a silver dollar. They were such buttons as states sometimes issue to hunters and fishermen. "Look. We are like sheep numbered," Agnes said angrily. She swore and spat on the ground and Kit turned her head aside and smiled. They were in the paved road, going down to the mill gate, and Agnes took the button from her coat and made a gesture as though to hurl it away into the darkness.

"God, I'd like to, I'd like to."

Her anger brought a smile to Kit's lips.

They were an odd enough pair, going along thus. Kit had kept her eyes open as she had lived along in the mill village. Unconsciously perhaps, in those first months away from home, she was already reaching out for something, feeling for it constantly, trying for it. She herself did not know what it was. It was a thing—call it a kind of style in life. She was wanting unconsciously to become a stylist in living.

To get it into her body. Already she was noting things, checking on things that would have meant little or nothing to Agnes. "All right, sister. You've got your dream. I've got another."

There were the Saturday nights when they went into town. As they worked nights they had also the Saturday afternoons. They had the Sundays.

A few times Kit went to church and Agnes tried to stop her. "Don't be a fish," she said; "don't believe anything these guys tell you." Most of the mill people went to little Baptist and Methodist churches near the mill village.

"Trust God. Look to Jesus for salvation," Agnes quoted. "Ah, cut it out. What the hell," she said. There had been strikes in other mills she had worked in and she told Kit that wherever there was a strike or trouble in a mill the preachers always stood by the mill owners. "Why not?" she said, and explained that the salaries, or at least a large part of the salaries, of such preachers were paid by the mill owners. She scolded, but Kit, without saying anything about it, sometimes dressed as best she could and on Sunday morning marched off, not to one of the little churches near the mill but down into the town. She walked about until she came to what looked to her like the biggest and most expensive church and went in. At first she went a little timidly. "I wonder if they'll throw me out?" They didn't and she got bolder. In such places she could see what young women wore who had money to buy clothes. She was getting points — not at all hearing the words of the preachers in the churches — noting how some of the rich or well-to-do young women of a North Carolina town dressed, walked, held their heads.

Something to practise in secret when she was alone in her room.

Or she was in the main street of the town on a Saturday afternoon with Agnes, the broad-shouldered, big-hipped, big-legged one. "There's one" . . . she did not say the words aloud to Agnes. . . . "There's one . . . that one just getting out of the big car parked there in front of the store." She noted the shining beauty of the car. That one held her head and her slender young body in just a certain way. "That's nice." Kit herself tried to walk so, hold her own head and body so. There was this passion in Kit, sleeping in her, it had been born in her — herself not knowing. It wasn't just the young woman who had got out of the car, Kit watching, absorbed, Agnes not noticing — it was also the car itself. Something perhaps always very American in Kit Brandon. "I'd like . . . I'd like, some day, to own such a car, to drive it." She had no feeling of anger toward the young woman who had got out of the car. "There might, some day, be a way." Her dream was far far away from the somewhat grandiose one that was in Agnes's head.

There was a particular Saturday evening when the two went into town . . . snow in the state of the upper South.

It might have been a town of northern Ohio, or of Minnesota. Pretty far away from the South, as the North commonly thinks of it . . . cotton fields, Negroes with banjoes at cabin doors. Agnes had an idea. "We'll have a drink when we get to town. I know a place."

She liked to go to places . . . some such place as could be found in any industrial town during the probibition era . . . little warm inside room, usually in a house quite near the main street section. If there were no men present, to sit with some other women with feet up on a table . . . smoke and drink . . . be mannish.

"Never mind about woman's dignity or this business of trying to keep yourself up to it . . . we're working women . . . this foolishness, trying to be dainty and feminine . . . it takes too much money to try to keep that up . . . it isn't my line."

Most of the other women in the cotton mill were shocked by Agnes. The proletariat, so called, are the great protectors of sex morals, of respectability. The middle class takes care of money morals. Agnes would have gone big with the daughters of some of the rich women of the town, if they had known her, had there been any way for them to know her. She would have been more in their line in that period, after the World War.

A few companions, to listen as she talked. She was always burning with ideas, her mind always busy. She saw constantly a vision of a new world, emerging or about to emerge, as she might have said, out of an old agricultural South. She had been born Southern, was one of the few people, born South, who never thought anything, said anything, about being of the best blood of the South. Ideas she had got from reading and from listening to radical speeches in little halls, a few other venturesome workers gathered in the halls with her. There were a few men and women, young ones, burning with enthusiasm, who got down from the North into such Southern industrial towns. The A. F. of L. leaders couldn't and didn't look with much enthusiasm on such workers. The wages were too insignificant, not enough in it, for the A. F. of L. leaders. Agnes felt that she had got a lot out of such speakers. There were, however, reservations in her mind.

She had spoken more than once of all this to Kit, who only partly understood. There was a tale she had told, of a strike in a mill at Marion, North Carolina. "I was there, in that one," she said. She explained that, being unconnected — her father and mother were both dead and she had no brothers or sisters — she had got out, when the strike got hopeless, had changed her name. Like a criminal she had got an alias. "Otherwise I'd have been put on the black list." The manufacturers passed the word about, from one to another: "Look out for so and so. He, or she, is a trouble maker."

The point about the particular strike, at Marion . . . she told the story of the excitement of the strike's beginning. She had got a little cynical. It was at about this time that the president of the A. F of L. gave out a statement: "We are going to organize the whole cotton industry."

"The hell you say."

The excitement of the early days of a strike, outside leaders, young radicals as well as the regular old-line labor leaders coming in . . . grand feeling . . . "See, we are brothers. We stand shoulder to shoulder" . . . fiery speeches made, gatherings of strikers . . . "I'll stand here till I die" . . .

As a rule it all turned out pretty sadly, Agnes told Kit.

Certainly the manufacturers weren't fools. There was a way to break down the morale of the workers. At Marion there had been several people, workers, shot and killed at the mill gate.

It was in the early dawn, the night shift coming off, day shift, already on strike, waiting, Agnes there with the others, to tell the night workers, "We're out, we're on strike."

The company was prepared, too. A mill, so threatened, Agnes explained, went to a so-called detective agency. Such agencies were in reality just strike-breaking organizations . . . tough guys employed . . . killers. Al Capone got his start as a strikebreaker. They at the mill gate too . . . ready.

Pity of it. Bodies of dead workers lying in the dust in a road at a mill gate. "Some of the rest of us ran. All those shot were shot in the back. Some of the rest of us just stood there, dumb. There is so much force against us, officials of the town, of the county, of the State, of the U. S. A. What the hell are we to do? We've never had the nerve to ask for much.

"All we want is just a little more of the stuff we make, a little more leisure, fair treatment . . . Jesus." Agnes always got high when she talked thus.

At Marion, the funeral of the dead workers . . . speakers from the outside world. A famous man, a famous writer, came down . . . rumors of the big massacre at Marion flying out, to an outside world. A big city newspaper had hired the big writer to come down. Agnes had heard, later, that he got $10,000 for ten articles written about that particular strike. He came and went. Others, speakers, officials of labor unions, etc., came and went. "Of course, afterwards, after the strike was broken, the mill started up again with other workers inside . . . people just like us . . . we on charity. The famous writer sent us down a barrel of apples. Wasn't that swell of him? I want to get drunk, smash something or some one.

"Ah, what the hell, Kit . . . let's talk about something else.

"Don't say no more," Agnes cried. Kit had said nothing. Agnes had done all the talking.

It had been bitterly cold for several days and then had got somewhat warmer and the snow had come. States like North Carolina, Kentucky, Tennessee, Missouri — called Southern, Oh, Thou Sunny South — can be colder than North Dakota, Idaho, Alaska. The cold gets you more. The world was white as Kit and Agnes walked down from the mill village. There had been a drizzling rain earlier that day. It turned to snow.

A kind of glory and mystery in the night, too. The two women felt it, each in her own way. The snow, very wet, had clung to everything as it fell, to the branches of trees that lined a paved road that led down past the mill gate, to the gate itself, now closed . . . little house there by the gate in which, on other nights, sat an old crippled workman on guard . . . an old workman who had been hurt in the mill and had got now this sinecure . . . to the heavy wire fence built around the mill yard, each wire outlined in white . . .

"Old Pete," Agnes said. She meant the old fellow who sat at night in the little house by the gate, "Old Pete's in his hole tonight."

White snow on the roofs of houses, in the mill village, along the road, roof of the mill itself . . . casements of windows, dimly lighted on this night of joy for workers Saturday night.

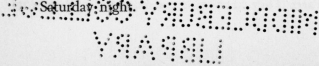

*"Saturday night and supper on the table. It's the happiest
time in a workingman's life."* (Old Worker's Song.)

White snow everywhere. There was an automobile standing before a little frame house beside the road . . . no lights
in the house. Some family was moving, in or out. It was all
outlined in white, spokes of wheels, hood of the car, the
body. There were pieces of furniture tied to the outside.
The car was an old Ford, Model T. Outlined in white two
or three chairs, a broken table, some wire bed springs.
Electric street lights shining down on a white shining world.
There was no sidewalk from the mill village down to the
town but the way was lighted. It was an okay road for
those who owned cars. The two women wore cheap, thin
shoes, tramping down to town in the snow. They were
both young. It didn't too much matter to them.

Except . . . "Damn it, now look . . . I got to get me some
new kicks again."

Something else, also new in modern life, something concerned with women. In Chicago, New York, Philadelphia
and other cities there were, when Kit was thus a young
kid, pretty puzzled yet, listening to Agnes' talk . . . labor,
capital, rise of the new world, we'll-make-em-come-to-us-
yet-one-of-these-days . . . establishments in cities, busy machines clattering away, catering to a new, and old, hunger
in women.

The hunger was not in Agnes. If it had ever been in her,
it had been put down. It was in Kit.

The establishments in the cities sent experts off to the big
style centers . . . smart men, smart women designers, thinking out new, striking, enticing ways to bring out the charm
of women in dress. The experts went to New York. They
went to Paris. They kept on the alert, bought or stole the

lines of new gowns, bought originals at high prices. The
most enticing ones were bid for, fought for, high prices paid,
then rushed home. It's there, in modern machines, the
ability to duplicate, endlessly, endlessly.

Cheaper, shabbier cloth, but keep the design and the colors. Make duplicates, plenty of them. The big mail-order
houses sending the word out too, even to remote villages,
to farms. In Paris today, in Beanville, Arkansas, three weeks
from now. "Hurry girls, hurry little working girls and
women."

Song of the Shirt, hell . . . make it the Song of the
Shimmy.

Flood the market quickly. Women's fashions change
quickly. There's something going on, unknown to women a
generation or two ago. Even girls in factories, or servant
girls, can rig themselves out now in the latest thing out of
Paris — even in Paris, Illinois. Quick, buy copies of *Deline-
ator, Ladies' Home Journal, Woman's Home Companion,
McCall's Magazine*. Take home a copy of *Woman's Home
Companion*, young woman. Keep up to snuff.

Stories too, in the magazines. After all, even poor girls —
sometimes, not often, but there's the chance — they marry
old rich ones. Damn it, a girl might as well get an old Papa
if she can't get a young one, if she's got some of *it*, eh?

There are men who like them warm. Others like the cold
ones. If you can warm up a cold one it makes you feel big,
like a conqueror.

There are dreams in women's heads besides dreams of getting a man. A woman wants her own foundation for living,
too. If a woman likes beautiful clothes it isn't always and
altogether as a way to the man hunt. The chances are that
women dress more for other women than for men.

And there is something else too . . . a thing not too often thought of . . . it is too easily taken for granted that having money, living in a fine house, driving a fine car, makes for sensitiveness, the possibility of tenderness. We group people too easily . . . new words rapidly coming into our American vocabulary . . . the proletariat . . . the bourgeoisie . . . the capitalists . . . separations too simple, too easily made.

Kit Brandon, as she walked in the snow along the road with Agnes, hadn't, as yet, any definite ideas about clothes, getting a man or not getting one. She was beginning to get, faintly, ideas of what might be done. There was her straight slender young body, white flesh, straight legs, slender ankles. She did not spend much time dreaming of strong male arms about her, the brave male protecting the shrinking female. She was getting along a little in a matter of growing importance to herself, beginning to want something that some man might — by a conceivable chance — she having aforesaid nice legs, arms, little hard breasts just budding, etc. — help her to get.

What nice eyes! They could be soft and apparently gentle and yielding at times. They could be hard shrewd eyes. Kit was having her being, her young womanhood, in the period immediately after the World War in America. . . .

"They sure gypped us in that war."

The thought not very definite in the minds of the young. The war had, for example, not touched Kit or any one she knew very directly. There was something in the air. "These big boys aren't so big, are they?" Doubts regarding not only great soldiers, so-called, but also great statesmen, captains of industry and others. There was no definite immediate organization of thought, for example, toward impulse to revolt, make revolution, a new start. Age of the so-called hard-boiled ones . . . they often enough a new kind of sentimentalists too . . . the wise crackers . . . hard boys.

All of this merely suggested here, as part, unconscious part, of Kit Brandon, what she would have been becoming. In her day the American intellectual world was being flooded with books . . . she hadn't read them . . . she came later to a time of book reading, trying to "improve" herself in that way as people do. "It may be that is the way, the hard sharpness," she was thinking.

All of this, hinted at, certainly not yet very definite in her. The young are often more open and ready to receive than people want to believe. It is so much easier for any one of us to think of another, of any one, as all one thing, easy to understand. It makes everything so simple and nice, doesn't it?

It, the thing here suggested, however, standing up in Kit. She was more intensely personal than Agnes. It may be that the thing Agnes had was more healthy, that it was something bigger — growing belief in revolution for example — growing readiness to give self, throw self away, fight, even perhaps to die for others but, again, this not all of Agnes either. There was a side of her that wanted to be more like Kit. Once that evening as they were walking along, she stopped in the road and stood for a minute, looking at Kit. The struggle along the road, in the snow at the side of the road, had brought a flush of color to Kit's cheeks that were, ordinarily, rather pale. They were under a street light. "Gee, Kid . . . God, you're a swell-looker, Kid."

And then there was the world the two were moving in that night. It was oddly, strangely, a world more mysterious than they knew, at least consciously. Men and women in a new American world trying to adjust . . . new mystery inside houses they passed, outside houses, inside factories, outside factories. The two young women, walking down thus through the snowy night, walked under electric lights. The states of the upper South had been made what they were, what they suddenly, in a single decade, became, by the coming of water power. Duke . . . the Duke fortune . . . a man named Duke, certainly a go-getter . . . in tobacco, organizer of the American Tobacco Company . . . the government busting that up . . . effort of another generation to stop the development of the next generation . . . Teddy Roosevelt, the trust-buster.

. . . Story of Duke, the old one, the wise one . . . what a doctor, from North Carolina, practising perhaps in New York, told him . . .

" . . . Boy, go get the water power of our State. It's a state of high mountains, cheap land, many mountain streams rushing down . . .

" . . . They don't see it. Go get it!"

"More money in that than in anything yet."

Power.

Power.

Power.

The Dukes the new kings.

Power hidden in streams, hidden away, far up in the mountains to be sent singing along wires, great steel spiders striding down out of the hills, across the lowlands, to towns, factories . . . big towns springing up suddenly.

The two mill girls also walking that night under the great steel spiders. The snow clung to them. "Look," Agnes said to Kit. The steel structures that carry high pressure wires went like an army of gigantic spiders off into the darkness and distance.

The two girls would be passed, even on such a night, by speeding automobiles. The lights of passing automobiles played over their figures struggling along in the snow. There was a car filled with young men. They called to the women:

"Come on. What about it? Want a ride?"

"Ah, you go to hell."

Laughter. A shout. Speed. Speed. Speed. "Here we go."

Speed in machines inside factories, infinite speed in power, being carried, high up, over their heads, to factories, outside factories, in the nights, in the days.

Let's say that, in winter, the days in upper South States become cold and disagreeable. All right. You have money and a fast car. You jump into the car, whirl away. Florida in a day and a half, maybe less . . . orange trees . . . Gulf Stream swinging in to wash on a wide sandy beach. "Did you bring your bathing suit? Why not?"

"Think of it . . . yesterday we were in Greensboro, North Carolina.

"God, wasn't it cold?"

Cars flying over roads at forty, fifty, sixty, seventy. Who knows yet what it's all about? Who's going to tell us what it's all about?

And in the factories the goods pouring out, shoes pouring out, nice slick foxy little gowns for women . . . just like the top-notchers in New York, on Park Avenue in New York, on Michigan Avenue in Chicago, on the Rue de la Paix in Paris, just like the top-notch dames in such places wear.

You have to know your stuff to see the difference, when they're new.

BIG SALE
WOMEN'S SMART GOWNS
MODELS RIGHT FROM PARIS
NOW   ONLY $6.72

You can get you a swell fur coat on the installment plan. Mystery in a snowy world walked in by two young women, oddly different, maybe, down inside them, oddly alike.

They got down into the town and their feet were cold and wet. That was tough, not so much on them as on the cheap shoes they wore. "Come on Kit," Agnes said, and led the way out of the main street. They went down to where a railroad crossed the main street and got into a street of shabby little stores, little hot stuffy restaurants run by Greeks where hot dogs were sold. You could get spaghetti in Italian joints.

On such a street, on most Saturday evenings, plenty of young fellows out trying to pick up something, the girls would have been hailed a half dozen times. "Hey, kid" — this to Kit — "shake that female Jack Dempsey you're with and come to me. Hot time, kid." Agnes would turn to swear.

The young bloods weren't out that night. The girls went along the street to a small frame house, set back from the street, piles of rubbish in the yard, and around the house to the back door. Agnes knocked and a woman came to the door. She knew Agnes. "Hello," she said, "come in," and presently they were in a warm inner room and Agnes had called for drinks.

Kit didn't want her drink. She took it. There were some

men in the room, sitting at a near-by table and they were also drinking. What they all got was white mule. It was a raw, terrible drink and burned Kit's throat. Funny to think it might have been made by her own father, back up in the hills. Tears came into her eyes when the raw stuff touched the tender flesh of her throat and Agnes laughed. "It's awful stuff but it's good for you sometimes," she said.

They were in the room and Agnes was talking again. She had been to the place one night with a certain man. He was, she explained, a radical from New York. She was trying, was always trying to work something out in her own mind. They sat at a little table in the little room, rather dimly lighted, the woman who had admitted them coming in and going out. There were five or six men at a near-by table and Kit sat so that she faced them as Agnes talked. She didn't hear much of what Agnes said. There was a young man over there, at the other table, facing her.

He was pale. He did not look well. He was oddly like the young man Frank, the consumptive who had been her first boy friend. She might have called Frank lover. She didn't.

The one at the table that night was like and unlike. He was dressed well, in well-made clothes. She even looked down at his shoes, could see them under the table. They also were well made. They were unlike the shoes on the feet of the other men at the table. He might be a young swell of the town. Drinking habits and drinking places in America during prohibition were not so swell either.

Agnes talked. She was so absorbed in her own words that she did not notice that she was not being listened to. She talked. The young man at the other table was so unlike his companions. They were all young men. They talked loudly. Once or twice the woman who ran the place had to come in and ask them to be more quiet. The woman was middle-aged, she looked frumpy. The other men at the table were unlike the pale one who looked like Frank.

Frank had died only a few weeks earlier. The young man at the table kept looking at Kit.

She was having thoughts about Frank, now dead, as Agnes talked. Agnes was talking of revolution. She was always at that. She was talking of a new world workers were some day to make. The pale young man at the table in the little shabby speak-easy might have been a young Duke, or son, say of some great cotton-mill baron, or a cigarette baron.

There are huge life-insurance companies in North Carolina. He might have been the son of a millionaire president of a life-insurance company.

He might have been, like the working boy Frank, a dreamer. "He's got it, I bet, like Frank had," Kit thought. She meant tuberculosis.

Odd to think about people — supposing the young man at the table to be something of the sort suggested above, getting the same disease a lad like Frank got. He'd have come to the little dump maybe just to be with people. "This rot-gut whiskey won't do me any good but what's the difference? I'm gone anyway."

Kit Brandon off on her own, a million miles from Agnes, talking away opposite her. She was thinking of her last evening with the dying boy Frank.

She had walked out with Frank on another Saturday evening.

It was winter time too, then, but it was warm. It was the last time he had been outdoors before he died.

He had got an obsession. He had sent her word: "I want

to see you. You come Saturday night." A woman who worked in the mill and had a room in the same house he lived in had brought Kit the word and she had gone to him.

They had walked out, going slowly, and had got finally into a little lane, leading into a field. It was a place, just outside of town, where there was a farmhouse on one side of a road and a barn, in a field, on the other. The barn was set quite far back from the road and the lane led down to it.

The farmhouse was quite dark. "Come in here with me," Frank had said to her. He explained that he couldn't walk far. They went into the lane and Frank told her what he wanted. "That other night," he said—they were in the lane, just off the road—"when I touched you the way I did, with my hands . . . I didn't have the nerve to ask you then but now . . . if I don't ask you I won't get another chance . . .

"Because I'm going to die soon, now.

"I want you to, with me, because I never did and I do want to before I die."

Kit had let it happen. "Why not?" she had thought that night. She had let him and they had got caught, just after it was over—a man, perhaps a farmhand coming along the lane. Fortunately, they didn't quite get caught. They had a chance to get to their feet.

"What the hell you doing in here?"

They hadn't said anything but had hurried away out of the lane and back to Frank's place, as fast as they could go, he being as he was. They sat on the porch together at the house for a time and he cried and told her something. "I didn't want it to be disturbed like that," he said. He had

tried to explain something of what he had wanted, a kind
of sealing together, of himself with her, a living in profound
nothingness with another — once, once before he died. He
had a kind of idea. "I might live on in you," he said.

As to whether or not Kit had understood what Frank
had meant that night she didn't know. She was in the little
speak-easy thinking of it as Agnes talked. Her thoughts had
been aroused in her by the face, the eyes, of another young
man at the near-by table, like and unlike Frank, now dead.
She and Agnes had their drinks and Agnes talked and then
paid the check. Agnes was a little irritated, perhaps, feeling
that her talk had been falling on deaf ears. She got excited.

She had been telling the story of another strike she had
been in and of how, after the failure of the strike, the workers were left stranded, as at Marion, North Carolina. All
the labor leaders, even the young radicals from the North,
had got on trains and gone away.

"Why the hell don't they stay with us when we're licked,
take what we have to take?" she said in a loud voice, and the
men at the near-by table all turned and stared. She and Kit
both became self-conscious. "Let's get out of this dump,"
Agnes said, and they had got up to go out when one of the
young men at the other table jumped up and tried to de-
tain Kit. The one who did it was a little drunk. He grabbed
Kit by the arm. "Look here," he said. "Say, you're a sweet
kid," he said. He held her by the arm and when Agnes
advanced to the rescue he threw out his free arm trying
to brush her aside. "I don't want you," he said, "I want this
one." The other young men at the table were laughing and
the pale young man, who was so like and unlike Frank,
was trying to protest. "Ah, Jim, Jim, let her alone," he was

saying when Agnes, with a quick wide swing of her arm, struck the drunken young man in the face with her fist and knocked him to the floor.

There was an outbreak, an outcry, a racket, and the woman of the place ran into the room. She protested. Two or three of the other young men, at the table with the drunken one, had helped him to his feet and were holding him. He was swearing and the woman of the place kept protesting. "Be quiet! Oh, please, please be quiet," she was saying as Kit and Agnes slipped past her out of the room and got out again into the street. They walked up and down the main street of the town. It still snowed and Agnes had become quiet. She had perhaps been hurt by two things, that Kit had not listened to her talk in the speak-easy and that the drunken man had made the sharp distinction between herself and Kit. As the two young women walked up and down the main street of the town, the snow still falling, snow clinging to the coats of people, lighted store fronts shining through the falling snow, Kit felt the night beautiful.

Agnes didn't. She soon wanted to go home. "We might as well," she said. She spoke of clothes ruined, shoes ruined. The night had turned suddenly ugly for her.

CHAPTER FIVE

THERE were all kinds of fellows in with Tom Halsey, more or less under his orders, some bold ones, some sly crafty ones, some brutes. They talked, whispered among themselves. "What the hell?" It was because of Tom Halsey's son, young Gordon Halsey. He had got stuck on the skirt—Kit Brandon.

There was that other woman, Kate, a good deal older than Kit. She was all right. She knew how to keep her mouth shut.

But just the same. It was an old, old idea—*cherchez la femme.* "They gab. You get in a jam and you are mixed up with some dame and, sure as hell, she runs out on you."

The old war between men and women. Many of the mountain men who worked with Tom Halsey . . . Tom was a pioneer, a bringer of a new and modern world into the mountain life, . . . they were of an older order.

You saw a mountain man coming into some little mountain town afoot. He strode along the road ahead of his woman, did not walk beside her. Many of the mountain men had big families. The children walked in the road behind, the girl children at the end of the little procession. When a son of the family had reached maturity, began to think of himself as a man, he stepped ahead of his mother and walked just at the heels of his father.

The women submitted. A mountain man did not do any work about the house. He did not milk the cow, feed the pigs, carry firewood into the house. He crept away to the woods to make himself a run of liquor; he worked in his few hillside fields.

But the new world had come, even into the hills. Paved roads were being pushed through. They twisted and wound along little river bottoms, under majestic hills, occasionally climbed over a hill and went on down into another valley. Industrial towns had come, some of them growing swiftly, towns of North Carolina, Eastern Tennessee, Eastern Kentucky, Southwest Virginia. Tourists in Fords, Chevrolets, Buicks, Packards went whirling along roads and through the hills. The industrial towns had come because of power in the rivers of the hills and because of cheap labor. There were still hundreds of square miles of country in the mountains apparently uninhabited, but not uninhabited. The tourist going along in his car looked about. "What a desolate country!" He was mistaken. There were many thousands, even hundreds of thousands of people, hidden away, in little hollows, on mountain sides, in mountain cabins no car could climb up to. The mountain people had lived thus for many generations. Books had been written about them, tales of mountain feuds . . . the Hatfield-McCoys of West Virginia, stories out of Breathitt County, Kentucky . . . sentimental yarns. . . . "Trail of the Lonesome Pine."

There were garages strung along the new big highways and these were often gathering places for Tom's men. How quickly they had taken to the automobile. They gathered before such places, sat about, some in overalls. A surprising number of them could not read or write. They were outwardly listless enough looking men. They talked slowly and quietly. As always happens, the mind of the man out of another world too much influenced by the reading of newspapers, popular magazines and novels, could not differentiate. The mountain men were thought of, by tourists passing swiftly through the hills, as all of a type. They were dangerous, secretive, sly. They spent their time hunting "federals" or shooting at each other. It was of course all nonsense. They were of every type, incipient poets, honest hard-working men, killers, horse traders, liars, men faithful to friends unto death, stupid ones, smart ones, God-seeking ones. It is true that in lonely isolated places things did happen. What Kit's father had, she thought, intended doing to Kit was not a too unusual thing. They lived in a country long out of the path of so-called American progress, a country long forgotten. The westward drift of population in America in earlier days had been along rivers and across the plains, over the Alleghanies from the East and down the Ohio, or along the upper lake region.

Then out into the fat rich plains, the prairie country, the great American agricultural empire. A man of Tom's crowd took a load of liquor into Ohio. He came back and talked. During the Civil War Mosby's raiders cut across river from Kentucky into the North. They would have been Southern boys, for the most part Poor Whites, fighting they did not know what for. They raided through Indiana and Ohio and some of them came back.

They came back shaking their heads. Talks at night by Confederate camp fires. "Boys, we can never lick that people. Why, look how our fields are desolated. Up there the barns are groaning, towns are growing, even while this war is going on. They are too big, fat, and well-fed for us."

Mountain man, of Tom Halsey's crowd, in a garage, talking to other mountain men. "Good God, Jim, Fred, Joe, Harry, here we are. We scratch the ground on one of these hills to raise a little corn. It gets up shoulder high and we think we've got a crop. Little scrawny corn stalks as big as my finger. Up there the corn is like trees and you should see their towns, the way their women dress, the houses they live in."

It was no wonder that the money crop of the hills, moonliquor, had, under prohibition, got so important. Tom Halsey, in organizing, drawing together under one head, a scattered industry of thousands of small units, had but followed in the footsteps of others in a modern world — organized steel, the oil industry, tobacco, the woollen industry. Control the illicit liquor business, control and organize crime. Although Tom Halsey did not have an office in an office building, board of directors' room with mahogany table, etc., he was ambitious. He felt himself in the American business tradition. He had thought about it, had his own pride. He felt that American business men, captains of industry, were really big men and that he was on the road to bigness.

The mountain empire in the very heart of America was long forgotten. In Old Virginia the big families, the F. F. V.'s, are nearly all in the Tidewater country. The Washingtons, Jeffersons, Madisons all lived in Tidewater. They forgot the mountain country, the mountain men. Daniel Boone lived out there, Abe Lincoln's people came from the hills. The mountain men were the adventurers, openers up

of Kentucky, of Tennessee, of what is now West Virginia
— land of coal. Once the mountain men tried to get out
from under the overlordship of Tidewater Virginia. They
organized the state of Franklin, a purely mountain state,
elected a governor and United States senators. They didn't
get away with it.

The men of Tom Halsey's crowd, bringers of the new era
into the hills, whiskey-making organized, put on a business
basis, on their hours off loafing before a roadside garage,
looked out over a lovely country.

The garage, let us say, is high up, near a mountain top,
where one of the new paved roads sweeps up out of one
river valley to pass over and into another. The men's eyes
are accustomed to the sight before them. However, and although the mountain folk do not often speak of it, not being
given to flowery talk, there is in them a deep love of their
hill country. Some of the men of Tom Halsey's liquor-
making, liquor-handling, liquor-running crowd, men who
under Tom began suddenly to make money, to drive
automobiles, to take trips down out of the hills and even
into the rolling hill country of southern Ohio and Pennsylvania . . . some of them had been as far away from their
home hills as Detroit . . . belonged to families that had
been in the hills since before the Revolutionary War. They
were sons and grandsons of men who had got the hill country love, love of isolation and independence, into their blood.
They were poor men but they were no time-clock punch-
ers. They didn't become clerks in stores and banks. "I am
poor but be careful. Do not tread too hard on my toes."
When a stranger came into the hills he was watched, but
the mountain men were not necessarily suspicious lest he be
a federal. The poorest mountain man, living in the most

isolated hollow of the hills, in the greatest poverty, often in a one-room cabin with a dirt floor, when such a stranger came to his door invited him into his house, invited him to eat, to spend the night, to stay, if he wished, in the poor hovel for a long visit.

A surprising number of the men in the American Southern Highlands are Scotch-Irish, so-called. It does not mean, however, that they are half Irish. It means that, in old Europe, an English king once sent mountain Scots into Ireland and gave them free land there but mountain people are like the French. They hate paying taxes. The English king tried to tax them and great hordes of them came to America. They were always whiskey makers. Their ancestors had made pot liquor in Scotch hills. They came through Pennsylvania and down through the valley of Virginia, the "Shenandoah" and to the hills because they were hill people. They were in the Whiskey Rebellion in Pennsylvania in early days. "What was all this business about taxes? What has government done for us that we should pay taxes?" For generations the material growth of America had gone on, a great boast, a great wonder, railroads built, later highways built, schools built, cities built. It hadn't happened in the hill country, in all the great sweep of mountain country, starting in the East, almost within sight of the capital at Washington, and sweeping westward, through Virginia, touching North Carolina, taking in a great part of West Virginia, Tennessee, Northern Alabama, and Georgia, Kentucky, and Missouri.

It is true that modern industry had done something to, if not for, the hill country. The great lumber kings had invaded the country. There had been thievery of great boundaries and ruthless cutting and slashing. An old story, the whole country may some day realize what a tragic story.

In the early days the mountain men, families, drifted into the hills one by one and settled there. They knew little of courts of law. Titles for land when acquired were often not recorded in the courts. After all Daniel Boone, at the end of all his exploring, his daring penetration into unknown places, when he was old and had settled on a piece of land, to enjoy in peace his old age, was gypped out of the land by some big land company. The big land companies were one of the earliest forms of American graft. Even the immortal Washington got in on that racket.

The early mountain man, coming in, picked himself a place with a bit of creek or river bottom. Hundreds and even thousands of cold mountain streams flowed down out of the hills. They were alive with trout. The forests were full of game. There was enough grass . . . the nutritious blue grass in the limestone hill . . . to feed a cow, a team of oxen or a horse. Pigs could be marked and turned loose to roam in the forest and in good years they grew fat on the fallen acorns.

A life that would have seemed barren to many Americans, in a land where riches came so rapidly, so much flat land, easily farmed, land to be had for the taking in an earlier day. Mark Twain's writing of the Tennessee land in "The Golden Age" . . . queer creatures, the mountaineers, so listless, so ignorant . . . nothing said about the beauty of Tennessee hills. Would they produce coal, would they produce iron? What other use is there for such land?

To city men, town men, men of fat Middle-Western farms, such a land would seem of no use. But there was something else to be said. Did not Thomas Jefferson declare that the best government was the least government? There was independence. Your mountain man did not bend the

knee. "Treat me with the respect due to my manhood
or . . ."

"Or, or, or."

Life was hard but good, too. A mountain man, grown
lean and hard in a hard land on hard fare, thought nothing
of walking twenty-five miles over mountain trails, through
the thick laurel, under the great trees, to some tiny settlement, to bring home tobacco, salt and sugar. He went with
his "passel of ginseng," called "sang," or with a few hens in
a "poke," slung over his shoulder. There was something
mysterious about the wild sang. It was wanted, a good price
would be paid for it, by some far-off people. The people
who wanted it might have been living in Mars. The mountain man didn't know, didn't ask. In many of the mountain
cabins, mere huts, the doors were left swinging open winter
and summer. Hens came indoors and laid eggs on the beds
or under the beds. The mountain man's children had fixed a
place for hens to set in a corner of his one-room house. His
pig wandered in and out at the open door. You can house-
break a pig, too.

Suspicion of government deeply rooted. Again: "What
right has government to say my children shall go to school?
What do we need of book-larnin'? What has government
done for me? I myself have no book-larnin', cannot read or
write, but am I not a man in my place?" Tom Halsey, the
man who became a mountain gang leader . . . he was a
rather small compactly built quiet man . . . blue-black hair,
black sharp eyes, an upshoot out of his people, more cun-
ning, perhaps cruel, determined, ambitious. How he got his
power over other men and, when he wished it, over women,
no one knew. He could remember when, as a boy, he went,
for the first time, with his father and other men to a town.

They went, the little caravan of mountaineers, some sixty miles, over stony winding mountain roads, half trails. The men carried axes to cut underbrush away. Up and down mountains they went, a team of oxen pulling a covered wagon, a few dozen jugs or kegs of whiskey in the wagon. They made good whiskey in that day, let it mature, didn't hurry it, didn't load the beer with sugar to hurry it, didn't make the later stomach-destroying stuff Tom got rich handling. The whiskey would be buried in straw in the wagon and a man with a gun walked on a mile or two ahead. If a federal appeared . . . they existed at the time too . . . he was to fire the gun. The whiskey was quickly hidden in the near-by brush. At night, when the little caravan camped by some clear mountain stream, it was again carried into the brush, hidden for the night under the thick laurel and rhododendron. When the men got down, near the town, it would be again hidden while they went on into town.

The caravan took all of three long days making its way down to the town where there was a store. There was a branch railroad that came up to the town. It was another three days getting home.

Could a man, several men, come over such roads, for such a great distance, merely to sell a few hens, a little sang? It was too difficult to haul the corn down. Whiskey was the distillation of the corn. Men wanted it. A man and his family wanted sugar, salt, tobacco, snuff. The women and children had to have clothes.

The little pilgrimage going down camped at night by a mountain stream. Tom Halsey remembered that. He remembered the mysterious darkness of the great forests, the cry of owls at night, the talk of the men. The men who would be so silent in town, among town men, now talked freely. When they got near the town the whiskey would be hidden and the smartest, shrewdest one among them . . . it would be Tom's father . . . pride in the boy in that fact . . . would be appointed the one to make the trade for the liquor. "We are mountain men, cannot read or write, but when we speak we tell the truth. It is good liquor. If you think we are dull and stupid, come, try swapping horses with one of us.

"The whiskey is hidden in such and such a place. Come, I will show you." Tom's father spoke of good times when he was a boy. His people lived in the hills of Tennessee. There was a war . . . it was the Spanish-American War . . . and thousands of young men from the North came to camp at a place called "Chickamaugua Park."

And did they want whiskey? Did they buy it? It was good times for the liquor makers in the hills. It may be that later, when Tom became a big business men, he remembered his father's talk of that time.

In the town something to be seen. There was, for example, the railroad locomotive. It was really a cheaply constructed bit of railroad that ran up to that mountain place, a mere branch road. There was to be a big lumber cutting started there. But, to the boy, the railroad engine had seemed wonderful and terrible enough. To Tom's mind it may have suggested something. Organizers of big business must have imagination too. They must be born with imagination. The business, the acquisitive instinct, that enables a man to grow rich and powerful, may be, after all, but a perversion, a twist of some finer instinct. Oh, the great world, off there in the distance somewhere, down along that poor little mountain railroad, great rich plains opening out down there, broad rivers flowing! Oh, the great cities being built! Oh, the great forests that still covered so much of a hill country!

The mountain country lay between the North and the South. It had long been the middle-land, the border-land between two civilizations. How many battles of the Civil War fought in the hills, mountain men on both sides in the struggle. Birds, from the North, going South, stopped their flight for a time in the hills. Some from the South stayed there, in the high cool places; from the North, in the warm valleys. Southern and Northern flowers and trees grew along mountain trails. There was snow falling on the mountain tops, far South, warm days in winter far North.

The forest that once covered the whole land to be remembered by all those who had known it. Tom's father became a lumberjack when the lumber kings came. He talked, sometimes, when Tom was a young fellow, growing up at home, of the forest. It was something mysterious. You felt strange sometimes. Tom's father could not find words for what he wanted to say. He did not know that man had got his notion for the cathedrals, for the Gothic, from the forests. The great aisles, leading away mysteriously under the trees. It was dark overhead, the branches of the great trees intertwined. "You didn't want to speak loud."

There was no underbrush in some places, on upper plateaus where the biggest trees were, and the ground underneath was soft. You walked always on a deep thick carpet of moss.

It was a great sponge. You sank in it to the boot tops.

An idea Tom Halsey never got, that his father never got. This great middle-ground between the North and the South, the Southern Appalachian Highlands, meant something terribly important to the whole country. It was the great stream source. What great rivers having their source in the hills. Once Pinchot, in Theodore Roosevelt's time, was trying to make the idea of forest preservation clear to a group of senators. He took a board and held it on a table, at an angle of forty-five degrees. He poured a glass of water down the face of the board and then took the same board and covered it with blotting paper.

Again he poured the water down the face of the board but it did not run off. The water trickled, a few drops at a time, slowly out at the base of the board.

To see the country as a whole, understand it as a whole, a faculty that, as statesman, Lincoln had, as warrior, Grant had. The lumber kings going into the Southern Highlands and stripping the timber away, often destroyed timber they could not get out. Whole mountain slopes were often destroyed to make a runway for tall timber on some upper plateau . . . the washing away of the good soil beginning, going on year after year, floods in the Tennessee, the Cumberland, the Ohio. Floods down the Mississippi . . . fair lands made deserts . . . countries have been destroyed thus . . . towns destroyed, farms destroyed. A lumber baron has made a million, two million, five million. It is a sweet picture. Kill the TVA! Kill the CCC! These things embarrass private enterprises. Suppose it were possible that, some day, a new impulse be carried to the point where all men, in youth, were compelled to spend perhaps three years, working in the forests, or in any work that would benefit the whole country, getting thereby a sense of the country as a whole.

The dream of a new conception of life and the land.

CHAPTER SIX

TOM HALSEY, a mountain man and the son and grandson of mountain men, was born with a talent. It was not altogether an accident that he became a success later. He was by his very nature a man of business, an organizer of men and affairs. In him there was the same sort of talent that has come to the surface in so many other Americans, some of them historical figures . . . important surely in the development of industrial America. Do not be too quick to condemn them. Wait. Have you had the opportunity for wealth and the power that wealth brings? For a long time the industrial organizers were America's heroes, looked up to by American youth . . . their glory is fading now. They were more influential in making young Americans than the Jeffersons and Lincolns. Is it worth while naming some of them . . . the Rockefellers, Goulds, Harrimans, etc., etc., etc.? A list of names could be made covering a long page.

Did I say their glory has passed? Do you live in any small or fairly large American town? If one of these great ones were to come, perhaps to live in your town . . . how wonderful. Are you sure that John W. Gates did not make more splash, that he was not more courted in Springfield, Illinois, than was ever Abraham Lincoln or say the poet Vachel Lindsay?

You begin small. There was an early American philosopher, Benjamin Franklin . . . "A stitch in time saves nine." . . . "Take care of the pennies and the dollars will take care of themselves."

Later product of that last, "Safety first."

There came a time when the young Tom Halsey left his father's house. He had already got his start. He had a calf his father gave him, and that grew into a cow. In a year when the moss in the old forest was thick on the ground two young pigs he had acquired grew into fat hogs at no cost to young Tom.

Be careful, be cautious, be shrewd. Do not mind too much using others. Be as fair with them as you can. Tom was never much of a talker. Don't waste words either. He went once to make some liquor with his father, when he was still little more than a boy. They were walking up a long mountain trail. They were going to a certain spot, beside a small mountain stream. You had to push through thick laurel to get in.

Tom's father had an idea. He spoke of it as the two made their way up the path. They had been up there some time before to set the mash, to make the beer for the run. It was to be a big one, the biggest they had ever made. The father walked in front, not looking back. "Now you look here, Tom" . . . the father spoke of his plan. There was a good and growing sale for liquor in the lumber camp where he had been at work. He had got off work for two or three weeks and had tramped home, over the mountains from the big lumber cutting forty miles away. "You will bring the stuff over there at night." He named a certain date. He was to go back to the camp in a few days. The idea was that the boy was to haul the liquor to the vicinity of the camp at night. It would take two nights and he would have to hide in the woods during the day. The father would meet him on the second night and together they would store the liquor in a place near the camp where the father could get it out, a gallon at a time. It would bring a good price. There was an advantage, the father being there, one of the workmen. The man at the head of the camp was sharp on bootleggers. The sharpness had driven up the prices.

The father was telling the son. He was taking him into his plan.

Well, not quite. They walked along in silence for a time and then the boy spoke and the father turned in the path to look at him. There was that quality in the young Tom. It was always in him. He did not get excited, speak sharply. He meant what he said. There was a certain finality that made others stop, take a look, wonder.

It was the sort of remark a mountain boy did not make to his own father.

"Uh huh. And me?"

A moment of suspense, there on the mountainside between the two . . . this after the father had stopped and was looking at young Tom. The two standing looking at each other, the silence, the challenge, not from son to father but, because it was Tom Halsey and even though he was but a boy, from man to man.

As though birds in the woods might be singing the words, the wind that blew among the trees carrying the words.

"And me? And me? And me?"

"Now there has come the time for the bargain between us."

The above words not said . . . just the, "And me . . . and me . . . and me."

But a mountain man, if he is a man, does not bargain with his son. He orders and the son obeys.

"And me? And me? And me?"

Young Tom, even then, would not have been defiant. He was handling his father as later he handled officers of the law, members of the gang he organized. His "and me" was rather an explanation. "You see, you do not understand. I am not merely a mountain boy, son of a mountain man. I am myself.

"I have certain plans, not very definite yet. You have to begin small, but you must take advantage of every opportunity. The time will come when I will command men, will command affairs."

The "and me." What an influence it has had in the affairs of the world, eh?

The father turned, after a long silent look at the son and went on along the trail up the mountain and the son followed in silence. He hadn't said, "If you don't split I won't do it, I won't play ball," but the words were implicit in his voice, the sound of his voice, a certain quiet thing in his eyes. Already he had the cow. It was his and he had sold the fat pigs. More than one mountain boy has left home, got himself a wife, set up for himself, on less.

The father went along before his son in silence. He was thinking. If he took some other mountain man in with him, to make the stuff at home, haul it to the camp, take most of the risk, he would have to share.

The boy had not defied him. He had asked a question. There were no other sons at home. The boy was already trained as a liquor maker. There was a quality Tom had from the beginning. If he got what he wanted he did not try to win moral or spiritual victories. It was as though he

said to himself . . . "Be careful now. A man wants to keep
his self-respect. Be careful. Give the other fellow a way out.
If he wants to feel big, you let him. You get what you're
after." There was nothing more said until evening, when
the two were coming back down the mountain and then
the father spoke, as though an idea had just occurred to him.

"Tom, my boy," he said . . . "It is all right. We will make
some money.

"By God, you shall have your share," he said.

Get a little and a little more. Don't waste anything at
first. Keep your eye on the main chance.

CHAPTER SEVEN

EVEN for the masters of the art of acquiring, for the men-handlers, organization-handlers, money-getters, power-getters, there are bad times. The hand slips. The brain doesn't work. A man becomes a captain of some great industry. He commands money, men, affairs. See how cool, self-possessed and quiet he is. He is not an artist. He does not make a fool of himself, say like a Vincent Van Gogh. He does not run across fields, shout, try to catch the glory of the sun on a canvas, give the sun to other men. He does not go God-seeking, wanting to give God to men.

He perhaps gets sick. He is in a hospital and there is a little blonde, a nurse. Look out, man! She is holding his hand. "I can see you are a man of feeling. How sensitive you are, so easily hurt.

"I am sure you are a man not understood. People think you are hard, cruel, without feeling. What a mistake it is."

A sigh. A look of longing in a woman's eyes.

Or it is a show girl. The man, the grizzled old warrior of money, has gone to see a show. "Ah, there is one." Inner excitement in the old fellow. What hope, what longing. It is generally understood that blondes do it best.

As it happened, however, Tom Halsey was one of the

lucky ones. A woman came to him when he was very
young.

She was not a woman. She was a young girl but, in the
mountains, young girls suddenly and mysteriously become
women. Tom was working in a field, a sloping field, planted
to corn in the spring, and the field went down to a mountain road. You went along the mountain road, perhaps a
quarter of a mile, to the Halsey house, a large and rather
comfortable log farmhouse. At the foot of the field, near the
road, there was a spring and locust trees grew there, spreading their branches out over the spring. The locust puts out
its leaves late in the spring. How delicate and feathery they
are. The honey locust blooms riotously and the trees are
covered with bees. They make a soft, sometimes loud, mur-
muring sound. Tom was hoeing corn, working it for the
first time, and an odd caravan came along the road.

But the caravan wasn't so odd. It was a sight Tom had
seen before. Some little mountain farmer had failed. He had
been living on a mountainside farm somewhere back up in
the hills, a man of fifty, with pale watery eyes and a little
scrawny red beard, now turning gray. It looked dirty and
the man was dirty. He had a wife and several children, some
of them quite young.

Why, what a producer. It was, in the mountains, a common enough sight. Look. There are twelve, thirteen, perhaps fourteen kids. The man has two half-broken-down old
horses and there is a wagon, the wheels tied in place by
ropes, and on the wagon, pretty much covered with younger
children clinging on, there are a few sticks of furniture,
some dirty torn blankets and equally torn and dirty bed
ticks. On one of the blankets, held in the arms of a girl
child of eight, a sickly looking pale child, there is a babe

and it cries lustily. The babe is not sickly. It will still be at
the breast of the woman, the mother, who sits on the wagon
beside the man. She is a huge fat woman who loooks like an
old Indian squaw. She may be that. She sits so placidly as
the wagon crawls creaking along, Tom, in the field, near
the fence and the spring, watching. She may be an Indian. There are still small fragments of Indian tribes in
the hills.

Tom is standing and looking. He looks with impersonal
eyes. The hill farmer on the wagon has had ill luck. He had
a crop of corn planted and there came a great rain. The
corn was planted on new ground in a sloping field and the
man and the children had worked all winter clearing the
land. It was a piece of cheap land, the timber having been
taken off some years before.

And then the great rain came, the water washed down the
hill and across the face of the field. There was nothing to
be done. The man stood helpless. He was a man who had always had ill luck. His wife was slovenly, a bad housekeeper
and a bad cook and as her children dropped from her . . .
they came regularly, one after another, easily, falling from
between her great thighs, they were all girl children. What
is a man to do about that?

There was the great rain, all the good soil in the new
ground washed away, the young corn gone, all washed
away. There were three young calves and three cows and
two sows, soon to farrow, in the field by the creek. It was a
long narrow field and the grass was good. In the mountains
when the great rains come, in country where the timber has
been cut off, small mountain streams become suddenly tor-
rents. It may happen without warning. The great rain may
be above you, far up some mountain. It may be the rain

comes at night, when a man is asleep. The calves, sows and cows were all drowned.

Last year the bean beetles took his beans. He had four fine hogs, fat, almost ready to kill. He had driven them down, out of an upper oak forest where they had grown fat on the fallen acorns. It was almost killing time but they all took the cholera and died.

What was the use? What was a man to do? The man had heard that in a distant town, far away, a hundred miles, there was work to be had for women and girls. Some of his girls were quite big now. There was a cotton mill in the town. It took such girls. It was no place for a man. They did not take a man of fifty, did not want such men, but a man must do something. Hungry children must be fed. The man sat sadly on the broken seat of his broken wagon beside his fat silent placid wife, driving his bony team. In the town to which he was going, a growing industrial town, the girls would find work. They would earn money. There were some five or six girls, now old enough to go to work. He himself would have to sit at home, with the fat wife, in a house in a mill village.

Or in the afternoon, he would wander about. There would be other men like himself, "mill daddies." His old woman was slovenly, a bad housekeeper. It might be that, in the end, he would begin working about the house, doing women's work, making beds, sweeping, helping with the cooking.

The wagon went its painful way along the road. There had been a dry time and there was dust. The wheels made crazy tracks in the road. Three or four older girls walked behind the wagon. The caravan passed, young Tom standing and staring, no word, no sign passed between him and the man, between him and the girls. It went down the sloping road, the crooked wheels catching on protruding rocks. Often the wagon came to a dead stop. "Why doesn't he make that fat old mother get out and walk?" There was a little creek to be forded and beyond a little rise just before you came to the Halsey house. The team struggled, the man slashing at them with a whip, Tom staring. "They'll never make it."

And how did the team manage to get up hills, up the sides of mountains? There were a hundred miles of such mountain road to be covered before the caravan reached the cotton-mill town.

Tom turned to go back to his work and then stopped. There was still another girl, belonging to the family, a slender pale woman child of fourteen or fifteen. She was coming along the road alone, stumbling along. She did not see Tom standing there.

She was bare-legged, bare-footed. She was ill. She stopped by the fence near the spring and struggled to get over, still not seeing Tom. Her cheeks were flushed, as with a fever, and she appeared as though drunken. Had the others forgotten her? She had become ill and had stopped beside the road to rest and was now trying to overtake the wagon, but she had noticed the spring just inside the field and was trying to get to it.

In such a family, one child would not be missed. She looked very ill. She might die. Something in Tom was touched.

Why, how pretty she was! Her illness had made her more pretty, even beautiful. She had got to the top of the rail fence, had one leg over — what a clear-cut lovely little face, now drawn with pain, lines of suffering showing on such a young face. She had yellow hair, a mass of it, fallen down over young shoulders. "She will fall," Tom thought. He sprang toward her.

It may have been his sudden appearance that startled her, threw her off balance. There was a little cry from her and she fell. She lay still on the grass under the fence.

And now something else happened. Tom had run to the girl under the fence, had picked her up, was holding her in his arms, and had faced about . . . she was unconscious, had perhaps struck her head in falling . . . he was facing the road and the Halsey house, and the wagon had struggled up the little slope and was before the house.

It broke down. There was a crash. One of the wheels had come off and the wagon with its contents, the few sticks of furniture, bedding, assortment of girl children of all ages, the fat old mother, the defeated mountain farmer, all were dumped in the road.

There were screams. There were cries. Tom, as he stood holding the unconscious girl child, saw his mother run out of the house to the road. At that time Tom was alone at home with his mother, a strong, rather mannish-looking woman. He laid the unconscious girl as tenderly as he could on the fence top, her arms and head hanging down on one side and her feet and bare slender legs on the other, and bolted over. With her in his arms he went, half running, along the road to the house.

It was Tom Halsey himself who afterwards told Kit Brandon of what happened to his young wife, the mother of his son Gordon who became Kit's husband.

He got to her house that day, and afterwards for several weeks she was ill there. It was not thought she would live

and several times Tom rode off to a distant town to bring a
doctor, sometimes at night. As for her family, the wagon
again patched, they went on their way, having spent the
night and a part of the next day at the Halsey place. To the
fat mother and perhaps to the father she was just another
girl child. Such a woman could drop another. It was easy
for her, and Tom's mother, although she looked mannish,
had a woman's heart. She was glad enough to get the girl.
"If she lives, she may be a comfort," she thought.

She did live and she became Tom's wife, but she was
never strong. Tom told Kit the story of his short life with
her and of her death.

He had got his own place and already he had got into the
liquor business in a small way. He had got his neighbors,
who were liquor makers . . . there were enough of them,
all small makers, little groups of men going in together,
buying a still . . . he had got them all to bring the stuff
to him.

He told Kit how it was with him at that time. His son
had been born and his wife was again ill. She had begun
nursing her child but one of her breasts had caked and he
had to take her off to a distant town to have it lanced. He
had wanted to take her to a big town, perhaps to the very cotton-mill town that had swallowed up her family . . . she had
never heard from them again after they disappeared down
the road . . . there was a hospital at that place . . . he hadn't
the money. He had got a mountain doctor who had done
his job crudely. His wife's breast became infected and there
was high fever.

Tom was in a fix. He was worried. He was frightened.
The doctor who had lanced the breast told him that it
would be dangerous to try to move her. He had come with

his young wife into a new neighborhood, some thirty miles from his father's house and had bought a little farm there. He did not know his neighbors very well yet and already he was in debt to some of them. He had taken their liquor to handle, had begun to build up a trade in distant towns. He had taken several trips with his loaded wagon at night but some of the money that should have gone to the liquor makers had been spent.

He told Kit of calling his neighbors together. "This is how it is with me. My wife is dying and the doctor says she cannot be moved, but I intend to move her. I must have money."

Beside the cotton-mill town there was another industrial town, some thirty miles away, but there was no hospital in that place. Tom had been there several times. There was a man of the town.

A note of bitterness, of contempt, crept into Tom's voice when he spoke of that man.

It wasn't a pleasant picture. He was a man of fifty-five. There may be more such men among successful Americans than we other Americans care to realize. He had made money rapidly after a long early struggle . . . a big man, with a big head, big shoulders and body. Once he had been a laborer in a lumber camp. Often such men, when they succeed . . . they have done hard, heavy manual work during youth and early manhood . . . they are inclined to eat hugely, drink hugely.

Later they sit all day and every day at a desk. They go on with the heavy living and while they still appear strong there is a gradual breaking down of something inside. Tom said that this one had got hold of some invention. It was a tool, widely used and useful to farmers, not of the hills but of the Northern plains, and was built largely of wood. He had understood how to get money from banks, how to advertise. Perhaps he had come South, into a Southern industrial town, because wood was cheap there and labor cheap. He had been married but had no children and his wife had died.

He prided himself on being a sport, on living flashily. His mind had taken that turn. He drove a big sport motor car and wore heavy homespun clothes imported from England. He had got him a big house, at the edge of the town where he had set up his factory and had guests down from Northern cities. "You must come down to my place. It is in the mountains, in the Blue Ridge.

"If you want to bring a woman along . . ." Laughter. He poked the man in the ribs or slapped him on the back. "You know . . . make it a vacation," he said. This was before prohibition but there was local option in the county and he had built a bar in the basement of his house.

The Southern industrial town was a county seat and before and after the coming of prohibition, the jail there was constantly filled with violators of illicit liquor laws. They were all poor men or the sons of poor men, laborers in the factories in the town, sons of laborers, mountain farmers, caught at the still, sons of these men bringing moon whiskey in to serve the town. The rich and the well-to-do and the sons of these did not get into jail. The whole town knew of the bar in the rich man's house. He gave money to charity. He helped support the churches of the town.

Tom told Kit, speaking bitterly, stories of how the man lived. He loved getting the sons and daughters of the town people, sons and daughters of merchants, lawyers, successful doctors into his house and getting them drunk. He had become somewhat jaded about women but still loved touching them, the young ones. He wanted to put his hands on them, stand close, run his hands over young female bodies. There are such men. Once perhaps they had something to give a woman. It got lost, was petered away.

"I'd do anything for you, little girl. Do you want a fur coat?" . . . his hands on her. Hands creeping down over hips, over breasts. Men of the town, the respectable women of the town, older women, leaders in the churches, knew of these things. The town was filled with whispers. Nothing was done. The young people continued to go to the parties at his house. It was a little hard to refuse. "Be careful. Do not offend this man. He has power."

He wanted to be known as a sport, a dashing figure of a man, but he was also frugal. Men who grow rich are frugal and careful in small things. For his bar he brought in liquors from Northern cities. . . . "You see," he said . . . he put on a white apron, became a bartender for his guests. . . . "You see, it is good stuff. It is the real stuff."

But at the same time . . . you understand . . . when people have become a little drunk . . . how do they know? It is really foolish to waste good liquor. Mountain moon may be had at a low price. It may be colored with prune juice. A bottle of imported liquor costing, I assure you, enough, may be refilled.

Tom Halsey drove at night . . . it was a Saturday night . . . in at the man's driveway and on past the brightly lighted house to where there was a big brick garage. There was room in the garage for several cars. Tom drove his team — the wagon well loaded, and it made racket enough. It was no wonder that, later, when he became a successful illicit liquor man, making plenty of money, he insisted on big powerful, silent cars. The house of the successful manufacturer was surrounded by several acres of land and was outside the town limits.

It was a summer night and the house and yard were filled with young couples. Some of the young men, seen by Tom, as he drove in . . . they strolled along paths, past lighted windows . . . were in evening clothes. Young women were in light summer dresses. It is so nice, with your hands, to feel the body of a young woman, under a light summer dress.

Tom was in a hurry. There was a negro man, dressed in uniform, who came to him when he had stopped the team near the garage and Tom spoke to him. He didn't waste words. "Look here, nigger, I'm in a hurry. You tell your boss. Goddam your black soul, you get him out here, and quick."

He said no more. The man went and presently there was the big man, the rich man, the flashy one.

He was angry. He was upset. "Why, yes. I have bought stuff from you but for God's sake, man . . . haven't you any sense?" . . . he made a sign towards Tom's team . . . bringing that in here. There are people here.

"I'll have nothing more to do with a man who is such a damned fool."

The two men were walking in a path near the garage. There was a light over the garage door and they went along the side of the building and stopped. Tom tried to explain. "But my wife is very ill. She may die. I must have money. I could unload it back here."

He even pleaded, but as the man did not at once respond his voice grew harsh. However he did not shout. He was sizing up his man. "He is pretty big." Tom was himself a small man. "He has led a certain kind of life for a long time now. He's probably soft." "That nigger of yours, in that uniform . . . there are 150 gallons . . . I want you to take it all . . . it is a hurry up matter with me . . . I tell you my wife is ill . . . I've got to have money and right now . . . It will be $300 . . . I know damned well you always have cash, plenty of it . . . you are the kind." His voice was growing more and more harsh. "You are the kind that likes to pull a big roll, flash it before people. Goddam you."

He was astonishing the man, throwing him off guard. "There are some bushes here." He pointed. They stood near the wall of the garage. "I'll unload it quickly enough. Your nigger can put it away. While I am unloading you will go into the house and get the money.

"If you haven't it on you. Have you?"

The man laughed. After all he had once been a lumberjack. If he had only taken care of his big body through the years. The man before him was after all small. "Why, you impertinent little runt!"

He got no further. Tom leaped and had him by the throat. He was like a wild cat fastened on to the throat of a horse. After all, the man would not shout. He would not dare. "Oh, these big bugs," Tom said, long afterwards, telling of the moment.

It didn't last long, a short struggle, the man's arms flailing about, hitting nothing, his breath going. Tom was close in where the big fists couldn't hurt him. His rather small hands were very powerful. "Will you or won't you? If you shout and they come I'll kill you and them." He let go the man's throat. He knew he had him. "If you go in there and don't come out with it, at once, I'll come in after you.

"I'm sorry," he said, "my wife's dying." The man went.

Tom drove home. He told Kit that he forgot about the liquor, did not remember to unload it. The way home was over very rough roads and the liquor was in glass fruit jars. They kept breaking, he said. There was a drip, drip, drip of mountain liquor in a mountain road. He lashed his team, nearly killing the horses. When he got to his house there were several men, mountain men, neighbors, loitering in the dark road before his house. Their women were inside. They were the men who had trusted him with the liquor but they were not there to collect. Their wives were trying to save Tom's wife, but it was too late. She died that night, just as he stopped his team before the house . . . steam arising in clouds from the half-dead animals . . . they breathed in gasps, nostrils vibrating . . . it was a pretty good team, young horses. His wife died but his son lived.

CHAPTER EIGHT

K IT thought that Tom Halsey must have seen the woman Kate before his wife died. She and her husband, a mountain preacher, lived in the same settlement in the mountains where Tom had his farm. At the time Tom's wife died, on the same night, a tragedy also happened to Kate. She was laid abed of her first child and it died. Tom may have heard of her loss. Almost every day he had been driving to a distant town. There was trouble in getting a food his babe would take. He had consulted doctors, had, at their advice, bought certain patent baby foods that were tried unsuccessfully. When he went hurriedly off to town thus, his way lay past a certain mountain cabin. It sat back from the road on the side of a hill, a flimsy little one-room structure built of unpainted boards. For some reason, unexplained, Kit telling Kate's story, knew that there were great masses of tiger lilies in the yard before the door and she thought that Tom might have noticed the woman, having heard her story, and after she had got out of her bed of illness . . . the husband would be away from home . . . he always was . . . he was a God man and terribly serious, even fanatic about it and would have been off somewhere working in God's vineyard, herding the strayed sheep, lifting the fallen. The woman would have been seated in the doorway of her little house, behind the masses of tiger lilies, head in hands, gazing off toward the distant blue hills, sunk in the terrible sorrow that comes to the woman who loses the first fruit of the womb.

Her husband was an uneducated man. He could just read and write. In the mountains there are many such men. They are not called to God's ministry by the church. God calls them directly. He had been, before God called him, a rather quiet, somewhat sensitive and frightened boy, and was one of a large family. His name was Joseph Lawler and his father, Ike Lawler, was a man well known and a good deal feared in all that section of the mountains. He was a big man, tall and with small shifty eyes and was notoriously lazy but, although he himself did no work, he worked brutally the few poor horses that came into his possession and he did the same with his wife and children.

The mountains were full of stories about Ike Lawler. His wife, a heavy fat woman, like Tom's mother-in-law, was always having children. As with the Indian woman, the mother of Tom's wife, they dropped almost casually from her. It was said that she once dropped one in a field where, under the eye of her husband, she had been kept at work until the last possible moment. There were fourteen of the children, twelve of them boys, and when a new one was born Ike Lawler did not waste time on sentimentality but made his wife get out of bed and get back to work at once.

He was, in a small way, successful. Although he owned little land, he was always arranging with others for the working of land on shares and often the fields, so worked, would be a long way from his house and Kit said . . . she must afterwards have spoken to some man, perhaps one of

Tom's later rumrunners, from that neighborhood . . . that
he would be seen by neighbors herding his family along a
road to their work. He himself would be astride a horse, a
long horsewhip in his hand, a whip he was passionately
fond of using on his wife or one of his children, the procession going along a road or across fields. He was also, in a
small way, a thief and was in the habit of going at night
with two or three of the sons to rob his neighbors' hen
roosts. He did not work, when so occupied, in his own immediate neighborhood, but started in the late afternoon and went
many miles, often into some mountain town. He himself
did not approach the hen roosts. He stayed hidden in some
near-by wood and sent the sons. If they were caught and
arrested it would be they who would have to serve the jail
sentences. In the mountains there was a story that, once,
when he had no horse or when the horse he then owned had
been beaten until it could not work, he hitched his wife and
two of his sons to a plow, himself for once taking the plow
handles, and that he thus plowed a field.

So there was this man and his family and it was a summer
day and the family were at work in a field. The field was far
from the Lawler home and was at the very top of a high
hill. It was flat up there and the field was new land. There
had been a stand of timber but it had been killed by the
process known as "ringing." In the upper field, where
the Lawler family were at work, there was a whole forest of
such trees. Dead trees standing up thus put out no leaves.
They turn gray. After a time they tremble in every wind.
There are no masses of leaves to keep the warm sun from
the good earth. The trees are but the ghosts of trees.

To break up such new ground, under the trees, between
the standing trees, is heavy and laborious work. The plow

point catches upon tree roots, there is a tangle of the roots
of smaller trees and bushes. The work in the field had been
done and the field planted to corn. The young corn was
ready to be hoed but Ike Lawler did not stay in the field.
He had his wife up there, one of the girl children and the
young Joseph. Joseph was then a boy of twelve and was
thin and sickly. He spent his days being frightened and his
nights having strange dreams. It was because of religion.
Going to meeting was almost the only diversion for the
mountain people and there had been a series of meetings in
a little church in the neighborhood.

Ike Lawler did not stay that day in the upper field. He
had others of his children at work in other fields. "I want
this field all worked out by tonight," he said. The fat old
mother was again pregnant. She grunted as she worked.
At noon there was, for each of the workers, a slab of cold
corn bread.

It was a hot day and as the afternoon began to grow long
there was, on the part of all three of the workers, a growing fear that the field would not be finished. They did not
speak of it. They worked more and more hurriedly and
feverishly. The thin-legged sickly boy Joseph may have gone
a little off his head. He began talking aloud to himself,
"Am I one of God's children or am I not?" he asked. "Will
God some day speak to me? If I die suddenly will I go to
Heaven or will I go to hell? Will God speak to me as he
did to Paul on the road to Damascus?"

It may be that he had begun to have ambitious dreams.
In the mountain churches men spoke of the call, direct from
God, to God's ministry.

There was a storm, coming quickly as storms do in
high mountain places. There were black clouds creeping up

over distant mountain ridges, plainly seen from the upper field. The black masses of clouds became spread out. They covered the sky.

It remained very still, very hot in the field. There was rapid movement in the masses of black clouds overhead while down below all was still. It would have been well for the mother and children if they had run into a near-by wood, where the trees were still strong and alive or down the mountain toward their home. They didn't dare. The old mother, heavy with child, went along the rows, working desperately, groaning, under the tall ghosts of trees, the children following, Joseph muttering. The girl child had begun to cry.

There was another quick change. It had been still and hot in the field but suddenly a cold wind began to blow and every moment it increased in violence. It made a low whining noise rushing through the branches of the bare dead trees and at once smaller branches began to break and fall. They were carried along by the racing wind.

The whole scene was like a stage set. The three people had been working with frightened abandon but they suddenly stopped and stood. Branches from the dead trees began flying past them and with every minute the violence of the wind increased. Now the black mass of clouds overhead was torn into ribbons.

As the three stood, carried suddenly thus out of one fear . . . the fear of not getting the work done . . . into this new fear, fear of the husband and father on the one side and God fear on the other . . . the father Ike Lawler appeared.

He had been at the house of a neighbor, one of his own stripe, and had been drinking there. He had traded horses and was astride a great awkward work horse he had got,

a horse very huge and very bony. He was beating the horse
with his whip as he rode down toward his family.

Being rather drunk, he was without fear of the storm. So
he had told the wife, son, and daughter to finish the field
and now night was coming and it was not finished. He had
mistaken the blackness that had settled down over the field
for night. "Why, what are you doing here? Why are you
standing and loafing? To work, I tell you, to work," he yelled,
riding down upon them. If he was not frightened the horse
was. It was a huge, awkward, bony old work-horse but had
become mad and unmanageable with fright. It reared, stood
on its hind legs, grotesquely.

The masses of black and gray clouds fell down over the
scene. They became a dirty flying gray mist that hid the
horse and rider from the three workers and then the rain
came with an even louder roar of wind.

It was a bedlam and Joseph Lawler always remembered
the scene afterwards. When he became a mountain preacher
and told of it the scene grew more and more wonderful.
He said that there was the man, representing evil, roaring
in the storm and that there was a moment when the wind
blew a little clear place in the blackness and that, standing
and trembling, he heard the voice and saw the face of God.
He declared that God spoke clearly to him but what it was
that God said to him he would not tell. He grew mysterious.
"It is not to be told. The words of God are not to be told
to mortal ears," he said. The horse, with its rider, the horse
maddened by fright and by the lash of Ike Lawler's whip,
rode down upon the others and the girl child, Joseph Lawler's sister, was knocked down and hurt. Later she died of
the hurt.

The great wind was blowing down the dead trees. They

began falling. The trees were like rows of dominoes set up on the floor by a child at play. One domino, at the end, is touched by the child's finger and down they all come. The falling limb of a great tree struck Ike Lawler and knocked him from his horse. He was badly hurt and later, after the mother, who by some miracle escaped, had got down out of the field and had brought neighbor men, he was carried to his house.

And where was the boy Joseph? How significant! Several men of the neighborhood brought up there by the mother found him, and even Ike Lawler was impressed by their story. Two great trees had fallen making a gigantic cross and there was the boy apparently stunned . . . it may have been no more than fright . . . he was uninjured . . . he may have climbed to the position in which he was found. He lay very still and white. As he lay thus he was exactly the figure of the Christ on the cross. He was unconscious but when a man picked him from the cross he spoke. "I saw God," he said, quietly enough. "God took care of me. He spoke to me in the storm."

It was enough. To the mountain people, even to his father, Joseph Lawler became something special. More and more, as he grew into young manhood, he lived a life apart from others and devoted himself to God. He became a boy preacher, speaking and exhorting in the streets of mountain towns and in cabins. He came along a mountain road and stopped before a cabin. "Come out. Come out," he called, "God is calling to you," and when the people had come out of the house he knelt in the road and prayed loudly for the people of the house.

He began to get a small following, among others the mountain girl Kate, who became his wife. She was the woman Tom Halsey had perhaps seen, after she had lost her child, sitting by the door of her house and looking out over the hills. She had followed her preacher husband in his wanderings over the hills . . . at first he called himself a Baptist but later he adopted the Holiness faith . . . and there were several others, among them two old men and a half insane old woman. The little cavalcade took pilgrimages, sometimes lasting for several days or weeks, through the hills. At night they would stop before some isolated cabin. Joseph Lawler had become more and more sure of himself, more and more imperious. He demanded food for himself and his followers and a place for them to sleep. "It is God's wish," he said. He had grown constantly more and more adept as an interpreter of God's wishes.

Kate was his wife — or mistress. The young preacher had not been legally married to his woman. "God has married us," he said to her and to the others among his followers.

That was also a story. Tom once told Kit Brandon about it. "I had a feeling," he said. He meant to imply that what he did was not very definitely thought out.

He was at home on the little farm he had got . . . this some days after his wife's death. He did not remember how much time had passed. His mother had come to his new home to take care of the babe. He was in trouble. As has been suggested, several patent foods, recommended by a country doctor and got from a drug store in a distant town, had proved ineffectual and his child was starving.

He was at work one day in his field but suddenly stopped work. He stood gazing at the sky. "There is no use crying out to God." He told Kit later that he did not remember much of what happened to him that day. It was late after-

noon and he had been hoeing corn. "God takes care of the
man who takes care of himself."

"God is on the side of the big battalions." Anyway Tom
Halsey was not literary. "If I stand here like this my babe,
my son, will also die." He threw his hoe into a fence corner
and started toward his house. He got down to his barn and
saddled a horse. "There is needed a woman who can nurse
my son." He may have heard that the woman Kate had lost
her babe. He mounted the horse and called to his mother.
"Mother, you bring me the babe."

His mother protested. "What are you going to do, Tom?
The baby is too sick to be moved."

She had come to the door of the house with the sickly,
starved child in her arms. He did not answer but, getting off
the horse, went to her and took the child from her arms.
The mother stood in the little yard before Tom's mountain
cabin protesting violently, but without another word to her
and with the child in his arms he mounted his horse and
rode away.

The young preacher, of the Holiness faith, whose following had grown, had got himself a tent in which he held
meetings, moving from place to place through the mountains. He was holding meetings in a field, near his own
home, at the time when Tom Halsey set out with his babe
in his arms. Tom was not very clear as to what had happened to him during the late afternoon and early evening
of that day. He may just have ridden rather blindly about.

And in the little tent the preacher had got, there was a
meeting being held. The preacher's wife, the woman Kate,
was there. She was a little ill. Her breasts were hurting. The
tent, a ragged dirty one, without walls, was a mere shelter.

It had been pitched close beside a road and was filled with mountain people. They sat, with heavy serious faces. The preacher had for a light a sputtering kerosene torch, hung from the ceiling of the tent, and the light from it played over the faces.

It played over the face of the young preacher. He was exhorting. He half wept. He shouted. Little flecks of spittle formed in the corners of his mouth. There were groans from the audience. A wailing woman's voice arose. "Oh, God, God, look down on me . . . speak to me as you once spoke to him," she cried. The preacher had again told the story of the storm and of his own direct and personal contact with God. He told it at every meeting, the story always growing and growing. The meeting that night had not really got well going. Presently it would be better. God's spirit would manifest itself. There would be screams, women rolling on the ground, cries from the throats of men.

The meeting was however spoiled. Tom Halsey, the sick child in his arms, rode along the road beside which the tent was pitched. He stopped his horse and getting down came into the tent with the child in his arms. He also may have been temporarily a little off his head. He had been passionately devoted to his wife. He stood in the tent, under the sputtering light, looking about, and then went to where the preacher's wife sat, rather apart from all the others. She was on the very front one of the rude benches. The benches were but rough boards laid on logs.

Tom went to the woman and sat beside her and immediately the thing happened. He began to look steadily at Kate and she at him. It was as though they spoke. It may be she did not look at Tom but at the babe. "My own babe has been torn from my arms by death. Come to my arms, come to my breast, thou hungry one." She became fascinated, staring, and the preacher, looking down at her and at Tom Halsey, was profoundly disturbed.

Well, and what of him?

It may be that thoughts rushed through the woman's mind. He had said that God had taken their child and had seemed almost cheerful about it. It was another thing to speak about in his sermons. "God wants me to go on doing His glorious work. He has taken my child, a little saint now in Heaven, to have there, as a shining thing, a shining light to me."

And so . . . bitter thoughts perhaps in the mind of the woman, the mother, sitting and hearing his words, a bitter hurting in her breast. As she stared at Tom and at the sick babe he held in his arms, tears came to her eyes.

And then Tom Halsey did something. He arose. He stood before the woman. The preacher, on his little raised plat-form, stopped speaking and a hush fell over the audience. The woman was clad in a simple cotton gown that buttoned down the front and Tom reached down and began to un-button it. She did not move but when he put the child to her breast, an ecstatic look came into her eyes.

There was a commotion. The preacher's words died on his lips and he sprang down from his raised place and stood before Tom and the woman. "Well," he said. He had gone white. His mouth opened and closed. As for Tom and the woman . . . it was as though they had both suddenly become aware that what had happened . . . such a personal, such a private matter . . . had happened in a public place. The woman arose, the child still at the breast and stood beside Tom. She was staring now, in a half-dazed way, about the room and at her husband. With the man, her husband, that

God man, she had once followed blindly, with blind faith, like the others in the tent . . . all now staring at her with fixed stares of astonishment . . . she had nothing to do. With Tom Halsey she could live again. He was connected with the child in her arms, at her breasts. The young preacher continued to stand, his mouth opening and closing. "Kate," he said, but she did not answer, did not look at him. She was looking at Tom, as though expectant. "What now?" She did not speak. She stood waiting.

She did not have to wait long. "Come on," Tom said, and led the way out of the tent, the preacher following. Men and women of the audience arose from their seats and followed. Tom led the way to where the horse was tethered and helping her on again put the babe into her arms. He sprang into the saddle before her. "Put your arm about me," he said, "you won't fall." The preacher had fallen to his knees in the dust of the road and was crying out to his God. "Don't let her go away with him. God, don't let her go," he cried.

The astonished people stood in silence as Tom and the woman Kate rode away into the darkness.

CHAPTER NINE

THERE was another adventure coming Kit Brandon's way before the big adventure of marriage. She had begun her flight . . . young, pretty, good-looking American woman on the move. She hadn't as yet gone very far, in a certain direction. There had been an alive pert little one, named Sarah, she had known in the cotton mill.

"Life's a game."

"Play to win."

"Learn to use what you've got."

"If you don't put it over on them they'll put it over on you."

She had got the American restlessness all right. Young American working man, factory hand. . . . "Say Bill, I'm going to pull my freight out of here. I'm going to Baltimore . . . to Frisco . . . to Cleveland . . . to Kansas City . . . I hear it's swell out there."

Labor turnover in more than one American factory as high as fifty, sixty, seventy-five per cent in a year. The word is that they have the same problem over in Russia.

As for the matter of a "certain direction," that's putting it delicately enough, eh? . . . Kit didn't count a certain threatened happening with her own father . . . by a certain mountain stream . . . after bathing . . . being bathed by the hands of another . . . in soft evening light when she was a child. It might have happened then, but it didn't.

She got out of the cotton-mill town suddenly one hot summer day, took a train to another industrial town of the upper South, got a job in a shoe factory there. They always manage to make a place for the young pretty fairly well-dressed ones, if they look strong enough to stand up to it. Kit had got the faculty, the trick — it is born in some women — of wearing clothes. There are some of them, as the saying goes, who can take almost any kind of rag, put it on, make it look like Park Avenue. She had it. It was partly study and observation. She had even changed her way of walking, of carrying her body, holding her head, getting a certain dignity and grace. As they say of colts at the race tracks, she was about ready to go to the races.

As for the shoe-factory town . . . she always thought of it afterwards only in this way as . . . "that place where the shoe factory is." It was a big town, set on the side of a hill. There were big hills, really mountains, climbing up back of the town and you were always going up and down hills. You stood in one of the streets and looked down on the roofs of the houses in the next street below. Far down below there was a river, very charming sometimes to see from above . . . the factory was down near the river and near railroad tracks . . . the river gleaming gold sometimes when the sun was setting, red sometimes, sometimes a dirty yellow, sometimes when the sky was overcast, steel gray. Kit didn't notice it much. She had a room with an Italian woman in a street also down near the river. The woman had left her husband and had a son, a clerk in a grocery store, who lived with his mother and he at once began trying to "make" Kit. He didn't get far although the mother was always singing his praises. "I tell you he's a good boy." He was a man of twenty-seven and unmarried. "When he was in school he was always the smartest one in his class." The father who had kept a fruit store had got into trouble with a married woman and, in danger of being shot, had fled and she had got a divorce. The woman wanted her son to marry and have children. "I like children about.

"I tell you he's a good boy. At the store they're simply crazy about him. So many people come in the store . . . they won't have no one but my boy wait on them." At night, when she was in bed, Kit heard the mother and son talking together in Italian. What an odd thing, the people, so near, talking in words she couldn't understand. It was new knowledge to her, that there were people, in strange places, strange countries over the world, talking in words you couldn't understand.

So much new knowledge to get. The son had sleek shiny black hair and black eyes. His skin was very dark. Soon he would be fat, a fat Italian man. It was easy enough to hold him at a distance, even to confuse him.

You had to learn the trick. Hold yourself back, learn to keep a kind of reserve. It was for Kit a time of slow awakening . . . "soon I'll be a woman." . . .

"A good many women are married even at the age I have now come to." Kit's point of view on men . . . it is certainly an important matter to any young woman of seventeen or eighteen . . . was, in an odd way, outside self, important and not important. Talk of it always, persistently, among the young women at the factory . . . in that place she made no close friends with any of the other girls, her

mood for the time to be alone . . . she went now and then
to the movies and there always the man and woman thing
. . . long lingering kisses. "Your arms about me, darling.
Oh, darling, how I have longed for you." In that place she
began something. Unlike a good many poor white mountain girls, brought up in such families as her own, she knew
how to read and write. "I had better find out more about
that." She heard from a girl in her room at the factory, a
thin big-nosed girl who wore glasses, about a thing called
the public library and went there one Saturday afternoon.

But how were you to know what books you wanted?
There were so many. There were open shelves and she
watched others, went as they did, in among books.

A woman spoke to her, an older woman with white hair
and a curiously gentle face. Kit thought at first she had
something to do with the place but was mistaken. She was
just an older woman sensing Kit's confusion. "May I help
you?"

"Yes." Confusion in Kit too, then a sudden impulse to be
downright with that one. It was the woman to woman thing
again, the instinct in other women to like Kit, in an odd way
to respect her. "I'll tell you. I'm a factory girl. I've never
been in a place like this before. I know nothing of books."
The woman smiled, but nicely, Kit thought. "Odd, my fight
in life is going to be with men, not with other women."
That thought not definite in Kit and yet the understanding of it in her almost from the beginning. "Do you want
a love story?"

"No." The woman smiled.

"Oh, so not that?" she said. "Well, let's look about. Will
it be something about people, or perhaps history?"

She was going along the rows of books and suddenly

stopped. Kit followed. Could it be that any one was familiar
with so many books?

History?

Kit had but a vague idea of what the word meant. How
many words also to know about. Words also opened out
new vistas in life. There was a sudden longing that morning
to be more like the woman who was being kind to her. She
had a quality, firm but gentle. "She's never worked in any
factory," Kit thought. The woman revolutionist, Agnes,
who had been Kit's friend and who was always talking
about the rich and the poor. . . . "The rich are pretty much
all skunks. . . . They have to be wiped out, done away with."
Such notions had never made a deep impression on Kit.
There might even be a certain advantage to the unbalance.
There could be such a thing as intelligent luxury, soft fine
fabrics out of which to make clothes, life on a certain high
plane of mind and body.

All of this to be sure, dim, oh, very dim, in Kit. The
woman took a book from the shelf. "It's a book by Theodore Dreiser. He may be our great novelist." The title of
the book was *Sister Carrie*.

The woman helped Kit about the making out of her application for taking the book out. The application had to
be signed by a property holder of the town and she signed
it. Her name was Holbrook. She did not work in the library.
There was a pile of books on a counter and the woman
went to an outer door and called a Negro who came and
got them. She was some swell.

"Are you going anywhere I could take you?" she asked
Kit.

"No. I am just going home."

"Well, come on. Let me take you. I'll enjoy doing it."

It was an old story, the rich woman, some woman the wife of the man who owned such a factory as the one Kit worked in. Kit's chance acquaintance was not like that but her associates were mostly like that. Such women can't avoid seeing young working women, many of them comely, even beautiful women. Such a woman may be childless. Mrs. Holbrook had a woman acquaintance who had no children and who kept fourteen Angora cats. She fed them on *pâté de foi gras*.

Talk among such women, at card parties . . . chatter, chatter, chatter, at garden parties, at teas . . . the servant class, the working class . . . the rich constantly doing more than the workers to build up the idea of the much-talked-of thing, class consciousness.

So comfortable to feel yourself a little removed . . . whence cometh all this D. A. R. talk, First Families of Virginia, Best Blood of the South? . . . above, high up, a superior class.

But alas and alas, for even the most wealthy, in secret moments, a kind of niceness, reality of outlook, persisting in spite of ugliness, alas even envy.

Things to give you a jolt. "Why is it that artists . . . we who after all have money to buy the books, the paintings . . . why do painters, the most real and talented ones . . . why do they, when they paint women, always seem to prefer to paint working women? Poets singing of them. There is a writer whose book I have been reading. He writes of the beauty of the hands of a washwoman.

"Why have I, alas, these fat pudgy hands and these thick ankles? It is strange that even royalty, kings and their wives and daughters, the members of nobility . . . they are so often such commonplace even ugly-looking people. Oh dear, oh dear.

"And sometimes these working girls . . . poor things . . . often so lovely. Why I never did any work with my hands in all my life. It is so confusing."

They went out and got into a big luxurious car and drove to where Kit lived in a little street of frame houses down by the shoe factory, the river and the railroad tracks.

The woman kept talking, evidently trying to put Kit at her ease. She needn't have bothered. Kit felt quite all right. The momentary confusion that had come when the woman first spoke to her was quite gone.

"My name is Mrs. Holbrook."

"Mine is Kit Brandon."

"What a pretty name!"

And, sitting thus, in the luxurious car, with the rich woman, Kit's mind drifted away from car and woman and to another woman, one she had known just before she left the cotton-mill town. That one was a gold-digger. She, Sarah, had got her hooks into a lawyer. Some man had already taught Sarah to drive a car and she had got the use of the lawyer's car and had taught Kit how to drive. It was, as Sarah said, "a pretty swell little runabout."

Sarah spoke of her man by his first name. "I'm going to get Joe to buy me one."

Sarah had even suggested with a laugh that it would be something pretty hot if she got Joe to get the money from his rich horsey wife to buy a car for herself and told Kit that she and Joe were planning a campaign to get the money. He was to say that he had lost it playing the races.

"That would be pretty hot, eh, she so crazy about horses."

Joe had given Sarah a key and would leave his car on some side street. Occasionally, when he had to leave town she had the car over the week end. She had taught Kit to drive and Kit had caught on quickly, instinctively.

"Say, kid, you are going to make one swell driver. You take to it like a fish takes to water."

Kit in the big car with the woman she had met in the library, the woman talking, trying to put Kit at her ease. She spoke of books, several of them piled on the car floor at their feet. They had, she said, something to do with a paper she was preparing for a woman's club . . . the woman was half laughing at herself . . . it was all so silly, a person like herself pretending to be a scholar. She was to prepare a paper on the Civilization of the Ancient Greeks. Kit was not listening.

The Greeks were, she gathered, a people, perhaps like the Italian woman and her son, people who could say words, speak in a way you couldn't understand. She was really thinking about the car. If she had been born a man, she would have tried getting a job driving for some such rich woman.

"Lord, how I'd like getting my hand on that wheel." Later, not much later, when Gordon Halsey, not being able to get her in any other way, proposed marriage, the thing that really induced her to make up her mind to do it, give it a trial, was that he had such a swell fast car. Odd that now the rich woman, and not Kit, was self-conscious. Kit was even a little aware of that fact.

It might well have been her mountain ancestry. The mountain people can do it. There is a quality in them, it was in her father, even in that slovenly woman her mother. "Here I am. I am what I am. It would be well for you not

to feel superior to me." It is a quality sometimes very confusing to outsiders, people not of the hills, particularly to
those coming from the outside, wanting to help the poor.
A mountain man or woman can look at you with an odd
impersonal stare. They can look out of their eyes as gypsies
look.

The woman who insisted upon taking Kit quite to her
rooming place kept talking. "I can't help thinking, often,
what an injustice.

"This place down here. How stupid that we have let the
railroads and the factories take our river front." She laughed,
self-consciously. "Not that I should say anything. It was my
father who first grabbed the river front here." She pointed.
"I dare say you work in the shoe factory. It was my father
who established the shoe factory here.

"And I must say I'd hate to give up anything I've got
because of his cleverness and greediness."

She let Kit out at her place. The Italian woman who was
scrubbing the little wooden porch before the house was
terribly impressed. She had a mop and a scrub bucket and,
after quickly putting them inside the door, stood, lost in
wonder, staring.

"I see you are not among the Greeks. You are among the
Romans," the woman said as Kit alighted, holding her book.
The rich woman had got back her self-possession.

"It is so hard to talk with working girls. I don't mean
they are not nice, as good as we are, perhaps better, but
one does not know what to say to them."

"Yes, that's so," Kit said, answering the woman's sally.
What did the woman mean by Romans? She was still thinking of the car. "God, but I would like to get my hands on
it." She had already picked up from Sarah some of the patter

of car drivers, giving cars the feminine gender. "I'll bet she could step. I'd love to get in her and give her the works." In her absorption she even forgot to thank the rich woman for her kindness.

She read the Dreiser book later in her bed at night. In that place she had a daytime job. Reading was at first slow and rather painful work. Even in so simple a story, simply told, there were so many words she didn't know.

And then too it was about a woman, of a sort she already had learned to know. It might have been Sarah's story. Sarah might also come to something like the woman of the book. She wished the story had concerned itself more with the lives of the rich.

She was sitting in the railroad station in the town of the shoe factory and by chance had the Dreiser book in her hand. There was a bag sitting at her feet. It was a Sunday afternoon and she had grown tired of sitting in her room. Downstairs, in the house of the Italians, the son was at home. It was no good going downstairs in that house. There was that embarrassment, the young man ogling her in that way he had. He wouldn't dare say anything but he would keep looking with his queer greedy greasy eyes while the mother talked. It was a bright warm day and Kit had come to a sudden decision. She had been lying in bed reading her book and suddenly got up and dressed. She packed a bag she had recently bought. "I'm going to get out of this.

"And why not get out of this town?" She had no friends in that place. It would be something, an adventure, a new beginning. She suddenly remembered having heard one of the girls at the factory speak of another North Carolina town a hundred miles away. "It's a fine place. There's plenty of work there."

When she had said good-bye to the Italian woman, who protested and even threatened to weep . . . the son wanted to carry her bag . . . dark sad Italian eyes — a hurt look . . . "Damn, I have missed my chance" . . . she turned him away with an abrupt no . . . he didn't know how to get past it.

She went into the railroad station, into the waiting room, to sit, the station was beyond the factory, on the bank of the river.

On Sunday there were no afternoon trains and the big waiting room was deserted. Any way, she might as well sit there.

It was for Kit a beginning, a start. She had got, in the railroad station, the young man who took her in his car to the town she had made up her mind to tackle next. Anyway it was saving railroad fare.

And she was curious. He seemed all right, was perhaps three or four years older than herself. He drove a good car although it probably didn't belong to him. She had been sitting in the quite empty waiting room of the station when he came in, a young man, such as you might see at a golf club or on a tennis court, dressed in light summer clothes. He had come in and tapped on the window of the ticket office. There was a clouded glass. There was no one there and he had turned to go out when he saw her. She had the Dreiser book in her hand.

She wasn't reading, although at once, when he approached her, asking her a question, she saw that he glanced to see what she was reading. Afterward, when they were in the car, he spoke of it.

"You aren't a highbrow, are you?"

"I don't know," she said.

"That book," he said. He said that when he was in college

he had heard some of the fellows speak of it. "I don't hold it against a fellow or a girl that he reads such books, these serious books, but I don't go in for them myself."

He had even tried to use the book, something he had heard of it . . . he said he had a sister who was rather a highbrow . . . he had heard it was about a woman who was rather free with men, not being married to them. "Is that so?"

"It may be so."

His young eyes looking at her. "How do you feel about such things?" She didn't try to answer that one. She let it go with a smile.

She had really been sitting in the station, not reading, looking out a window . . . there was a printed time-table on the wall and she had figured out that there would be a train in the late afternoon, at five.

There was the figure of little blond Sarah of the cotton mill in her mind. "On such a day as this she would be step-ping high."

Sarah would have gone to live with that man, the lawyer. It was bound to happen, inevitable. Outside the station window there were just the tracks between the station and the shore of the river. It was nice, far over there, low wooded hills and a clear blue sky. There were a few white houses among the trees, houses just seen, half hidden by trees . . . perhaps also in Kit thoughts of that Mrs. Hol-brook. Some women get so much. Mrs. Holbrook no doubt born to it. Sarah after it.

"Life's a game."

"If you don't put it over on them, they'll put it over on you."

There were a few boats on the river, young men with their

girls out for a ride. It may be that at the moment the thing predominant in Kit's mind was just the vague thought of distance. Always the thought of something nice out there, beyond the horizon.

Mrs. Holbrook beyond the horizon. Was Sarah also? To be a Sarah was also not so easy. Perhaps you needed to have something. Sarah, no doubt, had the feel for it, the not too much minding some one, some other person, close, touching you, taking. "I wonder if I could? I'm sure I want some of the things Sarah is going to get by it even more than she does." There was, however, something in Sarah's voice, in her manner, when she spoke of it, "pleasure," that must have been it, "in being in the arms of that man." Sarah had spoken with such enthusiasm of the hotel room, the luxury of the bed, the curtains at the window. "Gee, Kit, if we could have dresses made of stuff like that."

"I would have liked that but to have to pay for it that way."

"Are you by any chance Miss Overton?" That was the young man in the railroad station, who had got a sudden hunch. "Gee, I've got Dad's car. Now if I had a swell little piece, that would maybe come across.

"I don't like to be always buying it. It takes something that should be nice out of it." He really meant the satisfaction of winning it. "I got it from her with my personality" . . . a personal triumph. That about Miss Overton was of course a stall, a bluff, a way to cut in. He told her that afterwards when they were in the car. "You know, as soon as I saw you sitting in there, I thought . . . 'gosh,' I thought, 'I'd like to take her with me some place in my car.'"

Kit had made it not too difficult although she had thought at once, having decided she would take him on, that it

would be no Sarah and her Joe affair. "It may be only because he is too young, too much of a kid." He has asked,
with a rather nice boyish frankness, "Where are you going?
You are waiting for a train, aren't you?"

"Yes."

Then his proposal. She had told him where she had
planned to go.

"Have you bought your ticket?" She hadn't. "Then come
on, let me take you."

He hadn't been able to place her, get her number, that
was evident. Could she be just a little girl, ready and willing enough to be picked up by a man, any man who happened along. The town was full of young factory girls and
at least some of them were like that. There wasn't any
regular house of prostitution, and young fellows of the
town, sons of important citizens . . . they had to do what
they could.

It was an absorbingly interesting experiment for Kit, her
first of the kind, trying to figure him out, be nice enough
to him to get the ride to that town in his car . . . she might
even work him to let her drive.

"Life's a game."

"Work them to get what you want."

He was thinking . . . "I don't know about her." She
might be like his sister. There was that book in her hand.
"I've got a car outside here." He had really seen her through
the window of the room, had looked in from the outside
and seen her sitting there. "Gosh, there's something nice all
right." He even told her all of this when he had got her
into the car. "I was just driving past the station and thought
I would run in to set my watch by the station clock. All
of that, my coming in and tapping on the window, that

about a Miss Overton . . . it was all a bluff." "Well, you
smarty," Kit said trying to be girlish, even a bit kittenish.
He was a queer combination of caution and frankness.

For example, lying to her about his name. She didn't
quite know how she knew that but she did and she also
lied. He might be thinking that he would get her and that
later it might lead to some kind of trouble.

They had got outside the town of shoes and were on a big
highway, in an open car, very nice, very light and swift.
Almost at once she had got him to let her drive. They were
on the great North Carolina highway that runs down south-
westerly from Charlotte to Greenville in South Carolina
and beyond. Oh, North Carolina, the proud state, the bold
state!

No longer the old North Carolina. "Old North State"
of the Southern Confederacy, later poor state. "Valley of
Humiliation between the two Mountains of Conceit" . . .
South Carolina and Virginia . . . better forget all that.
That's all in the past.

The big highway Kit was on with her catch, her hands
presently at the wheel of the car, was something to excite.
You could ride all day on that highway, coming to town
after town, many of the towns but a few miles apart, big
towns and little towns, factory chimneys, mill chimneys
never out of sight. Much of the big highway was cement
hard and smooth, on such a summer Sunday the road full
of cars . . . where else in all the world but in America could
you see such a sight, cars by the hundreds, by the thousands, many of the cars very beautiful, the swift ride, the soft
hurling through space, when you have got it into you, have
the feel of it, in your own body, in your hands.

The purring thing down in front, under the hood of the

car . . . oh, American workmen, American inventors, you have done something here, oh mechanical age, this is your finest accomplishment.

This power, this swiftness sometimes in the hands of young girls, like Kit, in the hands of fat women of forty. Look a little out for them if they have not begun to drive when they are young . . . old men, come down out of horse-and-buggy days, old gray-haired women.

The long gleaming, moving, sometimes swift moving procession, Kit in it, a part of it. "Say, you are pretty handy with a car, aren't you?" her catch said once. She had just shaved a car that had come into the highway out of a side road, that had come without warning. She had whizzed past, throwing the juice to her at just the right moment, her catch sitting tense, his eyes closed. There was a heavy-handed farmer driving. "Gosh, I thought he had you. That guy ought to stay at the plow." Her catch was still puzzled. "Say, tell me, you ain't a highbrow, are you?" She didn't answer but smiled. He was thinking of the book she was holding when he found her. She would have to mail it back to that library place. His sister had been caught reading it by his father. His sister was a highbrow all right. He had heard there was some hot stuff in it.

When he was in college . . . he had been out a year . . . there were some of the fellows . . . they went in for such highbrow stuff. "I like this western stuff myself," he said. When he read a book he wanted action, something doing all the time. He had got it into his head that she was a school teacher. "Are you?" "I might be," she said. Well, it was possible, a school teacher also might be had. He decided to wait until night. "You wouldn't mind having dinner with me, would you, we'd go to the hotel?" She

wondered if that was the way Sarah's lawyer began with
Sarah. She said she would go. "Then we can take a ride in
the evening," he said, thinking that in the darkness with
her he could perhaps get his nerve up, perhaps kiss her, get
his arms about her. "You've got to work them up, get them
going a little." How transparent he was. They went to the
hotel and Kit had her bag checked. He suggested that. "Do
any of your people live in this town?" he asked her, but she
was noncommittal. "It might be," she said. She let him
buy her dinner in the dining-room of a big hotel, many
well-dressed people also dining. Kit being as cagy as she
could, watching others not to give herself away, letting him
talk . . . men and especially young men and young old
men love to talk of themselves . . .

What he was going to do in life. His father had a factory,
he was going in and try to work to be a sales manager. He
had forgotten that he had already told her his father was
a doctor. "Then I'm going to get me a swell little wife."
He described the woman he thought would make him
happy as his wife, making her as much like Kit as possible.
"Anyway I'm not going to marry for money." It might be
that he had noticed that her bag was a cheap one, her
clothes certainly not expensive. When she had dined she
excused herself for a moment, the suggestion being that she
had to go to the toilet, and going out of the dining-room, got
her bag and hurried out of the hotel. She would have to try
to find a cheap boarding house. She had a queer uncomfortable feeling. If she had been playing a game it was too
easy. She felt like a hunter of big game who had been out
shooting at rabbits.

CHAPTER TEN

TOM HALSEY, the man old enough to be Kit Brandon's father, was destined to be the big figure in her life. She did not know that. She was brought to Tom by his son, Gordon Halsey, who was the man child Tom had once brought to the mountain woman Kate, wife of the inspired mountain preacher, the man child Tom had laid to Kate's breasts.

Scattering and shattering thus a meeting of God's children, hushing the cries and groans of mountain men and women touched by the finger of God, creating thus a so-human situation that did in a way knock rather galleywest the power over people of the preacher. "By God, before I'd let any man get away with a thing like that with my woman."

"Say, if he's so big with God as he claims, why'd God let that happen to him?"

Tom getting more than that, an almost slavish follower in the woman Kate . . . male triumph over the female.

Kit's first meeting with Tom was at Kate's house. Kate had grown middle-aged and the babe she had nursed was now a man, at least in years. He was a young sport, a woman-getter he hoped, a rich man's son. He wanted to think he was truly all of these.

He had not been sent to Harvard, or Yale, or Princeton, had never been a football hero, although he might have been and done something of the sort except that Tom hadn't got his real start early enough. Young Gordon was physically big. He might have been splendid football material and, as for Kit when she met Gordon, she was certainly not the rather naïve mountain girl who had taken the first mill job. Mill girls also educate each other. They do it also in shoe factories, overall factories, five-and-ten-cent stores, in Macys and Wanamakers, why not?

A mountain girl, ex-mill girl, getting keen. Get always a little keener. Why should the daughters of mill owners, storekeepers, daughters of professional men, novel writers, etc., etc., have anything on you, cotton-mill girls, overall-factory girls, shoe-factory girls, big department-store girls . . . when it comes to handling men? You've got to learn it, haven't you, girls? They sure try to get away with it with you too, don't they?

Sharpen your wits. Life's a game. Women know. Working women, particularly the ones that have the looks, the ones that have what it takes, have opportunities. They should learn to know a lot.

At least girls, to be on to a guy like young Gordon Halsey . . . not so smart after all . . . son of a rich man, wanting to be both a very very respectable one and at the same time more or less the tough one . . . in with the best people but also thought to be, well, cheek-by-jowl with the so-mysterious underworld . . . men of crime, men of mystery, hard guys . . . like Cal. Coolidge going out West and putting on a cowboy uniform . . . young man half balanced so between two or more than two worlds . . . belonging really to no world . . . say like a lot of us modern novelists and story

tellers too . . . wanting to be both poet and rich man.
But let it pass.

Gordon Halsey, living as he did in one of the states of the
Upper South, would perhaps already have begun to think,
and when occasion arose speak of himself as of an old Southern family, best blood of the Old South. He would have got
that far out beyond his father. Poor lad. Look! He doesn't
get away with it. Society, American society in his time, having taken to arms oil thieves, timber robbers, water-power
highwaymen, had gagged at taking Al Capones, Legs Diamonds, Waxey Gordons. Not that Tom Halsey cared too
much. He did care. As Tom had grown richer he had also
changed but more of that later. The fact surely did hurt the
son.

He, the son, would have tried to put it over on Kit
Brandon. He had found her working in a five-and-ten-cent
store. For some reason, certainly not understandable to him,
she got him hard. "What, am I really going to fall for her,
just a little shop girl?" Look out, boy, it has happened before.

It wasn't because she was so warm, a hot baby. There is
another sort of challenge.

"Say, there's one not so easy to get, to knock off. If I
could get her I'd prove myself, even to myself, a real ladies'
man, eh?"

The cooler, more self-possessed ones also tempt.

Gordon having made a campaign for Kit, having chanced
into the store where she had got a job . . . she feeling her
way in a perplexing enough world, having already, since
leaving home, been cotton-mill worker, shoe-factory worker
and now five-and-ten-cent-store girl . . . Gordon having
chanced into the store one day, having got his first look at
her, the first once-over, in there . . .

Big, yellow, high-powered, sport-model car parked in the
street outside . . .

Other girls in the store checking on the car and on the
young man in rather flashy, broad-checked homespun
clothes — English tailored . . . like a big league baseball
player or say like Jack Reed, American-Russian Revolutionary hero, when Jack was a young man in America before the World War, big, loose, free-swinging shoulders
like that . . . the similarity would have stopped dead right
there . . . splendid young body, this one, without the Jack
Reed flair for glowing sincerity . . .

He walking down one of the aisles of the store . . .
Woolworth's . . .

Who do you think built the Woolworth Building, Woolworth Tower in New York? Say, the Empire State has put it
in the shade, eh? . . .

And now look, so soon Rockefeller Center hanging Empire State on the ropes. Those boys, Al Smith, Young Rockefeller, Woolworth, etc., do step fast, don't they?

Kit in the stationery department in the Woolworth
store. "Go to counter number eleven, please." Kit even
getting literary. There were a few books, reprints at bargain prices, detective stories for tired clerks who work for
tired business men, mystery stories, stories of quick passionate love.

Gordon Halsey strolling. As it turned out he forgot what
he came in the store to get. It may have been pants buttons.
The girls in the store were staring. They whispered, one to
another, confusing Gordon with stories that had already by
that time begun to be whispered about the father . . . his
secret power, his individual daring. "Look, Mabel, look.
That's him. That's Halsey, the big liquor man. Gee, I bet

he's rich. Look at them clothes. Look out there in the street
at that car he's driving.

"Oh, oh, oh, oh, oh, oh! Gosh, Mabel, ain't he handsome?"

Young Gordon Halsey . . . big bumblebee buzzing, about
to alight on some slender-stalked flower. Buzzz. Buzzz.
Buzzz. Look out, swaying, slender-stemmed blossoms in the
Woolworth garden. Kit was the prettiest. She had that *it,* or
seemed to Gordon to have it. He had forgotten what he
came in for. He bought a book . . . picture on the paper
jacket outside . . . young man, in appearance something,
vaguely, like himself . . . like figures in advertisements of
men's wear houses in the back pages of *The New Yorker,
Esquire,* etc. The man in a flashy car had stopped to pick up
a girl in the street. There was a swell-looking rich man's
house in the background, the girl, walking along, a little re-
motely like Kit. Title of the book: *Hitch-hiking to Dream-
land.* He held it up before her, smiling. "How much?" Was
the guy blind? There was a big placard saying how much.
He bought also some picture post-cards, taking his time to
select them. He got an eyeful.

He began his campaign. He came again and again and
again. Other girls in the store noticed. She had him going.
He'd got Kit's name from another girl and she came to Kit
with advice. "It's a chance, all right, but make him step,
kid."

"Kid, you got him hooked."

"Don't stand for no nonsense, kid."

"You're telling me."

He'd be trying of course to put it over on her, make her
come across, say just for a buggy ride in that big yellow
car. "You know how they are. They're all alike."

It went on for a month, two months, three months and he

had begun to get desperate. At last he came to a decision. "My God, I'm in love. I'm sunk." The trouble was that he couldn't marry, didn't dare marry again, without consulting his father. He had already tried marriage once, and the marriage had turned out a mess. He had got a gabber, one who talked too much . . .

It had cost money to get out of that and Tom Halsey had got him out. There had been, on the part of the lady, an attempt at blackmail. "I talk too much, do I? Well, you wait, if'n I don't get what I want I'm going to talk more. I'll talk a lot." Tom Halsey himself had to handle her. It wasn't that young Gordon was in on Tom's racket. He wasn't. Tom didn't want him in. The young man was, in a sense, Tom Halsey's Achilles' heel. He wanted the boy to be outside, go straight, get to be maybe even a gentleman. He wouldn't have put it that way. "You can have all the money you want, all you need, but when it comes to certain things, like let's say marriage now, I'm sorry, but, young man, you'll have to consult me."

It isn't such a nice position to be in, as a man, say in the eyes of your woman. A man wants to be his own man. Tom Halsey, although, since he had got into the liquor business in a big way and since prohibition, had been making a lot of money,—although he already had a lot, he wasn't a snob. He wouldn't be demanding for his son the daughter of some rich man, best blood of the Old South, etc., etc. Tom hadn't had his money quite long enough for that but there were ideas in his head. Kit found out what they were later.

He'd be wanting, demanding, for Gordon, not a dizzy blonde like that first one his son got when Tom kept his hands off, one who wasn't even faithful to him, although God knew she had enough money spent on her, on clothes, etc. . . . it had been because she was careless, had been hot-southing her man too openly that Tom had been able to get the goods on her and shut her up. He had got her to leave the state, go out to Reno, do the necessary out there, enough money to live pretty comfortably for several years . . . confessions to two or three specific cases of hot-southing her man signed, sealed, and stowed away by Tom.

He didn't want any more of that.

Gordon took Kit to his father. He wrote a letter and was called on the phone. "I feel so and so but will do just what you say, Dad." "All right, boy. Be at such and such a place at such and such a time. Have her with you." They went to Kate's place.

It was some two miles outside of a certain North Carolina industrial town and there was a very neat little white farm-house with green blinds beside an unpaved dirt road. It was a nice little place and, although after his first marriage Gordon seldom went there, he knew it well. He had spent his boyhood there, seeing his father from time to time, sometimes not seeing him for long periods. While Tom was building up his organization, before he got money enough to be safe from such nonsense he simply had to serve a few jail sentences himself. Once he had to put in six months on the road. He was in a chain gang although they didn't call it that. They called it a road gang.

The little white house was well kept. Kate was a neat housekeeper. There was a high hedge at the front, facing the road, and the lawn was always kept neatly mowed. It was a very innocent-looking place. There were several tall pine trees, close to the house and almost hiding it, and the road was one not much used.

There was in fact a kind of network of little roads. Be-

hind the house there was a huge apple orchard and several
barns, sheds, etc., and beyond . . . Kate owned a large farm
of more than 400 acres . . . Tom had bought it for her . . .
it stood in her name . . . she kept, for such legal purposes,
the name of that preacher to whom she had been married,
not by the law, but, as he said, by God . . . beyond all this
fields, never plowed, kept in grass. She rented some of the
fields to a neighbor who got them at a low price by keeping his mouth shut. He was a dairyman and pastured cows
in the fields. Beyond there were other fields, and others and
others. There were a few small patches of woodland.

There were farm roads everywhere. You could approach the
house from the north, south, east or west. The house had
become a kind of office for Tom although he was not often
there. It was his pay-off place.

Kate, now grown middle-aged, was tall and inclined to
gauntness. She was a striking-enough-looking figure. There
was a kind of stoicism, a firmness. She had become the sort
of woman men did not trifle with. Young Gordon had not
had a happy childhood. She was such a strange quiet one
and although she adored Tom's son, and had always hu-
mored him and even spoiled him, he was afraid of her and,
even after he grew up and went to town to live in a hotel
and be a man and a sport, he thought of her as rather a
woman of stone.

"I've often wondered," he said sometimes. He spoke of
her to some acquaintance he had made, never naming her.
She became in such talks a mysterious woman, connected
with his father, far off somewhere. He was a little more
frank with Kit . . . after he was quite sure he was in love,
telling her, as all men do tell the woman, his story of his

childhood. "Gee, I tell you I was a lonely kid, girl." The appeal to the mother in the woman.

In other conversations, with friends, he made or tried to make it all more mysterious. It might be a smartly dressed hotel clerk with whom he played pool or billiards, or the man at the wrestling arena. Gordon had money in that.

Or one of the two or three sporting sons of rich men with whom he sometimes went about. "So, as I was telling you, there was this woman. My own mother was dead. Dad got this woman to take care of me. D'you know, I've often wondered. We lived in this house and he came there sometimes. He'd spend the night there. I'd be sleeping upstairs and they'd be downstairs.

"I tell you she was like stone. D'you know I think, if my Dad had told her to go kill some one, she'd have gone and done it like a trained bird dog goes to get a quail you've shot.

"She raised me all right but I don't know her. God, I wonder sometimes if she and Dad. . . . After all, she's a woman and my Dad's a man. I'll say he is."

Gordon always talked a little too freely. After all, he'd gone to school in the town where he lived later. His first wife had been gabby. That was the reason he'd have to get his Dad's O. K. before he could go through with a marriage with Kit.

If he could only get Kit without marriage. He couldn't. God knew he'd tried hard enough. After all, she also had something of Kate's quality. You can't force things with that kind. "If I could get her I'd feel I'd done something. It's a man's job, okay." He was quite sure and not at all sure about Kit. Gordon was twenty-four and Kit Brandon was eighteen.

Was Gordon Halsey something Kit wanted? Could she get, through him, something she wanted? The reader should bear in mind that Kit Brandon was and is a real person, a living American woman. How much of her real story can be told? You, sitting and reading this book, have also a story, a history. How much of that could be told? How much do we writers dare let ourselves go in the making of portraits? How close can we keep to truth? How much do we dare try to be true historians?

The association of the historian, chances of association, somewhat limited.

And then, too, another danger, always the danger of the historian's imagination also thrusting in. Who has not asked himself the question . . . "Do I know my own wife, my brother, father, son, friend?" Moments of intense loneliness, known to all people.

Illuminating moments come. We see another, for perhaps only a flashing moment, see and understand all, a whole life in the moment.

There was no doubt that Kit, since we left her, working in the cotton mill, had changed. These factory girls, living with others in little mill-town houses, the houses often crowded, people living thus crowded together, married and single people who take rooms with the married, the quarrels, love-makings, heard through thin partitions of rooms, life boiling, simmering, becoming hot . . . "I love you" . . . becoming cold and dry . . . "I hate you" . . . "Why have you betrayed me into such a life as this?" . . . weariness of older workers, dry barrenness that comes with too much and too long weariness, carried into houses, into bedrooms . . .

Experiences in the mill, things seen, heard, felt. A feeling of restlessness had come over Kit and she had suddenly left the mill town and had gone to the other town of the Upper South where she got the place in a shoe factory.

Before she did that there were the talks with several girls. They may have felt in her the adventurer. There were walks with women other than Agnes. There was the flashy little blonde, Sarah, the gold-digger, with an upturned nose. She talked with Kit, the two walking home together from the mill on a spring morning.

They went along the same road in which she had walked with Agnes when the pavement was hidden under deep snow. The little pert one, Sarah, suddenly grew serious. These half-children sometimes learn things fast.

The sun had just come up over in the east, across fields, a little summer mist across its face, making it big, a glowing red. On a distant road a young farm man walked along a dirt road behind his team, going to some field for the spring plowing. All of life isn't in the mills, in the little crowded houses in company-owned mill towns. Oh, the hunger sometimes, in girls, in young men workers . . . feeling bound, imprisoned . . . for the big outside world, hungering for it as young girls and boys, in American country towns, particularly before the coming of the automobile, went instinctively in troops on summer evenings to railroad stations to see trains come and go. Sense of bigness, hugeness, in every thought of their country, America.

The horses were huge, heavy and all white. They looked like elephants, off there in that light. The young farm man went swinging along. He was singing, his voice just heard across the fields. He looked seven feet tall.

What unspoken thoughts in the two girls. After spring came the hot summer and the hot weary nights, so long,

so long, in the mill, the little houses in the daytime when
night mill hands tried to sleep, so hot, so hot. Kit had been
through one summer of it.

This other seemingly so nice, so inviting, the out-of-doors,
the wide world. The little pert one, Sarah . . . she was always starting something with some man, say with a room
foreman. It was whispered in the mill that the room foreman, in the room where she and Kit both worked, had already had her . . . she suddenly now, walking with Kit,
growing serious. "D'you know I like you." Kit not answering, she smiled. Kit had reserve, didn't throw herself about.

"I'll tell you what, let's not go home this morning."

"What d'you mean?"

The little blonde explained. She had some money. As it
developed . . . she afterwards told Kit . . . she had got it
from a man. She was made for that, born to it . . . to get it
from a man. She was liking Kit . . . women always did
instinctively like Kit . . . and was wanting to help her, put
out a hand to her.

A man had picked Sarah up in the street, on the Saturday
night before, had got her into his car. He was a rich
man's son and was married and she had got from him ten
dollars. It wasn't so much. She felt she had given the
money's worth. "I don't care if you know. You aren't the
kind that talks."

She wanted Kit to go into town with her, have breakfast
somewhere in town. "Come on. We'll go to the hotel, to the
Jefferson Davis." The Jefferson Davis was the swell hotel
of the town. "What, in these clothes?"

"Yes. We can go down into the ladies' room." After all the
girls and women in that mill were mostly well enough
dressed. The management insisted on that. Although it

was not openly said, you could be discharged for slovenli-
ness in dress. "We don't want our employees looking shabby.
It gives a wrong impression." The two girls were in the
spinning room and there was no occasion, except in the dead
hot nights of midsummer, to soil clothes. The dirtier work
in the mill was in the cotton cleansing room where the dirt
and filth were taken out of the baled cotton as it came from
fields and gins and only Negroes worked in there. It was
called "nigger's work," a place shut off from the other
rooms, the air filled always with clouds of lint and dust.
Kit's companion went along beside Kit, talking rapidly,
even a little hysterically. Kit had suddenly decided to go
with her. They turned about and went in the direction of
the town. "All right," Kit said, breaking into sudden laughter. She felt suddenly free and even gay, the weariness from
the long night of labor quite gone out of her body. How
pretty Sarah was! There was something she had, a great
mass of shining yellow hair, very silky, and big blue eyes.
She had, like Kit, an alive slender young body. There were
freckles on her cheeks and across her little nose. She was a
kind of Billy Burke of the mill, a Billy Burke at twenty, in
her first loveliness. Her face suddenly got a little drawn and
as the two walked, getting to the outer part of town, passing
houses of the town people, the houses for the most part
very quiet, the people still asleep . . . there was a Negro
man scrubbing the porch before one of the houses . . . "I
tell you what, Kit . . ."

Sarah started to say something and then stopped and
then again began talking rapidly. Although she was still
very young this wasn't the first mill at which Sarah had
worked, the first town in which she had lived.

She had wanted to travel, to see the world and she had

been daring. Kit felt that. "I'm not going to stay here long either," she was already telling herself. Sarah had come to the town and the mill some months before, hitch-hiking from another town.

She had seen things, done things. "I don't care if you know," she said. Already, although she was so young, she had been with a half dozen men. "You don't have to get that way, have a kid and all that. You have to know things." She was wanting to educate Kit, give her knowledge.

"After all, why is it, why is it?" The words were like a little cry out of Sarah. They were going along in quiet morning streets. "Say, kid, you think of it. Gee, God, it's tough, having to be a mill girl.

"You look at what happens to us." All a girl had to do was to look around, she explained. There were the working women, many of them married, the mothers of children. They had been honest girls, honest working girls, and had perhaps married . . . some honest-enough working man, some fellow in the mills. "Say, now, a loom-fixer," Sarah said. "Gee, God . . . she has a kid by him and then, as soon as she can stand on her feet, back she goes, into the mill." Sarah became profane. "You know what it does to a woman, having a kid like that and then going back to work too soon . . . on your feet all day or all night?

"It plays hell with your figure if nothing worse.

"There isn't any goddam grubby millhand going to get me and don't you let it happen to you either, Kit.

"I'm not going to have a lot of kids just to make a lot more slaves for the kind of big-bugs we work for."

Kit listened, absorbed in what Sarah was saying. The little blonde was saying things that had already come some-

what vaguely into her own mind. She had never put her
own thoughts into words. "God damn 'em," Sarah said, and
then she laughed.

They were passing a big house, set back from the street,
a box hedge in front, facing the sidewalk. They could see
over the hedge and across a wide lawn to a stately stone
house. "I guess one of the big bugs lives in there," Sarah
said. "Let them have the kids, eh," she added. "But I'm
not going to give up having some fun." She grew serious.
"I wonder why . . . I wonder why one girl, or a woman
either, is born, say now a big bug, and another isn't." The
two girls had stopped before the house with the wide green
lawn, cut off from them by a hedge over which they could
see. "D'you ever get religion?" Sarah asked. How in earnest
she was! Kit had got suddenly a glowing liking for her.

She wasn't like Kit's other woman friend in that place,
the big woman, Agnes, always dreaming of some kind of a
social revolution, a sudden swift change in the whole social
structure, justice ruling, something of that kind. Kit had
listened to a lot of Agnes's talk. She had never listened as
intently as she now listened to Sarah.

"D'you ever get religion?" Sarah didn't wait for an answer. "I did once but I tell you what, I got over it quick.
It's the bunk," she said. "I guess it's swell enough for a
girl who hasn't got the real stuff," she said.

She was looking at Kit, the two standing before the big
house. They stood for a moment thus, looking at each other
. . . it was for Kit one of those moments of revelation, a
whole new viewpoint on life presented . . . like a door
jerked open for her . . . moments of revelation that come
sometimes to the young. They went on along the street.
"I guess its O. K. for that kind, for the ugly ones, for the

ones that haven't got any looks. If you haven't got what it takes to get what you want, I guess its O. K. to leave it up to God.

"You might as well leave it to something. If you're a girl and haven't got any looks, you're sunk anyway.

"But if you've got the goods and you and I have," she said. She said she had been a good deal of a sucker, the first time or two she had been with men. "I don't know whether you know what I mean or not.

"Kit, kid," she said, "I guess maybe they'd have a harder time shaking the apples off your tree than they did off mine." She laughed again. As they went along Sarah began telling of the man from whom she got the ten dollars. She said he was all right. "He didn't try to bunk me," she said.

He had thought at first that she might be a quite innocent young girl. "I look like that, don't I?" Sarah said, throwing up her head and turning to Kit. They both laughed. Kit thought she was swell. Being with Sarah that morning had given her a sudden fine feeling of new freedom, of adventure. "It's the way my nose turns up and the freckles on my nose," Sarah said. The man she had been with was a young lawyer, partner in a law firm with his father. His father was successful and the son had married a rich girl.

But there had been something dry and dead about her. He told Sarah that she was a horse woman, thought of nothing but fine saddle horses, cared for nothing else. "She ought to sleep with a horse," he said to Sarah.

He had got fed up on her horseyness and on her. "We've got a kid. Well, and that's all right," he said to Sarah. He thought, at first, when he had picked her up, that she might be an innocent girl. "Are you?" he had asked; "because, if you are, I'll drop you right now.

"If you are not. . . ." He had proposed that she drive with him to a town a hundred miles away. He said he had noticed her walking along the street and had followed. Then he went to get his car. He watched his chance to speak to her when he felt it was safe. She had been walking about, looking into store windows and had turned into a side street. "I was really out to pick up a man," Sarah said. She declared she had done it more than once but with a toss of her head said that she had always been choosy, wouldn't just take any bum that came along looking for something. She told Kit all about the night with him. She thought he was all right, wanted only a little warm affection. He had given her the ten dollars, apologizing, as he did so. It was about all he had left in his pocket when the hotel bill was paid. They had stayed until late on Sunday morning, having dinner in their room, with a bottle of wine he managed in some way to get. "He was a funny guy all right, but nice," she said. He had asked her, "So you're a working girl, eh? You are in the mill, eh?

"So that's all right," he had said. He had certainly talked in a way that had at first startled and then amused Sarah. "I like these square-shooting guys," she said. He had declared it was all quite regular, in good form, a man like himself, from a so-called good family, meaning, he said, a rich or a well-to-do family, married and dissatisfied with his wife . . . "she being a cold fish," he said. Afraid, he said, to go ahead and break things up, tell her to go to hell or to the horse barns, without the guts to do that.

"We all do it," he said. "Gee, it was just killing to hear him," Sarah exclaimed. He explained that his father was the lawyer for the mill in which Sarah and Kit worked and that he also owned the controlling interest in the newspaper

in their town. "That's so we can control public opinion in
case some of you little girls get upstage and want your just
rights," he said. He said all of these things, Sarah explained,
while they were lying in bed, lying and talking with a queer
look in his eyes and a queer twist to his lips. "But just the
same he wasn't kidding, he meant it," Sarah declared. She
said she had sure liked him fine. "He wasn't any rough guy
either, one of the kind that don't know how to treat a
woman. In the morning we had a swell breakfast in bed.
He had it sent up to the room.

"It was so comfy and nice up there." A girl, Sarah declared, was a damn fool who wasn't smart enough to get
everything she could out of life.

There were a few extra dollars in his pocket and he had
suggested, if she didn't mind, that she take a train home.
He would drop her at the railroad station. The ten dollars
was a gift. It wasn't much, he had said, for the joy she had
given him, but there would be more.

He had asked her, "You'll be sensible, won't you, kid,
you'll take the money?" and, "Sure" she had replied. She described the hotel room he had got. It was so big, warm, and
light. It had seemed to her luxurious. "I hadn't given him
anything so precious. I liked him. He was nice. He wasn't
rough. Gee, Kit," she said, "to think of it, I'd be working in
the damn mill every night for a week to make what he
gave me."

She said she was going to see him again and that she
might quit the mill. He had suggested something of the
kind. Even if he was taking something away from her it
wouldn't be any worse than something they take from you
when you worked as she and Kit did in one of their mills.

The two girls went to the hotel and walked in, Kit's heart

thumping. She had never before been in such a place. What admiration she had for Sarah, who did everything so boldly, asking a Negro boy where the ladies' room was and if the dining-room was open. "Is it all right for me to park my car out there, at the side door?" she asked the Negro. Kit thought it was a grand bluff. There were two or three cars parked near the side door of the hotel. The colored boy in a bright blue uniform kept bowing and scraping to them. He was, "Yes, Missing," in great shape, as Sarah afterwards said. The dining-room wasn't open at such an early hour but there was another room, called a grille. They went in there and breakfasted in state, Sarah carrying it off with a wink. "I guess it's easy enough, if you've got to throw it away anyway, to get something for it," Sarah said, and Kit understood what she meant. She meant the youth and the beauty they both had. She meant that there was a market for it.

CHAPTER ELEVEN

WHEN Kit went with Gordon Halsey to Kate's house, really to pass inspection by Tom Halsey, the illicit liquor business was in its first full flush of success, as was the oil business when the elder Rockefeller, Mr. John D. himself, got in and the steel business when Andrew Carnegie began. The prohibition law had been passed the year before and the Anti-Saloon League was in its full glory. In old Virginia in the hall of the lower house, and for that matter in the state senate, old stamping ground of Patrick Henry . . . "Give me liberty or give me death" . . . of Thomas Jefferson . . . "The government that governs the least is the best government" . . . in this place as in many state capitals, men like Virginia's Bishop Cannon were in control . . . they were holding the whip . . . politicians were in terror of them . . . Women's Christian Temperance Union in control . . . money pouring in to the Anti-Saloon League from big industrialists . . . the saloon gone . . .

Oh, pride, oh, cock-sureness! "The saloon must never come back." Now it will become fashionable, a real mark of distinction, to have a stock of liquor in the home. "We, the rich and the well-to-do, can have it now. These others, of the lower classes, the workers, they cannot get it. It costs too much. You'll see they will be better workers now."

"Not that I think there is anything wrong with liquor, in the hands of the right people."

But wait, little one, it won't be long. Soon the workers will have it too. There will be stuff made that can sell even at fifteen cents a drink.

The old corner saloons in the cities, saloons in small towns over the country . . . tough places, eh? Well, there was something to be said. Is it, after all, completely a woman's world? The coal miner, coming to the surface of Mother Earth on a Saturday evening. At last a shave, perhaps even a bath, in a washtub in a shed back of his miner's cabin. God knows kids enough sprawling and puking on the floor inside the cabin. "Here's my week's wage. I am holding out a dollar, a dollar and a half, two dollars. Yes, I'm going down to Jim's.

"Yes, I know but God-damit, you look here, old woman, I work too. You talk about working your hands off here at home, over our kids. Yeah, I know.

"But what the hell, woman, even if I get a little spiffed, this one night a week, something warm down inside me for once? . . . All right, just as you say, then. Sure. Maybe I come home a little unsteady on my legs, singing as I make my way up the hill in the mud.

"What the hell, song on my lips for once anyway. My head muddled, eh? Well, sure. What of it? If I had much of a head would I be what I am? You knew when you took me on as your man I didn't ever represent myself as any Einstein to you, did I, woman?

"Ah, shut up a minute, will you, old girl? There's the money on the table, all I've earned all week . . . yes, risking my life every minute of the week and here's a dollar-fifty in my hand. Into my pocket and presently into Jim's till it

goes. Sure I used to be content to stay at home with you,
when you were young, hadn't all these kids, when you were
a damn sight prettier and, when it comes to that, a damn
sight more stuck on me, too.

"Anyway here goes . . . an evening . . . some warm
friendly talk with other men like me, other workers, other
slaves, their chains kicked off for a few hours. What the hell
if later I come back up the hill here, probably in the rain,
with Frank and Harry and Will? All right, maybe a fight
. . . maybe just the three of us, arms about each other's
shoulders, singing maybe . . . big feeling of real friendship
for once anyway. 'Harry, old pal, I know you're one that
will stick by a friend come rain, come snow. Put her
there, Harry.' That feeling. It's good, woman, even if it's
all nonsense, even if it's only, as you say, Jim's booze talking in us.

"Damn it, woman, maybe there's something about men
you and no other woman rightly understands and never
will.

"Nor the W. C. T. U., nor the politicians, nor the ones
who have the money and can do as they damn please anyway. Why should they know? How can they know?

"Well, so-long, old woman. Get sore again if you think it
will do you any good."

And there are the Farmers too, hard-working little farmers of the West and Middle West. Down South they closed up
the saloons early in the movement . . . afraid the Negro
would get himself a drink, maybe get ugly, asserting that
he's as good as any man because he does a man's work . . .
all that nonsense. "There'll always be a way for us whites to
get what we want."

Kansas went out early, too. They drank Peruna out there. D'you ever try it?

French workers, German workers, over in old Europe, sitting with wives and children in little cafés or beer gardens, wife and kids getting in on what fun there is for a working man. Perhaps a little music. You and the old woman and the kids, anyway the older ones, sitting at tables, maybe outdoors under trees, thumping on tables with beer mugs.

Little farmers over here with bad years behind them. God knows with discouraging enough outlook ahead. In Jim's, or Joe's, or Pete's, with others, of a Saturday night. Some of the factory boys in there too.

"Say if we small farmers and farm hands could ever learn to get together with the factory boys, there'd be something crack up in this country, eh? Boy, we'd make the politicians hump, eh?

"But hell, when it comes to the politicians, maybe they're all right. I guess they only try to do what they think they can get away with, same as all of us. If we got together, had now say this socialism or this communism, we'd still have the politicians.

"But boy, we could crack the whip at their heels, eh what?"

Kit went to Kate's with Gordon, in Gordon's big yellow sport-model car. They went to Kate's little white farmhouse, of so many approaches, the house half hidden behind the trees in front, apple orchard with old trees, long untrimmed, shaggy nice old trees filled in the fall with many little gnarled apples, big red barns. From the rear of the house, as from almost any point in that North Carolina country, you could see in the distance low wooded hills and in the far distance there was a big paved road that came up out of a valley and went twisting up over a hill. It was a cement road and after a rain, when the sun came out, how it glistened.

"I want to go fast, fast, over any road, into the distance, into the beyond. Do I not love my country? It is vast. How am I ever to know it a little if I do not go fast, fast?

"Fast. Fast.

"It is so vast."

Gordon and Kit went into Kate's by a side door and came at once into a fairly large room that had been arranged as a sort of restaurant or tea room.

But, after all, men in the illicit liquor trade did not sit in tea rooms. There were a few small tables with chairs, such as might have been seen in the back rooms of saloons before prohibition, tables at which sat farmers and workers playing cards, heavy fists thumping on tables. There was one picture, a campaign portrait of Chief Justice Hughes, on the wall . . . a left-over from the Wilson-Hughes presidential campaign . . . and a large couch against a blank wall. It was evident that the room had been made by taking out a partition between two rooms. It occupied a space that had been, formerly, when the house belonged to a farming family, the dining-room and parlor. There was a closed stairway leading up from a little hallway, the door to the hallway standing open and beyond the hallway a bedroom. As it turned out, that was Tom Halsey's room although he seldom slept there. There was no desk and only one chair but he conducted conferences with men in the room, made arrangements and gave orders. He or his guest sat on the edge of the bed.

The upstairs, probably taken by bedrooms, was Kate's.

Although they were not married she was known among
Tom's people as Kate Halsey. It wasn't in the mode for
fellows in Tom's racket to inquire too closely into other
fellows' personal relations. The point went deeper. Was she
okay? Did she keep her mouth shut? At that time Kit had
never before seen Kate and did not see her at once when
she entered the room with Gordon. There was a large long
kitchen, running the whole length of the back of the house,
with doors into the large room and into Tom's room and it
was equipped with the very latest in kitchen improvements,
an electric stove, electric dish washer and clothes washer and
a huge electric refrigerator. Kit and Gordon had entered by
a side door into the large room and there were some men sitting at one of the tables and playing cards. They did not
speak to Gordon nor he to them. The table was by a small
fireplace in which there was a pile of dead wood ashes. Gordon went to sit on the couch. There was a small table with
an electric lamp near it and on the table a newspaper was
lying. It was an old newspaper but he picked it up and turning on the light pretended to read. Kit sat beside him and
as she sat thus the men at the table turned, one at a time,
and each took a long careful look at her.

It was an uncomfortable moment. Kit was uncomfortable
and so also, very evidently, was Gordon. "So this had been
his home, where he had spent his boyhood, this place?"
She felt at once a certain sympathy for Gordon. Already
he had told her of the woman Kate and of his father and she
was eaten by curiosity. Would the father be like the men
sitting at the table and one by one turning to stare at her?

How unfriendly they seemed in their attitude toward
Gordon! "Will his father be like one of these men?" There
was at once a feeling of relief. "After all I'm not yet married

to him." She had held him off. "I'll see. I'll think about it." There was the temptation. It was evident there would be plenty of money, what seemed to her fairly oceans of money.

And most of all there would be a big fast sporty car to drive. Already she had managed that and when they were in the car . . . two or three evenings a week for several weeks it had been going on . . . there was a long trip on Sunday afternoons, often lasting until late at night . . . on all such trips she was at the wheel.

It was better so. He was pleading, pleading. "Oh, Kit, it is such a hard time for me.

"Do you not love me, Kit?"

"Well, I don't know. I can't tell yet."

There was one thing certain. She loved his car. When you are at the wheel of a car and there is a man with you, trying so hard to make you . . . he can't do much.

His arm about your shoulders sometimes. "But, Gordon, I can't drive comfortably with your arm there." She had been learning.

You do not put them off too abruptly, get cross, speak sharply. You smile or laugh. There is a thing you do with the eyes. It's best when you are in some safe place, in a hotel dining-room. Kit had learned to be at her ease in such places. Gordon had surely done that for her, taking her about blowing in his money. She now knew what to do with the knives and forks, the little bird baths they put down before you with the dessert . . . she had been terribly puzzled at first.

You can do something with the eyes. You pretend you are afraid . . . Kit wasn't, not of Gordon . . . all of his little tricks were too obvious, too easy to see through. You can make the eyes say things . . . "Oh, man, man, I long for you so but I am a pure young girl and so afraid. I do not dare, for a minute, surrender to my own feeling." All of that implied by a look you now and then give him. Any woman who is a woman knows how. Working women, who are good-lookers and pursued by men, have to learn fast.

Or they will go under.

Under what?

Some man, of course.

And then what? "Well, I've got what I was after." Perhaps all men were not like Gordon, but he was typical of a lot. Kit sensed that.

"The hunt is up. I am matching myself against this neat little piece.

"If I get her, win out, I will have proved something.

"That I am a real hunter, bring down my game when I go after it. We men, we have sometimes to prove ourselves real men."

"But don't you care for me, even a little?"

"Gordon, you know I do." She did care. There was a side to him, a kind of boyishness sometimes. The old thing, the story of so many marriages . . . they are often enough not unhappy marriages . . . it is possible, even probable, that women can come to maturity, do often come to their own kind of maturity, quickly, in a way men cannot.

As some trees come to early maturity while others come slowly, oh, so slowly, if they come at all . . . the thing implied, often a quick natural growing.

Something in women closer perhaps to earth, to nature.

In working women often the seeming phenomenon, the constant contact with other and older women and with men, the kind of fine comradeship that does grow up be-

tween such women, as in Kit's case with Agnes and with
Sarah . . . "Get wise, kid, get wise. Get wise fast."

Was there something to be held on to at all costs . . .
the thing taught many girls?

"Look here. You've got something they want. They'll be
after it, hot after it. You must remember you are a poor
girl, just a working girl. It's all you've got. When you let
go of it, be smart. Be sure you get something for it."

All of that to such young women as Kit Brandon had been
often said, whispered, with girlish giggles, said outright,
plainly, as by one like Agnes.

"But don't you care for me a little?"

"Well say, why do you suppose I go out with you?"
His pleading. "It is so hard for me." It was true, she in her
own way knew, that he did suffer in his longing for her.
She felt it in him. No woman is ever really hurt by that
knowing, even when it is connected with a man not at all
desirable to her.

And Gordon Halsey was, in his own way, desirable. Often
his pleading, when they had driven to some other town on
a Sunday afternoon, had dined in a hotel . . . he took her
always to the best places . . . he had learned something of
ordering a dinner . . . his boyish eagerness, the hurt look in
his eyes . . . his wanting her to stay there with him, in the
hotel for the night . . . as Sarah with that lawyer of hers.

"But there's my job, Gordon."

"Oh, the hell with that."

He offered her money. "Now listen, Kit, I'm not trying
to buy you. I've found out you're not one who can be
bought. You need it."

She did need it. "If I am to go about with him in his car
and to such places." She had taken his money and had built

up her wardrobe carefully, with growing understanding of her own needs, keeping in mind always that it was better not to display her new and more expensive clothes at the store, to the other girls in the store.

They were interested, absorbed, giving to her the sort of sympathy such girls and women can give to their fellows, to one of their fellows trying to play the game, to win in the game. "Do you think he's getting to her? Is she putting out?"

"No, he's not, not from her."

"I tell you what, Kit's too smart. I tell you, she's a smart kid."

"You know I care for you. If not, why would I waste my time, going out with you?" A man can't get too close, begin kissing, all that sort of thing in a car when the woman is driving. He had kept wanting her to stop by some dark roadside at night but she wouldn't. "I'll tell you straight, Gordon. If I marry you I'll marry you." She meant that at the moment, a kind of loyalty, woman to her man implied. "I guess, if you really want me to be your wife, you won't want me trailing off after other men, as that other woman did."

That kind of talking helping to hold him too. Whether or not it was talk just invented, as a part of the game she was playing, she didn't herself know. She was becoming constantly sharper, keener, no doubt, from the first, too keen for him.

Were her words to him altogether lying words? "I care for his car, for his money."

She did care for something else too. There is a thing, quite natural, strong in many women. "It may be that I can

make him be what I want, if I know what I want" . . . the
maternal, the feeling of maternal strength in the woman.
The very fact that he couldn't, didn't dare come quite
straight with her, about his father for example, having to
bring her to the father for a kind of inspection, Gordon
not being that far his own man . . .

The bluff he put up to her. "I want Dad to know you,"
the implication that it was because he wanted to arouse in
his father affection for her, that he was proud of her.

He perhaps was that. She was, she had no doubt of that
. . . he had once shown her a photograph of the other one,
his first wife . . . Kit was the best thing he had found
or was likely to find.

The silence in the room to which Gordon had brought
Kit continued for what seemed to her a long, long time.
The men at the table, silently at their card playing, continued to turn from time to time, one after the other, to stare
at her. One of them suddenly spoke. He called and his voice
coming out of the silence made both Gordon and Kit jump.
"Kate," he called. "What about some beer here, Kate?"

The woman Kate came presently through a door that led
to her kitchen and at the time Kit had the feeling that
Kate was a good deal like a spider running out of some hidden hole at the base of its web. She changed her mind about
Kate later, came to admire her.

She gave at first so distinctly the impression of a hard,
ruthless woman. There were the heavy lines in her life-
bitten face, a kind of rigidity. You felt something, a question . . . "Who, or what, has done this to you?

"You have been hurt, deeply hurt. Will you now begin to
hurt others?"

Kate had been carried away from her man . . . the son
Gordon did not know that story, knew only that she was
not his mother . . . that mountain God-man ruthlessly
robbed of his woman by Tom, as Tom was afterwards to do
all things, with a sort of quiet ruthlessness. "There is a
babe at your breast, woman. What more do you want?"

Why, indeed, there is something else wanted, something
very deep, often very subtle, hidden away, in all women
who are women. It is the desire, the hunger, to bear the
child within the woman's own body, feel the movement
of it, the pain to be faced . . . act of creation. "Here is our
woman thing. No man can ever go through this, feel this."
Afterwards to mark the child's growth, hope for it, dream
for it. The child that had been Kate's child was not her
child.

There was in her, as Kit later found out, a kind of blind
loyalty. Such a woman must give of herself, blindly, to some
man, the one-man woman. She had not been able to give
what she had to give, to the other, the God-man . . . God-
men are rarely woman-men . . . so she gave it to Tom
Halsey.

That the giving was not quite wanted, that it was accepted
only in a certain way . . . the woman to be used, put aside,
then again used . . .

"Very well, then, I will be your servant.

"I am the one-man woman. My man is my man." There
was hurt enough in the woman who called herself Kate
Halsey. She didn't parade it. A few such people, men sometimes, women sometimes, hurt, kicked about by life . . .
the artist man for example, the poet, the painter who does
beautiful work, giving himself in all cleanliness, a D. H.
Lawrence, a Rembrandt, when his world so carefully built

fell down upon him when he was an old man, a Vincent
Van Gogh, in America the poet Vachel Lindsay, examples
of artist men so hurt . . . run, Vincent Van Gogh, to the
woman in the house of prostitution with your ear in your
hand . . . "Here, woman, if you cannot take me, take this
bit of me." There are some such men, some such women,
who get out of such hurts a kind of inner laughter but
others cannot get it. The hurt endures.

The woman Kate came into the room where Kit sat with
Gordon. The curtains of the room were drawn, although it
was still light outside . . . Kit and Gordon had arrived in the
early evening of a summer Sunday. Electric lights were
turned on. Kate came bringing bottles of beer and glasses
and without speaking set them down before the men and,
without looking at Kit or Gordon, returned to her kitchen.
One of the men growled at her. "Thanks," he said.

At that time, in the early days of prohibition and of the
rapidly expanding illicit liquor trade, men like Tom Halsey,
who had quickly spread themselves and the organization
they had got together out over certain territories, were determined to control there, opportunity grasped in firm hands,
much as nations put out strong hands to control trade areas,
usually so-called backward countries . . . certainly backward
in the ability to grasp and hold . . . spheres of influence
established . . . ruthlessness in nations . . . ruthlessness in
men, in the illicit liquor trade war outside the law. Against
the high-jacker and his gang, who held up your liquor cars
or trucks on the road, there was no legal redress. It was
necessary to maintain your own army. Such men as Tom
had become often brought into their territories tough guys,
even city gun men. There was property to be protected. Oh,

sacred property! There were now and then men who must
be put out of the way. Two of the men playing cards in
Kate's house when Gordon and Kit came there were of this
sort. The third man was a countryman, a tall fellow in overalls, a mountain man . . . he may have been learning the
gun man's trade. He had a long, rather serious-looking face
and small gray eyes set close together.

He and who else?

There was one of the men in the room that day who had
secret ambitions. He was one of the two city gun men
brought in and his name was — or at least he spoke of
himself as — Steve Wyagle. He was known as Shorty, being
short of stature, a swarthy-skinned man, ancestry somewhere
in the south of Europe, a fellow with blue-black hair,
cut close to the head, thick-necked, the hair growing far
down over his low forehead, a scar, evidently from an old
knife wound, running down from near his left eye and
disappearing behind his neck. The cut had not been prop-
erly mended. There had been a rough, careless job of sew-
ing. White and red puckers of flesh showed against the dark
brown of the skin.

He was ambitious. He was secretly at work. He looked at
Gordon Halsey, who had brought a woman to that place.
He was having himself a good look at Kit. He had heard
tales. "This Tom Halsey, the big shot here, he has a weakness. It is his son and the son has a weakness. It is women.

"And now the son has got himself a new skirt, eh? The
other one he had was a talker. All women talk. She came
near getting Tom and the whole crowd into trouble.

"Now there will be a chance for me. If Tom doesn't speak
out, tell that son of his where to get off, kick this new dame
of his out of the picture, I'll do some talking myself. It will

be a chance for spreading dissension. Perhaps, if he lets his
son get away with this I'll even put up a spiel to the big
shot himself. I'll have my say about this woman business and
I'll do it where some of the others can hear.

"And then, if he doesn't kick her out, I'll put it up to the
boys. I'll show this Tom Halsey who is the big shot here."

The man Steve Wyagle, sitting and thinking, turning
occasionally from his card playing for another look at Kit.
Kit was also thinking. She had been brought to the place
. . . she knew vaguely, although it had never been definitely
put up to her, that she had been brought there to be inspected by Tom Halsey, Gordon's father. Well, where was
the man? Why didn't he show himself? The man she was
presumed to be about to marry was sitting beside her, obviously nervous. He kept the newspaper before his face, pretended to be absorbed in it. That would be, always . . . one
might as well face the truth . . . about his speed. He was a
pretender. He would be always, now pretending to be tough,
now to be more or less the gentleman, now a sport, now a
man in love. He would be the sort almost any woman could
knock off, terribly in love today, quite cold tomorrow.

"He hasn't got me yet."

"But there is something else too." It is likely that all
morals, all moral codes are the inventions of men. Kit had
something — the grand unmoral nature of all true women.
There was hunger in her, it had been growing in her. "I
want what I want, good clothes, above all a fine fast car to
drive.

"It is all right to talk about the nobility of labor, the sort
of talk I used to hear on the lips of Agnes . . . I guess it
was O. K. for her, talking that way, feeling that way, but

I'm different. You have to try to get a few things you want for yourself. It's all right, I guess, this talk about the nobility of labor, but what's noble in this wearing yourself out as a clerk in a five-and-ten?

"Or in a cotton mill or shoe factory?

"It must be that all such talk comes from those who never did any real work."

There were those like the revolutionist Agnes.

"Well, all right, but I'm not Agnes."

There was that in Kit that demanded something out of life while she was young, felt the power of youth in herself.

And there was another angle. As she sat in that room with the not-very-cheerful-looking card players and the nervous Gordon she was aware of a growing fear in her. She had been to movies, had read newspapers. The young Italian man, in the place where she had the room in the shoe factory town, was addicted to detective stories and she had read several of them. When you read such a book you got excited, were held tightly, but afterwards it all faded away. You could remember nothing at all of the characters in the book. Your knowledge of people was in no way extended. There was, in fact, after reading, a queer sold-out feeling in you but something remained.

If not people at least thoughts coming back of a murder on some lonely road at night, or in a lonely farmhouse — blood flowing, a dead man or woman. The women were so often young and beautiful. Kit began to be afraid. There were such things as gang killings, people not wanted put out of the way. How did she know the man, Gordon's father, wanted his son to take another wife?

Something else. There were gang rapings. Groups of men,

roughs, usually after drinking, sometimes attacked young
girls in small American towns. Almost every town had in
its history some such story. The stories were whispered about
among the girls in the factories. There was even a story in the
Bible. Some girl had told Kit to look it up and read it.
"It was in the Old Testament, Genesis XIX."

Lot in the house in Sodom — gang of the boys outside.

"Behold, now, I have two daughters who have not known
man." Big night for the boys.

There was fear but it passed quickly. Kit sat up very
straight beside Gordon who had slumped and sat with the
newspaper still held before his face. She had, at the moment,
something of the quality in her bearing that had made Tom
Halsey a leader. She was neatly but not flashily dressed, in
a well-fitted suit, certainly well-tailored, and there was something quiet and steady in her eyes. "They don't rape my
kind. I've got something they won't dare try to touch."

There was surely something ridiculous in her attitude at
that moment. She was unarmed. The three men at the table
were all physically powerful men. They were not sensitive
to attitudes.

A door opened and Tom Halsey came into the room
through the door that led into the downstairs bedroom and
walked straight across the room to Kit and Gordon, and
Gordon immediately jumped up. He tried to be at ease, to
be cheerful, a kind of hail-fellow.

"Why, hello, Dad."

"Hello, Gordon." Tom was smiling. How much affection,
how much contempt there can be in the attitude of a father
toward a son. "Hello." Gordon was muttering an introduc-
tion. He sat and then quickly got to his feet again. The news-

paper he had been holding fell to the floor. The three men at the table were staring but Tom Halsey paid no attention to them or to the confusion of his son. He had the detached air of a doctor coming into his waiting room. There are several people sitting and he nods to one of them. "Will you please come this way?" He walked to the door of his bedroom and opening it stepped aside and Kit, who had followed, went in.

"It's a bedroom, you see," he said when they were both inside and the door closed. "I'll have to apologize but it is also my office." If Kit Brandon had been learning, picking up points as she went along in life, so had Tom. If you are in the illicit liquor business in a big way, if you want to be a big shot in the game, you'd better learn. You'll be meeting all sorts of people who must be handled. Better step carefully, learn fast. In Tom Halsey there were also secret new ambitions. They all get it, the successful ones, big stockmarket riggers, big shots in finance and industry. "Look here, I'm in this game now but I'm going to get out when I get mine. I'm going to be respectable and respected."

"There's only the one chair, you see. You take it. I'll sit here, on the edge of the bed."

There was a second door to the room and it led into the kitchen and at once Kit knew that the woman Kate, she had just seen for the first time, was in there, standing in there, not moving, listening.

Antagonism in the men she had seen in the other room, antagonism in Kate. There was Gordon's father, Tom Halsey, sitting on the edge of the bed. Silence. "So he's having himself a good look, appraising me.

"He and his son can both go to hell for all I care."

It was well for Kit that she had been born a mountain

lass, daughter of mountain folk. They all have it, the mountain people, Gipsies, American Indians. All can sit in the
presence of others in prolonged silence . . . poker-faced.
Tom Halsey would have been thinking of his son as he sat
looking at Kit.

"So he thinks he wants this one. That's strange." This
out of a contempt for the son he wouldn't have dared admit to himself. There was this other thing, growing in him.
"If I make good in this game I'm in, pile up a lot of money,
I'll be wanting something I can't get in my own self. It's a
tough game. I'll have made too scaly a record. I'll have to
get it through my son . . . respectability, a Halsey thrust
up out of the muck.

"I wish he were better stuff. In this matter a man must
work with what he has. But the woman his son gets and by
whom he may have a son must be O. K."

"This looks like a firm little thing."

Tom had sense enough to know that his Gordon was not
likely to cut in on one of the so-called established families
in the section of country he had marked down as his own,
for which there would be a constant, a ruthless war, under
cover, with other ambitious men. "She might do for what
I want for my son."

He was looking at her not coldly, not warmly. "My son
tells me that you and he are planning to be married," he said
finally and Kit answered in a tone much like his own.
She smiled. "He may be planning. He has spoken of it.
I'm not planning."

"You may take that. Put it in your pipe. Smoke it." Kit
said nothing of the sort. She may again have been thinking
of Sarah . . . luxury of the rich that Sarah had spoken of.
"I wonder if he lives here, in this dump, men like those

fellows outside there for companions? It doesn't look to me like a life I want."

Tom arose, from his seat on the bed. "Let's step outside," he said, and they went out of the room, through Kate's kitchen, as Kit had already guessed, the woman Kate standing just outside the half-closed door. She made no effort to conceal the fact that she had been standing, looking and listening, and Tom did not look at her.

He led the way out onto a back porch and into an orchard. Kit smiled. "Well, this is good," she thought. She was thinking of Gordon, behind his newspaper in the room with the three men, of his sitting there and waiting, wanting, she thought, to be self-possessed, to create an impression of strength. How many men in the world always wanting to seem to be what they cannot be, never getting the idea that strength is in acceptance of limitations, not in stretching them!

What a splendid big game hunter Gordon would have made! How much false hair grows on the breasts of some men?

At the same time, in Kit, something very feminine. The father would walk with her, trying to get her number, he deciding whether or not he wanted her for his son's wife, leaving the son to sit in there. There is a mother in every real woman. "Don't you think we'd better call Gordon? He and I will be getting back to town."

Tom stopped and stood looking at her. There was Gordon's flashy car parked near the house. They were in a path that led through an orchard, crossed a bridge over a small stream, and led into a wood. The day was growing old and dusk was coming on. Tom took no notice of the implication of her remark, that she and not Gordon's father would make the decision about her marriage, that just the same she was sorry for Gordon, did not like leaving him sitting in that room, the woman Kate and the men sitting in there no doubt having guessed what the son's visit to his father was all about . . . they making a kind of tame and impotent bull of him who so wanted to be thought of as so very male, so very bullish. Tom stood for a moment looking at Gordon's car. "I'm afraid he likes to advertise the fact that he has plenty of money to spend," he said. He went on along the path, Kit beside him. "Oh, all right," she thought. "If he is willing to rub it into his son why should I worry?"

Kit with Tom Halsey walked along a path through an old orchard, the path grass-grown. She got curiously alive that day.

"So there is a way for a man to get at a woman other than, well, let's say Gordon's way." She didn't think any such thoughts definitely. They were implicit afterwards, in her talks regarding her life . . . the curious jumping from moment to moment. "I was sorry for Gordon."

"I thought his father was a man, all right. In all that happened after I met him I always did think that."

She would have walked with the man that day a little defiant. It was all right, in a way, the idea of marriage with Gordon. It meant for her . . . well, what did it mean? She had no notion that he would be what is called a faithful husband. Several of the girls in the five-and-ten had spoken on that angle. "There couldn't any woman bank on that guy.

"He'd be after some new skirt inside a year.

"Any girl that flattered him a little could get him."

It was a little rough, his being left, sitting in there . . .

in the room in the house where the three tough ones were
playing cards.

On the other hand, nothing so swell about staying in the
five-and-ten. Pretty soon a girl is worn out, begins to look
tired, hasn't got any pep.

You get to the place where you'll just take anything
that comes along. Then kids come, yourself dragging along
through life. If you want to kick loose you can't get a job
any more. They all want the young good-lookers. It was a
good thing that one like Gordon didn't know what he had
to offer. If he was really smart he'd know he could pick 'em
like apples off a tree. What, a swell car to drive, putting it
over on other women? Money to buy clothes? Perhaps in
Kit, that day as she walked with Tom Halsey . . . on the
spot with him, as it were . . . a kind of something, not
very clearly defined . . . something all American women
very passionately deny . . . it may be they don't really
want it . . . it might be called, "manhood."

What do you mean, a big he-man?

No, not that . . . Christ, not that.

Women plastering themselves all over the place. What's
done gone with a certain old, old, oh very old, relationship
between man and woman? Tag! You're it!

It may well be that, in certain periods in man's stumbling
progress through, let's say history, he not too aware . . . she
always sheing and sheing . . .

Being always more sensibly aware . . . this not to say
she is necessarily top hole . . .

Not really wanting to be . . . always a little self-consciously hurt when she is shoved up there . . . you know, on top . . .

It may be that the man, Tom Halsey, had it for Kit Brandon. I thought so more than once as she told me her story. They walked through an old apple orchard, the sort of old apple trees that are left for years untrimmed, producing every year smaller and smaller apples, a forest of sprouts growing up from each limb, then across a bit of meadow and a bridge. They got into a small wood and went through it to stand by a fence in a place that gave a view of distant meadows, the land going up and up, softly rolling toward distant hills. There was a paved road to be seen, a cement road, a thread of grayish white against the green of meadows. It was getting on toward dark and the cars . . . people of near-by towns were out for a late Sunday drive . . . headlights of some of the cars were already lighted . . . there was a flow, a swift moving procession. The cars came from behind a hill, almost black now in that light, moved across a high clear place, disappeared temporarily behind a little hill, emerged again, the headlight of one car making a patch of light in which the car before it moved . . . swiftly . . . seemingly swift . . .

The moving lights, people hurled thus so easily, swiftly, through space . . .

Story of the modern American world . . . significant of what was going on out there, across darkening fields . . . an age when man, in his concentration on one phase of life, the mechanical . . . much, oh much achieved . . . the automobile perhaps the finest expression of it all . . .

"I want" . . . (in a material world) . . . "I want."

The overbalance, science gone a little insane. "Let's go to the moon or to Mars next."

O. K. Go on child-man. We'll see what you get out of that.

Kit and Tom . . . he was silent. The silence between the two went on for a long time but Kit wasn't impatient. This business of the young, among our American women, wanting the young among our American men. "God knows I'd like to get a mature one if I could, one who would mean something to me . . . not just what one like Gordon means by it." There is no doubt that, from the first moment he laid eyes on her, Tom Halsey had a certain respect for something in Kit, as he had for something in the woman Kate.

He wouldn't have been thinking specially, "Will she do?" There would have been little or no doubt of a kind of firmness, of reality, in her. The nonsense, already in the man's head, about his son . . . "Through him, or a grandson, I may get the Halseys established . . . big people, respectable people" . . . he was later to speak of this matter a good deal to Kit . . . it always went over her head . . .

He must have accepted her from the start. They stood together by the fence on that night for a long time, darkness coming . . . the time may not have been as long as it seemed later to Kit . . . there might even have been a kind of bond growing between the two.

There could have been something. They had both been born and had spent childhoods on poor mountain land and the land lying there before them that night, most of it embraced in the farm Tom had bought for Kate . . . it would have been good rich land.

Forests covering it in an earlier day, in a day not so far away from the two, then settlers coming, trees hacked down, the generations following each other.

Westward going, westward going, westward going.

A kind of obsession in that, too. There was too much land left wasted and unused behind the generations.

The coming of the machine, science, mechanical progress, the overbalance. They certainly were not aware. Kit thought she got a growing liking for Tom Halsey from the first. It would break down but slowly in her.

She wasn't bothered by his silence and just stood near him, they both looking off across the land toward the distant road, high up across the wide space, until he was ready to return to the house. They had got half way back, were again in the overgrown farm road that ran through the orchard, before he spoke. It was quite dark in there and from the house, all the shades being tightly drawn, no lights came. He touched her arm and she stopped. "I guess you and Gordon will go through with it." It was dark and she didn't look toward him but suddenly she knew that he was right. She would go through with it with Gordon, would have herself a swell fast car to drive, money to buy things she thought she wanted. His voice, as was usual with him, was very quiet. Something began. He afterwards talked to Kit more than to others. Something like feeling, exasperation, crept into the voice. "He won't stick to you. He won't stick to anything. You may be able to make him be something."

He walked on ahead of her and she followed. "You don't need to come into the house. I'll send him out to you. It may be we can do something together." He didn't say to her what was in his mind. Perhaps he had become again a mountain man and liked her being a mountain woman, one of his own people. "It may be we can do something together." She found out later that he meant she might have a son by his son, one who would come close to his own wishes.

CHAPTER TWELVE

K IT got her automobile. She got a fast little roadster
which Gordon bought for her. She thought sometimes of Sarah and her lover. After she left the place
where she and Sarah had worked together she never
heard from that particular attractive little female. Had Sarah's
racket worked? Did she hold on to her lawyer lover? Did
the lawyer's wife find him out and maybe wreck her husband's little holiday? Sarah had talked very glowingly about
the hotel room where she had stayed with her pickup that
first night and now Kit lived in a hotel, the best in a town
of perhaps 75,000 people. She had a suite there, with a bedroom of her own and also a living room. She could lie in
bed in the morning, pick up the telephone beside her bed,
order breakfast sent up. She had been married to Gordon
Halsey some six or eight months and all of these wonders
had happened.

The rooms were fixed up to suit her own fancy. What
dresses she bought, what furnishings for her bed, hangings
for windows, couch covers, fur coats, shoes, how many
pairs of shoes!

One automobile? Why she could have any one of dozens.
It was like being married to an automobile salesman. To be

sure she couldn't exactly own them. Tom Halsey had cars working out from a dozen centers of activity. There was liquor being run northward from a long seacoast, North Carolina, South Carolina, spots along the Gulf of Mexico. In a city like New Orleans there were many ways for small craft, from West Indies Islands, to dash in or creep in. Big towns of the North, Pittsburgh, Youngstown, Akron, Toledo, Cleveland, Detroit, Indianapolis, St. Louis . . . count them over on your fingers and toes . . . all the good stuff coming in didn't come through Canada . . . there were all the rich and the well-to-do, wanting the best. For the poor the alki cookers among the foreign-born in industrial suburbs of cities. These under the thumb of the big shot in any one of the big towns. For the poor the alki cookers of such places and the mountain moonshiners. In the Southern cities they nearly all drank raw moon. They said they liked it. "Give me some good moon for mine."

"Good moon indeed." Tom once explained it all, smiling in the soft way he had got into. "Yes, I dare say they did make some good moon in our hills once." In Northern cities and towns they had a kind of illusion about the mountain moon and that helped make a market. They had read books and stories about mountain moonshiners, the gun-toting, hard-eyed mountain man. "Yes, sah, I'z sure proud of the liquor I make." "Proud hell!" Tom knew. He rather enjoyed telling Kit, wising her up. He had accepted her. "If there is any one of the cars I own you think you'd enjoy driving for a time, let me know." He had caught her love of driving, her passion for fast and powerful cars. "She's a square shooter," he thought. "She isn't one of the gabby kind." In the presence of her husband's father Kit never did talk much. She sensed his desire to talk . . . to a woman

. . . knew, in a way in which women do know such things, that he had chosen her to play a certain rôle in his own life. He came to the hotel where she and Gordon both lived . . . after the first two or three months they had got separate suites, a fact that Tom Halsey knew but didn't want to let himself know. It might have been indicative of a breakup between his son and Kit and he didn't want that.

He came to the door of her suite, usually in the late afternoon, and knocked on her door. Kit would be sitting and reading a book. There was a slant she had at that time. It might all have been due to the flood of possession that was coming her way at just that time. She tried to explain it afterwards but couldn't, not very satisfactorily. There was a queer feeling, a kind of sense of obligation, money flowing freely to her, possessions flowing so freely. "There wasn't a thing in the world I could think of I wanted, or thought I wanted, I couldn't get.

"I could go into a shoe store, not the kind of cheap-john place we girls in the factory or in the five-and-ten had to go to but one of these places where they sell only expensive shoes.

"I could just go in and sit down." The whole thing had fascinated her for a time. Clerks were bowing to her, kneeling at her feet. "Yes, Mrs. Halsey." "Yessing me all over the damn place," she said. She liked it for a time. I gathered she did not write to Sarah or to Agnes the revolutionist, did not go back to the five-and-ten where Gordon had found her. "What was the use? If I had gone in there the girls would only have thought I did it to rub it in." Even if Sarah, for example, had won out in her racket, had been able to hold her lawyer, or some other who had money, she would have been feeling, in the presence of Kit . . . well, Kit was legitimately married, she had been made an honest woman.

And there was her own family. There were other children in that family. It might be that her father, with his slovenly wife, was still living in the mountain cabin from which she had escaped, other children born, perhaps children wanting shoes, decent food, young girls, it might well be, having happen to them what she thought had come so near to happening to her at the hands of her father.

"You can't. It's no use." Kit was meaning to say that if money, possessions, flow in to you as they did to her at that time, there isn't anything you can do about it. She did not put it into words but had the conviction that, if you get into the stream of it . . . there is always unaccountable wealth lying about . . . people have never learned how to use land, houses, towns, clothes, possessions of any sort. You get caught as in a stream during a sudden flood. There you are. Better swim with the stream.

If you go trying to help others you become, almost inevitably, patronizing. There might be a few people in the world who could do the thing. There was that woman Kit had met in the library, that time when she was in the town where shoes are made. "I don't know. Maybe one like that could do it," Kit said. "I knew I couldn't."

You went into the shoe store, where they sold only the most expensive makes of shoes. Kit must always have known that she had very slender beautiful feet, slender graceful ankles. Shoe clerks never miss the chance to tell women customers such things. The clerks yessing her. They were kneeling at her feet. A kind of gaudy feeling came. It might well be that the shoe clerk was the son of some Southern so-called first family, the family having gone broke. "Why, my grandfather owned 600 slaves." "Oh, yeah!" A kind of nice . . . for the time nice . . . inward laugh. "Gee, and to think I once, not so long before, worked in a shoe factory." They hadn't made any such shoes in that place. It was a place where they made cheap shoes, for working men and working women. They made thousands of pairs of shoes for one of the big mail-order houses.

"Yes, I'll take that pair. Send them over to the hotel."

"Yes, Mrs. Halsey. And will that be all today?" Such bowing, such politeness. "Boy, you'd better be polite to me."

"Oh, Mrs. Halsey, here is something, a sample pair, in a new style . . . there aren't many women who could really wear them.

"Do you mind . . . I'd love to see them on your feet."

She fell for it. She didn't quite fall for it. There was, no doubt, during that period in her life, a something that did save her. It was a kind of basic common sense.

Just the same you can ride high, ride fancy, for the time.

There is always a fly in the ointment. It is the thing basically wrong with material wealth. It may be that wealth is at bottom no good. All people who have much material wealth must at times have a feeling that began to come to Kit. Wouldn't it be wonderful if all people should some day find out that there is, at bottom, no fun in being rich . . . rich in material possessions, money, land, things, while there is in the world one other human being who is in want? You go to the theatre, into what is called society, to the houses of others who are also rich, to an expensive restaurant. How nice! Who can doubt the joy to be got from the feel of warm well-made clothes, women being made beautiful by beautiful clothes . . . women should be

beautified, it is the secret longing of all feminine hearts
. . . joy of feeling with the fingers beautiful and costly
fabrics?

You come out of some such place. There are the poor or
the hungry in the streets. Are you to become blind?

Can you build up some feeling of being a specially de-
serving one in yourself or will you take the other road?
"These people I see shuffling through the streets. They are
of an inferior stock." Surely in this notion the basis on which
was built the idea of Southern aristocracy in America — something to put against the fact of chattel slavery while it
existed. "I am brainier, wiser, shrewder.

"I am an artist. I am a person of taste."

You go into a Southern city and see there, walking along,
a very beautiful woman. You are with a Southerner. "Look,"
you cry, "how beautiful she is."

"What, a nigger beautiful?"

Or . . . "Can there be such a thing as a beautiful factory
girl?"

It is necessary, almost imperative, to build something . . .
"culture may be a way out, to make me feel more comfortable." Oh, the American women, who have had a little
luck, perhaps have got, through marriage, some man to
devote his life to money making. Women in literary clubs,
speakers brought in, a blindness got . . . oh, blessed blindness. Kit said that for a time she did it, tried to do what
is called "improve the mind." She said she took *The New
York Times,* read the Sunday book supplement, went and
bought books. She would be reading one of the books when
Tom Halsey came to see her.

This before there was a kind of break-up between them.

This before they did really get at each other a little, come for a time to a kind of understanding.

There was, at first, the question of money — how was it to be got from Tom to Kit? He made his son a generous, a more than generous, allowance, but there was in Gordon, as Kit soon found out, something not in his father. He was tight. When he had got hold of money he didn't want to let go. Kit thought that from the beginning, after Tom Halsey began to clean up, rake it in, and after he began to pitch money into the lap of his son, Tom having, as Kit also found out, a romantic notion, hidden away somewhere at the back of his head, something about a family established . . . there was a kind of humbleness in him . . . although he tried hard to stay in the background, never to push himself forward, was very careful to avoid publicity, a thing bound to destroy any man in his racket . . . humbleness based on the fact that he was shrewd enough to know that his own past . . . he having served time in jail as a small bootlegger and rumrunner, that he had himself no chance to do what is called "make it." . . .
Respectability, standing, even at the last, perhaps in a grandson if not in his own son, the Halseys beginning to be established, looked up to by respectable people. "I don't believe he ever asked himself the direct question," Kit said . . . this when disillusionment had come to her, long after the time of which we are now speaking . . . Kit getting a kind of notion into her head that may possibly, in these days, be penetrating many American heads . . . "He was puzzled. I don't think he ever thought about how some of the people he wanted secretly to be like, or to have perhaps a grandson to be like . . . you know," she said, "people like bankers, cot-

ton-mill owners . . . fellows like that, big-bugs who lived
in grand houses . . . he never stopped to ask himself, 'How
did they get theirs?' "

There was, as suggested, the question of the passage of
money, from Tom to Kit. Tom, she said, didn't want to
come right out and ask her. Tom's particular romantic slant
so bound up in an odd way with the son could certainly
not be fed in that way.

"Say, Kit, what about it, does your husband, my son,
loosen up?"

Gordon didn't. He paid his wife's hotel bill. He wanted
her to come and ask him for money. I gathered that he was
one who likes, in the presence of other men, to appear generous and open-handed. "Come on, boys, have a drink. This
one's on me." Kit . . . she certainly got wise faster and
faster after marriage to Gordon . . . said he was a check
grabber who always missed his grab. "I'd have seen him in
hell before I'd ever have asked him for a red."

She said that Tom liked to come to her room to sit and
talk. He told her a good deal about the organization he had
managed to build up, what men in his organization had to
be watched, who among the many men working for him and
with him were anxious to replace him, become the big shot
in his territory. She gathered that there were spies everywhere, men who came to him, told him what in secret was
going on within his organization, the spies perhaps watched
by other spies. In the tangled mess he had to try to keep a
clear, cool head. "You try to let them, if they will, kill one
another off. If they won't do it, you take a hand yourself."

Kit said that Tom, the big shot, so-called, in the first few
months after her marriage to the son, often sat with her for
hours. He had decided to trust her. He wanted some one

he could trust. He really wanted to ask her whether or not she had got pregnant by his son but there was in him a kind of delicacy about putting the question bluntly as there was about going into the matter of money. He sat with her and talked, very quietly, she said, often smiling softly as he told of some man within his organization he had to get . . . she thought afterwards that there must always have been killing going on, he not taking a direct hand . . . she thought he didn't take a direct hand for a long time. She said, "I was pretty green. I thought I understood a lot more than I did understand."

He sat and talked but he always left money with her. "He saw to it that I had plenty of money."

It was in a way amusing, Tom's method of giving her the money. He never gave it to her directly. When he left her presence . . . she had got his number . . . he never spoke of money to her. He had been sitting on a chair or on a couch in her living room. It is likely that during this particular period of Kit Brandon's life adventures, when she must have spent a great deal of money for clothes, for shoes and hats . . . she did not confine her purchases to the Southern industrial town but took several trips alone to New York . . . she took magazines like *The New Yorker* . . . went into select and expensive shops there. . . . She had read carefully some magazine . . . picture on an advertising page of some pretty hot baby, about her own age, perhaps stepping out of the door of an expensive-looking mansion, the woman she saw in the advertisement clad in a mink coat . . . an advertisement designed and written no doubt by some hack advertising writer, a fellow with his own ambitions . . . he no doubt figuring that if he could cut a bit deeper into the American advertising cake he could move

say from Brooklyn to Bronxville . . . hot dog . . . getting
a bit higher up in American life.

Words in the advertisement like this . . . "Slim, straight
swagger lines. A coat with casual informal elegance that
appeals so definitely to smart women, $2650."

"Boy, that for me. I'll take me a look into that." There
always remained in Kit a kind of sensible occasional going
back to the living language she had acquired as cotton-mill
girl, factory girl, five-and-ten clerk . . . taking, very sensibly, what she could get. The chances are that all through
her flush period, being Gordon's young wife, the father
hoping for a son from her, she really dressed for the man,
Tom Halsey.

She thought there was something in him that knew when
she was, as she said, rigged out top notch. When he had been
with her and he had gone she took a look, in the chair or
couch where he had been sitting. He always left it, tucked in
somewhere, not to be too easily missed. There would be
three hundred, a thousand, sometimes as much as fifteen
hundred or two thousand. "I never would say he wasn't a
pretty swell guy," she said when she was explaining all this.

But there was something peculiar, to the outsider very
interesting. Tom Halsey must always have had to fix a good
many men. There would have been county officials, federal
men to be seen. For a time, at least for several years after
prohibition came, there was more money to be made, less
risk to be run, in being an enforcement officer than in being
in the racket itself.

Tom had got a notion in his head. Money must never be
directly passed. Why? More than once the same thing has
popped up in the dealings had with politicians by big industrialists. Old stories of little black bags, the box of cigars

left in a hotel room. There is a thin layer of cigars at the top
of the box and below, hidden away under the cigars, so and
so many bills. You go into Senator Strathaway's room. It is
well to take some one with you, say a clerk. "Why the senator isn't here. He told me to meet him here. I brought him
this box of cigars." You open the box, let the clerk see the
cigars neatly laid there in the box and at that moment in
comes the senator. There is a little casual conversation and out
you go. You make a motion with your hand. "Senator, I
brought you some of my own imported cigars. I thought you
would like them."

It makes it all so very nice afterwards. There is an investi-
gation. The senator has suddenly too much money. You are
on the witness stand. "Did you or did you not, on a certain
occasion, go to the senator's room? Did you leave something
there?"

"Yes, I did. It happens I took with me my secretary. I
took the senator a box of cigars. It just happens that I opened
it in the presence of my secretary.

"And it happens also, sir, that there was in the room at the
time another. It was a hotel bell boy. He came in with a
telegram and just then the senator came in. They all heard
everything that was said. They all saw me leave. They saw
the cigars. I have always admired the senator. It is a habit
of mine to leave cigars with men I admire."

It was amusing to Kit. Afterwards she saw and heard a
good deal of it. "Of course he had to pay his way." She even
thought that, in Tom's mind, the fact of not actually passing
the money in some way cleared him. It was as though he
had said even to himself, "You see, I have not paid the man
any money.

"It happens that I was out driving in my car and I met him, a federal man or a county official. He was in his car and we both stopped. We had a conversation but nothing was said of money. He may have said something like this . . . 'well, I expect you to take care of me,' but what of that? He did not mention money nor did I. It happens that we were standing and talking at the side of the road, near a grassy bank, and I suddenly had the impulse to go and lay some money on the bank. I did not see him pick it up.

"It is obvious, is it not, that I never gave him a cent? I could go into any court in the land and swear to that."

Kit had got money, an expensive mink coat, another of squirrel . . . it always reminded her — a little guilty feeling in her — of the squirrels chattering at evening and in the early morning in the woods near her father's mountain cabin when she was a child . . . gowns and more gowns . . . two or three evening gowns, rarely used . . . her husband wanted her to put one on when she went with him to prize fights or to a wrestling match but she refused . . . expensive shoes a plenty.

Oh, what beautiful shoes are made for our American women! Where in the world can they be equalled for beauty? They are so trim — trim as were the clipper ships Americans once built to race through the seven seas. Go forth American Women. Sail blithely the seven seas.

Kit did most of her fast sailing in a trim little sports model car. From the first that was the best thing she got from her marriage, the car of her own. It took her away from marriage, let her at times forget. All day and every day she kept the car parked in the street before the hotel. She got the hotel doorman to keep a place for her, not directly in front of the hotel but across the street, where she could see it from a window of her suite. Her husband did not like driving with her. "She drives too fast." He said it made him nervous.

Effort to have and keep a feeling of loyalty to him. It must have gone on for some time. "I would like to give him a fair break. He has taken me out of the five-and-ten, out of the factories." When she was alone in their common suite, this before she told him bluntly to get one of his own . . . "If you want to get one next to mine O.K. . . . only we will keep the door between the two closed." When she was alone in the hotel suite she liked the feeling that she could look out of the window and see the car parked in the street below. She went and looked at the mink coat hanging in a closet, ran her hand over the soft fur, saw the gowns she had bought hanging there, the expensive shoes in a shoe bag hanging on the closet door, opened drawers to look at soft costly lingerie.

Then to the window to look at the car in the street below. She laughed. "It isn't so bad to live like this — on the trigger as it were." She had picked up on the floor of the bathroom of the suite, when she still shared it with her husband, a letter. "Well, well!"

But after all it wasn't unexpected and in any event she had never been very warm to him. It happened that, on the day she found the letter . . . it was late morning and he was up and gone . . . he had gone into the bathroom before leaving to arrange his tie . . . quietly, quietly, not to awaken her . . . she was awake all the time . . . she was always pretending to be asleep when he was about . . .

. . . At night saying . . . "but I am so tired. I am so sleepy, Gordon."

The letter had been kicked back under the edge of the bathtub. "Oh, my darling . . . I am so hungry to see you." There was a good deal of that sort of thing in the letter. Kit stood naked reading it and presently, when the first queer little shock had passed . . . she knew instinctively, as women always know, what one of the women in the crowd she and Gordon were always being with it was. She thought of the factory girl Sarah. The little thing now after her Gordon was rather like Sarah.

A little shock and then a sense of relief, too. "Now I can have it out with him." A certain pretense she didn't much like could be dropped.

He wouldn't dare venture an open break. He would be afraid of his father. She looked down at her own slender naked body and then reached for a towel. The letter . . . it had got wet from her wet fingers . . . the words in it were written in pencil . . . her wet fingers smeared the letters. She tore it up and sent it down the toilet. "I don't want any evidence. At bottom he will be glad enough. I'll give him a real break."

He could go ahead, get him a little hot one like Sarah, come in when he wished at night. That day when she found the letter, when she had torn it to bits, sending it down the toilet, standing over the toilet to watch the little rushing cascade of water that carried it away, she had already bathed but she ran fresh water into the tub and took another bath. It wasn't the touch of the letter. The woman who was now after her man, the one she had happened to marry, was like Sarah and she had rather admired Sarah. No doubt Gordon had said words to the woman. "My wife is a cold woman." She had been cold. She dressed slowly, going now and then to a window to look down at the car parked in the street. She had already phoned to have it brought from the garage. She was alternately smiling and then frowning, hating as all people do the necessity for plain speaking, trying to think . . . "Will I put it on the grounds of finding this letter or will I be honest?" It might work better to be angry. She was for a moment sorry that she had destroyed the letter. It would have been more simple to thrust it at him. "Here. Take this. And now get out of here." Although she had destroyed the letter it was the tone she finally adopted, thinking it would make it all somewhat easier for him. He could lie, as he did, say he knew nothing about any letter, did not know who had written it, etc., etc. There was to be sure an angry scene but it turned out as Kit wished. She did not have to sleep with him, feel his arms about her at night, go with him to prize fights and wrestling matches, run about with his crowd.

There still remained the father, Tom Halsey. She had reckoned on Gordon's not telling him, knew he wouldn't, but there was something else. She felt, in fact knew, that Tom had hoped for a child from his son's marriage. She was not pregnant. There were moments in the months after her separation from Gordon . . . before others they kept up the appearance of things being as they had been . . . in the month after the secret break Kit spent more and more time abroad in her car, sometimes driving all day alone, ranging far and wide . . . there were moments when she thought, "I could get me another man as he has got a woman." She might become pregnant. There were opportunities offered. She had stopped her car, being alone, beside a road on the crest of a hill and a young man, no doubt a salesman, came along. He stopped his car and walked over to her car, saying he had lost his way.

It was a bluff, his wanting a close look. He hung about for a few minutes, trying to make conversation.

She could have had him. There were plenty of others. Often she stopped for lunch at some hotel in a strange town, men in the dining-rooms giving her the eye. "Shall I?" She wanted, or thought she wanted to hang onto the advantage she had got, keep the flow of money from Tom Halsey coming her way. "How easy it is for any woman to fool any man," she thought.

She had it out with Tom one afternoon when they were alone together, when he had come to her rooms at the hotel. He drove her into a corner. "I have been here several times. You were not at home." "I see that you and Gordon have taken separate suites." Should she tell him about the letter?

"No." He would stick to Gordon.

"I know what he is like, but he is my son.

"There was an undertaking. When you married him you knew what he was like. You undertook to hold him. It was a job you tackled."

Kit was sitting in her room looking at Tom who was looking sharply at her. She put her head down into her hands and her shoulders shook. "Now I will have to think fast.

"This is not a Gordon with whom I have to deal." She began telling a long broken story of the efforts she and Gordon had made. They had been bitterly disappointed. She said she had been to a doctor but the doctor had said there was nothing wrong with her. She had even prayed, she said. She sat, not looking at him, and there was a long unbroken silence during which something came into her head.

It was an idea. It may have been that the idea had been in

her, had been growing in her. It was that if she could not
serve the man sitting there before her in one way there
might be another. She did not look at him but still sat with
her face in her hands. "What a bluffer I am." She made her
shoulders shake. "I am quite sure it is not going to happen.
I have wanted it too." She was remembering the long swift
drives of the last few months over many roads, often until
late at night, her husband abroad with his crowd, attend-
ing his prize fights and wrestling matches. He would be
sleeping with that new little thing he had got. It may be
that she had already got a feeling that was later to be so
strong in her. It concerned the clothes she had got to wear.
There was no place to wear them.

Money flowing in . . . nothing to do with it.

The queer loneliness of her position. "It might after all be
better to be in the factory or in the five-and-ten. There
would be people to talk with." She had been having some
such thoughts.

Thoughts also of Gordon and his crowd, his partner in
the boxing and wrestling arena venture, a little sharp-faced
man with watery eyes and a big nose. In the presence of
women he was always putting a hand up over his mouth,
whispering behind it. There was a finger missing from the
hand. He would be whispering some sex story, giggling,
the other women in the party protesting and also giggling.
The man's name was Harry . . . "Oh, you Harry, you dirty
thing, Harry." Well, the man was dirty — in some queer way
all the men and women among Gordon's friends and ac-
quaintances were dirty.

There were sometimes wrestlers and fighters brought up
into the Gordon suite. They had seemed cleaner.

There was a little cry in Kit that day she sat with Tom.

She managed to get a kind of broken half sob into her voice. "If you want Gordon to get another woman I'll get out.

"I'd like to stick to you, though."

She did not want him to question Gordon. "He has been hurt by it just as I have," she said, meaning to make it seem a mutual sorrow.

She did not look up when she heard him get up from his chair and start toward the door and at the door he turned and came back to her. He touched her shoulders with his hand. "What do you want? What do you mean by sticking to me?" he asked, and in a broken voice she tried to tell him. She wanted him to let her become one of his drivers. "You have done so much for me.

"I would do anything to be of some use to you."

She said the words and waited. It was odd. She had not thought definitely of what she wanted until she began speaking. To be sure she had heard, from Gordon and others . . . when he was with his own crowd Gordon was always speaking of the dangers in his father's racket, always acting a bit mysterious, trying to give the impression that he also constantly plunged into danger. He did not speak of it as his father's business. "In our business," he said, "you never know from one day to another when you will be bumped off."

"And you want that . . . you want to drive for me?" Tom said.

"Yes," she said. Still she did not look at him. She heard him moving toward the door. "You know what risks you will run?"

"Yes," she said again and, "I'll see," he said. She thought he would let her do it. He had agreed to the marriage between herself and Gordon, wanting to use her. That was his way of life, to use others. If he could not use her in one way he would in another. When he had gone she got to her feet and half danced about in her room. "I'm going to get a real chance now," she thought. She looked forward with joy to the possibilities of a life of danger to be taken on in exchange for the queer half-dead false life she had been living since her marriage with Gordon.

CHAPTER THIRTEEN

KIT had begun a new life. She quit being a wife. It is likely that Tom Halsey never discussed with his son the matter of what he thought was wrong between Kit and Gordon. His attitude toward the son may, from the first, have been mixed, elements of sincere hatred and contempt overlaid with hope. "Why don't he? Why don't he?"

Why don't he what?

"Why don't he be, or try to be, what I am not, what I want him to be?"

It may be that he had hoped, through his son's new wife, to arrive at something deeply desired. It is unlikely that he had ever in his life thought much outside self. You can't if you are out after success.

You have got to go get it, go get it, go get it.

He may have thought . . . "She has gone up-stage on me." That night when Gordon brought Kit to Kate's house and he walked with her he had accepted her.

"She is, on the whole, rather like me.

"She isn't a softy. She knows what my son is.

"All right. I'll take her on."

Kit felt that, after the talk she had with her husband's

father . . . she had tried to work the feminine line on him
. . . that business of putting her face in her hands, making
her shoulders shake . . .

It hadn't worked. She decided that was true after he left.
It was all mixed, a puzzling mixture of thoughts and emotions in her, too. She had put up the bluff of crying while he
was with her but after he left she did cry.

There were so many things to be decided. He hadn't said
whether or not her proposal that, if she couldn't serve in one
way, as a breeding animal to make new and nobler Halseys, she might serve in another, would be accepted.

And then, a day or two later, he did accept. He came
again to her room, stepped inside the door, smiled, a funny
cold little smile, as though to say . . . "O. K. then . . . no more
long intimate conversations between us . . . You want in
on my racket. Very well . . . I'll let you in." The above words
certainly not said. "You go to see Kate," he said. "She'll
tell you what you are to do.

"Good-bye."

He left as he had come and for a long time she saw no more
of him and but little of her husband.

Her bills at the hotel . . . there was a garage connected
. . . gas and repairs for her cars, meals charged to her
room . . . she still occasionally bought gowns, shoes, etc.
. . . these also charged . . . the bills were paid by some one.
She thought it would not have been Gordon. "Not that tight-
wad," she told herself. For a time she did not go to Kate and
had the feeling, as regards Tom, that he was in some queer
new way keeping an eye on her. As he had spies by whom
he checked on others, so also on her. As he had disposed
of one woman for the son's sake, so now another.

He would be wanting to get something on her. There was

in the man, as there is and must be in all men in any civilization founded on gain, man always trying to climb up over
the shoulders of man, a part of the show of success in such
a life so often centered upon some woman . . . women
enough apparently eager for it . . . so often the successful
man, big money maker, making of his woman . . . wife or
mistress, a kind of clothes rack . . . there was hatred a-
plenty. Kit knew it as regards Tom. The knowledge was
down inside her, stirring down inside her as though he
had impregnated her, not with the grandchild wanted from
her but with an unspoken threat.

"If my son is not man enough to put you in your place,
I am."

It would have been the very foundation of Tom Halsey's
philosophy and no man has ever lived who did not have to
form some kind of philosophy by which to keep on living,
that life is a game, nothing more. If you can win, you win.

You draw close to others only to use them. What else is
there to it all? The racket Tom was in was tough enough.
Who would know that better than himself? Unlike the big
business man, company promoter, Wall Street stock jobber,
organizer of huge chains of retail stores . . . small merchants in thousands of towns swept ruthlessly aside . . .
water power magnates, power sleeping in rivers grabbed,
huge blocks of heavily watered stock thrown on the market
. . . the people in turn grabbing it . . .

"You can't let yourself be sentimental about the suckers.
We are the builders. Wait. You'll see. In the end we are the
benefactors. There is a new kind of world coming. We are
making it. We are making it."

None of that for Tom. It did not matter how he had begun, he had landed, as leader, man of power over other

men, in a business outside the law. There is no doubt that
he occasionally said to himself, as he had once said in conversation with Kit, as Al Capone, big shot in the criminal
world of Chicago, is reported to have said . . .

"Well, they wanted it. I only gave them what they
wanted."

Others enough saying it.

Novelists saying it . . . "I admit that I am just a commer-
cial writer. I'm no highbrow. I give 'em what they want.
I only hand them out the rosy pap they want, the suckers."

Writers for the movies . . . "I'm only doing this to get
some dough. When I have got what dough I need I'm
going to do some straight honest work."

Merchants doing it. Politicians doing it. Capitalists doing
it. Newspaper publishers doing it.

Oh, for the higher life.

Tom wouldn't have had even the satisfaction that must
have come to Capone, people making a half hero of
him, romanticizing his obvious cruelty as their fathers did
that of a Jesse James or Billy the Kid . . . the newspapers,
movies and radio speakers, shrewdly enough, playing up to
the passion always in masses of people for some sort of a
big man.

Oh, how easy, easy, to make fascism here . . . hunger of
people to find and follow the big shot, getting thereby some
little feeling of bigness in self.

But Tom Halsey was not a big big shot. He was a little big
shot. He knew that. He was cautious, careful, quiet talking,
doing in the meantime very well by himself.

He was suspicious of women.

There was the woman Kate. It is unlikely that his son's
suspicions in regard to the father's relations with the woman

who had suckled the son were founded on anything.
Kate was Kate. She was the woman who makes the
final, the absolute surrender to some man. It is unlikely
that she ever got from Tom Halsey anything beyond this
privilege of surrender. It is a privilege deeply desired by some
women.

There came an odd period in Kit's life. It would be hard
to say how much she ever knew of what went on in her at
that time. She did not, at once, as Tom had directed, go to
Kate. For the time being she stayed as she was, living
in the suite in the hotel, driving in her car. She took
long drives to neighboring towns, sometimes staying over
night in some hotel in some strange town. She talked at
length later of that period in her life. She had an experience
that must be common to many people. It had happened that,
in the conversation with Tom, when she told him of the
hopelessness of his looking forward to a grandson as a result of the son's marriage with herself, when she told him
she had been to a doctor who had told her that she was all
right, she had done something people often do when they
are lying. She had purposely prevented conception happening as a result of her always reluctant relations with Gordon, not as she afterwards frankly said, wanting a son by
him, but in the moment when she was telling Tom that she
had been to a doctor, when she was sitting before him, her
face in her hands, her shoulders shaking by an effort of her
own will in trying to convey to him the impression that he
was facing a broken-hearted woman, she had made a slip.
 "I was momentarily a damn fool. I gave him the name of
the doctor I was telling him I had been to see. It would be
as funny as hell if it hadn't been at the moment such a seri-

ous slip. You see, he hadn't asked me for the doctor's name.
I just put it in. There is a thing happens to you when you
are lying. You get to thinking you are good and then you
slip."

There was an office building in the industrial town of the
Upper South in which Kit lived with Gordon. It was near
the hotel in which Kit and Gordon lived. It was a building
for the most part taken up with the offices of doctors. Kit
said . . . "I'm damned.

"The truth is that of course as soon as we were married
and Gordon thought he had me, he found out he didn't.

"He kept going after me for a while but presently found
out that he wasn't getting anywhere with it."

Kit explained her technique. She said that when she could
no longer get away with the game of having a headache
or trying to put it over on him that she was ill of women's
historic illness when she wasn't, she tried the game of
being just listless. "I sure gave him a dirty deal," she said,
and I gathered that there were several rows, Gordon tramping angrily up and down in their bedroom. "He slugged
me once," she said.

"Of course he was a lot stronger physically than I was.
I was sitting in a chair, in my nightgown, and he came
over to me and putting his big hands under my arm pits
jerked me to my feet. I had sure been pulling the lada-dada
on him. He jerked me up and then he hit me. He knocked
me down.

"Then he picked me up from the floor and threw me
across the room and I landed on the bed. . . . It was the
only time he came at all near getting me," she said.

"So I was talking that time to his father, handing him
the bunk. I guess I had been pretty lonely for a long time. I

used to sit a lot by the window in our little living room and
look down into the street, you know, always quite a lot
going on down there . . . maybe just a young mountain
boy come into town and trying to make him a pick-up of a
young town girl. She might have been a girl working in the
big cigarette factory there was in that town and she was off
for a Saturday afternoon. She'd be walking up and down
the main street as girls do, you know, wanting to be picked
up and not wanting . . .

"She wouldn't anyway be wanting that country boy with
his Jaky ways and he'd be trying but afraid to really go right
up to her and I'd be sitting there and watching that and
other things going on in the street. I had got fixed on my
mind the name of a doctor that was on the window of that
office building, so I sprung it on Tom when I was giving
him that line about not being able to have a child and
how it wasn't my fault.

"I gave him the doctor's name. I just put it in when I
was talking. The doctor's name was Ashley.

"You see, it turned out, he was a dentist," Kit said.

She began to drive for Tom, getting, as he had suggested,
her orders through Kate. She never did get Kate's attitude
toward herself very clear. "I think she liked me. She might
have done me dirt if Tom had told her to, but I don't
know. She'd tell me where to go, what drive I was to
make, where I was to deliver the stuff, she'd give me money
for expenses . . . I got as much as fifty to a hundred dollars for trips. . . . She never asked me for an expense account. . . . 'Oh, I guess thirty-five will cover it' I'd say and
then, sometimes, when I was leaving her . . . we never mentioned the names of either Gordon or Tom when we were

talking . . . we just talked business . . . she'd stand looking at me.

"I'd be by the door going out to get into my car. I always
went into her house by the kitchen door, never into that
room where I went that time with Gordon. Sometimes I'd
hear voices of men, some of Tom's crowd, talking in there.
I'd stand by the door looking at Kate and she'd be looking
at me.

"I think she wanted to say, 'Cut it out . . . get out . . . this
is too thick for you,' but she didn't say it.

"She must have known about Gordon and me, that I was
through with him, that I'd never go back to him, you know,
in that way, that something in me couldn't, and perhaps she
knew that Tom would only wait until he had something
on me or was ready to get rid of me in another way but
knew also that I was bull-headed too.

"She'd stand looking at me with a funny troubled look
in her eyes and I'd look at her and then I'd go."

At first Kit didn't act as pilot for strings of liquor cars
as she did later but took out single loads. When she began
driving, making a business of it, the late fall had come.
Thanksgiving had passed and Christmas holidays were
ahead. Birthday of the Christ to be again celebrated.

There was a good deal of so-called good liquor, imported stuff, brought in from the West Indies, landed in
some of the innumerable bays and inlets along the gulf
coast or on the North or South Carolina coast . . . Tom
Halsey's grip on his own territory at that time being strong
enough so that it was better for other big-little shots to
make a deal with him . . . otherwise danger always of
high-jacking, some of Tom's crowd doing the job . . .

Better pay the price. Get it through.

Plenty of big business men, politicians, professional men, big and little, even sometimes judges in law courts where you would be tried and sentenced if they caught you taking it to them . . . all of these clamoring for it, in big towns, little towns, in clubs, in hotels. Interior cities in Pennsylvania, Ohio, Indiana, Illinois, Iowa clamoring. All of this during the Harding-Coolidge times. Plenty of money flowing.

You went to a certain town and to a certain hotel and a man came for you in a car. He might be a local man, even a deputy sheriff of some interior county. There were a good many deals made with such men, in some cases all of the officials of a county taken in. Tom Halsey was an adept at such work. The idea was that there would be no selling or delivery of liquor to the citizens of such a county. "We'll see to it that you do not get into any trouble with your local people." There was always some money passed. Such local deals didn't cost so much.

Kit would be taken out to some country road, perhaps to some lonely farmhouse, and there was a big car, loaded and waiting. This might be at nine or ten in the evening. In the weeks of waiting, after Tom told her to go to Kate and before she did go, she had been making an extensive study of road maps. She said . . . "I was green at first, had to take risks, keep to the big highways, take a chance on just getting through anyway, but after I went into the business, as I was alone most of the time, often having to stay for three or four days in some little town, some load I was to pick up having been delayed, I had plenty of time to study."

She became an expert on the roads of several states, knew

short-cuts and the condition roads were likely to be in in all
kinds of weather. When she was in a small town waiting
. . . one of Tom's men or one of the law officials who had
been fixed had come to her and had passed her word that a
load she was to handle had been delayed and that she might
have to wait two or three days . . . she did not stay about
the town but sent word that she wanted a car and spent
the time in studying the roads in that section of the country.
Often on such days she drove three or four hundred miles,
taking notes in a little book she kept. She was like a river
pilot in the early days of steamer travel on the Mississippi.
As he studied forming and shifting sandbars in the river,
stages of the water, snags that might drive a hole through
his boat's hull, studied cut-offs, knew when they were safe
to run, studied tall trees and bluffs along the river, getting
fixed in his mind points by which to steer on dark nights,
so she studied road construction, detours, marked down
places into which to dodge when pursued by law officers
who were not fixed or couldn't be fixed, she knew which dirt
roads were clay and almost impassable in wet weather and
which were sand and could be run over, knew even, eventu-
ally and after she had been for two or three years, sometimes
acting as pilot for fleets of loaded cars, sometimes herself
taking a load . . .

She knew where on some main road there was a sudden
and just noticeable by-pass, a little dirt road that ran up into
a wood, where you could dodge up, cut off your engine and
lights, get out of the car and creep down near to the road
. . . "If they get the car and the load they won't get
me" . . . lie low, watch the car or cars of the law go roaring past . . .

. . . "Where the hell's that bitch got to now?"

. . . Knew even farm roads, leading past perfectly innocent farmhouses and barns.

"On clear nights, if there was a moon, you could turn
off lights, slip in, slide past house and barn, get out of the car
to open farm gates, go down across a meadow, through
a strip of woodland, open another gate. You could get out
on to another road. They'd be after you maybe back there
on the road you'd left."

There might be some honest federal man or local sheriff
who was out laying for you. He had parked a car across the
entrance to a narrow bridge, was stopping all cars on that
road that night, some deputy he had with him having
slipped the word to some one in Tom's crowd.

There was in Kit an odd loyalty to a vague thing she called
"the crowd." It wasn't that she ever knew many of the
men of Tom's crowd personally. She didn't. There was however a kind of belief, a feeling running through all the men
she met so casually. "We take care of our own." Many of the
men in Tom's organization had been poor mountain whites.
They were often illiterate. Some, like Kit, had been factory
hands. They felt themselves at war, against some vague
thing — society — the law-and-order people.

"Laws for themselves. Laws by which to gouge and rob
us," they would have said.

She was, had been all her life, deeply lonely. It is likely
that, after she went to work for Tom, knowing in a vague
way that he was out to get her, there was in her no
special loyalty to the so-called big-shot of that particular
section of America's outlaw world, partitioned as it was all
over America — little big shots and big big shots . . . the
big shots, little and big, getting the gravy but neverthe-
less . . .

Men of the so-called criminal classes. . . . There is a man lying in hospital. He has been taken for a ride. He was thrown out of a car on a country road or on some quiet suburban street outside some big city. A man with a sub-machine gun riddled his body with bullets. He was picked up and hurried to a hospital.

The law speaking . . . "You tell us. Come on, buddy, you tell us."

"You go to hell. My own crowd'll take care of this."

Loyalty to some vague, never definitely defined thing. "Well, what else have I got to be loyal to?" There is a loyalty somewhat of the same sort in factories. It is so little understood, not taken into account by union labor men, by reformers, by radicals, by revolutionists. Little factory girls and often badly treated factory men. "No, I'll not go out on strike. I don't trust those who ask me to go on strike either.

"Sure I know the boss has gypped us.

"I guess maybe I'd do the same if I was in his place. I dunno.

"I got to be loyal to some one.

"I guess maybe he ain't such a bad guy."

When Kit began, got into the game, it was a year when there had been early and deep snows all over the Upper South mountain country. She went rigged out now, she said, to her first job. There was . . . it lasted, all through her connection with Tom's crowd . . . a notion that she was in some way closely connected with Tom, to them the big shot. There was even a notion that she was Tom's daughter.

She played up to it.

And there was something else. She got it, understood it

shrewdly. If you are a woman and associated with the sort
of men she did at that time associate with . . . she thought
it went for most men . . . and if you wear fine, well-tailored
clothes, an expensive fur coat, becoming hats, expensive
shoes, there is something happens to them in relation to
you.

"It gets them. They can't get gay." Kit had got her own
sort of cynicism all right. "Most men, when they are out on
the hunt, as most men are most of the time, go after working girls. You look at the foremen in the factories where I
worked. They nearly all did it.

"And nearly all the rich young fellows and the sons of
the well-to-do merchants, etc., in the towns where the factories are.

"And even the cops in the towns."

To the end it was Kit's notion that the law enforcement
officials, great and small, and particularly during the prohibition era, were not too far removed from the law break-
ers. "And the people who buy the stuff, too," she said. "If
we're so bad what about the ones who pay for the stuff we
run to them?"

And there was the notion Tom had once or twice brought
into his conversations with her — this before the break between them, while he still thought of her as the possible
instrument for the creation of a new and more highly respected race of Halseys — he having built up the money
foundation for such respectability . . . he also not being
lacking in shrewdness . . . the notion that, almost without
exception, the founders of almost all the so-called great
families in America, from colonial times down, had been
law-breakers.

It was a fact, obviously beyond denial, that all through her law-breaking days . . . the thing at first manifest throughout all the ramifications of Tom's organization . . . gradually getting across to the public in one whole section of America, a section embracing several states . . . that Kit's flair for clothes helped her. It helped to create the tradition, the half-mystical romance that surrounded her figure. She felt it in country and city hotel clerks, in men in hotel lobbies, in workmen in garages, in the often illiterate men of Tom's crowd, in tobacco-chewing deputy sheriffs, who had been fixed. All of these she thought paid a kind of reluctant but real respect to what the clothes she wore led them to think she must be.

"They thought I was some kind of a strange, new sort of big shot."

And there was for her also the satisfaction of at least having some use for the clothes bought with the money that had been showered down upon her. After all there had been no point, no fun, in doing what Gordon had, crudely, wanted her to do . . . the putting on of evening clothes to go with him to a prize fight or a wrestling match or in strutting about in really well-made clothes before the members of such a crowd, men and women, as he ran with.

Surely much more fun, excitement, even self-respect . . . a thing she always did passionately want . . . in really using the clothes to some purpose . . . to appear, say on a rainy November or early December night, when it was raining after a time of snow, at some lonely seeming farmhouse, hidden away on some little dirt road near a town in Southwest Virginia or East Tennessee . . .

Being like a professional model, stepped out of the advertising pages of *The New Yorker*.

There was a car loaded and ready to be run out . . . it would be high-priced imported stuff, bound say for Cincinnati or Charleston, W. Va. . . . to be got through before daylight the next morning . . . it raining hard . . . there would be tricky mountain roads to be got over, heavy fogs lying over the mountaintops . . . the better to serve her purpose. There would be the ride out to the farmhouse from some rather dreary small town hotel, at which she had arrived early that afternoon. She would have come by train.

Oh, the dreariness of some of the rooms! There would be the kind of cheap furniture common to so many hotel rooms in the smaller towns. There would be a note for her. Like a criminal she constantly changed her name . . . Kit Brandon, alias Mary Wetherby, alias Sally Smith, alias Mrs. Eugene Masters, alias Mrs. Erskine Hemmingway. After she had taken a few trips she worked out a little scheme. She sent herself a telegram that would arrive ahead of her. Let's say her run was to be from some little town on the northern border of North Carolina and her load was to be delivered in Charleston, West Virginia. The telegram read . . . "Jim, your husband, badly hurt in accident at Charleston, West Virginia. Come at once."

She was stopped by a policeman in one of the streets of Roanoke, Virginia, on one of her early trips, was rather hurrying through a street along which many cars were parked . . . It was a wet rainy night and a uniformed policeman stopped her . . .

Men were backing cars out from a curb ahead. There was no chance to give her own machine the gun and run for it. The car was loaded with rather expensive stuff. There was a policeman in the road and two others standing near by on the sidewalk. She was green then, new at the game and her heart began to beat heavily. Her hands were trembling.

It turned out to be a false alarm. "Please drive carefully through here," the cop said. There was some kind of children's entertainment going on in a church. The incident however started her brain to working. The telegram was to flash on any federal man or cop who might stop her to search her car. She never did use one of the telegrams but once and then it worked. This was after she had got better at the game, her nerves steadier, herself leaning out of the car, speaking politely to the man who had stopped her. She made her voice as closely as she could an earnest pleading one. "Please read this."

The man was standing in a dark road with the telegram in his hand, his flashlight making a brilliant spot of light on the yellow paper. "Please, please, don't stop me, don't delay me."

"What is your husband?" the man asked solicitously.

"He's chief of police in Charleston. I've been away on a visit. His car was struck by a fire truck going to a fire."

It happened that the federal man had blocked a narrow bridge, not far from the place where she was stopped, and the man to whom she handed the telegram sent another man with a car to clear the way for her.

She was in one of the little hotel rooms. In spite of the reputation she was presently to get . . . the romanticizing of her figure by the newspapers . . . herself heralded as a desperate character, bold, beautiful, dangerous, etc., etc., she never did carry a gun or any sort of weapon. Often, in the fall and winter months, she arrived in such a place when it was raining or snowing. She had brought books and sat reading and looking out at sad-enough small-town streets.

There was the dreariness of such rooms, the curious smell that gets into the wall paper, into the chairs, into the often half-soiled bed coverings and window curtains, smell of generations of travelling salesmen, an old cigar butt pushed into the corner of the little clothes closet by a slovenly maid, an empty corn liquor bottle with the cork gone left in the rickety chest-of-drawers. She went to sit by the window that looked into the street. "God," she said in speaking of that time, "if I hadn't to look forward to the excitement and danger of the drive ahead, I'd have gone crazy."

There was from the first something creeping in on her. On fair days she could escape, make an arrangement for a car, get out of the hotel, drive in country roads, build up her knowledge of that particular section, but there were many days not fair and it wasn't wise for her to be too much seen . . . small-town men, retail merchants, lawyers, etc., often with little enough to do . . . the winter days in such places passing drearily, respectability that would not permit them to get drunk except occasionally in secret . . . no movies in the daytime . . . no fishing in winter in near-by streams. . . the hunting season at an end . . . they sizing her up . . . "Say, did you see that? Now, who the hell can that one be? What's she doing here?"

"Boy, there's some swell-looking dame. Boy, wouldn't you like," etc., etc.,

Curiosity aroused. It was better to keep, as much as possible, out of sight. The less people notice you, think about you, the better. There was a curious persistent loneliness, it growing on her, getting into her being like a disease, only broken by the excitement of her work.

She thought of things read in newspapers, stories of criminals hiding out. Some man of the criminal class had made a haul. He had held up a bank or a bank messenger, had kidnapped the child of some rich man, had got a lot of swag, had got away with it.

Time to lie low now, keep out of sight. Kit, always an imaginative one, always a bit more mental than physical, found herself, in imagination, being some such a one. She had books with her but couldn't read. She moved restlessly about in the narrow quarters of some such dreary hotel room, sat by the window with a book in her hand, tried to concentrate on its pages. If, as sometimes happened, she had to stay in such a place for two or three days, the weather bad . . . it might be a place of two or three thousand people, the hotel a flimsy frame building . . . she got half hysterical. She tried to explain it. "It wasn't outside. It was inside me," she said. As suggested, she identified herself with some imagined desperate person, that is to say with some real criminal, who has done some desperate deed and was in hiding. She tried to reason with herself. "Suppose I am caught, arrested, thrown into jail . . . what of it?"

She had no family with standing in this or any community to be lost. "It just happens that I am in a certain business? There would be no such business if people didn't want it. I am the same girl who once worked in a factory, who worked in a five-and-ten. I haven't hurt any one, stolen anything. There was in her no feeling of being morally corrupt. She sat sometimes asking herself questions. "Would I give up what I have got, go back, say into a shoe factory or a cotton mill, live, as I did live, often as lonely as I am

now, work for some mill owner for ten or twelve dollars a
week?" There was always, in Kit, as perhaps also in
Tom Halsey, consciousness of some kind of power in self. In
some vague way she knew that, even when she had been half
illiterate, there had been a kind of consciousness in her. It
might possibly have come out of her mountain ancestry. "I
am a woman walking the earth as men walk the earth." In
great numbers of the workers, among whom she had formerly lived, there was a curious humbleness that was
not in her. She was, after all, Southern and in great
numbers of Southerners, particularly among the poor, the
white poor, there is a kind of humbleness . . . it might
have come down into them out of old slavery days . . .
feeling that there are certain people, rich, holding seemingly important positions, large estates, plantations, mills,
etc. . . . "They aren't the same as we are."

"The hell they're not."

She had never said it. She felt it.

The thing Kit had often felt, never quite defined in her
own mind, was defined often enough in things heard.
When she was a mill girl or a clerk in the five-and-ten,
others talking. The others read newspapers. They went to
the movies. The rich, the ones up above them, mill owners,
politicians, prominent men and women of all sorts in the
mill towns were like the movie stars in Hollywood. "Their
doing what they do is not like our doing it." The idea was
in some indefinable way like that. "They must be smart.
I'm not smart." There was a politician accused of stealing
a million dollars from the state. He laughed. "Why, you
are mistaken. I didn't steal a million. I stole two million."

There were the poor, often scrupulously honest, curiously
religious, who gave him a kind of admiration. They went to

the polls and voted for him. "After all, he's smart. He's a big man."

Or he got into trouble, denied his guilt, was tried, convicted and they were sorry for him. They said of the man who owned the mill, "It's not his fault." There was for Kit the persistent question . . . "Would it have been better for me to stay where I was, in some factory or in a five-and-ten . . .

". . . wearing myself out for some guy?

"No, I don't care. I'm glad I'm what I am."

She turned for relief to the world outside, to the window of the hotel room. There were a few people going along in the street. It rained. The hotel stood at a street intersection and on another corner was the town post office. There was a filling station on a third corner.

There were little pictures of life, caught thus, as though she looked through a magnifying glass. On certain of such days her brain seemed terribly alive. "How curiously separated I am from everybody.

"Is there a wall between me and others?

"I had a husband but he was no husband, a father but he was no father. I had a few friends" . . . She thought of Agnes, Sarah and other workwomen to whom she had once felt close. "There is something that separates people, curiously, persistently, in American life." She did not think the thought definitely. As is true of so many other obscure people in America she felt it. There were times when she terribly wanted a man, not primarily as sex comrade, but as real comrade, someone to creep close to, feel close to, perhaps even a little to command her, direct her. If it were true that she had—as the newspapers afterwards, when she became more or less notorious, persistently proclaimed — her own beauty there was a desire to have her beauty mean something definite and real to another, unlike herself a male being.

There were afternoons when she sat thus in such a hotel room and cried. She became annoyed with herself. She tried to concentrate on what life there was in the street outside. A farmer drove up and parked his car in the street and got out. He was quite an old man, tall, poorly dressed. His car was an ancient Model T Ford. He got out and started to cross the street and his wife also got out of the car. She was fat, old and awkward but he did not offer to help her. She stumbled and half fell and then caught, with her old hand, the door of the car. "Why doesn't he help her? Why doesn't he?"

The wife followed her man across the street and in at the door of the post office. It was something to think about.

"Are there people, all over the world, always from the beginning of life to the end of life, lonely? What makes it so?

"Is the man, down there in the street, merely brutal?

"No.

"It may be he is only one who can't break some shell about himself. It may be I am like that.

"Will it ever happen to me that some one will come and break it for me?"

There was a young man, hardly more than a boy, who worked in a filling-station. He wore his cap on the side of his head. Cars kept coming and departing. He filled gas tanks; he made remarks to people. People leaned out at the windows of cars and laughed at him and with him. Now he was wiping a windshield. What a fellow! He did a little jig, whistled, sang snatches of songs. It was good to see him, to sit watching him — good, good. He was like a little bird hopping about, chirping, picking his crumbs of relationship.

Presently in the rain there came along the street a young woman. She had on a bright green raincoat and carried an umbrella. There was no car stopping at the filling-station at just that moment and the young filling-station man had gone inside his brightly painted little house but he had evidently been watching through a window.

He hopped out. He greeted the woman. She was young and quite pretty. She came to him and there was a moment of conversation and then he took money out of his pocket and gave it to her and she started away but he called her back.

He looked about, up and down the street. "They are married. They are a young bride and groom," Kit told herself. He caught her into his arms and kissed her. She protested but she was glad, happy. She made a pretense of hitting him, slapping him with her open hand, and then, half running, disappeared out of Kit's line of vision and the young filling-station man stood in the rain before his little house and danced another jig.

The night came. It was a relief. At eight-thirty the man, a deputy sheriff, came for her. He told her afterwards, when they were in the car going to the place where they were to pick up her load, that he had told the hotel clerk that she was employed by the government. He had given the fellow to understand that she was a detective.

"How cute!"

She didn't like the man, detested him. He perhaps tried

to make up to her, get her friendly, but she sat in the car
in silence or answered his sallies with monosyllables. She
was rigged out all right, not gaudily, but the clothes she
wore had a certain air. He was awed, felt embarrassed, was
glad when they had got to the place to which he was to
take her.

There was a farmhouse, and she went in, the deputy ac-
companying her to the door. "Well, I'll say good night. This
is the place I was to bring you." He had done his job, had
brought her to the place. He was to have told her any
important news of the road, if there were any federal men
about, any roads he knew of being blocked. He knew of
none, was glad to escape, had earned his particular little
cut in the graft. It was time for him to get back to town,
sit away the evening perhaps at the back of some drugstore with other men of the town, looking as important as
he could. Men would come in, merchants and others, to
discuss affairs, politics, prohibition, etc. He would be asked
questions. The thing to do was to look mysterious. It made
the others think you knew a lot of things you weren't going
to tell.

"Good night," Kit said coldly enough.

"Gee, I'll bet she's a big-timer all right."

Kit went on, into the farmhouse.

There were people sitting in the farmhouse waiting for
her arrival. There was the farmer, an unsuccessful man, a
man of fifty, unshaven, a little frightened. He owed money
at the bank in town and felt he had been forced into this
new thing, this law-breaking. Nowadays there were all sorts
of mysterious people appearing at his house. They came usually at night.

His house was on a little-used dirt road that led up into hills. A man, a young fellow, had arrived there on the night before, had driven his car into the farmer's barn. It was at three in the morning and raining. He had come to the kitchen door, knocked loudly and it happened the farmer's wife was ill. His daughter had to go downstairs and after the farmer built a fire in the kitchen stove the daughter had to get the fellow something to eat. "This is another new one," the farmer thought. He was a rough-looking one, young and strong and with one eye gone. He demanded bacon, eggs, and coffee. He stood in the kitchen swearing. "God damn such a night."

The farmer went out into a shed to get wood for the kitchen stove, leaving his daughter in the kitchen with that fellow. She was but half clad. She was pretty. The farmer had two sons but they had left home, had gone to some distant industrial town to get jobs in factories. He came back into the kitchen, his arms loaded with firewood and there was something wrong.

There was a curious something in the air, fright, indignation. The daughter was leaning over the stove and when the farmer entered she turned her face to him. The fellow had said something to her, had even perhaps touched her with his hands, as Kit, when she was as yet little more than a child, had once been touched. Pictures out of life thus repeating themselves.

"But why did I let myself get into this?"

The farmer's wife had not been well. She was a small thin woman with a curious yellow complexion. The doctor said it was her liver. Doctor bills to be paid, interest on the loan at the bank in town to be paid. The farmer's sons did not know what he had let himself in for. The youngest one would say nothing but, if he knew, the older one would raise hell.

"All right, give up the damn place then."

There would be a quarrel between father and son.

"I won't. This farm belonged to my father and before that to his father. I am master in my own house. I'll do as I please."

The man had a suspicion that more than one of the fellows of Tom's crowd, coming to the house in the night, had said insulting things to his daughter. She was like her mother, a silent one. Once when he was awake at night he had heard the daughter crying in her bed.

Kit came into the house, felt the atmosphere of the place, as she more and more in her loneliness began to feel such things, said little, stood a moment by the fire.

"Is the car ready?"

"Yes, Miss."

The daughter in the room, looking at her, at her clothes. The daughter was a young thing, not more than sixteen, with a slender young body and a strange frightened look in her eyes. "She could be real pretty," Kit thought. She was embarrassed by something in the child's eyes. It was admiration, envy. The farmer was awkwardly pushing a chair toward Kit. "Won't you sit, Miss? It's a terrible night out." Outside the rain was turning to snow. The roads would be dangerously slick. It would be a tough night for Kit's drive.

"All the better," Kit was on the road. She was driving rapidly, recklessly through snow, half-rain. To get out of North Carolina into Virginia there was a high mountain to cross. Then she had to cross another to get from Virginia into West Virginia. Silent sleeping towns to go whirling through.

She would be driving a very powerful car, heavily loaded. There was a slogan she had made for herself in regard to driving. "If you come to a dangerous place, a slippery road, sheer drop of perhaps several hundred feet at one side of the road, don't cut down on your speed. Aim it! Shoot! Go across at speed!

"Control with the motor, not the brake."

She had got a kind of philosophy. "If you are going to get smashed you're going to get smashed." She knew, felt Tom Halsey, as in some way of his own, having her on the spot.

"All right. I'll show him.

"I'll show him who's the best driver he's got."

Well enough she knew that there were plenty of so-called tough fellows in Tom's crowd. "All right. Let's see if any of them can make a better record than I can in getting the stuff through."

The night was black but she was clad in the warm luxurious fur coat. At last there was some sense to the expensive mink coat she had got with the Halsey money. There was a high plateau to be crossed, the road covered with ice so that she had to keep one wheel off the pavement, finding partly unfrozen mud mixed with gravel in which at least one of the wheels could get some traction.

"Give it to her. If we smash, we smash." She had got a kind of personal feeling about the machine she drove. It seemed beautifully alive to her. There was an exhilaration, a kind of half madness. Sometimes as she drove thus, every moment taking the chance of throwing her life away, she talked aloud to the machine. In a sense she loved it. "Come on, boy," she cried. There was a kind of drunkenness — half insane determination to get through. From the very first she began to establish a reputation in the minds of others of Tom's crowd. Word of her exploits was whispered about. "God, what a driver.

"She puts the stuff through," was the word whispered about.

CHAPTER FOURTEEN

KIT had been driving for two adventurous years.
There was a notion she had got.

It concerned the roads at night. She was always
running at night, in or out of some city or big
town. She worked winter and summer through rainstorms,
moonlight, through hot nights, cold nights, road-frozen
nights. She was more and more alone. She grew in realiza-
tion of the loneliness of nights, the laying-up, hiding-out, in
lonely little hotels. She got a feeling that there was no day,
only nights.

She had got into the habit of reading books. What else was
there to do? She was becoming more and more known and
it was better not to be seen abroad in streets of towns. She
read books that told about early adventurers in America,
the pioneers who went out of the East to open up the West,
western railroad builders, builders of bridges, books about
men who bound all of America together, by railroad and
telegraph lines.

The pony express riders on western plains. Sometimes at
night, when she was half hiding out in some little town and
darkness had settled over the streets she crept out of the

hotel to go to a movie. She said that at such times she put on one of the cheap little dresses she always carried in her bag, such a dress as a working girl ought to wear. Men spoke to her, tried to pick her up. There were many little adventures on such nights.

There was one with a shy little man, perhaps ten years older than herself, and she thought the whole thing was due to loneliness. The man might have been a clerk in a grocery or a drug store.

He followed her out of a movie where he had happened to sit beside her and, realizing that he was following her . . . he had looked at her with such a shy hungry look in the theatre, she did not return to her hotel but went walking in the sleeping residence streets of the town.

The man followed. She didn't quite know herself what she was up to. She thought it might have been kind of defiance of Tom Halsey, whom now she so seldom saw and never spoke with. Occasionally she returned to the hotel where she had lived with Gordon and where she still kept her suite of rooms. Either Gordon or Tom paid. She didn't know which. Once or twice she saw her husband, who seemed afraid of her. "How are you?" he asked, meeting her in the hotel corridor. There was a look of fear in his eyes. She didn't know what he was afraid of.

"Oh, I'm all right. How are you?" He hurried away.

She thought Tom might have one of his spies watching her. She wanted to defy him.

And there was something else. Since she had given up living with Gordon there had been no intimacy with any other man. She didn't herself understand the particular adventure she got into. It was in a small Ohio town, near the Ohio river. She afterwards thought it was the town of Marietta,

Ohio. "I can't be sure," she said. She had become like a travelling salesman or a member of some small wandering theatrical troop, one who awakens in the morning, always in a strange room, stretches and lies wondering, "Oh, Lord, what town am I in now?"

She went along a street of the Ohio town, walked slowly through several quiet residence streets, past little lights, followed by the man. "Shall I let him pick me up?" She had looked him over in the little movie theatre. He was rather small and neatly dressed, with bright eyes and a sharp little face. She had on, as suggested, rather commonplace working girl's clothes and a little cheap hat. There was a kind of sickness, brought on by loneliness.

And here was the other feeling. A new desire had come. She did want in some way to defy Tom. "I have played square with him, taking all sorts of chances for him. I'm helping him to get rich. What right has he to get up-stage on me now?"

Suppose she double-crossed Tom for a change, got herself pregnant . . . she had been careful, not to let that happen with Gordon. . . . "If I got that way I felt I could bluff Gordon out, make him lie low.

"I felt I could even make him claim it to Tom as his own child."

She didn't think it all out. It might have been just sheer loneliness, wanting to break it, to get close to some one. . . . "I didn't care at the moment who it was."

She had got into a quiet little street near the outer edge of the town, into a place where the street ended on a high sloping bank that led down to the Ohio River. The bank was grassy. The whole adventure was a little uncanny and strange.

The man had followed her, keeping a half block behind and she turned and walked back to him. When she approached him she felt him as frightened, as about to turn and hurry away but she spoke to him firmly. "Come here," she said.

She led him back along the street and down the grassy bank into the darkness toward the river and there, in the darkness, no word spoken between them, she half forced him to draw close, holding him, embracing him . . . he full of half fears . . . then wonder . . . that it could be so easily achieved . . . a kind of queer boyishness, as sometimes, earlier, in Gordon . . . in him too . . . this mixed with fright. Blind, dumb effort of perplexed hungry humans to draw close.

"It was all terribly silly," she said, speaking of it afterwards. There was her own peculiarly boyish frankness, telling of the half success, half failure, of the embrace with the strange frightened man, in this silence by the silent river, and then of their climbing back up the bank to the street's end, she holding fast to his arm and then of releasing him. "He half ran away," she said, and there was a picture made of the little man escaping by running away along a dark small town street and of Kit standing and watching him go.

She would have laughed, a very bitter little laugh, as he disappeared.

The adventure had been followed by a sleepless night. She was back in her bed at the hotel, propped up in bed reading. She laughed a little, cried a little. In speaking of the adventure of the night she was glad to get off the story of the frightened small town man . . . she thought he was probably married, a very respectable little merchant or clerk. . . . He like herself, not a sensualist but wanting something warm and real outside his own little narrow money-grubbing life . . . and to talk again of the road.

There was a kind of ecstacy in that, in the cool adventures. The American roads, asphalt roads, twisting their ways through states, over mountains, over rivers, at night through sleeping towns, the half mystery of the night, plunges into darkness, through strips of forests, now out into the moonlight.

Books read in the hotel rooms, stories of early adventurous American men. She at times felt herself some such a one.

There were the truck drivers on the roads, the men who had begun to move great vans of goods across country at night, going on as she did in all kinds of weather. She met such a truck on a winter night in the high mountains, the road icy. It ground along over the edge of some sheer drop of several hundred feet. Nearly all the truck drivers, working thus at night, as she did, were young as she was. She flashed past such a truck on an icy night, dry snow blowing in clouds across hills and in the light of her car lamps saw some young workman Kit thought was taking chances at least as great as any taken by the early American adventurers of the books. She saw and felt something she wanted. There was a young truck driver, slender and strong, narrow hipped, in a leather jacket and cap. His truck was stuck on a steep icy hill and he had got stones to scotch the wheels, to keep it from slipping off into space. He stood there, hands on hips, in the light from her car headlight, dry snow, driven by icy winds, whirling about his figure. Something in Kit jumping. "There! Will I get me, sometime, one like that?"

Not a buyer or seller, not an exploiter, merchant, lawyer,

not a schemer of any kind. There was the sharp sting of sadness. "If I wasn't so outside, away from people, a marked person, always hiding out, I might have a chance."

There was another sort of adventure, inevitable in the work Kit was doing. Not all of the law officials of the counties through which she dashed at night could be fixed. She was occasionally picked up, the road or bridge blocked. You had to try to bluff your way through if you could, if there was a chance, to smash through. You couldn't always. She was arrested, thrown into some little county jail and immediately called for a lawyer. A wire was sent to Kate and presently a man appeared.

He was one of Tom's fixers. He knew how. There was a hearing, perhaps an agreement made between Tom's fixer and the county prosecuting attorney. She was let out on bail and then didn't appear for trial or she pled guilty of having and possessing and paid a fine.

There was a jail sentence but it could be set aside and if she had been taken, acting as a pilot car for a convoy of cars, she carried no liquor and could play the innocent.

There was however, for Kit, another side to the story. She was in jail. Sometimes she had to stay for two or three days. At that time all of the little jails in the mountain states of the upper South were kept filled with mountain men. There would be a dirty little room, often without outer windows, no toilet arrangements. There was a pot, pushed under a cot that was covered with dirty bedding. She sat on the edge of the cot. There was a hole in a door leading into a corridor and men, friends of the jailer or of some deputy who had brought her in, came to look at her.

There were remarks thrown at her . . . coarse laughter. She could glance up and see eyes looking in at her. She did not dare sleep but sat on the cot's edge in silence, well clad . . . if this happened in the winter, in an expensive fur coat.

There were words heard whispered out there, in the corridors of the jail, "That's her." There was a kind of awe in the voices. She was becoming well-known, notorious. Already her picture . . . "Kit, the rum-running queen" . . . it was faked . . . she was made to look like a tall slender young society girl, a débutante . . . it had been in newspapers of big towns that circulated out through the country in which she worked, that Tom dominated. There was a story of her great wealth. She was a beautiful young society girl who had gone into the game as an adventure.

She was a dangerous woman, always armed and was said to have killed two or three men. In one of the papers there was a story that she had diamonds set in her teeth.

It was dangerous. It was all bad. She kept her face covered from photographers and became sullen and silent when approached by some small town newspaperman wanting to get a flash story to send off to a daily in a near-by larger town.

She was bailed out of the jail or her fine was paid. Smart lawyers could fix things. There might be federal men, higher ups, who could be seen. Tom had always managed to keep himself rather in the background but she was known in the racket as Kit Halsey. When up for trial she always gave another name but even her own lawyer smiled. There was that persistent story that she was the daughter of Tom, the big shot.

"My name is Mary Graves."

"Oh, yeah?" a newspaperman leaned over and whispered to her lawyer. "It doesn't matter. I am nobody. I have nothing to lose."

But it did matter. Kit went to see Kate. Was it time to get out of the racket? She thought it was. She waited.

"I had some money stowed away all right."

It wasn't a question of money. There was something else. "I wanted to get away and I didn't want to."

There was the matter of Tom, something between herself and Tom. She was determined not to be scared out. There was a kind of growing hatred, a growing determination. For a time after her marriage Tom had taken her into his confidence. "Suppose I did lie to him about that doctor, that time I told him I was all right, that it wasn't my fault I didn't have a kid." She had been a good driver for Tom, had time and again risked her own life. No other driver he had got his loads through as she did. She had become an expert as pilot for convoys of liquor cars, had on one occasion taken her own life deliberately into her hands and had wrecked a pursuing car filled with officers, this to enable a big shipment carried in six cars to get away.

She knew that when keeping her on got too hot for him Tom would throw her to the dogs. She knew she should quit, get out of it. She wouldn't. "I didn't know what I was going to do. I was no longer just a working woman. I had been spoiled for that.

"There was a way in which I liked the racket too well to give it up." She went to see Kate.

It was a summer night, the moon shining, and she left a town in which she had been waiting for orders and drove some two hundred miles, arriving at Kate's house at two in the morning. The house was dark and she had come in, the lights of her car turned off, by a back way. She parked her car near the small grove of trees, where she had once stood talking with Tom, and went toward the house.

The house was quite dark and altogether silent. Would Tom be there? She rather wished he would, was in a defiant mood. "Look here, Tom, what's wrong between us?" She remembered two or three times when, since her separation from Gordon, she had been in Tom's presence.

The first time was at Kate's house, when she had come there for a settlement and had gone into Kate's kitchen. Tom was standing in the kitchen but when she came in he walked away, into his own room. That time she had been embarrassed, remembering the lie she had told him, but the second meeting was different. She had acted as pilot for a string of loaded cars and had got them through to a certain farmhouse in Ohio, near a certain town, not far from the city of Cincinnati and having got them through was about to leave when Tom appeared.

He had driven into the farmyard that night, a bright clear warm winter night, and was getting out of his car as she was about to get into hers.

The incident had been ridiculous. It had infuriated her. At that time she had never lost a car intrusted to her. She had already made a record for getting cars through. He stood in the farmyard, the drivers of the several cars of the convoy standing about . . . it was their presence that made the incident so exasperating. If she had been alone with Tom it would not have mattered so much.

There was what she thought an unnecessary insult. She saw him standing there and walked over to him. She

thought, "What's the use of our being like a couple of kids?"
She thought, "What's the use of our being like this?"

She was remembering the confidential talks had in her
hotel suite, his telling her, always a little vaguely, of his
ambitions, hints thrown out as to his ambitions . . . these
including herself.

She walked over and spoke to him. "Hello, Tom" . . . and
he uttered a little sound and again walked away from her.
"Huh!" he grunted. It was as though he had spat in her
face.

And there were the other men, other drivers for Tom,
standing, listening and looking. She went back to her car
and drove away wanting to spit at him, fight him, scratch
his face.

"What a fool I am to bother. Why don't I chuck it, cut
out, go on my own?" During the week before one of the
men of Tom's crowd, a mountain man of forty who had
before prohibition been a little mountain farmer, had spoken
to her. There had been hints thrown out. Two things were
in the wind. She had been told that there were new federal
men, come into Tom's territory under a new leader. It was
said that their leader had got men into Tom's crowd, was
getting some of Tom's men fixed as Tom fixed law-enforce-
ment men.

It was said that the new man was after the big shot, after
Tom himself.

And there was something else. The mountain man who
talked to Kit spoke shyly and carefully. He was being canny.
She saw there a side to Tom's operations she had not heard
about or thought about. There were great quantities of moun-
tain-made moon . . . pretty raw stuff it was . . . being made

in the mountain country of the upper South and more and more Tom and his crowd had begun to dominate the industry.

It was the story of every big American industry. Tom had grown more and more greedy. The little makers in the hills, the old type of mountain moonshiner of romance, was being wiped out. In the patter of the communists he was being "liquidated." In many of the mountain counties Tom had made an arrangement with the local officials. He and his men helped catch the smaller offenders, they "turned them up." There was a small maker, turning out his twenty to thirty gallons a day, back somewhere in the thick laurel in the hills, and a sheriff got a phone call. "A man will meet you at the red bridge on the Clare Ford road at ten tonight. Bring about three deputies."

The little makers were thrown into jail. They were serving time in road gangs. The number of arrests made in this way helped some local sheriff to make a good record of arrests.

And when such a man, usually some young mountain man, had served his time in jail or on the road and was again free he was approached by one of Tom's men.

"You are broke, eh? You think perhaps you will try another little run?

"You will get caught. It is no good."

It was suggested . . . the man was given a hint. . . . "Why not get in with the big one?"

The man could go to work for Tom at some big still. There were two or three thousand-gallon stills at work constantly, all through the prohibition times, in some of the mountain counties, stills quite safe from capture . . . there was an immense market for the moon among workingmen

in all of the industrial towns of the Middle West . . . the
great coal mining regions of West Virginia, Kentucky,
Southern Ohio, Indiana and Illinois. . . . North Carolina
moon, Tennessee moon, North Georgia moon . . . train
loads of sugar and containers were being shipped into Tom's
territory . . . the old slow method of making the moon
from grain was out . . . the raw alcohol could be extracted
from sugar quickly . . . just enough grain was used to give
the raw stuff some slight flavor. It was fighting liquor, man-
stabbing liquor, gal-gitting liquor.

It went out of the mountain country in great convoys. It
was good business. A man could be quite safe working for
Tom but more and more Tom had cut down the earnings.
There were men working about stills, hauling in sugar and
containers . . . after all they did face the possibility of arrest,
of going to jail . . . it was known and felt that, if the pinch
came, it would be the little man who would be thrown to
the dogs . . . there were men doing such work for a dollar
and a half, for two dollars a day.

The mountain man who spoke to Kit was some such fellow. He had been an independent maker. Now he was one
of Tom's men, working at one of Tom's stills. He had been
cautious. "I am not speaking for myself. Although I have a
wife and five kids, I'm not kicking."

There was the suggestion . . . the new federal man,
leader of the new crowd of federal men come into the mountain country, was said to be foxy. He was a small man,
sharp and shrewd, and the mountain man, talking with Kit,
had heard he couldn't be fixed.

The man kept assuring her of his own loyalty to Tom's
gang . . . he was being shrewd and cagey but, he said, he
liked the chance to talk about it all to some one he knew

was also loyal and as he talked Kit had the feeling that he
might himself be a federal man or that he had made an
arrangement with them, had agreed to work with them.

She was however a little torn, a little puzzled. In the beginning during the organization of Tom's crowd there had
been a generous distribution of the swag taken. Men of
Tom's crowd always went about with money in their
pockets. Cars were bought, mountain women got new store
clothes, children of mountain men got shoes.

But there had been this change. Tom was taking always a
bigger and bigger cut. More and more he was ruling by
terror. It might be, Kit thought, as the mountain man talked,
always declaring his own loyalty, that he had been sent to
her by the new leader of the federals . . .

Or he might have been sent by Tom himself. "He'd like
to get something on me," she thought.

There were these thoughts, questions in her mind, that
night when she went to Kate's. Could she question Kate,
would Kate talk? She had felt a liking for herself in Kate.
When the mountain man had talked to her he had spoken
guardedly of a certain man. "I am not sure about this. I've
only heard."

It was the man Steve Wyagle, known as Shorty, the city
gun-man, the one Kit had seen sitting with other men in
Kate's house that time she first came to Kate's with Gordon.

There was a whisper going about that he was planning to
try at least to elbow his way into Tom's place in the organization and might even be playing in with the new federal
men. If they got Tom, broke up his crowd, Steve could
organize a new crowd.

If the new federal man got Tom and a few of his followers he would perhaps be satisfied. He would have made a reputation for himself with the government, would have pulled off a big stroke. He would be sent away to work in some other section of the country. It would be time then for a new man to step into Tom's shoes, build up a new organization. Promises no doubt made. "You see what Tom's doing. He's keeping it all.

"If we get rid of him we can all make money again."

Kit at that time had never seen the new federal man who had evidently created a new force within Tom's crowd, the force of fear, of suspicion. He had got men within the organization into a new mood. They had begun to look at each other with eyes into which had crept suspicion. "Is he one of us, or is he a federal man, working inside the organization, getting evidence that may send me to prison for years? Or is he in with Steve Wyagle?"

Steve Wyagle was a tough one, a killer. Kit had never seen the new federal man when she went to Kate that night but later he did speak to her.

There was one time when she had returned to the town and the hotel where she had lived with Gordon. She had spent the night there and in the morning was getting into her car, in the street before the hotel, when the man stepped over to her car and spoke to her.

For some reason she was at once on her guard, knew who the man was. He spoke to her softly, smiling up at her, a rather small, slender, neatly dressed man, he was with a diamond pin in his tie. She noticed that he wore rings on the fingers of both hands.

"Mrs. Halsey," he said, raising his hat and smiling and ——

"Well," she replied. "If I am Mrs. Halsey what do you want of me?"

He leaned over toward her and spoke quickly, a little stream of words flowing through thin lips, she staring at him. "I think you know who I am." He smiled.

"You had better be very very careful. You had better come to see me, or you could phone." He took a card from his pocket and laid it beside her on the seat of the car. "There's my name and my telephone number.

"You had better see me soon. The game's up," he said, still smiling, still speaking softly. He had curious gray eyes, very pale, and there were little brown spots on the eye balls. "You go to hell," Kit said to him as she drove away, speaking boldly enough but in her also he had created fear. There had been three or four men lounging about the front of the hotel. They might have been some of Tom's crowd. The federal man might have got them, frightened them into working with him, helping him gather evidence . . . promise of immunity when the big break came. He might have said to them, "See. You watch this." The whole conversation with herself, to men standing even a few feet away, might have seemed friendly.

As though he were giving her instruction.

He could have stepped back to them. There were so many men in Tom's crowd Kit had never seen. He could have addressed them . . . "You see. She also is working in with us."

Kit was furious after the incident. It hadn't happened that night when she went to Kate, but already she had had the conversation with the mountain man.

Did she want to warn Kate, warn Tom through Kate? Her relationship with the older woman was a curious one. The two women had never talked to each other. It is likely

that the same loneliness, the persistent hunger for some kind
of real companionship in life that had driven Kit into the
absurd embrace with the clerk she had found in the movie
theatre had also driven her to Kate. She had never had a real
woman friend or a man friend. There had been too many
nights spent alone, on lonely roads, in lonely hotel rooms,
always lying low . . . secrecy had become more and more
necessary as she had become better known, since her name
had been played up in newspapers. Once she had the beginning of a kind of friendship with Tom Halsey. He had, at
least partially, taken her into his confidence. It might be that
if she warned Kate and Tom through Kate, the friendship
could be re-established. There was a kind of persistent admiration for Tom. She thought afterwards it might have
been rather romantic. "Perhaps I only wanted a man I could
feel was a man."

"Hell. What the hell, Tom? Come out of it." Kit had got,
naturally had to get, being in the work she was, having to
deal with sheriffs and deputy sheriffs, with the men of
Tom's crowd she did meet, a new and bolder front. She felt
that she would not be afraid to face Tom, have it out with
him . . .

"I'm a woman and you're a man. Let's forget it. Sure I
ran out on you in the matter of having a kid by your lousy
son. I lied to you about that but I've sure been a good workman for you.

"If you're so crazy about having a grandson, to carry on
the Halsey name, on the money we are all making for you
in this racket, you know, Tom, respectable Halseys, asso-
ciating with the best people, the very kind of people who
buy the stuff we run out to them . . .

"Why not tell Gordon to get a divorce? I won't put a

straw in his way. Tell him to get some other skirt. Tell him
to get a gentle soft one, not another like me."

It might be that the trouble with Tom was that he had
it in his head that in the end she would try to hold him up.
He was getting more and more crazy about money, constantly getting more greedy. It was also an old American
story, the man who by being bold, daring or crafty had got
a million and who, having got it, wanted two and having
two wanted five, ten, twenty million.

Kit went softly over to the kitchen door of Kate's house
and knocked. She had got herself into an exalted mood,
hoping that Tom might be at the house, that she could have
it out with him. When she had knocked . . . the car in
which she had arrived was parked out of sight from the
house . . . she stepped away from the door and stood in a
spot where in the moonlight she could be clearly seen from
a window.

It was for her one of those times . . . all people have them
. . . a resolution made . . . you are prepared to assert yourself, have your say . . . it is all thought out.

And then — whiff — it doesn't work out.

Kit stood in the yard at the back of Kate's house until
Kate came to the kitchen door and the two women went
into the kitchen. It was time for a settlement between them
. . . so and so much money to come to Kit and she got it.
There had been a light turned on for a moment and then
it was again turned off. Kit stepped out of the house and
Kate stood in the doorway. She was a curiously stern looking
figure standing there, Kit quite close, so that she could see
the heavy hard-seeming lines of the older woman's face.
Kate was a tall gaunt woman. How hard her eyes seemed.
Kit hesitated.

Again she spoke. What had gone wrong with her? She
had suddenly the feeling that her voice had gone wrong.
She had intended to ask a question, quite casually, but being
suddenly uncertain, her voice became sharp and demanding.

"Is Tom Halsey in there?" She pointed. She could see the
tall form of the woman Kate stiffen.

"I want to see him. I've got to see him. I think he's in
there. You tell him to come out here. I've got something to
say to him."

It was all wrong, wrong. Kit had intended to take Kate
into her confidence, tell her about the conversation with the
mountain man, about the new leader of the federal men
who had come into Tom's territory determined to get
Tom.

She had intended to take advantage of the opportunity to
get closer to Kate and through her perhaps to re-establish
her old relationship with Tom, and her own stupidity had
spoiled everything.

She had made a demand. There had been, in the tones
in which she had addressed Kate, something like a threat.
Kate did not answer for a moment and then she spoke softly.

"When Tom Halsey wants to see you I guess he'll send
you word," she said in her low even voice, and without more
words stepped back into her kitchen and closed the door.

CHAPTER FIFTEEN

TOM HALSEY did send Kit word. At that time Kit had been taking with her a certain young man . . . sometimes when running single loads of expensive liquor into some Middle Western industrial town or city, sometimes when acting as pilot for convoys of cars, taking perhaps a big shipment of moon out of the mountain country and into the coal mining districts of West Virginia or southern Ohio. The young man was in reality just a boy.

He was a college boy, from one of the older Virginia colleges . . . it was during the college vacation time that he came to work, as a driver, for Tom's crowd and he was sent to Kit.

She was to teach him, put him through his paces, teach him the trick of acting as pilot for convoys of cars, the roads, stations, almost always in a barn on some lonely farm, where liquor was stored. He was a gray-eyed, slender, eager young fellow, not physically very strong and at once, after he came to her, Kit took a fancy to him.

It was a curious feeling, having the boyish young fellow with her . . . he was with her on almost every trip she took for two months . . . something like a mother feeling coming to her . . . really it was a little absurd, her having the

feeling . . . she was not much older than the boy . . . she
thought of him as a boy, not as a young man. He was a
Weathersmythe from one of the eastern, the tidewater counties, of Virginia.

He talked. There was a shy eager outburst of speech. They
went, running a car of expensive stuff through the night,
over the mountains, say out of North Carolina and into
Ohio. It might be a load of imported stuff, smuggled in
somewhere along the North or South Carolina coast . . .
Tom having contracted to get it through. Kit let the boy
drive. He was like herself, instinctively a fine driver. His
presence broke her loneliness.

They had delivered a load, in some Ohio industrial town
. . . it might be going into the cellar of some rich manufacturer, such a man as would be strong for law and order
. . . down on all lawlessness in others . . . and then Kit
and the boy lit out, disappeared into the morning blue.

No load now, no immediate danger of arrest.

Kit kept wondering about the young boy, her companion.
But he wasn't so young. He might have been a year younger
than herself.

He wanted to talk. He belonged to a family, known,
understood to be one of the F. F. V's.

Kit got it all out of his talk. He had in him something she
herself understood. The danger of the trade into which he
had got . . . his getting in with Tom had come about
through an acquaintance with some boot-legger, some man
in the college town who sold stuff to the college boys . . .

The man passing the word on to Tom. "Yes, we'll give
him a try." The boy excited by the constant danger of arrest.
There were other young fellows of the sort who had worked
for Tom but none of them had been sent to Kit.

She was at first a little suspicious. "Well, we'll see." She had that feeling, very strong in her now, growing in her, that Tom wanted to get something on her. She and the young Weathersmythe would be, perhaps for some weeks, constantly together. It might be that Tom was being foxy, trying to get something on Kit as he had on his son's first wife.

Making that one hot-foot it off to Reno, a little money pitched to her. . . . "So that's that. Good-bye, Miss Skirt."

Kit and the boy were alone together night after night. When they had delivered a load they went to some little town, stopping on the way at another town. They had breakfast together at some small town restaurant and Kit sent off a wire, not to Kate but to a business man of the town near which Kate lived.

The wire would be handed by the business man to a second man who would see that it got to Kate. If you knew how to read it, it would tell you where to find and get word to Kit . . .

Another load to be got or a convoy of cars to be piloted.

Kit was suspicious, not of the boy . . . he at once won her confidence, even her affection . . . but of Tom. When they were approaching some little town, where they were to hide out and wait, she dropped the boy at the town's edge and went on to the hotel. He had his bag and walked in, registering after she had been assigned a room. They were both tired and sleepy and Kit slept until late afternoon.

She awoke, dressed, had her room put in order and then . . . this after they had been together for some days . . . he came to her.

She had warned him but he came along the hotel corridor and tapped softly on her door. "Come on," he whispered, "there don't any one know us here." He wanted her to go with him to the hotel dining-room or to a restaurant, stood in the doorway to her room, whispering, an eager smile on his young face. He had begun at once to call her Kit and, as his name was Alfred, she called him Alf.

"Ah, come on, Kit. What the hell? Let's take a chance. It's so nice out." She had explained to him carefully, time and again, that it was better that they not be seen together but he was so eager, standing there in the hallway of the shabby little hotel. His lips trembled with eagerness. "We'll have something to eat and take a walk. It'll be dark soon." She sent him downstairs and went down to join him.

They walked together in the streets of towns, in quiet residence streets, Kit for the most part silent and curious, while the boy talked. She had told him of the danger of the game into which he had got. "With me, Alf, you see, it doesn't much matter." She was trying to make him see his own situation as something different from her own.

"I haven't any people, don't even know where my people are.

"If I am arrested, thrown into jail . . . my name getting into the newspapers, you see, it won't matter."

She kept urging him to get out of the game at once, but he protested.

"You don't know how it is at home."

There was his father, such a stodgy self-important one. An aunt kept house for his father. He described her, a short fat very red-faced woman of fifty-five, a manager, he said. She had inherited some money . . . really paid the expenses of the house and had paid the boy's expenses at the Virginia college.

The boy described the life in his father's house. His own

position there was a curious one, the father, Kit gathered, rather overawed by the aunt, his sister. There had been some money in the family, money coming down from young Alfred's grandfather but the grandfather had not trusted his son and had left the money to his daughter.

It was all something new to Kit, a peep into a kind of life of which she knew nothing.

And so, the Weathersmythes were of the Virginia aristocracy of which she had often heard. For two or three years she had been living her own kind of solitary life, often enough staying in some Virginia town, sometimes at night walking alone in the streets of some such town.

Houses of the rich and well-to-do among Virginia families passed during some such walk. She might even have stopped some man or woman on a sidewalk. "Can you tell me, please, who lives in that house?" There might be a big old frame house with a wide lawn in front, perhaps girls, young women, no older than herself sitting on a porch in front or coming down a gravel walk to the street.

Her own fancy keenly alive. The notion, firmly fixed in the minds of so many who like herself had come out of a poorer class, that there was peace and happiness to be found . . . happiness in a way inevitable, assured in the houses of the rich and the well-to-do.

A kind of envy, hunger for something of the sort in her own life. She listened to the talk of young Weathersmythe, a little shocked, but with rapt absorbing attention.

He began telling her the story of his grandfather, who was a Civil War veteran.

He was one of Mosby's men and young Weathersmythe thought of him always as a heroic figure.

He, the grandfather, had gone into the Mosby organization during the Civil War . . . that strange band, largely young Southern bloods, raiding all during the war back of the Northern armies. They were half guerillas, half warriors. They were horse stealers. When Lee's army was in rags and on half rations they were dressed in the best of gray broadcloth, had money in their pockets. . . . Once a band of them robbed a Northern army paymaster of some hundred and fifty thousand dollars.

It was split up among them and they bought more and more gaudy clothes, better and better horses. They sent North, by way of some army sutler, for the best of clothes, boots, hats. They fought desperately, killed and were killed with cruel abandon. Once they went, a little band of them, on a dark night, into the very heart of a large camp of Northern troops, their own horses tied to trees, somewhere back in a dark wood, and brought out as captive the commander of the camp.

It was a strange, very exciting and exhilarating kind of warfare, often degenerating into plain robbery, the bands forming, raiding, then dispersing, and young Weathersmythe spoke of it all with fervor. There was a life . . . fun, danger, fine clothes, good horses, women, admirers. He had been a boy when his grandfather was an old man and other very old men, also Virginians, who had also been Mosby men, sometimes came to his grandfather's house. The boy lived there with his father and his aunt, his own mother being dead. The old men came and sat on the porch before the house. It was at the edge of a town in the Shenandoah Valley and there were rich and fertile fields, belonging to his grandfather, stretching away behind the house. The old men came and sat with the grandfather and they talked of their young lives and young adventures.

They were in the streets of some town, Kit and young
Weathersmythe, Kit going along in silence listening while
her new companion talked and it grew late. "It is better
not to stay out too late," she said. "We will attract attention when we go in." She was thinking of the hotel lobby,
some lounger, perhaps also in with Tom's crowd, who
might be about. Since she had become a character, a half-
celebrity, her name in newspapers, she had grown more and
more cautious. She made the young man wait until she had
gone alone into the hotel and to her room but she could not
escape him.

He came again to the door of her room, wanted to be
admitted and with a smile she let him in and sat with
him for hours, a chair drawn up to a window that looked
into a sleeping small town main street, the boy on the floor
at her feet.

He talked. He was dissatisfied with his own life, angry
about something. His story came out.

It was an old story, the son of a well-to-do, respected and
respectable man . . . boredom with respectability. There is
something such young men want. As the boy talked to Kit
at night, in some hotel room . . . often he stayed with her
thus until two or three in the morning . . . he was telling
her the story of his father, of his own birth . . . always she
half expected when he was with her thus that there would
be a knock at the door, some man or group of Tom's men
standing there.

"Now we have you where we want you."

Tom laying down the law to her. "Now we will clean this
up." The fear in him that she, being still his son's wife,
would, if anything happened to him, be dangerous. A man in
Tom's position was always in danger of being bumped off,
taken for a ride . . .

He was a gang leader but clung to the notion that through his son there would come into being a new generation of Halseys . . . respectable Halseys . . .

. . . Even in time perhaps a claim set up . . . no one particularly interested in disputing it . . . the Halseys also numbered among the F. F. V's.

An absurd enough notion. Kit had got it all from Tom's former talk with her. She had a curious determination . . . not being particularly interested in the money Tom Halsey had accumulated, not wanting him to defeat her.

She thought it was that feeling kept her in the game so long, after she knew that it might cost even her life.

In a hotel room with her was a boy dispelling the F. F. V. myth. He told her the story of his father, as a young man, of the age perhaps that the boy was when he was with Kit.

So he, the father, had also gone forth on his adventures. There was a story . . . the boy had not known it when his grandfather was alive . . . he told Kit that it was thrown into his teeth when he was a lad and went to the Virginia town school. There was the suggestion thrown out that he was an illegitimate child.

He wasn't. "My father and mother were married all right," he told Kit. They were sitting in one of the hotel rooms at night. In all the relationship between the two there was, on the boy's part, no move, no suggestion or attempt to draw close to her as young man to young woman. She thought afterwards that young Weathersmythe might have been quite sexless . . .

. . . Or that he was so constantly excited by his own notion of the adventure of the life they were leading to-gether, so anxious to draw close to her, have her as a friend

on another plane, that the man and woman impulse was
quite crowded out.

He sat on the floor, in the hotel room . . . it often a
shabby enough room . . . talking. He talked first of the
grandfather, the Mosby man . . . the man he had loved, for
whom he had the boyish passionate admiration . . . making a hero of him. The grandfather had been, Kit gathered
from the boy's talk, one of the most daring of the Mosby
men. He had come to Mosby as a private in the ranks but
had been made, for his daring, first a lieutenant and then a
captain. Such men were sent out, often alone, to get in-
formation, to locate the smaller bands of enemy cavalry, to
burn bridges, steal horses.

There had been one such undertaking, notable enough
in the life of Alfred's grandfather. There were the Northern
troops, in pursuit of Mosby and his men, camped, of all
places, at the Weathersmythe house, in the very house before
which Captain Weathersmythe, now an old man, sat talking
of the adventure, the boy listening, wide-eyed.

Captain Weathersmythe setting out . . . "They are at
your house, the bastards. You're the man to get the lay of
things" . . . Weathersmythe not now decked out in gray
broadcloth, high boots of fine leather with spurs jingling
. . . "Not another troop in the whole Confederate army
rigged out as we are. No wonder all the young bloods want
to join us," . . . no pistol at side now, no swagger gray hat,
turned up so saucily with a feather in it. He had let his beard
grow, had got into a suit of ragged and dirty blue clothes,
taken off a Union prisoner.

He went to the camp of the Union men, the men camped
on his own good Shenandoah Valley farm, the officers living

in his house, his eyes open, his brain busy enough. "In such and such a way we will come down upon them at night. We can hide our horses in this hollow, beside this little stream where the Balm of Gilead trees grow. They have got a picket here, where the path comes down out of the wood, but we'll get him. I'll go ahead and get him with my own naked hands. I'll choke him into silence."

There was a troop of Northern cavalry and among them, of all people who do you think?

"An Adams . . . ha! . . . one of the New England Adamses. He is an officer among them."

Dream of taking, as captive, or of killing, an Adams. Memory of old John Quincy Adams, after being President, coming back to Washington as simple congressman and sitting in the Congress, that waspish stern old man, goading the slave owners of the South also sitting in the Congress . . . an Adams, Lincoln's Ambassador to England.

The young Charles Francis, Jr., commanding a detachment of cavalry bivouacking at the Weathersmythe house in the Valley.

Mosby a dramatist, wanting the publicity that would come with the capture or death of the young Adams . . . the North given another shock.

"Ha! This will be something to curl their hair. Don't fail me now, Weathersmythe." Young Alfred's grandfather had gone there, to his own house, to find out how many men young Adams had, passing himself off as a Union soldier from Ohio escaped from a Confederate prison.

Taking the risk of being recognized by some of his own former slaves, still about the place.

The Adams there, in that house, sitting in one of the rooms. . . . It was the dining-room of the house . . . writing let-

ters. He might be writing to his father. Ambassador to
England. "Damn the English. They've done us dirt enough
. . . not giving us the recognition that would have made our
success sure . . . a dirty commercial-minded lot, the damn
English . . . they are really also Yanks."

An Adams writing letters. That lot always writing,
writing, writing. Weathersmythe shown in to him, to be
questioned. "Ha! I'll throw you off the track." "Did you
hear anything of Mosby's men as you came through to
us?"

"Yes, sir." There is an old Negro man, former house
servant in the house, standing by the door. He is being
servant to an Adams now but he knows his Captain
Weathersmythe. The Negro frightened by the presence of a
Weathersmythe. "If I make a sign he'll kill me before they
can kill him."

The gorgeous risk of it . . . death if there is a flutter of
suspicion. He had trusted the fear of the ex-slave. A story
told, that he, the Union prisoner, had picked up as he crept
toward the Union lines . . . of Mosby and his men gone
off on a raid. "They left two nights ago. I was lying beside
the road and saw them go. I heard their talk."

"No, sir. I don't know. I heard them say. . . ." He named
a town, a hundred miles inside the Union lines. . . . It was
a place where stores for the Union army were kept.

That and the young Weathersmythe, with Kit . . . such
a gentle seeming boy with his rather slight body and sensitive face . . . this in the night, the little hotel in which they
were staying very quiet . . .

She had to caution him. "Don't talk so loud, will you, boy,
please, boy," she pled. He made her feel very gentle, very

motherly. He told the story of the night raid of the Mosby men, his grandfather among them, he knowing every little country road, every cowpath in that section of the valley.

The sudden descent out of darkness, the alarm, the killing of many. It was odd, a bit uncanny, the enthusiasm of the young Weathersmythe . . . talking, talking, in the half darkness of the room, a young boy's romanticization of war, of killing. Kit had a woman's half revulsion. Sometimes after such a talk she had the notion that the boy also wanted to kill . . .

There was a hunger for revenge in him. Kit got his story in fragments. His mother had been a mountain girl, from a county south of the valley county in Virginia that was the home of the Weathersmythes. The grandfather had come back to the farm after the war and had gone to work.

The Weathersmythe slaves were gone. The place was in ruins but the Weathersmythe who had been a Mosby man put his own hand to the plow. He sold off some of the Weathersmythe land, worked day and night. The former wealth of the Weathersmythes was gone but the young Civil War Weathersmythe had re-established the family.

He had got down, from the hill country to the South, a mountain man, also a Civil War man, one of Lee's men who had surrendered with Lee at Appomatox, and it was this man's daughter who became young Alfred's mother.

It had happened. There was the son of the Mosby man . . . he was at the age young Alfred was when he came to Kit. Young Alfred himself going in secretly for a kind of adventure, Kit thought he had romanticized as perhaps long before his grandfather had romanticized the work of Mosby. After all, the Mosby might have been a kind of Tom Halsey, the same kind of force in him . . . ability in him to make men do what he wanted them to do.

It developed that young Alfred, before coming to Kit, had seen and talked to Tom, and Kit thought that Tom had perhaps been pleased and flattered to have such a one in his band. He might later be useful to Tom. The Weathersmythes were more or less prominent in the state and the boy's father was in state politics.

The boy had been born to the mountain girl, daughter of a poor white farmhand on the Weathersmythe place, and Kit understood that the marriage had not taken place until a few weeks before young Alfred was born and that there had been a struggle, the mountain girl's father coming at night to the Weathersmythe house, a scene between him and the Mosby Weathersmythe, young Alfred's father called out of his bed . . . confronted by the girl's father . . . "is this story true?"

Alfred's father denying, protesting, accusing. A hint thrown out that the child, so soon to be born, might well be the son of some other man at work on the place, the father of the girl angry . . . he having come to the house with a shotgun over his arm. . . .

How much of the story had been born later in Kit's imagination and how much in the imagination of the boy, she didn't afterwards know. She was herself the daughter of a Poor White. She said . . . "He told me such a lot of things. He was a born story teller. He made everything seem so vivid. It was like reading an exciting story in a book."

Young Alfred did tell her of how once, in the vacation time after his first year in college . . . it was after his second college year that he came to her . . . he went off secretly, trying to find some of his mother's people.

He had found them although his mother was dead, but Kit gathered that he had not made himself known. They were very poor and ignorant people in the hills and young Alfred, although on his mother's side he was a Poor White, was also a Weathersmythe.

Such a queer mixture of pride, arrogance, gentleness. The young man was torn by many conflicting emotions. Kit, in speaking of him . . . he remained for some reason a very vital figure in her own adventure in living . . . admitted that she did not understand the boy who for a time was her companion. She said . . . "He never asked me about my own people." She thought that a part at least of the story that remained in her mind might have been formed out of other stories she had heard.

There was, in any event, the scene in the Weathersmythe house. There would have ben another Weathersmythe, Alfred's father, confronted by Alfred's mother's father, the shotgun hung over his arm, this in the night, the Mosby Weathersmythe standing there, Alfred's father accusing, the Weathersmythe denying . . . he would have known he was lying.

A mountain man angry. After all the Weathersmythes, gay young dogs, Mosby men, feathers in their hats, gay broadcloth clothes, shining boots that went up to the knees . . . they a little like movie cowboys of another age in America . . . the real cowboy after all being in actuality little more than a hired man who all day long, month after month, must follow tame enough cows and steers through barren dry country . . .

. . . it is to be borne in mind that although Alfred Weathersmythe's grandfather had been a Mosby man . . . gay dog,

F. F. V. with feather in hat, doing daringly enough, the grandfather, on Alfred's mother's side, had been one of Lee's men.

He would have been with Jackson at Chancellorsville . . . in the long secret march with Stonewall Jackson that time . . . odd that there had been so little talk of Stonewall being an F. F. V. . . . that strange religious, murderous genius . . . praying and killing, then again praying . . . man of such fine abandon.

Young Alfred Weathersmythe's grandfather, on the mother's side, marching with him . . .

Then again at Gettysburg, standing to it there.

And again when Grant came down with his ever-increasing hordes to pen Lee in at Richmond and Petersburg . . . the crater . . . the persistent grim thrusts of that other genius of grim war, Grant . . . curiously gentle man, called "Butcher Grant."

Alfred Weathersmythe's commoner grandfather standing before Alfred Weathersmythe's grandfather, once F. F. V. young blood, gun in hand, Alfred's father going a little cheap . . . Kit Brandon had the impression that the father of her friend, young Alfred, always had been a cheap man and that the son knew it.

. . . Gun of mountain man brought down to firing position.

"You are the father of the child my daughter is going to have. What are you going to do about it?"

F. F. V. young blood meeting the commoner. It may well be that a commoner who has been four years with a Lee is no longer a commoner.

Alfred Weathersmythe's other grandfather, the Mosby one, speaking up.

"Put the gun down, Jim."

Kit understood, got it from fragmentary things young Alfred said that there had been an offer of money. He had got the story from some of his mother's people, that time he went to them . . . an offer of money made and refused.

Then a mountain man getting proud. He spoke to Alfred's father, ignoring the grandfather. "All right. You marry her. Let her have the child. You can keep it and I'll take her away."

As it happened the mother died soon after Alfred was born and he grew up in his grandfather's home knowing nothing of all this.

And then the story came to him, not from his father, his grandfather or his aunt, but from other boys, in a Virginia town where he went to grade school and then to high school.

So he wasn't then a pure Weathersmythe, an F. F. V. There was the bad blood, so called, his father just a common soldier with Lee's army . . . certainly not a dashing cavalry man. Mosby man with feather in hat, every man in the little band trying to out-jeb the Jeb Stuart. A kind of shame and self-consciousness in the boy. This in secret. His father, grandfather, and that so executive aunt, always marching him off to church and Sunday School when he was a small boy . . . he had always been slender and not strong . . . the aunt, he told Kit, was a determined religionist.

There had come a kind of hatred of his father . . . this mingled with a curious reverence for the grandfather, the Mosby man. When Kit urged him to get out of Tom's gang, have nothing to do with it . . . she pointed out what Tom

was probably up to, taking the boy on to learn her own
trade. The boy's father was in state politics — later in
the state legislature. At that time, as every one must know,
who knows later Virginia history, the legislature of Virginia was dominated, almost absolutely, by the Anti-Saloon
League, in the person of Bishop Cannon, Methodist church-
man . . . he even sitting day after day in the doorway to
the hall where the legislature met, United States senators,
governors, members of Congress as well as state legislators,
fearing him, kow-towing to him. This in proud Virginia.

And at home the boy's father . . . a lawyer in a Virginia
town. While the boy was in college he served a term as
county prosecuting attorney.

The boy described him to Kit. He was a small fat man and
a constant hard drinker, although he did not drink in public. The boy said he was always having what he called
"illnesses," staying at home sometimes in his room for days.
He drank and talked aloud to himself, the aunt protecting
him from the outside world. She fought with him, tried to
take his liquor from him but he lied to her, said it was all
gone, that he hadn't any . . . he had become very canny
about hiding it. The household in this mood, sometimes for
days . . . people of the town knowing and not knowing . . .

He was after all a Weathersmythe.

The aunt sometimes giving way to tears and sometimes
to anger. There were bitter quarrels. The aunt owned the
house in which they lived. What money the elder Weathersmythe had left had been left to her. He recovered from one
of his bad times, the boy said, and went abroad. He was in
court, prosecuting mountain men for making perhaps the

very liquor he had been consuming the week before. He was strutting before other men, speaking of his family.

"I am a Weathersmythe."

The boy Alfred told Kit that he didn't care if he was caught, running liquor for Tom Halsey. He told Kit that he had himself tried drinking for a time but that he didn't like it. It gave him only a silly sick feeling. It seemed to Kit that, in coming with Tom's crowd, he half convinced himself that he was being an adventurer like his grandfather, and that half he had done it hoping to be caught, and the family disgraced.

CHAPTER SIXTEEN

AND so Tom Halsey had sent for Kit. It was after the boy Alfred Weathersmythe had left her and she was a little uncertain about what he was doing and it was after the time when the new federal man had spoken to her in the street and when she knew vaguely that there was trouble for Tom ahead.

She was waiting, she hardly knew what for. She was told that the boy, Alfred, was now attached to Tom's person. There was a story that Tom, like a city gangster or a Huey Long, had begun going about accompanied by a guard.

Had the boy Alfred been made one of his guards? The idea amused and startled Kit. She was told to go to Kate and went on a night in the fall.

It was a clear night and Kit was nervous. Her relations with Kate had also changed and there was that story, told her by the mountain man, member of Tom's crowd, about the attempt of the ex-city rough, Steve Wyagle, to elbow in on Tom's game.

Kit went to Kate's somewhat grimly. She was in a curious position. For two or three years she had been making what had seemed to her a good deal of money. For perhaps a year there had been the secret longing to get out, begin a new

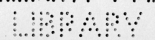

life, but there was also the question to be settled . . . if she
began a new life what sort of life was it to be? Like the
boy Alfred Weathersmythe and others of Tom's crowd
she had known it was the excitement of the life of the rumrunner that had held her. Young Weathersmythe was not
the only young fellow, of some so-called "good family" who
had dipped into rum-running or some other form of boot-
legging. Kit for example had heard from young Weathersmythe a story . . . it had been told to the young man's
father by a Chicago man who had come to his house on
some matter of business . . . the boy in an adjoining
room listening while the two men talked . . . the amused
cynicism of the Chicago man . . .

. . . The boy's father, at that time ambitious to become a
member of the legislature of his state, political follower at
the moment of Bishop Cannon . . .

. . . He also cynical enough.

. . . The father had begun the conversation with the Chicago man . . . they sat in the Weathersmythe house, the
two men with a bottle between them . . .

. . . The Chicago man . . . "You are, as I understand
it, strong, that is to say politically, for prohibition?"

. . . "Yes." Laughter . . . the boy unknown to the two
men sitting in a near-by room, the door open, reading a
book. If he had got a kind of hatred of his father, a hatred
based partly on a growing feeling that the father had been
cheap and unfair with his mother, partly on boyish hatred of
hypocrisy . . . if he had this feeling he had at the same time
the feeling that his father was clever.

He was a man who enjoyed drinking, even getting drunk.
Young Alfred told Kit that more than once, when the father

was on one of his secret sprees, he had seen him coming out of his room, his hair disheveled, staggering along a hallway to the bathroom . . .

. . . and then, perhaps a week later, the same man up before the voters. He would be making a prohibition speech . . .

. . . In some way making the people like it, the church in his legislative district endorsing him, preachers working for his election . . .

. . . When he had been prosecuting attorney, his perhaps prosecuting, getting sent off to jail, some man from the mountain district of the county from whom he had himself bought liquor . . .

. . . In some way making the man stand up to the deception, making him accept it. "If you say a word I'll simply call you a liar . . . I'm after all a Weathersmythe."

. . . "Damn the Weathersmythes," the boy had once said indignantly to Kit.

. . . "It will be your word against mine. If you lay low I'll get the judge to go light on you."

. . . He wouldn't have bragged about being a Weathersmythe, would have been too smart for that. He would have made the force of the fact that he was a Weathersmythe operate on the mind of the mountain man. The mountain man would have been a poor and no doubt illiterate man from the hills, not, after all, unlike young Alfred's mother's father or unlike Kit's own people.

The two men talking in the Weathersmythe house.

"Yes, of course, politically, I am for prohibition. I'd like to see any man get elected to office in this state just now who wasn't.

"What, with all the moralists for it, the church people all strong for it?

"That old fraud of a Bishop holding the whip over us."

Young Weathersmythe's father telling the Chicago man, also a lawyer . . . in the Virginia county of some legal matter connected with the settling up of a Virginia estate . . .

"I was in Washington. I was in Senator Blaon's office." Laughter. "You know what a strong prohibitionist he is.

"He is one of our great fighters for the principle of prohibition.

"Of course we had a drink." More laughter.

"Do you know what the old cuss uses as his racket? He has, you see, this bottle he keeps in his desk. . . . He is a great tippler. So it is perfectly legal stuff, issued you see for purely medicinal purposes, prescription of a doctor, etc., etc., etc.

"So he must keep refilling the bottle. You see I took him some myself. He is a man raised on our corn. He likes it. He keeps refilling the bottle. You see he feels that, if by some accident they catch him, he will be quite secure. He buys nothing from the Senate boot-leggers. We fellows down here keep him supplied."

Laughter of the two men, such respectable citizens, in a Virginia house. The Chicago man told a story of a young man graduated with honors from the University of Chicago. He had come into the office of the Chicago lawyer. "He had a sample case with him, wanted to establish a trade with me, had a good sales talk.

"So he let me sample his goods and we got into talk.

"He had been educated to business, told me that he had

after graduation looked over the field. He decided quite calmly that the liquor business was the best business going at the moment.

"There would be a risk of course but in what business is there not a risk and as for legality . . ."

The bright young college graduate, in the office of the Chicago lawyer had held forth on the subject of legality. What great business was there in America that had been built on legality? The college boy had studied the history of the great oil companies, steel companies, railroads, mining, power, public utility companies. "There are more immediate profits, quick returns, in the liquor racket for the man who has no stake." The fellow was like Tom Halsey — shrewd mountain man and shrewd college boy . . . "When I have got a stake I'll look elsewhere. This racket won't last. I'm in to get what I can while the getting is good."

It was like the stories, always being whispered about college campuses all over America, of young women, also anxious to get on, caught up by the American cry of "progress, advancement . . . get on in the world . . . put it across" . . . young women making their way through college by working nights at the oldest of all women's trades.

Kit felt that she had been spoiled for returning to the life of a working woman. Business was a mystery to her. She had got a kind of prejudice against all buying and selling. She had herself never bought or sold any liquor. If there was in her a hunger for marriage with some man she was in the position of innumerable other American women . . . she had not found the man she wanted.

She arrived at Kate's house at night and Kate came out and got into her car. She did not tell Kit where they were going. "Tom wants to see you." Kate fell into silence, speaking only to direct Kit along roads.

Tom Halsey had arranged a meeting with the man Steve Wyagle. Kit thought . . . during this period of her experience as one of Tom's crowd . . . after all a minor member of the crowd, unknown to most of the others . . . leading as she did such a solitary life. She was, it is true, known to them, a figure the newspapers had picked up, made into a half celebrity . . . she thought that but for the fact that she was the wife of Tom's son she would have gone through the whole experience unnoticed by him . . .

The power of the man Wyagle had, she concluded, been growing. He had been going about among Tom's crowd, talking of Tom's growing greediness. It was even possible that Steve had made some arrangements with the federal man. There were such arrangements made all through the prohibition times, officers of the law making deals with the lawbreakers. "You turn such and such a one up, help us get the evidence we need.

"We'll take care of you."

With Tom Halsey gone, perhaps serving time in some federal prison, there would be a chance for the new man. Kit and Kate drove along a road, getting some fifteen or twenty miles from Kate's house . . . it was a bright clear fall evening . . . and turned into a little wood road. They parked the car, leaving it in a little opening among trees, Kit growing constantly more and more nervous. She kept looking at Kate but Kate's face told her nothing. The conviction was growing in her that she was being taken to some out of the way place. It might be the end of her.

"But would the woman Kate give herself to a thing of that sort?"

The two women walked in silence along a wood path coming at last to a fence at the wood's edge and once, while they were still in the wood, Kit put her hand on Kate's arm. Her own hand trembled. She had grown pale. Her voice trembled.

"Where are we going, Kate? What's up?" she asked, but Kate did not answer and, as on another occasion when Kit had become frightened by the possibilities of what might happen to herself through Tom, she grew a little angry.

Kit had never carried a gun but now she wished she had one. There was a small flashlight in the pocket of her coat and she took it out and held it gripped in her right hand. There was no need for it. The night was clear and there was a moon.

"Be quiet," Kate had said to Kit, her voice suddenly harsh, and the two women approached the fence at the edge of the wood in silence. There were some bushes growing at just that spot and they got behind them.

They stood thus, Kit didn't know for how long. There was a clearing in the wood and in the clearing an old barn and in the bright moonlight Kit could see the remains of the foundation of what had once been a house. It was one of Tom's liquor storing places but Kit had never been there. She stood, half angry, half afraid, beside Kate, occasionally looking at her. Thoughts were racing in her head. Formerly, all through the first year and a half of her employment by Tom she had felt Kate as her friend. Now she was doubtful. She was frightened.

Had the woman Kate brought her to that place on Tom's

orders to put her "on the spot"? She kept looking furtively about but there was only the silence of a wood at night, a silence broken only by the little steady sound of insect life. Once an owl hooted. The sound came from far off, some-where in the distance.

There was the long silence and then it was broken. Kit saw that Tom Halsey had out-smarted the ex-city rough, Steve Wyagle. The man had been induced to come to the spot, to the old barn in the clearing in the wood, accom-panied by three of what he thought to be his own men, men pledged to him in the effort that was to be made to unseat Tom. There had been some kind of assurance given the man Steve. "You come with three of your own men and I will come with but one of mine.

"We will have a talk. We will talk things over." Steve Wyagle came along the woodland path, the three men with him, and went into the clearing and Kit saw that one of the men was a fellow who had been with Steve, one of his com-panions on that first Sunday evening when she had gone with Gordon to Kate's house. She remembered the impres-sion got at that time, an impression of cruelty in the man's eyes. With his three companions Wyagle crossed the open space before Kit and went into the barn.

There was another time of silence and again Kate trem-bled. If it were true that Kate had brought her to the place to put her on the spot, to be killed, these were the men to do it. She looked about prepared for flight through the wood, and her hand gripped the flashlight. She thought vaguely of Kate, anger sweeping over her. "If I start to run and she tries to hold me I'll hit her," she thought. Kate stood close to her. Kate's eyes were watching her.

And then Tom Halsey came and he was accompanied

only by the boy Alfred Weathersmythe. They came along
the woodland path passing close to the bush back of which
Kate and Kit stood and went into the clearing. They did not
enter the barn but stood silently in the clearing.

It was a tense moment. Kit had a sudden and intense
return of an old admiration for Tom. He stood, silently,
in the clear place, to all appearances unarmed and then
Kit saw him lean over and whisper to young Alfred
Weathersmythe. It was not until afterwards that she thought
her way through what was happening that night, what was
about to happen.

Tom, having taken the boy Alfred to be ostensibly one of
his bodyguards, having him about day after day, had evidently, from the first, had something definite in mind.

He had intended making a killer of the boy. That had
been his purpose. Kit did not know how he did it — but she
knew that there was always something almost hypnotic about
Tom's quiet power over others.

And he had got the boy and certainly the fact would be an
advantage. There was murder to be done. It was to be done
by a Weathersmythe. Kit thought that he might have
worked on the romantic folly of the boy. "Are you a brave
man? Do you dare to be brave?"

The boy foolishly thinking of himself as another like that
grandfather, the Mosby man. Once when he was a small boy
he had asked the grandfather — "but could you kill a man
if you met him, say when you were riding in the road —
if there was just you two?"

"Yes. If he was a Yank." The grandfather had been stern.
What a foolish question to have asked!

In the clearing the two, Tom and the boy, stood . . .
Kit sure afterwards that the boy, like herself, must have

been trembling with fright. She said she got a sudden conviction of what was going to happen. "I wanted to run to them, to cry out to him — 'Stop it, stop it!' " She wanted to cry. She did start forward but Kate, putting out her hand, gripped her arm.

They stood in silence and then Steve Wyagle, the city rough, professional killer, walked out of the shadows of the barn and toward Tom. He was accompanied by the three roughs, lieutenants of his own as he thought but, even at that moment, Kit knew he had been out-smarted. Tom had got to his three companions, he had bought them off.

"Hello, Tom," Steve said, cheerfully enough, stepping forward. What a fool he was! He said no more. It was evident that both Tom and the young Weathersmythe were armed and as Steve stepped toward them, the boy shot and at that moment Steve's three companions grabbed his arms.

They had got his arms and held him, and while he struggled Tom put his hand on young Weathersmythe's shoulder and led him forward until he was within a few feet of the struggling man. The boy seemed paralyzed and Kit thought that even from where she stood with Kate she could see his body tremble.

He stood thus and Tom spoke to him, his voice still quiet, commanding, and Kit said that he even seemed to help the boy raise his arm . . . "Shoot," he said sharply, and the boy did.

He shot again and again in a kind of hysteria of shooting. He stood over the fallen man and poured bullets into him, keeping it up until the gun he held was empty and then turning he bolted past Kit and into the wood and Kit, also half hysterical and forgetting Kate, ran after him.

Kit got into her car and driving out of the wood got into a country road and sitting there in her car saw, in the bright moonlight, young Alfred Weathersmythe's figure running in the distance. There was a long dip in the road and she saw the figure come up the crest of a distant hill and disappear. . . . She threw the car into gear and followed and presently overtook him.

The running figure was Weathersmythe and when she had run the car alongside him he stopped.

He had become dumb. How white he was! He stood in the road trembling and Kit got out of the car and helped him into the seat. "No. No," he kept protesting. She drove slowly along the road until she came to a little wooden bridge and then stopped the car beside the road. He had begun to cry like a small child, and she took him into her arms and held him, caressing his face with her hand. She tried to talk to him but he would not answer. "Why did you do it, boy, why did you?" The feeling that had been growing in her as regards Tom, a feeling of distrust and suspicion, had become an intense hatred and she sat with the boy in the car, her arms about him, swearing violently. Words she had heard, remembered, intense bitter words, filthy words rose to her lips. She herself trembled.

She got out of the car and taking the boy by the hand, led him into a field. There was a rail fence but she did not climb over. She took the rails, one at a time, and threw them aside, being suddenly very strong, the boy standing dumbly to one side. The rails of the fence were something on which she could lay her hands. She gripped each rail, raised it over her head and hurled it from her, still cursing.

They got into the field and walked a short distance along the bank of a little creek and something inside Kit began to get more quiet. She had hold of young Weathersmythe's hand, leading him and he still kept muttering. "No. No," he continued saying. As Kit grew quieter she noticed that there was a cut place on his head. In running through the wood, after the shooting, he had struck his head against a tree. She stopped and made him sit at the edge of the stream.

There was, for Kit, one of those odd moments that come into all lives. She had been terribly excited and was filled with a feeling new to her. For the first time in her life she hated sincerely, wholly.

"He has done this to this boy. He has worked on him, in some way induced him to do this thing." She had no feeling of regret for the death of Wyagle. A useless brute had been snuffed out. She imagined Tom's working, as he would have worked, on the mind of the boy, making him think the deed he was to do was something heroic. The boy was to prove himself to Tom as perhaps his grandfather, the Mosby man, had in his time proved his courage and the coldbloodedness that is also a part of war to himself and others.

There was in fact a war on, a curious civil war, brought on by prohibition, Kit herself having joined up, the officers of the law, in spite of the fact that many of them were crooked, had sold out, were, after all, on the right side. Kit, sitting beside the boy in the field, at the stream's edge that night . . . he had become ill and was lying on the ground beside her, very white now, his lips still muttering the words, "no, no" . . . she kept leaning forward and wetting a handkerchief in the stream . . . it seemed to her that her mind wandered . . . she recalled a story the boy beside her had told her . . . it concerned his grandfather and the Civil War . . .

It was a story of Sheridan and the struggle in the valley
of the Shenandoah. There had been some of Mosby's men
taken in a fight and they were pronounced outlaws by Sheridan. Some five or six of them were led out and shot and
later, it was decided by Mosby that he would treat some of
Sheridan's men in the same way.

"It is war. They have shot in cold blood five of our men.
We will shoot five of theirs." Young Weathersmythe had
heard his grandfather tell the story . . . some forty or fifty
of the Mosby men, with five prisoners getting off their
horses at the edge of a wood. It was in the evening. The
grandfather had told of the scene, the Mosby men having
come out of a wood road. There was a falling field before
them and in the distance, across the valley to the West from
where the Mosby men stood beside their horses . . . the
men had dismounted and stood at their horses' heads. . . . In
the distance the sun was going down. "The sky was as red
as blood," the grandfather had said.

"You have to remember that the Mosby men were not
regular troops," young Weathersmythe had said to Kit that
time he was telling her the story. He explained that they were
irregular troops. They met. Word was sent to them to meet
at some point, usually at night. They went on a raid and
then, when they had returned from some such raids . . .
they were in a surprising number of cases successful . . .
their leader Mosby was a shrewd quiet man . . . as young
Alfred had spoken to Kit of him she found herself confusing his figure, as described by the boy, with that of Tom
Halsey . . . the same quiet ability to command men, to in-
spire fear in men, obedience in them.

The Mosby men, on the particular evening with the prisoners. "We are going to kill them, shoot the bastards." The grandfather had described the sun going down across the valley on that evening. Their leader Mosby was not with them and another man, with a major's commission, was in command. He spoke to the men who had charge of the prisoners, pointing . . . "March them out there,' and the prisoners were led out before the dismounted troops. "Well, who wants to do this job?" Silence among the Mosby men. Alfred Weathersmythe's telling Kit the story long afterwards, his determination to make of his grandfather a hero. . . . "Not one of them wanted to do it.

"It was a duty to be done. Would you have done it?"

It was the boy asking Kit the question, in a hotel room at night, he looking up at her with troubled eyes. His grandfather had done the job. He had shouted to the men holding the prisoners to turn them loose and, as they ran down the falling field, had followed them on his horse, shooting them one by one. The boy, imaginative, questioning, making the scene as he told it very vivid in his own mind and in Kit's mind. "He was doing his duty. He had the guts to do his duty.

"They had shot some of Mosby's men.

"Would you have done it, Kit; could you have done it?"

The boy in the hotel room, excited by his own tale, putting his head to his hands and muttering, "no, no."

He kept muttering the same words as he now lay beside Kit, her own mind confused, jumping back to another scene when a certain tubercular cotton-mill lad had lain beside her in another field, by another stream. She had sat, that time, holding the boy's head while the blood flowed from him, coloring a stream. The boy now beside her was also bloody. The blood kept running from the cut place in his head. He was very ill. Suddenly he sat up and leaning forward vomited, and as suddenly, he arose.

He stood for a moment looking down at Kit and then as though the sight of her was something terrible to him, he dashed away from her through the stream and ran away across fields and she sat quietly and let him run. On that night she had some vague notion that he would go to the law officers of some near-by town. He would tell what had happened. Kit sat on the grass in the field watching him run. She watched until he had disappeared. There was a wood beyond the field and she saw him run into that. She did not know afterwards how long she sat in the same place. "I saw him run," she said. "He didn't, as I thought he would, go to the officers. I don't know where he went.

"I never heard or saw any more of him," she said.

CHAPTER SEVENTEEN

GORDON HALSEY came to Kit in the hotel suite where she had once lived with him as his wife. He had two revolvers. He knocked and when she admitted him he came in and sank into a chair. He took an automatic revolver from his coat pocket and laid it on a little writing desk in a corner of the room. Then he took another from his trouser pocket and Kit broke into laughter.

Why, how pale he was. Gordon had grown fat and he was much agitated. He began to scold about his father. "He wants me to bring you to him," he said. What a funk he was in! He was angry. "What have I to do with all this?" He leaned forward in his chair and Kit noticed that his lips were trembling. He had been speaking in a whisper and had asked her to go lock the door and when she had done so . . . smiling . . . the terror that had so evidently taken possession of him affected her in two ways. She came and stood near him. When he had appeared at the door her first inclination had been to deny him admittance, tell him to get out, to stay out, but something, the curious look of terror in his eyes, had aroused her pity and that had been followed by amusement. For a moment he had been to her as he was, a little at least, before she had married him, a helpless child. He spoke in a loud whisper.

He was telling her a tale. "And so they have also got to you?" she thought, standing and looking at him. He had been approached by a federal man, it might be by the same one who had, some weeks before, spoken to her. There had been hints thrown at him, questions asked. He told Kit that two men had come that very afternoon to his hotel room. There had been threats made, possibility of a term in prison hinted at.

"For what? What do I know? What have I done?"

"Why, you have done nothing. You never did anything," Kit said.

He began to beg Kit to go away with him. "I have it all fixed," he said. He had got a car . . . not the big sports model car he had driven when he courted her but an old Ford. He had even left off his so sporty-looking English-cut clothes and was almost shabbily dressed in a worn suit. She wondered where he had got it. "He has had one of the bell boys here in the hotel get it for him," she thought. The suit was old and worn and it had a curious shininess. It was one of the kind of second-hand suits sold to workingmen in little stores on side streets of industrial towns. "They mend them. They clean and press them," she thought.

What a fool he was! He had got also a shabby-looking car and had it parked somewhere in a side street. "And so, you have got money hidden away." She knew her man. For years he had been getting money from Tom. He would have hidden much of it away, no doubt in safety deposit boxes in banks . . . not all in one town . . . she knew because in a small way she had done the same. He had put the idea into her head when they were first married, when there was at least something of a relationship between them. She stood

before him as he talked . . . it was late in the day, a fall day
and growing dark . . . and he was pleading with her. He
wanted her to cut out with him, leave the country.

"You really be my wife, Kit," he pled. He began a long
story, leaning forward in his chair, his face in his hands,
looking not at her but at the floor, talking in a whisper, the
two revolvers lying on the writing desk near her. It was true,
he said, that he had done her wrong, had played around
with other women, had lied to her. He began speaking of
his boyhood, in the house with the woman Kate. What
chance had he ever had?

"I never had a mother," he said. He was filled with self-
pity. Kit went to sit in a chair by a window, saying nothing, letting him talk. She was both amused and hurt. "What
a pitiful figure for any woman to call husband," she thought.
He said he had thought it all out. As to the business his
father was in, he had had nothing to do with it.

"You know that, Kit. You know it as well as I do." There
was something, to Kit, almost comical in the situation, his
sitting here in the room with her, telling of the wrongs
done him. He appealed to her, looking up from the floor.
She had moved silently to the chair by the window and he
turned his own chair to face her again but did not look
directly at her. He had got suddenly lonely and afraid. It
was the federal men and their talk with him that had started
it all and now he had turned to Kit. "I'll cut it all out, honest
I will, Kit." He meant his running about, sleeping with other
women, paying them with money got from his father. He
wanted her to go with him, at once, somewhere out into
the West. They would buy a farm, a cattle ranch, he said.
Kit gathered that the federal men, in their talk with him,
had suggested an idea that had frightened him more than all

the rest. The government had got a new technique. When it was difficult to get evidence against the leader or his better fixed lieutenants of one of the gangs that infested America all through the prohibition times, the government tried getting them on income tax evasion. They had already got several big shots on that charge.

And what of Gordon Halsey? He had never made any income tax returns and all the time he had been getting large sums from his father. As he talked to Kit that evening, saying they would creep out of the hotel, one at a time . . . he told her where he had parked the shabby looking Ford . . . as for his other car . . . he owned and had been driving a Lincoln . . . the government, he said, could have it.

The government men might be watching it. He had been very canny, had told them nothing. How were they to find out how much money he had and where he had it hidden? He and Kit would go away in the Ford. They would drive all night. He had cash enough with him to last them for weeks. When they got out West they could take new names. Although he had not treated Kit as he should have done he had really always loved her.

"I thought you didn't really have any respect for me," he said, looking up at her, and instantly she had, for a passing moment, the thought that she would like to go to him, perhaps take him into her arms. He was after all nothing but a stupid boy. "I wonder," she thought, as the impulse passed, "how many men are like him."

Could it be that all men were such silly children? Kit was in a curiously serious mood, had been in the same mood ever since the night when young Weathersmythe, under the influence of Tom, had killed Steve Wyagle. She had come back to her suite in the hotel in the Southern industrial town on the night after that had happened and had not left the suite since.

She had had her meals brought to her room and twice . . . she was a little vague as to how long she had been there . . . she thought it might have been for a week but then immediately afterwards concluded it couldn't have been for so long.

There had been notes sent to her, two of them. They were brought by the waiter, a Negro man, who also brought her meals. They were on the tray under a dish. They told her to go at once to Kate but she had not gone. She had torn up the notes and smiled. Was Tom Halsey also becoming afraid?

He had done that thing to her and to the boy, young Weathersmythe, had got her to come to that place, to watch him as he made the boy kill that man. Perhaps he had wanted to show her his power.

He had been getting himself into what he thought a safe place. If there was too much inquiry made as to the death of Wyagle there was the boy, the actual killer, son of a prominent family in Virginia, the state where family meant so much. The killing had taken place in the state, in one of the border mountain counties.

"They'd better not go too much into that."

It was evident that they hadn't. There had been but a short newspaper item about the finding of a man's body. If the old barn, in the clearing in the wood, near which the body had been found, had been used formerly by Tom's crowd as a place to store liquor during its passage across the state there had been no liquor found when county officers went to inspect the body. The man Wyagle was almost unknown. No one in that county had ever before seen him. There were no large towns in the mountain county.

A little item in the newspapers . . . a body found . . .
evidently that of a stranger. The man had been shot to death
but there were no guns found. It was presumed to be just another illicit liquor killing. The body was found by the man
who owned the farm. "Yes, and he knew more than it would
be comfortable for him to tell," Kit thought as she read the
item. She knew that Tom never stored liquor without first
making arrangements. The farmer would have been paid
to keep others off his place, keep an eye out. He wouldn't
be told too much. He would be paid for silence.

He would have been afraid not to tell the officers of the
county about the dead body found on his land. He would
have been afraid to express any suspicions as to the killers.

Kit had wondered, reading the notes telling her, commanding her, to report to Kate, if Tom had also grown
afraid. It had been the purpose of the federal men, come
into Tom's territory, determined to break up his particular
crowd . . . as long as prohibition lasted there would be such
crowds . . . Kit knew that . . . if the federal men succeeded in breaking up Tom's crowd, got Tom, another Tom
and another crowd would take over the business.

There was money in it, plenty of money to be made in the
game. There was no evidence that prohibition had lessened
the demand for liquor.

Kit sat in her room, listening to the pleadings of Gordon,
her husband . . . the thought that he was, at least legally,
her husband amused and in a queer way hurt . . . not
thinking of him . . . he went on pleading . . . he had got
the idea into his head that they would run away somewhere
together . . . go out West. . . . He would become a West-

erner . . . out in the place where gals are gals and men
are men . . . he had been reading Western magazines,
going to the movies . . . already perhaps he had begun
thinking of himself as a man made into a new man by getting on to a horse . . . she wondered if he had ever been
on one . . . riding across open plains . . . talking with a
Western drawl . . .

She smiled, these thoughts flitting across her mind as Gordon talked on and on, pleading with her. Now he was
boasting of his hidden wealth . . . now declaring his own
innocence of any wrongdoing. "This income tax thing, Kit
. . . it's for earning, now ain't it, it's for what you earn, Kit.
I haven't ever earned anything. You know I haven't." She
wanted to tell him to go out of the room, not to bother her,
but didn't. He was too much the pitiful figure sitting there,
pleading with her.

Her mind ran away from him to his father and he kept
on talking, his words sometimes not heard, sometimes
mingled with her own thoughts.

It was evening of the fall day and the lights in the room
had not been turned on. She was in a grim mood. When the
first of the notes, telling her to report to Kate, had been delivered . . . the Negro waiter saying nothing . . . the note
left on a tray under a dish . . . she had been inclined to
obey. After the shooting of Wyagle by the young Weathersmythe she had wanted to do something to Tom. She
thought of going to the federal men, finding the man who
had spoken to her, the leader of the federals, the man who
had managed to stir up fear and uncertainty in Tom's
domain, of talking to him, at least of telling him about the
killing. She couldn't. How could she do that without involv-
ing Weathersmythe? There was no doubt that Tom was

not only a capable leader of men, he was also smart. He had outsmarted her.

And there was something else. She hated being disloyal. There still remained in her the feeling . . . the gang . . . Tom's crowd . . . men she did not know . . . an organization . . . men like her own people, mountain men, poor whites like herself, had been enabled to buy clothes, live a bit more freely, make money. The privilege of making money, by almost any method, did mean something . . .

Kit had no religion, no real friends, had never had a real lover. It was as though she had said to herself, "I have to be loyal to something." This vague thing called "the crowd," "the gang," in newspapers sometimes called "the mob" . . . Tom Halsey's "mob" . . .

"God knows I haven't got anything else."

"I could go to Tom, watch my chance . . . he might not expect it of me . . . he knows I have never carried a gun . . . I could shoot him, kill him. It would only mean some other man to take his place. They'd get me but I would have got him. I could shoot him, stand over him with a gun in my hand and watch him die."

She had got the first note from Tom on just such another evening as the one on which Gordon came to her and after reading it and after the waiter who had brought her dinner had left she had decided to go out and to a store to buy a gun. She dressed for that purpose, not in any of the better clothes she still had . . . her rather expensive wardrobe having been renewed from time to time, but in a special dress she had bought.

It was a little black dress, loose and coming down to her shoe tops and there were a black sunbonnet and cheap black stockings and shoes. She had got the outfit once in a town in Ohio. She had been driving through the town, returning from one of her trips, no liquor in her car and she had gone into a little shabby store.

It wasn't a store. It was a place where some church women of the town were holding what they called a "rummage sale." She had been curious and had stopped her car and going into the place had bought the outfit. "It might come in handy," she had told herself and had been amused at the thought of making herself up in the outfit . . . something like the fiction women detectives about which she sometimes read in detective magazines . . . a beautiful young woman, very daring, so rigged out, going into some den of vice, etc., etc. . . . when she had lived with Gordon, as his wife, he was always keeping magazines about that were filled with such stories.

She had put the outfit on, that evening after she got Tom's first note, a little amused at herself. "I won't take the hotel elevator down to the street. I'll walk down the stairs and so out."

She had got ready to creep out of the hotel, thinking to go buy a revolver with which to shoot Tom but hadn't gone.

The hotel was being watched. Her own suite was being watched. No one had told her so. She had the conviction that it was so. There was something in the air that told her.

"There is a trap being set. They are going to try to get all of us, me too. I don't care much."

If it were true, what of it? She had thought about that. "Suppose I do have to serve a term in prison? I am in a prison now."

Even in a prison there might be something. There might be some women in there who would become her friends. She had a terrible need . . . it growing in her . . . of something . . . a relationship . . . some man or some woman, to whom she could feel close. Just at that time she had . . . it was she felt the strongest thing in her . . . the hunger to give.

What?

Herself in some way.

There had been the months and months of loneliness. If she succeeded in shooting, in killing Tom Halsey, it would also be her own end. American gangs were organized in that way, each leader, big-shot or little-big-shot, like Tom, having, inside the gang . . . the gang organization was not unlike political organizations . . . there would be some man or group of men in the organization who would re- venge the killing of the leader . . . the killing, if accom- plished would be, for her, a kind of giving of herself.

Loneliness.

The loneliness, so pronounced in Kit at that time, was not so unlike the loneliness of many Americans.

Loneliness of the radical in a capitalistic society, of the man who wants to fight it, who does feel in himself a kind of social call . . .

Immediately the thing called "respectability" gone. Such a one, a Eugene Debs for example, may be the most gentle of men. He becomes in the public mind something danger- ous, is pictured as Kit had been pictured, as a dangerous one.

. . . The life of the artist in any society.

. . . Life of the labor leader and for that matter loneliness also of the lives of successful Americans, even the very rich, the leaders of a capitalistic society:

"Man cannot live by bread alone:

. . . The leader, the successful one, in any competitive society having, as an essential to his success, to climb up over the shoulders of others. This or that man, standing in the way, to be swept aside, if need be ruined:

. . . His trying to justify it all. "It is a law of nature. The strong must survive. The weak must perish."

Kit had got herself into a state, had been in a state ever since the killing of Wyagle by Alfred Weathersmythe. It was dark in the room where she sat with Gordon. He had become silent. Already he had told her why he had come to her on that particular evening. His father had sent word to him. "You bring that wife of yours here to me. You do it tonight." Gordon was afraid to obey. He was afraid not to obey.

He was in a jam, sunk, so he had come to her. His childish mind had built up a new childish idea . . . that the relationship between them . . . that never had any reality . . . could be re-established, made real. They would run away together, go out West. They would get a ranch, raise cattle. He would become something he had seen depicted in the movies, a cowboy . . . one who knew nothing of cows, had perhaps never been on a horse. He would wear spurs and a ten-gallon hat, have a rope hanging on the pommel of his saddle. He would lasso steers, ride proudly into western towns while she . . .

She would be a meek and faithful wife to him.

Kit had got out of her chair by the window and was walking up and down the room. She had not slept for several nights. How American her husband was. Her thoughts may not have been so definite. Oh, what have American women not had to stand from American men! She began to laugh and her laughter startled Gordon so that he jumped to his feet. He was half angry. "What are you laughing about?" he asked angrily.

She did not answer. "Sit still," she said to him. Although there were no lights in the room a little light did come in from the hall through an open transom. "Yes, I guess we'll get out of here," she said, and when he did not answer but sat staring at her, an old look, she had long since grown accustomed to seeing on his face, came back. She could see his face dimly in the soft light. It was a look, half fear, half desire to assert something. She went into her bedroom and began packing a small bag, putting into the bag the little cheap black dress and then, coming back into the room where Gordon still sat in silence, she picked up one of the two revolvers he had brought with him. "I guess I'll take one of these," she said. He had become very meek. "You hold this and stand where you are," she said, handing him the little bag. He was like a frightened child. "What are you going to do?" he asked. She did not answer but went out into the hallway leaving him standing in the half darkness in the room. He had put the second revolver in his pocket. "He is the kind of man who will shoot some one if he isn't watched," she thought.

She had no definite plan but one was forming in her mind. Tom Halsey wanted her to come to him. All right, she would go. She had a hunch, a feeling. There was something definite about to happen. There would be, in some way, an end to the life she was in. There was in her also a determination, a kind of cold desire. She wanted to face Tom Halsey, in some way pay him out for what he had done to young Weathersmythe and through the boy to herself. She went along a hallway and presently saw a boy in uniform, one of the hotel bellboys. He was one she knew, a boy who had been often to her room, had done many errands for her. He was a slender young fellow with sharp crafty eyes.

She spoke to him sharply. Already she knew what was the situation in the hotel. At least she thought she knew. The manager of the hotel had been making money out of Tom and his crowd. Now he would know that his own situation . . . if it were true, as she suspected, that there was to be an effort, on the part of the federal men, to close in on them . . . he would have become frightened. She made a motion with her hand to the bellboy and led him back into her room. "Is the hotel here being watched?" she asked when she had closed the door. Gordon still stood where she had left him. There was still the frightened look on his face.

The bellboy said it was. Speaking hurriedly he told her that he had been told that both she and Gordon were to be ordered to leave. He had got that straight, he said. They would have been ordered out before but that the leader of the federal men had told the hotel manager that if either Gordon or herself left the hotel secretly he, the manager, would be held responsible.

There had been threats made. The bellboy grinned. The manager of the hotel, one of a chain of hotels, was, he said, frightened. If anything happened to bring the hotel into prominence, as harboring Tom Halsey's crowd, he would lose his job. The bellboy had got hold of the story. It had been whispered about among the boys. The manager was a man of thirty-five, a tall man with shiny black hair, always kept plastered down tightly on his head, and with a little black mustache. He had always been excessively polite to Kit, fawning on her. "Are you finding everything all right, Mrs. Halsey? Is there anything we can do for you?" A hundred times he had stopped her as she came in at the door of the hotel. He bowed to her. He had long arms and long hands. He was one of the kind of men who are inclined, when speaking to a woman, to caress. He caressed her with his voice, put a hand on her shoulder. "We have but one desire, Mrs. Halsey, to make you feel at home here. We want all of our guests to feel at home."

With a kind of delight in the situation of his employer the sharp-faced little bellboy was grinning and stowing the ten-dollar bill into his pocket. "All right," Kit said, smiling at him. "I guess we'll relieve your boss."

She made a proposal to the boy. Was there a way for him to get herself and husband out of the place without their being seen? The boy scratching his head. "There is a fifty-dollar bill in it for you."

"Ouch!" he said, still grinning. For a moment he stood uncertain and then telling her to come and, first opening the door and looking out, led the way down the hall. "You understand we have to take a chance," he had said and she nodded in approval.

They got safely out of the hotel although Kit thought that their departure was known shortly after they left. The boy led them down back stairs, through hallways . . . once when they heard the hotel elevator stop at a floor they were on, the boy led them into an unoccupied room, where they stayed concealed for some minutes.

Again they were in what Kit thought was a room where hotel laundry was kept. This on the ground floor. Her husband stood near her in that place and she could feel his body trembling. "What a man!" she thought again. She herself was cool. A kind of coldness and determination had taken possession of her. When they were in the laundry room the boy disappeared and Kit understood that he had gone to make necessary arrangements. He had explained the matter to Kit, ignoring Gordon. "The kid has got Gordon's number," she thought . . . and had suggested that the necessary arrangements would cost some more money. "So he is going to get all he can. The little devil has thought this out as we have been creeping down these stairs." "All right," she had said, smiling at him.

"There will be another fifty when we are in the clear," she said.

"It is after all Tom's money. It came from him."

The boy brought uniforms for them to slip on over their clothes, the white uniform of a cook for Gordon and a blue waitress uniform for Kit and thus arrayed they were led by a back door into an alleyway and, having given the boy his money, they were left there. The uniforms were taken off in the shadow of a brick building that was the hotel garage, Gordon still silent. He trembled so that Kit had to kneel down and pull off the legs of the cook's trousers. It was the uniform of a fat man. Had Gordon not been so frightened he could have walked out of the trousers.

Kit had a continual inclination to begin laughing. She took Gordon by the hand and led him along the alleyway and into a street and they went along streets Kit had never been in before. There was a street of darkened stores and presently they got into one of factories and before a small house, inside of which she could hear the voices of Negro women, talking and laughing; they found the car Gordon had bought.

There was some difficulty in finding the key, Gordon fumbling nervously in his pocket. He spoke for the first time. "Do you think we will get away? Do you think so?" Kit thought he spoke with the voice of a frightened child and when at last he had found the car key he dropped it in the road and she had to get down and fumble about, running her fingers through the dust of the unpaved street to find it again.

They were in the car and moving. She drove to the edge of town and, then circling the town, made for the road that led to Kate's house. She thought that Gordon did not know what she was doing. Again he had grown silent. He had taken the gun out of his pocket and it lay in his lap. He sat in silence until she had turned the car into the yard by a roadway that led to the back of Kate's house . . . the house as usual was, as seen from the outside, dark and silent . . . and then, when she had got out of the car, he began to plead with her.

"No. No," he said . . . he was still sitting in the car seat . . . the car was an old one, without side curtains, and he sat in the front seat . . . he had picked up the gun and held it in his hand . . . "no, no," he said, pleading with her . . . "I did not mean this. I did not mean here."

Kit did not answer but, reaching up and grasping his coat collar, jerked him out of the seat.

CHAPTER EIGHTEEN

K IT had got her limp and frightened husband into Kate's house. They were in the same room to which they had been shown that first time Kit had come there with Gordon, when she was being inspected by Tom . . . to see whether or not she would make a fit wife for his son. In spite of a kind of a tenseness in her, that grew after she had half dragged Gordon into the house, he all the time protesting, she had to smile, thinking of herself as such a candidate for wifehood. She kept smiling, the same grim little smile that had been on her lips all evening. Kate had admitted them into the house, Gordon holding the revolver openly in his hand . . . she thought he was unconscious of it . . . and she with a hand on the one she had stowed in the pocket of her coat.

They were both armed and that thought also amused Kit. As Kate had shown them into the room Kit had noted that she looked sharply at Gordon, checking his frightened appearance and seeing the gun that hung half limply in his hand. This was in the kitchen, they having entered the house through the kitchen door, and seeing Kate thus sizing up Gordon, Kit had smiled at her but there had been no smile in response and the fact had a little irritated her. She

wanted to say something . . . "Oh, for God's sake, Kate, have
a heart. At least, if you are going to bump me off in this
place have a laugh with me." She said nothing and, led by
Kate, they went into the same room in which she had sat
with Gordon the first time she came to the house. Kate
went back to the kitchen leaving the two sitting on the little
couch in the room. "Well, you can go to hell then," Kit
thought.

She did not think afterwards that she was particularly
afraid. There are times in life when you accept. She accepted the fact that she might not leave the house alive but
within her, like a little spark glowing, there was a hope that
she would get a chance at Tom, pay him out, not for what
he had done to her . . . she felt that if she was in a bad spot
it was her own doing . . . but rather for what he had done
to the young Weathersmythe.

She didn't know why that had hit her so hard. It had. It
had stayed with her, changed something in her. Now there
was in her no illusion about Tom and his occupation.

It wasn't, she thought, because his occupation was illegal.
She thought that had little to do with it. "I guess most any
way there is to make a lot of money would be illegal if there
were any real laws," she thought. That night she simply sat
and waited, her husband Gordon beside her on the couch.
He had slumped down, was white and silent. The gun still
hung in his limp hand.

There was a little light in the room, the curtains, as always
in that house, tightly drawn, the light coming from a tiny
electric light on the wall . . .

Little green house in Washington, in which, during the
Harding administration, men met to divide spoils . . . they
also in the illicit liquor business . . .

No doubt little houses in Chicago, rooms in hotels where men like Al Capone met their followers.

Kit could hear voices in the next room. They would be coming from the bedroom next to Kate's kitchen, Tom in there with some of his gang. He would be having his killers about him now . . .

"There is this woman, this Kit . . . she's out there . . . she is with that fool son of mine . . .

"She knows too much. I have told her three or four times to come out here but she hasn't come.

"Now she is here. We had better clean this up."

"If it is true that these government men are going to close in on us they will have a hard time convicting us if none of our own crowd squeals on us."

"But do you think she will squeal?"

"Yes, I think she will."

It would be simple enough. Tom would have one or two of the killers take care of her. When she was dead, her body thrown into a car, left somewhere far off, along some country road.

"As for that son of mine, I'll get him out of the country.

"He is a fool, but, after all, he is my son."

Perhaps the other men in the room looking a little doubtfully at Tom, thinking . . . "It is that son of his will get us stuck. He is the one who will squeal." They would say nothing.

Kit was sitting beside Gordon in the dimly lighted room and thinking hard. She thought of the woman Kate, wondering a little. There had been a time when she and Kate had been something near friends. It was an odd thing in women,

that faithfulness, willingness utterly to give up self, she felt
was in Kate. She was quite sure that Kate would, of her own
wish, never hurt any one. "It's strange . . . she is at bottom
a good woman.

"Will I ever feel as she does, such an utter attachment to
some man?"

Kit sat up straight on the couch and looked at her husband. He sat, or rather half lay, on the couch, one arm hanging over the side, the other in his lap, holding to the gun,
his face now very pale. In that light it seemed not white
but yellowish green. His eyes were closed.

And at that moment the door that led to Tom's room
opened and, accompanied by three other men, Tom came
into the room. They came silently, the three men going to
stand by the wall near the door and Tom standing in the
doorway. Kit had a thought. She always afterwards remembered it. As Tom had come out of the bedroom, accompanied by his killers, so a man named Wyagle had come out
of a barn, in an open place in a wood. "Wyagle's dead now,"
Kit thought. She had a sudden sharp feeling, a hunch. Not
herself but Tom Halsey was going to die. She did not think
of herself now as the killer.

An absurd thing happened. There was Gordon, sitting
like that on the couch and he sprang to his feet. He sat down
and again sprang up. "Oh, Papa. Hello, Papa," he said. His
voice was high and shrill. He said it three or four times and
then again slumped into the chair and sat as before with
eyes closed.

It was absurd, ridiculous. It was to Kit something almost
wonderful. She laughed aloud and got to her feet. If she
had had a desire, a determination to kill Tom it had left

her. To her, at the moment, it seemed a final, a kind of absolute humiliation of the man Halsey. "And so . . . you are the leader of a gang . . . you have bad men, killers about you . . .

"You are Tom Halsey, the strong quiet one."

Her thoughts were broken by the voice of Tom, speaking to her. He spoke sharply. "And so he will now take it out on me because his son is like that," she thought.

"If there were any chance that he would not have wanted me killed he will now. He will want killed every one who is now in this room."

"Come here, Kit," Tom said sharply, a new note of exasperation in his voice. She walked toward him and when she had got to where the men were standing by the wall, they stepped forward and pinned her arms to her side. One of them reached into her coat pocket and took the gun she had brought from the hotel, the gun she was to have used to shoot Tom. "And so," she thought, "his Kate has sharp eyes."

Kate would have noticed the bulge in her short coat when she had let her into the house. She stood, held thus, before Tom who half turned, as though to lead the way into the bedroom. She would be led out that way through Tom's room and Kate's kitchen. She would be taken outside, killed out there, her body thrown into a car. "I guess maybe they'll choke me." She stood silently and there were the absurd words uttered by Tom's son running through her head.

"Oh, Papa. Hello, Papa." Kit had to control herself to keep from throwing the words into Tom's face. She stood before him smiling.

CHAPTER NINETEEN

THERE was a diversion. It was all really very simple. Kit was there in that place, facing Tom, the men holding her. There was no violence. They held her and she didn't resist. She stood, still smiling at Tom, really wanting to laugh . . .

"Oho, big man, bad man, with your gang of other bad men, killers!"

The fellows holding Kit were certainly ugly enough looking brutes.

"Can a man be a brute and a killer and have a sense of humor?"

Kit's husband back there, was now sunk helplessly back on the couch. He was still holding the gun in his hand.

"Papa! Papa!"

Kit wanted to shout the words at Tom, throw them into his teeth. She looked hard at him and smiled. Perhaps he didn't see the smile in that light. He would be annoyed, humiliated.

"So this, Tom Halsey, is the son, at whose hands you are to establish a family, get the Halseys up into the ranks of respectables, establish an American family?"

Perhaps.

"Oho, oho!"

Men all over America struggling. "You wait. First I'll get rich and then I'll do something."

"I am a business man. I will work and scheme, pay workers who work for me as little as possible. I'll get rich. Then I'll become a man of leisure, travel, see the world, get culture.

"I will establish a family."

"I am an artist, a painter. I'll show you how to do it. The game is to paint portraits of rich men or their wives. Flatter them, if they are business men make them look strong-jawed, steady-eyed . . .

"Fix up their daughters or their wives. Boy, you know how to make them look.

"Buckle on to the dough. Get it. Put it away. Then become a real painter, eh."

"I am a writer. Hurra! The thing is to go in for the pulps, or go out to Hollywood. You can get a thousand a week out there.

"Look. It is like this with me. I am really, you see, a man of the people. I love the working classes. At heart I am a communist.

"I will go out there, get some of this dough.

"Then I will devote myself and my talents to the cause of the down-trodden.

"The Workers! The Workers! Oh, in my heart, how I love the workers."

It is of course absurd to think of the woman Kit, at that time not yet thirty, very slender, very straight-standing . . . not in the popular American Hollywood sense beautiful, but in her own way beautiful enough, with, at the moment, certainly, a fine dignity, quite convinced that, perhaps within a few minutes, she would be wiped out, disposed of, possibly in some rather brutal manner . . . caring certainly . . . not certainly at the moment afraid.

Certainly in her, at the moment, rich contempt. Is it in many, many American women, making out of modern America something like a matriarchy . . . so many men success-ridden, touch lost with the real sources of manhood?

The thought of Gordon's cry to his father taken up, spread through his gang. If you are a general commanding armies, leader of an American gang, a Hitler, a Mussolini, you must not let yourself be put in a ridiculous position.

In the room there was this moment, Kit's great moment, and then Kate, who during all this had been in her kitchen, came rapidly into the room and crossing to Tom spoke to him, saying some words Kit did not hear.

It may be that Tom was confused. He started quickly across the room and then turned and spoke to the men who were holding Kit. "Come here," he said and led the way into the kitchen, leaving Kit standing . . . her gun had been taken . . . alone again in the room with Gordon.

She did not look back at Gordon but went through the

door and into Tom's bedroom. There was another dim light in there and on the bed she saw a rope. "So they had intended to bind her." She was to have been thrown thus into a car, taken somewhere by two or three of Tom's roughs . . . no doubt insulted, perhaps violated, killed, her body thrown into some thicket. She had brought the little handbag from the hotel and it was in the room where Gordon sat, on the couch in there, and she went in and got it.

Gordon still sat dumbly on the couch but spoke to her in a loud whisper. "What are they going to do?" he asked but she did not answer.

She returned to Tom's room, having no plan. There was a window in the room and she went to it, ran up the shade and tried to open it but it was apparently nailed shut. She pushed with all her strength and then gave up. There was the sound of low voices coming from Kate's kitchen and she went and stood near the door, having some vague idea of a struggle. If Tom and his men came in through the door she would, the moment the door was opened, rush at them. She would scratch and bite, would fight them. "I might as well get done with it," she thought. They might kill her at once.

There was no more sound of the voices coming from the kitchen and she went quietly through the door and through the kitchen and got outside.

It was all a miracle to her. There she was. In one moment she had been quite sure she was to die and now there she was, out of that house, the hands of those men no longer holding her. It was quite dark and she slid carefully along the side of the house to a corner and stood waiting.

The moments passed. As often happens with people in sudden danger she had been quite cool but now her body began to tremble and her legs were so weak that she sat for a moment, her back against the wall of the building. It was a dark night with rain threatening and she could see nothing. A wind, such a sudden wind as often precedes a rain, came up and she could hear it in the branches of the trees in the apple orchard back of the house.

She did not know afterwards how long she waited thus. It may have been but for a minute. There was only the sound of the sudden wind in the trees and then, from the orchard and from the road in front of the house, there came the sound of shots and she could see the little sputter of light made by the discharge of guns.

It was at that moment that Gordon Halsey came rushing out of the house, coming as she had through the kitchen door.

He was shouting but this time he did not address his father as "Papa." "Father, father," he cried, and plunged into the darkness toward the orchard and the shots.

Kit did not stay. She ran. Dodging across a little strip of lawn beside the house, she forced her way through a low hedge, and got into a field. She ran along, keeping parallel to the road and came presently to where there was a wood, also near the road. There had been a raid planned by federal men, Kate's house no doubt watched for days . . . Kit didn't know how many of Tom's men had been at or near the house when she came there with Gordon.

There were many things she didn't know. In the wood

near the road were several cars parked . . . the cars that had
brought the federal men from town . . . and there was a man
standing near one of the cars, the lights out but the engine
running. She could hear the soft steady purr of the motor, a
sound that had always thrilled her, that had always made
her feel strong, as though a motor might be, well, say something of what a husband might be to her, and as she stood,
unseen, unheard, watching the man intently, his form but
dimly seen, her mind racing, he turned on the lights of the
car and walked away from it, down along a short woodland
path and into the road. It was the road that ran down to
Kate's house and he stood there listening. He had heard the
sound of the shots.

Kit didn't hesitate. She ran to the car and jumped into
the driver's seat. "The luck's with me tonight," she thought.

The car went with a roar into the road and turned away
from the direction of Kate's house. It was a good car. Kit
felt that. She almost struck the federal man standing there
in the road. "Look out — you fool." She didn't say it. "Hey!
Hey!" he cried. As she flashed past him she saw him pull a
gun out of its holster but he didn't shoot. He had been taken
off guard. He might have thought she was one of the federal
men, going into town, say for a doctor or an ambulance.
There had been the sound of the shooting.

Kit didn't know what the man thought. She was at the
wheel of a good, a powerful car. She drove furiously. She
did not know until later that several of Tom's men were
taken that night and that Tom was killed.

He was killed by his own son. Gordon had been over-
come with fright, finding himself alone in the house. Some

one of Tom's men, a watcher, had crept to the kitchen door and had warned Kate of the coming of the federal men. It had been a case of all the men in the house and others, who had evidently been waiting outside, trying each to save himself. They had tried to creep away in the darkness and some of them had succeeded but Tom Halsey had found himself facing two of the federal men.

This had happened in the apple orchard back of the house and he had turned to run, the federal men shooting at him. He had thought to do as Kit did, get through the hedge that ran alongside the house and into the fields but, as he ran, two or three of the federal men at his heels, he had met his son, now more and more frightened, gone half insane with fright and Gordon had fired.

He had shot his own father and having done so plunged into the arms of the men pursuing and with his father, who died in a hospital in town the next day, was taken a prisoner to town.

There were several cars loaded with prisoners and among them Kate. She had been found, seen by the light of a flashlight, standing, as Kit had stood earlier, with her back to the wall of the house. She had no gun. As she had been, so habitually silent for so long during her life with Tom Halsey, so, after her arrest and during the trial of other members of Tom's crowd and herself, she remained. She said nothing. "I know nothing," she said. Like Gordon Halsey she was sent off for a term in prison. The fact that the bullet that killed Tom Halsey entered his body from the front as he ran from the federal men made it quite certain that it was the son who had killed Tom Halsey.

CHAPTER TWENTY

KIT was in a little wood. As the mountain men said, she was "in the laurel." The wood was in a hill country, north of the town where Kate had lived and from which Kit had escaped. She took it for granted that Kate and perhaps, for all she knew, all the rest of Tom's crowd were in jail. It was not until some time later that she learned of Tom's death. She hadn't gone very far in the police car, driving it some thirty or forty miles and then leaving it beside a country road. She had struck out afoot.

She had some money, some three hundred dollars . . . she counted it at daybreak sitting in the wood. Fortunately she had clung to the little bag and had with her the black dress and the black sunbonnet and she put these on. It was the sort of garb you sometimes see on poor country women. Such a woman buys such a dress . . . it may be she has lost a child . . . it is a convention; it is also necessary to dress in black at a funeral. Afterwards it becomes her "best" dress. She wears it when she goes to town, when she goes to church. Kit put the suit and short coat she had worn when she went to Kate's house in the little bag and hid it in the wood. All of this was on the morning of her escape.

She felt free and was happy. For weeks she had been wanting to give up the life she had been in. She had held on wanting, in her own curiously tenacious way, to get even with Tom Halsey, do something to him, to pay him out for what he had done to young Weathersmythe. She had tried to think and talk herself out of that feeling but hadn't succeeded. "What is it to me? What have I to do with it?"

There had been something that held her and she had even gone to the length of wanting to kill Tom with her own hands, to shoot him, stand and watch him die and now the feeling was all gone. It had been unpleasant enough.

She did not know that he was dead . . . did not find that out until, in a restuarant in a small near-by town, she picked up a newspaper and read the story of Tom's death. The son, her husband, was in jail.

There was, in the same morning newspaper, a reference to herself. She had escaped but the officers were on her track. There was nothing said about her having run off with the car belonging to the federal man. That story would have made them look too soft and easy, she thought. She had a feeling, common among habitual law-breakers, of contempt for all officers of the law. Even in the popular detective stories her husband had been fond of reading, the law officers were usually fools. It might well be that the federal man in the road when she had run out of the wood with the federal car had not recognized her. The newspaper story she read said nothing of her being at Kate's house when the raid was made. "The notorious Kit Halsey was not taken but the police know of her whereabouts and it is expected she will be taken in a few days."

Kit felt again a sudden sharp sting of bitter loneliness. "The notorious Kit Halsey . . . the police know of her whereabouts." How men like to talk, bluff, say things that they think will make them seem wise and important.

Kit had come into the town after changing her clothes in the wood. "What shall I do now? Where shall I go?" She had come out of the wood and got into the road, this in the early morning. She had looked carefully about. There was no one in sight. What a clear sweet morning! The wood into which she had got on the evening before was on a high plateau. It was fall and the leaves on the trees in the wood and on other strips of woodland beyond were turning yellow and red but they had not begun to fall. She stood looking about. It was just such a country as that in which she had lived as a child, the same great hills going away, little farms stuck on hillsides. She was in the Appalachian hill country, her own country. On the night before, in the police car, she had driven blindly, not thinking, not caring where she went. There had been just the mad desire to get away from Tom, from Gordon . . . yes and from Kate. "I want something new now." The feeling common to thousands of young men and women in a civilization dominated by commercialism. "I don't want to buy and sell. I want to do some work that has some meaning."

It was good to be abroad in the fresh morning air. Not during that day, nor the next, when her adventures in that particular place ended, did she have much fear of being found and taken by the officers of the law. She had a hunch, a feeling. "No, they won't find me. I won't be taken."

From where she stood, in the upland road, she could look down into a broad valley where there was a town. "I'll go down and get something to eat." She went along the road and got to a paved road that led into the town. Cars kept passing her. She had seen the chimney of a factory from the

road above and as it was early morning she concluded that
the cars, all rather shabby looking, must belong to country
men, mountain men who were employed in the town's factory. None of the drivers offered to pick her up and she went
on into the town and stopped before a small hotel, near a
railroad station.

There was a restaurant, very evil smelling, dead flies under
the windows, and run by a fat man in a very dirty white
coat. She went in. She thought, "I'll get on a train and go
somewhere.

"But where?"

A fat dirty-looking man with fat dirty hands was standing
across a counter from her and she ordered some coffee and
sat at a soiled table. "No, I won't have anything to eat." The
morning newspaper was lying on a table. It was then she
read of Tom's death and the taking of the others.

There was a little adventure in the restaurant. Kit had no
change and gave the man a twenty-dollar bill and he stood
looking at her and whistling. "You get it changed for me.
I want some change," she said and he crossed to the railroad
station but presently came back saying he could not get the
change. Several times he had looked directly at her. The
black dress she had bought at the rummage sale was really
shabby. It was worn and faded and fitted her loosely. She
wore the black sunbonnet but the restaurant man could
look directly into her face. She met his gaze calmly. An idea
came to her. "Is there a train going north from here this
morning?" she asked, having some notion of going to some
city, perhaps in Ohio . . . she had often taken liquor into
the larger Ohio towns . . . Ohio, the home state of the anti-
saloon league, had always been one of the bigger consuming
states. . . . "I want to go to Columbus, Ohio," she said, but

the man said the morning train had already gone and that there would not be another before evening. "You'll have to take the six-eighteen tonight by Cincinnati."

She ended by taking a room at the hotel . . . it was the sort of place used, as Kit later concluded, by sports of the town, a place of assignation really, where rooms could be had for fifty cents. She followed the fat man up a dirty stairway and into a room that looked down into the street, saying that she had walked a long way and that she had a sister ill at Columbus but was sure the man did not believe her story. He had concluded that she was a woman keeping an assignation and her man hadn't appeared. Young women did not wear such clothes as she had on. "It's all right," he thought. "Her guy may show up." At any rate she had money and could pay her way. He stood at the door of her room grinning at her, and then closed the door slowly and as though regretfully and went away.

Kit stayed in the shabby room during that day and spent the night there and in the afternoon had another adventure. She began thinking of the woman Agnes, known long before in the cotton mill town, Agnes the radical. "I'll write to her and I'll go there," she thought. She had some vague notion . . . "I have some money. I might get Agnes to go in with me." She did not want to return, as a worker, to some cotton mill. "I'm through with the liquor business." It wasn't that she had any particular moral revulsion. It was the always hiding out, never knowing people. She might buy a farm. After all she had been a farm child. Why couldn't she and some person like Agnes . . . Agnes was at least strong . . . "She'll be wanting to change all the neighbors. She'll be preaching to them about their rights . . . She'll be always talking about politics," Kit thought . . .

Why shouldn't she and Agnes work together on the land? Kit had money stowed away in safety deposit boxes in several Ohio and West Virginia banks. She was a little vague as to how much money there was.

She went down into the street, this in the late afternoon, and, stopping in a drugstore, bought a writing tablet and some envelopes. She went to the post office. It was opposite a courthouse . . . the town was evidently a county seat . . . and there was a jail back of the courthouse.

There were two men who had evidently been arrested by the county officers. They were being taken out of a car and led across the courthouse lawn. They were young fellows. "They'll be mountain boys," Kit thought. They might well be young mountain men who had been making liquor for the Halsey crowd, caught now . . . there would be some of Tom's crowd, taken in the raid, who would buy their way through by giving names. There would be a general round-up. Kit had the odd, really absurd feeling that it was all outside herself, as though she were in an audience and saw a play going on in a theatre. She went into the post office and wrote the letter to Agnes, standing at a little desk and using the dirty sputtering pen she found lying there.

It was late afternoon of the bright fall day. The clerk in the post office from whom Kit presently bought a stamp was a little old man with a small womanish face. He stood looking hard at her. Surely he also could see, looking directly at her thus, that she was not the little old farm woman her dress would indicate. There were two or three men standing in the post office and Kit looked quickly about. They had been talking together but the talk ceased and they also stared at her. A neatly dressed man . . . Kit had noticed that two of the fingers of one of his hands were gone . . . spoke to another man and passed out. She could see other men passing up and down the street outside. Now there were two men left in the place and in a moment they also went into the street.

Kit had mailed her letter to Agnes . . . she never knew whether or not it reached its destination. She had decided to leave that part of the country, perhaps that evening, and had told Agnes to address her care of general delivery at Dayton, Ohio . . . it was another city she had often visited; she had delivered loads of liquor there . . . she had started to walk out of the post office when she noticed a poster on the wall.

It was a poster concerning herself. It had been put up that day. There was a picture of herself, got no doubt from some newspaper, and a description. She was of such and such a height, always neatly and well dressed. Kit stood before the poster reading it. She had forgotten that she might be watched. A little shiver ran through her body as she read.

So they had cooked that up. She was wanted. She was a dangerous and desperate woman. She was wanted for the shooting of the man Steve Wyagle.

There had been some man, of Tom's crowd . . . a quick thought came to her . . . it might have been her husband Gordon . . . he would be one to swear to anything to get himself out of trouble . . . they had thought that up . . . she was to be accused of the killing of Wyagle.

A thought came to her. Would the young Weathersmythe

also be involved? She reached up and tearing the poster from the wall rolled it into a tight roll and held it in her hand.

She turned, stood a moment uncertainly, and there was the man, the post office clerk with a little old womanish face at his window and again staring at her. How long had he been there? Had he seen her tear down the poster?

She went out of the post office and into the street. It was a bad moment. There was the courthouse opposite the post office and back of the courthouse the jail and there in the street, before her, was that man, the one with the two fingers gone from his right hand, and he was talking to two men who sat in a car at the curb.

The two men were in uniform. They were highway police. Kit walked past them. She had in her hand the poster, rolled up, her hand gripping it. The man with the fingers missing was talking to the two men and one of them got out of the car and stood on the sidewalk. All of the men stopped talking together and stood looking at her. "So this is the way it happens," she thought.

It was such a silly business . . . If she hadn't gone into the post office . . . "I wonder why I have stayed about here? I should have lit out, kept that car, highballed it out of the state."

The officers would have seen the poster in the post office. Perhaps one of them had just put it up. She walked past the men, her hand gripping tightly the roll of stiff paper.

Nothing happened. She went on along the street and got

into other streets of houses where people lived. It was a
bright clear fall afternoon, and women were abroad. Two
women stood by a fence talking and there was a boy in a
yard raking leaves.

Kit got out into the country and walked until she got into
some low hills. The hunger in her had grown and she was
in a sharp reaction from the fright in town so that for a
time she was weak and trembling.

"Oh, why was I not born into a different way of life? Why
do I not now live in some comfortable house in a town,
perhaps with children of my own? Why are some people
born, sons and daughters of the rich or well-to-do, while
others must spend lives in factories or in coal mining
towns?" Kit had for the moment lost all desire for the adventurous life. She wanted only to disappear into the mass
of people, no longer to be notorious, an adventuress. She sat
on dry grass in a wood and looking suddenly down saw,
still gripped in her right hand, the poster that pronounced
her not only a breaker of laws, but a desperate woman, a
killer.

CHAPTER TWENTY-ONE

IT was late afternoon of the following day, and Kit was again in the wood where she had changed her clothes. She had begun smoking during her life as a rumrunner and had an occasional cigarette. All day vague projects concerned with the life she was now to lead kept coming and going in her mind. It was true that the so-called Halsey gang was now broken up. Tom Halsey had got his. So all his plans . . . to make his pile, get out of it, begin another kind of life, have grandchildren, perhaps go to some city of the East, get into some "respectable" business, establish a family . . . all had ended by a stupid shot in the dark, a shot fired by his own son.

The son was now in prison. He would be begging off. If the federal men, who had accomplished the breaking up of the Halsey crowd, wanted to go on . . . get Kit for example . . . there was no doubt they could get Gordon to swear to anything.

She hadn't shot Steve Wyagle. Young Weathersmythe had done that. She thought of the Virginia boy. If still alive he would be trembling in his shoes now.

But after all, the only one who could bring him into it

was Kate. Kit had told Gordon nothing. Kate would tell the federal men nothing. Kit began walking up and down a woodland path. She lit a cigarette, took a few puffs and threw it away. It was a dry time and once one of her cigarettes, half burned, started a little fire among dry leaves which she put out with her foot. She was blue and discouraged, not because of fear that she would be taken, but because of the uncertainty as to her own future, what she was to do. "I may have money enough to live for a year or two but I can't just sit still." The thought came that she might go to some other part of the country, get into some other crowd, like Tom's . . . they would take her on . . . she knew the game.

"No!" She said the word aloud and was startled by the sound of her own voice in the quiet wood.

There was a little sound, far off. Some one was coming through the wood. She put out her cigarette and went and got behind some bushes and presently a young man and woman came along a path.

It was a pair of young lovers and Kit thought they might both be twenty-two or three. They were a young town couple and had driven a car out from town. It would be parked somewhere, at the other side of the wood. He was a neatly dressed young man . . . he might have been a clerk, and she a quite pretty young woman. They stopped near where Kit had concealed herself. She was behind a large tree where thick bushes grew.

The young man was pleading with his sweetheart. "I can't, darling, I can't wait any longer."

He had her in his arms and was kissing her.

"But we couldn't. Oh, I wouldn't dare."

"Yes, we could. It would be safe here."

After the adventure of the day before, when she had torn the poster from the post-office wall, she had walked about for two or three hours and then, when night came, had returned to the hotel near the railroad station. She had not slept or eaten since she had left Kate's house. She was not hungry. She was not sleepy. She had spent the night in the hotel room and it had been a not too disagreeable night.

The hotel proprietor had got that notion in his head. She was something fly. She had come there to meet some man. . . . Why else should any woman come to that particular hotel? He had been passing the word to men who came to to the place. They came to drink or to meet women. The hotel was the speak-easy of the town. The proprietor would be a man with a certain political pull.

"Say, I say Jim, there's something pretty swell up there in room eleven. It's the front room at the head of the stairs." (Life has many pleasant little phases.) A wink. "She came here to meet some guy and the guy got scared out and didn't show up.

"Gave me a line about going away on the evening train but I notice she didn't go.

"Jim, she's got dough too, plenty of it."

Two or three men had come up the stairs during the night to try the door to Kit's room, and there had been one, a drunken fellow, who had knocked loudly. "I say, kid, what about it? Are you in there? Say kid, what about opening up, having a drink with me, eh?"

To be sure Kit hadn't answered. The man had gone away. He was drunk. He went downstairs and sat in a

chair. He went to sleep. Kit wasn't frightened. She was too
busy thinking. She had got her twenty-dollar bill changed
when she had bought the stationery and at dawn she left
the hotel and returned to the wood where she had left the
clothes she had worn on the evening before when she went
with Gordon to Kate's house. At the desk in the hotel the
next morning there was a young girl of twelve or thirteen
and Kit thought her quite pretty.

"And I owe also for a cup of coffee," Kit said to her. How
pretty and clean looking the child was. "Can she be the
daughter of the man here?" Kit was asking herself. "God,
what a break she's going to get," she thought.

Kit crept away through the wood, leaving the lovers,
something inside her hurting. 'I don't want to know what
happens." How strange it was. It was so Gordon Halsey had
talked to her, when she was a clerk in the five and ten.

"I can't wait. I can't wait."

"The hell you can't." She had anyway been too slick for
Gordon.

She had got what she thought she wanted, a swell car to
drive, clothes, money to spend. The young girl she had just
seen in the wood with her lover . . . she had shiny black
hair and a slender small body. "I wonder if she'll have sense
enough to stall him off, keep him hanging.

"Or will she fall for his talk and, in the end, perhaps get
sold out?"

What a queer mixed-up thing life was, people always
being driven here and there by forces they themselves
couldn't understand, some being hurt, sold-out by life, others
apparently lifted up.

There was the fixed idea . . . you must try to make something of yourself. The obvious way was to get money, by some method, get the things you wanted.

"But what do I want?"

Kit still had definitely the belief that she was not going to be taken, that she would get away. When she had got clear of the lovers, who were so absorbed that they had heard or seen nothing of her, she began thinking of getting away from the absurd disguise she was wearing. She had concealed her bag in the wood. I wonder if I could find it. She had put it in a hollow log.

She began searching the wood, carefully, slowly, once almost walking directly into the pair of young lovers. The young man was walking along a path, apparently angry, and the young woman followed at his heels. She was crying. "So he's trying that on her now, eh?"

After a long search Kit found her bag and put into it the black dress. There was a gray travelling suit with a light-fitting little gray coat and she put them on.

It was growing late in the afternoon and she walked down to where there was a young man at work in a field near the wood's edge. Kit almost betrayed herself by walking into the man's presence. She got down behind a fence.

The man was cutting corn in the field. He was a strong-looking big-shouldered young fellow and worked rapidly, using a long knife he held in his right hand and gathering the heavy stalks into the crook of his arm. He was in faded blue overalls and was shocking the corn.

Kit sat by the fence, out of sight, watching. Beyond the cornfield there was a small frame house, newly built, unpainted, and back of the house a tiny barn, also new, and

presently, from the house . . . it had but one floor and could
have but two or at the most three rooms . . . came a young
woman.

She was the wife of the young farmer in the field and was
pregnant. Kit saw her come through a gate, near the
house, and could hear her making her way through the
still standing corn. She walked down one of the corn rows,
the broad dry corn leaves making a sharp rustling sound
as she brushed through.

The young man in the field heard her approaching and
stopped work. He stood waiting for her appearance. He had
his back to Kit.

It was all terribly important to Kit. She was in a certain
mood. It was as it had been in town on the day before when
she had seen the young mountain man being taken to jail.
She was again as she was then. She was like one of the audience in a theatre, sitting and watching the progress of a
play.

The young woman had come into the open place near the
wood's edge where the corn had been cut and near where
Kit was concealed.

"Come on now," she said to the man, "it's enough for
today.

"It will be dark soon now. I've already started your supper."

The young man laughed. "O K., Bess. I'll just tie up this
shock." He tied the shock and went over to her and for a
moment they stood together, facing Kit. She was concealed behind a rail fence looking through between two
lower rails. He began playing with her, rather awkwardly,
shyly, and presently she saw one of his large hands creep
down until it touched her rounded, distended body. She

laughed and drew away from him and giving her a hearty slap on the buttock he went off toward the house followed by his wife.

It was growing dark. Kit had stayed on in the wood. "I'm getting out of this country tonight," she told herself. She continued smoking cigarettes, but as it grew darker, realized that the smoking was a mistake. She was walking up and down in an open place back of the fence and could see over the top of the uncut corn to the little farmhouse.

It stood on a little rise of land and beyond the house there was an old orchard. Kit could see what she took to be the foundation stones of another and larger house that must formerly have stood on the knoll. Although she did not know it the foundation stones were all that was left of a large house that had once been the home of a wealthy slave owner. It had been destroyed by a marching Northern army during the Civil War.

The young man had gone into his little house with his wife, but presently came out followed by the wife and opened a gate that led into an orchard. A cow came through. "So they have got a cow." Kit was remembering her own childhood in another little mountain house. She stood smoking another cigarette, absorbed, watching, and presently realized that she had been seen. The woman stood pointing and the man got up from his milking and also looked.

Kit threw her cigarette away and went back into the wood but did not leave the place. She made her way by a circuitous route, night coming rapidly on, and approached the house.

When she got to the little hill on which the house stood

it was quite dark. She got to the barn and then, getting suddenly bolder went around the barn and got near the back door of the house. The woman was cooking the evening meal at a stove near the door and the man sat at a table waiting. The table was spread with a cheap but clean cloth and there were an open door and an open window. Kit went to within ten feet of the door and stood watching. She was in deep shadows. "It's a good thing they do not keep a dog," she thought.

"But what am I doing here?" She did not know afterwards how long she stood thus, acting the part of a jack-the-peeper. There was a little hurt place in her throat. "What a fool I am," she thought. There was a quick, rapid review of her own life, as factory and shop girl. Then as clerk in the five-and-ten; the coming of Gordon Halsey, her own cleverness in managing him, getting him into a marriage . . .

Her determination not to have a child by him . . .

Her hunger for expensive clothes, for fast cars to drive . . .

Her going into the work with Tom . . .

"What did I want? What have I always wanted?"

Inside the house, the woman stood by her stove. She was frying something in a pan and the young farm man was seated at the table watching. "They have just got a start. It may be he has worked hard and has got a little money. He has bought some land here.

"It may be she had a little money and could help him." The scene was to Kit like some book she was reading, a story perhaps of simple lives, of simple people.

"Well, what about it, old woman?" the man said laughing. He got up and went over to his wife, also tall and

strong-looking, and she began to threaten him with a long
fork she held in her hand, but he paid no attention to the
fork. Again, as in the cornfield, the man ran his big hand
over the woman's body until he came to the place where the
unborn child lay and the woman suddenly turned and
kissed him. He went back to his place at the table.

Kit went silently past the house and into the road. She
had thrown away the little bag that had contained the
clothes she now had on. She went along the road. It was not
the same road she had followed on the day before when she
had gone down in the town but like that road it led down
and into a paved highway.

There was a filling-station on the highway and several
cars stood parked before it. She approached. She had no definite plan. She could hear voices inside the filling-station and
a thought came to her. She knew that many filling-stations
along highways, in the time of prohibition, were also retail
places for the sale of liquor. "This is one," she thought.
There was in her mind some idea of getting some one to
drive her out of the country. "It would be absurd if now,
after escaping from Kate's house, after my foolish gesture
in tearing that poster from the wall of the post office, I'd
do something that would end in my being taken."

She had a conviction she wouldn't. She had got quite near
the filling-station and stopped at the side of the road. There
was a car standing near and in the dim light that came
through the window of the filling-station she could see a man
sitting in the car. He looked like a man of perhaps thirty,
slight and well dressed. He was a young town man. "I must be
quite near a town," Kit thought. She was in an odd dreamlike
state. She stood beside the road looking at the man who

turned in the car seat and looked at her. The car was a light runabout with the top down.

As Kit stood thus, looking at the man who also looked at her, there was a loud roaring sound in the road and two motorcycles driven by men in officer's uniforms came rapidly along the road and stopped at the filling-station. "There they are," Kit thought. "They are after me. I am going to be taken." The men had gone into the filling-station and Kit walked deliberately over to the car where the man sat.

"They are officers, aren't they?" she said pointing and the man smiled and nodded his head.

"Why?" he asked.

Kit hesitated. "I might as well take a chance," she thought. She knew that the taking of Tom Halsey's crowd had created talk. It had been hailed as a great triumph for the prohibition forces. "Just the same such places as this filling-station go on," she thought. There would be new men now supplying all such places. She was sure that the filling-station was in reality a speak-easy. She spoke rapidly to the man in the car, saying she had come to the filling-station to meet a man. "I don't want to be recognized," she said.

"If I could sit with you in your car until the officers go."

"Get in," he said, and Kit went quickly around the car and got into the seat beside the man. He would have the impression that she was some woman, perhaps from a near-by town, out to meet a lover, perhaps a married man of the town.

There had been a sudden real fright, seeing the officers at the place. "Is it a speak-easy?" she asked again pointing. "Yes," he said.

He was very curious and sat facing her in the car seat. "Will they raid the place?" she asked.

He said he didn't think so. He laughed. "Let's wait and see. They won't disturb me. There's a reason."

There had been several cars parked before the filling-station and now men began coming out, getting into cars and driving away. One of the men called to the man with whom Kit sat. "Coming, Tom?" he asked and "No, not yet," Kit's newly acquired acquaintance answered.

Kit and the man sat there in the car and waited. "You were to meet a friend here, some man, eh?" the man asked. "What kind of looking car does he drive?"

"It's a Packard," Kit said, and the man laughed. "O, ho," he said.

The officers had come out of the filling-station and had got their motorcycles that had been left leaning against the wall of the building. They were about to drive off and Kit was beginning to feel easy . . . there had been the sudden terror run through her after she got into the car. "They have made a bluff searching the place. They really wanted a drink," Kit's companion whispered and at that moment one of the officers put his motorcycle back against the building and walked over to the car. He had a flashlight in his hand and flashed it in her face and in the face of her new acquaintance. "Now I'm a goner," Kit thought. She thought: "There isn't an officer within two hundred miles that isn't on the lookout for me." It would be a real feather in the cap of some road cop to take her. She could in fancy see the headlines in newspapers . . . "Queen of the Rumrunners, taken by Officer Jones." She suddenly began to swear softly and her companion looked at her in astonishment. "Well, what the hell?" he said.

There was the officer standing in the road before the car with the flashlight in his hand. "Oh, it's you, Joel," he said

and turned away. The man of the filling-station came to his
door. "Good night," he called to the officer. He laughed.
With a loud roar one of the officers, on his motorcycle went
off along the road, but the other pushing his motorcycle
came again toward the car in which Kit sat. "You oughtn't
to be hanging around places like this," he said to the young
man in the car.

"Oh, yeah," Kit's acquaintance said. He laughed. "You
keep that flashlight out of my eyes." He leaned out of the
car. "Did you like your drink?" he asked, and "You go to
hell, Tom," the officer answered, preparing to mount his
motorcycle.

"I hope you have a big evening. I wish you luck with
her," he called as he rode away.

CHAPTER TWENTY-TWO

K IT felt that she had really got free. As the two officers rode away from the filling-station she thought
. . . "that's the last of it." It couldn't be possible
that, after twice being almost in their clutches
and they having missed, they would get her. "I won't be
around for them to get," she told herself. It had been absurd, her hanging about. How amusing if the two who had
just left were out looking for her. Her long experience with
officers of the law, eluding them, out-thinking them, outrunning them on the road, had made her contemptuous.
The man, in the car, who presently told her his name, spoke
to her. "I don't know why I think so but I've a hunch," he
said. . . . He seems a smiling alive man. The man of the
filling-station stood but a few feet away. . . . Joel spoke in
a low voice, quickly. "I've a hunch you've no liking for
police."

"No," she said, and then added quickly, "Let's get out of
here."

"O.K.," he said and started the engine of his car. The man
of the filling-station was coming toward them. He spoke
. . . "That's a hot pair," he said, making a motion with
his thumb. The sound of the two motorcycles could still be
heard in the distance.

The filling-station man laughed. . . . "They're after a woman.

"They couldn't catch a cold," he said. He stood beside the car and Joel shut off his motor. "What woman?" he asked.

The man explained. "It's that woman . . . you know Joel, the good-looking dame, the one who ran the stuff for Tom Halsey.

"You know they got him, they shot him." He was looking at Kit. "They say she's hanging around. A farmer back here claims he saw her today. It's probably a pipe. He says she was in the woods, back of young Hal Johnson's place." The light of the car was on his face and Kit thought . . . she was curiously cool . . . she smiled . . . she saw the man smile . . . "Oh, he'll be all right," she thought.

He was something she had been, and still was, one outside the law, beating the law, making his living by being outside the law. It would please him to see any officer of the law made into a fool. "Hello," the man said, "I thought you came out here alone. I didn't know you had a dame with you. Excuse me," he added.

Kit's new friend laughed. "She's a friend of my sister's. It's Miss Hunter," he said.

"Oh! Excuse me!" The man walked away, he was confused. He went into his little house and Kit was on the road with Joel. She had a new hunch. "I'm going to tell him," she thought. "It was me they were after, at least I think it was. I was in the woods back there," she said. There was a sudden outbreak of words. "I've got to get out of here. I want you to drive me!" Joel did not speak for a moment. He did not look at her.

"O. K.," he said at last. They were driving along a paved

road, going in the opposite direction from that taken by the
officers. "This is rich," he said. He became suddenly joyous.
"God, this is good." Kit thought he had been drinking.
He spoke of that. "Look here, do you know who I am?"
He drew the car to the side of the road and stopped. "I'm
Judge Hanaford's son. I'm his drunken son, no good," he
said.

Kit had never heard of Judge Hanaford, and Joel caught
the puzzled look on her face. "You've never heard of him,
eh?" he said; "well now, that would be a disappointment
to him."

For hours Kit drove Joel Hanaford's car, stopping once at
another filling-station into which he went to get a bottle of
moon liquor, getting the money to pay for it from Kit. He
had already told her that he had no money and that the car
he was driving did not belong to him. It belonged to his
sister, he explained and said that the sister was married to
a doctor. He kept breaking into little spasms of laughter,
wriggling in the car seat.

He broke into speech, telling Kit his story and stopping
from time to time to drink from a bottle and Kit had a feeling that she might have known him for years, that he might
have been some one to whom she had been close for a long
time, "like an older brother," she thought. She said something of the sort to him and he turned upon her. "Ouch!"
he said and began explaining that he didn't like the idea.
"There are too many women take me that way," he said. He
sighed. "It's my cross," he said. Kit had got in with a queer
one all right. Like young Weathersmythe, this one was a
Virginian but he told Kit that he was not one of the first
families. As they drove along in the night, Kit at the wheel,

every turn of the car wheels taking her farther from the scene of her activities as "Queen of the Rumrunners," herself feeling that she had seen the last of that life, trying to think a little into the future, Joel Hanaford sat beside her talking. Once she spoke to him about the drinking . . . he kept going back to the bottle . . . but he reassured her . . . "I know just how much to take," he said, "how much will keep me comfortably stewed" . . . as they drove along thus he told his story.

Like Alfred Weathersmythe, Joel Hanaford was a Virginian, but he declared to Kit that they . . . the Hanafords . . . were not one of the so-called "proud Virginia families." "You don't have to look up to us, woman," he said. "No one has to look up to us."

Kit got the story of the Hanaford family in little snatches as they drove, her own mind busy. It was to come back to her later, like something remembered out of a dream. She was obsessed for the time with a certain feeling — had been lonely and this new man, come upon so accidentally, seemed to break her loneliness. There was something about the man . . . she thought all of this out later . . . so friendly . . . he sitting there in the car beside her . . . as he drank he seemed to grow pale and he leaned back in the car seat, sometimes sitting with closed eyes. Once he was for a long time silent and his rather slight body leaned heavily against Kit's and turning she saw his small head, covered with thick reddish brown hair, and his small tired-looking face.

She had a curious desire to run her fingers through his hair. She would have liked to take him into her arms and hold him. He was tired, something inside of him tired. She felt that.

He kept talking. His father was a judge. Like young Weathersmythe's father, he had been a prosecuting attorney but, unlike the Weathersmythes the Hanafords had, Joel told Kit, no heroes in the family. There was a grandfather but he had not been a Mosby man.

He, the grandfather, had also been a soldier in the Civil War, but he had deserted. He had been a mountain man, poor and ignorant, and when, during the Civil War, he deserted from the Southern army he ran away and hid in the hills.

And then the war was over and he reappeared. He became a day laborer in the town in which his son was later to be first a prosecuting attorney and then a judge. Joel Hanaford seemed to Kit to tell the story of the Hanafords with a kind of bitter pleasure. It might well be, she thought afterwards, that he spent his life telling and retelling it.

It was a common enough story. The poor but worthy son of such a man as Joel described to Kit, determined to rise. He, Joel's father, had worked his way through school and college. He had won the favor of the people of his community. "Look at him," people said. Joel told Kit that he thought his father must have been the kind of boy and young man always being pointed out by mothers and fathers to other young men of his town, young men born into families that could offer their sons greater opportunities.

"Son, you look at John Hanaford. Look at what he has had to fight against and look at how he's getting along." John Hanaford, his son declared, had won all of the prizes, first at the town school, and then at college. He had done all the things such a young man should do, had peddled newspapers, to keep himself afloat while going through the town school, and later, at college, had waited on table in students' boarding houses.

And he had got on, had become a successful lawyer, a successful politician, and had married into one of the so-called better families in his town.

"And so there he is," Joel said to Kit. He talked quietly, continually smiling . . . Kit thought afterwards that it was a decidedly bitter smile . . . during the drive with him she was puzzled, and didn't understand the man. . . . She did and she didn't. She thought he did something rather fine to her.

There was the feeling of warm friendliness she got from him. There was no doubt he knew who she was. From the first moment with her she had the feeling that under no circumstances would he betray her.

He tried to explain why. Joel Hanaford had been brought up, had gone through boyhood, in the town where his father had made his struggle. "It wasn't that Dad bragged about his rise in the world, not directly," Joel said. When young Joel had got out of high school the World War had come on and he had gone into it. He had been wounded and gassed.

He had come home a wreck. "So there I was, in our house." He had begun drinking. Kit gathered that things had gone all wrong between the father and son. He tried to tell her about that. While Joel had been in the army his father had become more and more successful. He had been prosecuting attorney in his Virginia county . . . always, as the son told Kit, sending men off to prison. Joel hated the notion. "I guess they think they have to do it. I wouldn't. They get to like doing it." There was a big cotton mill in the town and Joel's father became attorney for that. He was made judge.

The son had come from the war a wreck and there was a political campaign on. There was a meeting being held in the town, speakers on the steps of the courthouse . . . this before the father became a judge.

The speaker had spoken of his own sacrifice, for his country, made by sending into the war his only son.

Joel's father was making a speech. "I happened along," Joel told Kit. There had been some reference on the part of the speaker . . . he was after the soldiers' vote. "I gave my son to my country," the father said.

Joel Hanaford sat up straight in the car seat. He trembled. He was trying to explain something to Kit. He was so excited that some of his excitement got into her and she stopped the car beside the road. He was trying to tell her of a sudden cold and deep disgust and wrath that had taken possession of him that day when he had stood in the crowd and listened to his father's words. He had wanted to cry out but had kept silent and had walked away from the crowd and the speaker unnoticed.

He had gone home to his father's house and had waited for his father's coming. In all of the young man's tale he did not mention his mother.

He had gone home and presently his father came and with him was another man. It was the owner of the cotton mill in the town. The mill man had got very rich during the war. The two men came to the door of the house and were met by the son. Kit understood that Joel's one sister, the one who afterwards married the doctor and whose car

she drove that night, was present. There had been a scene
between the father and son.

"It is disgusting. It is revolting," Joel had told his
father, speaking of the speech on the courthouse steps and
the father's use of himself, now a half-physical wreck, for
political purposes. Kit felt that she could see the scene at
the door of the Virginia house. She imagined Joel as speaking quietly enough. "I'm a wreck. I can't make my own
living. I have to take your money." The cotton-mill man was
standing with his mouth open and listening. It was the
influence of the mill man that later got Joel's father his
judgeship.

"If my name is ever mentioned again, in such a public
way . . . in order that you . . . and this man here . . .
may go on . . . putting other young men through what I
have been in . . . for your ends . . . I'll go out into the
public streets and denounce you, or I'll simply kill both of
you."

Joel Hanaford was delighted that he had been able to help
Kit escape. After he had told his story he became silent and
as it was almost morning Kit thought they had better find
a place to sleep.

Joel had been sleeping, his slight body leaning against
Kit's, but when she stopped the car at a filling-station he
awoke and as soon as they had left the filling-station took a
long drink from his bottle. He seemed at once alert and
awake and when Kit suggested going to a hotel he agreed.
"You notice, young woman, how fresh I am, how alert, eh?"
They had stopped in the street before a small hotel. "It is
this does it. I keep stewed half the time." He took another
drink from his bottle and put it in his pocket. He kept smil-

ing and his half laughing eyes awoke a kind of gladness
and even gaiety in Kit. "I wish I could take him with me,"
she thought. "I'd like to take care of him."

They went into the hotel and registered and were assigned
two adjoining rooms by a sleepy clerk. The hotel was another small, half shabby one. "The clerk thinks we are
lovers, eh?" Joel said as they went up the stairs. He stood
at the door before his own room speaking to Kit who was
at her door and the clerk went away down a flight of
steps. Joel kept smiling at her. "I guess you want to make
a getaway," he said. "You don't want some man like my
dad to get a crack at you.

"I don't blame you," he added, "but after you are gone
. . . of course I know who you are . . . after you are gone
I presume I'll get good and drunk.

"I'll be lonesome. Do you know what that means?"

He did not wait for Kit to answer but went into his room.
Kit had barely got her door closed until he rapped and
she reopened it. He stood there in the hallway, in the dim
light, and looked at her. There was what Kit thought a kind
of comical seriousness. "Look here," he said . . . he was not
smiling now . . . "you aren't on it, are you?" he asked,
and his face was so serious-looking that Kit broke into
laughter in which he joined. He stood grinning at her. "I
didn't think you were," he said, "but, you see . . . well, I
thought I ought to offer."

He took off his hat and bowed and still laughing Kit
stepped over to him. She took his head in her two hands
and kissed him on the cheek and as he stepped away from
her he scowled. "Oh, I see. It's like that."

"Oh, Lord," he said, "it's always like that with me and
women." He was going toward his own door but stopped

and again spoke to her. "I wish it wasn't like that with you," he said, "but you see I'm only half a man and you want a man.

"If I was a bit more a man I'd be asking you to marry me," he said, and again bowing, went into his room.

Kit stood a long time at her open door that night thinking. She was exhilarated. It wasn't, she told herself, that she was particularly attracted to the curious human being she had found and who had helped rescue her from the police. She thought it was something he stood for. There was a kind of bitter resistance to life in him that she liked. He had been defeated but he was mature. She stood at the door of her room, looking into the empty hallway. Beside Tom Halsey, that other man she had at one time admired, Tom with his childish determination to get money, to be a big shot, to set up a respectable family, beside this new man it seemed to her that night that Tom, even in his best days, before the growth of greediness in him, was no more than a child. There was an idea in Kit's head . . . a kind of dawning of light. It did not get itself very definitely expressed in her. It was as though in her there was something trying to become definite.

Kit closed the door of her room but did not undress. She stood by the door thinking and occasionally smiling. She was thinking of the odd attractive figure of Joel Hanaford.

Then she thought of another figure, the young farmer, a worker with his young wife in the poor little house. The woman standing by her kitchen stove, cooking food for her man come from his day's work. In fancy she saw again the man approach his wife, the rough worker's hands on her pregnant body. Kit kept smiling. "I'll not be here I guess when he awakes," she thought. Her mind made a quick plan. She would presently go downstairs and leave money for him in an envelope. Then she would cut out. There was in her mind an almost definite notion of a new kind of adventure she might begin. She felt warm and alive. Young Hanaford had done that for her. She had been carried out of herself and her own problem and into the life of another puzzled human. There were people to be found. She would get into some sort of work that did not so separate her from others. There might be some one other puzzled and baffled young one with whom she could make a real partnership in living.

mending 9/14/70